Tastes Good Enough to Die For

They waited outside, huddled together in groups, noses turning red and voices filled with speculation as they wondered what was going on.

Lucy shivered. "I should've brought my espresso with me. At least my fingers would stay warm."

The distant shriek of a siren heralded the arrival of the fire department. Everyone craned their necks as the truck came to a stop at the curb and four firefighters emerged.

"Everyone, stay back," one of the men ordered. "Keep the area in front of the building clear."

As they all edged away, two of the crew circled around back while two entered through the front door. After what seemed like an eternity but was probably only twenty minutes, the incident commander gave the all clear and everyone filed back inside the patisserie, relieved the alarm had proven false.

"Who do you suppose pulled the fire alarm?" Lucy asked as they followed Rachel Brandon and her crew inside and headed back to their table.

"No idea." Phaedra took out her phone. "I just hope whoever did it is caught." She glanced at the table with a frown. Espressos, check. Lucy and Marisol, check. But something was missing.

"Where's my cupcake?" she asked suddenly. "The one Hannah brought out for me and Dad. It's gone."

"It was here when we left," Lucy said.

"Looks like Rachel's assistant grabbed it," Marisol remarked, and they followed her gaze.

Sure enough, Anna Steele held the dark chocolate cupcake aloft on its plate as she made a beeline for Ms. Brandon on the other side of the shop. She caught Rachel's eye and called out, "I got you the last dark chocolate."

Rachel gave her assistant a dismissive wave. "Not now, I'm interviewing Hannah."

Anna visibly deflated. "Oh. Okay. Sorry."

"I can't believe she stole your cupcake!" Lucy glared at Anna. "And Rachel doesn't even want it. Want me to get it back? Because you know I will."

"No. It's okay. Dad will be disappointed, but he'll get over it."

"You're too nice," Lucy grumbled. "And way too understanding."

Phaedra shrugged. "It's a cupcake, Lu." She watched as Anna turned away, plainly disappointed her offering had been rejected, and licked a dab of ganache from her finger. "Let her have it. It's not the end of the world—"

Before she could finish the sentence, the plate tilted and slid out of Anna's hands onto the floor, sending the cupcake rolling. Perspiration broke out on her forehead, and her face went deathly pale.

"Something's wrong," Phaedra breathed, and shot to her feet in alarm. "Anna? What is it? Are you okay?"

But Rachel's assistant didn't respond, didn't even seem to hear her. "Dizzy," she panted, her breath coming in short gasps as she clutched her chest. "Heart beating . . . really fast . . ."

As everyone looked on in horror, Anna staggered forward, teetered unsteadily, and collapsed face-first onto the nearest table.

The Jane Austen Tea Society Mysteries

PRIDE, PREJUDICE, AND PERIL
A MURDEROUS PERSUASION
CYANIDE AND SENSIBILITY

Cyanide *and* Sensibility

A Jane Austen Tea Society Mystery

Katie Oliver

BERKLEY PRIME CRIME
New York

BERKLEY PRIME CRIME
Published by Berkley
An imprint of Penguin Random House LLC
penguinrandomhouse.com

Copyright © 2023 by Katie Oliver
Penguin Random House supports copyright. Copyright fuels creativity, encourages diverse voices, promotes free speech, and creates a vibrant culture. Thank you for buying an authorized edition of this book and for complying with copyright laws by not reproducing, scanning, or distributing any part of it in any form without permission. You are supporting writers and allowing Penguin Random House to continue to publish books for every reader.

BERKLEY and the BERKLEY & B colophon are registered trademarks and BERKLEY PRIME CRIME is a trademark of Penguin Random House LLC.

ISBN: 9780593337653

First Edition: December 2023

Printed in the United States of America
1 3 5 7 9 10 8 6 4 2

Book design by Alison Cnockaert

This is a work of fiction. Names, characters, places, and incidents either are the product of the author's imagination or are used fictitiously, and any resemblance to actual persons, living or dead, business establishments, events, or locales is entirely coincidental.

If you purchased this book without a cover, you should be aware that this book is stolen property. It was reported as "unsold and destroyed" to the publisher, and neither the author nor the publisher has received any payment for this "stripped book."

For my dad, who loved to read. I miss you every day.

Seldom, very seldom, does complete truth belong to any human disclosure; seldom can it happen that something is not a little disguised, or a little mistaken . . .

—JANE AUSTEN,
EMMA (1815)

One

Phaedra Brighton knew she was dangerously close to losing control of her car on the twisty, ice-slick road.

She tightened her grip on the wheel and drew in a calming breath. It was early December in the Blue Ridge, after all. The snow-dusted mountain peaks and tree branches rimed in ice offered a singular beauty—but danger as well. Branches snapped and pines fell under the weight of ice and snow. Winter made driving perilous, especially on infrequently traveled rural roads.

Like this one.

In spring and summer, a thick, impenetrable fog settled over the peaks and valleys. In autumn, a buck or doe might hurtle out in front of an unwary driver. But December meant snow, and hitting a patch of black ice could send a car spinning treacherously close to a guardrail overlooking a heart-stopping drop.

A sign loomed up ahead. DELAFORD WINERY. TWO MILES. Relief washed over Phaedra as she realized she was nearly there. She slowed the car and wished, not for the first time, that she was home and tucked up in bed. Not traveling halfway up the side of Afton Mountain so early on a Friday morning.

Oh, what she'd give for a bracing cup of Keemun right now . . .

When her mother, Nan, asked her to dress in her Regency finery and act as a guide for the annual Historic Holiday Homes tour, Phaedra regretfully declined. With morning and afternoon lectures scheduled at Somerset University, a peer review awaiting comments, next quarter's funding to finalize, and midterms to grade before winter break, Professor Brighton had zero free time.

Instead, she'd promised to drop off four dozen of her sister Hannah's cupcakes for visitors on the holiday homes tour. Cupcakes Hannah couldn't deliver herself because Saturday was the grand opening of her new patisserie, Tout de Sweet.

At least she'd get a peek inside Delaford.

The historic home was a jewel in the crown of local Virginia architecture and the final residence on the tour. And like every home on the tour, the interior would be as lavishly decorated in traditional holiday style as the exterior.

At the next signpost, Phaedra slowed the car and turned cautiously into the winery entrance. She had no desire to hit black ice and send her sister's cupcakes, beautifully decorated and stowed in the trunk, flying.

Hopefully the sun would show its face soon and melt all of these icy patches into harmless puddles.

The drive, branching left to the winery, or right to the historic family residence, was paved and treated with sand. She turned right.

To one side, a parking lot was already half filled with vehicles, as well as a large, fenced concrete area.

A helipad, she realized. Impressive.

She followed the curving asphalt and admired the fountain, turned off now for the winter, and caught her first glimpse of Delaford.

Despite the breathtaking backdrop of mountains and sky

behind it, the house, with its turrets and arches and mullioned windows, captured her attention. Although "house" was hardly the proper word for the sprawling stone edifice before her.

This? This was a castle. A magnificent stone edifice straight out of *Ivanhoe*. It lacked only a moat and a drawbridge, perhaps a few knights poised on the battlements shouldering bows and releasing arrows against encroaching marauders.

Brushing aside such fanciful thoughts, Phaedra shut off the engine and slid out of the Mini, hampered slightly by her ankle-skimming Regency dress. As a teaching tool it was invaluable; but the thin silk offered little protection against the cold. At least the steps, like the drive, had been treated and showed no trace of ice or snow. Carrying in four boxes of cupcakes shouldn't be a problem.

As she debated whether to risk carrying the boxes in at once or make a couple of trips, one of the tall carved doors swung open.

It wasn't Lady Rowena who stood there, or Rebecca, as she'd half expected; but a young woman with curly dark hair and friendly but inquisitive blue eyes.

"Hello." She regarded Phaedra expectantly. "You must be Professor Brighton. I'm Anna Steele, Rachel Brandon's personal assistant. I love your outfit."

"Thank you. It's period appropriate, and my students love it," Phaedra admitted, "but it's not very warm." She indicated the boxes on the back seat. "My sister's cupcakes for the tour. I wonder, would you mind . . ."

"Of course. Let me help you." She took two of the boxes, balancing them carefully in her arms, and led the way up the steps and through the front door. "The dining room is through here. Rachel's getting ready for a photo shoot for *Home Channel* magazine later this morning."

Phaedra followed, glimpsing ancestral portraits swagged in fresh greenery and a twelve-foot Christmas tree towering at one end of the entrance hall. A handful of people decorated the lower branches, already fitted with white lights, and carefully hung up a selection of antique, handblown glass ornaments.

She set the boxes down at the end of a lengthy dining table. "This is stunning."

"Would you like a quick tour?"

Before Phaedra could reply, a brisk voice rang out. "I'm afraid there's no time for that. Anna, go and sign for the champagne delivery, please."

As Anna excused herself, a perfectly coiffed woman in a navy-blue St. John suit strode into the room. Highlights gleamed in her dark blond hair. "Rachel Brandon," she said as she extended her hand. "You must be Professor Brighton. Nan said you'd be dropping off the cupcakes for our afternoon tour guests. Thank you."

"My pleasure."

The owner of Brandon Advertising and host of the Home Channel's *Home and Hearth* show was petite, yet she commanded the room just as Delaford commanded the mountainside. A firm grip belied her small stature.

"Your home is lovely."

Rachel produced a gracious smile. "Thank you. I hope the tour raises money for the Historical Society. Giving back is so important. I'm also a spokesperson for the Foster Child Foundation. It's a wonderful organization—I was a foster child myself."

"Oh. I had no idea." Phaedra eyed her with renewed admiration.

"Both endeavors are so close to my heart. I just hope the weather cooperates, at least for today." She glanced out the window. "The forecast is calling for more snow on Sunday."

"Two to four inches," Phaedra said. "But the sun's peeking out, so the roads should stay clear until then."

"I hope so. We're expecting quite a crowd." She glanced up as Anna returned. "Take these cupcakes into the kitchen and get them plated. Where is Clark what's-his-name?

He's supposed to interview me at"—she consulted her wristwatch—"eight. It's already five after."

"He just called. The roads are a little treacherous—"

"Professor Brighton arrived with no problem. I expect solutions, not excuses. If he isn't here in five minutes tell him he'll have to reschedule."

Phaedra bit back a smile. Looked like Clark Mullinax, reporter for the *Laurel Springs Clarion* and the bane of her high school existence, was in for a singular challenge with Rachel Brandon.

"I should go," she told Rachel. "I have a nine o'clock lecture to give and exams to grade before winter break starts. I'll be back later this afternoon to help set up. It was wonderful to meet you, Ms. Brandon."

"And you as well. I'll see you later."

As Phaedra retraced her steps across the cavernous entrance hall to the front doors, Anna Steele, cell phone pressed to one ear, caught her eye. She lowered the phone to her chest. "Thanks for bringing the cupcakes. Sorry I couldn't give you a tour."

"It's fine. I need to get going anyway. See you this afternoon." She opened the door, gave Rachel's personal assistant a wave goodbye, and returned to her car, her duty done.

She slid behind the wheel and, with a last admiring glance at the broad, sun-warmed face of the castle, headed for Somerset University.

Cars crowded the faculty parking lot as Phaedra arrived at the university. She pulled into an empty space beside Professor Mark Selden's dark green Triumph. With its "ET-2BRUT" license plate, the Shakespearean scholar's car was hard to miss.

After a chilly trip down Afton Mountain, the Mini was finally warm and she hated to leave its toasty interior. She reached for her briefcase and reminded herself to get the heater checked the next time the car was serviced.

Her steps were brisk as she crossed the south end of the campus to the Humanities building. No one lingered outside the doors or sat on the benches along the tree-lined quad. Those who ventured across campus walked quickly. Although the sun was out, the air carried the unmistakable sting of winter.

Phaedra entered the building and went straight to the faculty lounge. She was in serious need of a warming cup of tea before giving her first lecture of the day, "Women Writers of the Nineteenth Century." As she waited for the Earl Grey to steep, she glanced up at the bulletin board.

Notices and holiday-related items crowded its cork surface. Parties, among them a Twelfth Night celebration, featured heavily. She was surprised to see that Professor Selden was sponsoring and cohosting the event at Dean Carmichael's house.

A frown puckered her brow. On the surface, Selden and Carmichael had little in common. The dean, a former journalism teacher and a graduate of Northwestern University, had worked his way up the academic ladder. Mark was British, Oxford educated, and born into privilege.

For that reason, she'd initially assumed him to be a snob of the first order.

Which just went to show how wrong first impressions could be. Their guarded, somewhat prickly friendship had grown, slowly, into something more. Something almost, but not quite . . . romantic. Romantic-*ish*, Phaedra corrected. She refused to assign more import to her relationship with Professor Selden than actually existed.

After all, he was a well-respected Shakespearean professor, and she was a noted Jane Austen scholar and professor of English literature. Professionalism was paramount. Which was why she'd always striven to keep her personal and work relationships separate.

But Mark's passion for Shakespeare had sparked a renewed enthusiasm for teaching within her, and now she wondered if perhaps some of her personal rules of conduct shouldn't be relaxed a bit. Or jettisoned altogether.

"What's got you so deep in thought, Professor B?"

Marisol Dubois, her teaching assistant and one-third of the Jane Austen Tea Society book club Phaedra chaired, studied her curiously. Her green eyes were bright and inquisitive and missed very little.

"I'm caffeinating myself before my morning lecture."

"Why? You can deliver that lecture in your sleep. Standard first-year stuff."

"I got up early to run cupcakes over to the Delaford Winery."

Phaedra removed the tea bag from her paper cup and suppressed a yawn. "For the Historic Holiday Homes tour."

"Hannah's cupcakes?" Marisol asked. "I don't suppose you brought in a few extra . . ."

"No, sorry." Phaedra took a cautious sip of tea. "How was your date last night?"

"Not worth discussing. He had tats and spiky hair, so I assumed he'd be edgy and interesting. He wasn't either."

"Assumptions can be tricky." Phaedra regarded the murky brown liquid in her cup and grimaced. "Like assuming this tea would be drinkable." She dumped the remainder down the drain and tossed the cup and tea bag into the recycle bin. "I'm headed upstairs. See you later."

"There you are." Lucy Liang, the third Tea Society member and a professor of modern and postmodern literature, was all angles, from her short, dark hair to cheekbones that could cut glass. "I went to your office but you weren't there. Where've you been?"

"Delaford Winery."

Lucy raised her brow. "A little early, isn't it?"

"I wasn't there for a tasting. Although I hear their wines are spectacular. Hannah asked me to drop off four dozen cupcakes for the Historic Holiday Homes tour."

"Oh, right," Marisol said. "Her new patisserie opens tomorrow, doesn't it?"

Phaedra nodded. "Yes, it's the grand opening. And you're both invited."

"We'll be there," Marisol promised.

"Wait," Lucy said. She held out a small brown package covered in Chinese characters. "Auntie Roz brought you a present. From Shanghai." She handed it over. "It's jasmine-scented green tea."

"My favorite." Phaedra breathed in the delicate scent of jasmine and the grassy notes of green tea. "I can't wait to try it. Please thank her for me." She tucked the package in her briefcase and headed for the door. "I'd love to stay and catch up, but I need to run. Lecture. See you later."

"Meet us for lunch?" Marisol asked.

But Professor Brighton was already gone.

"Phae, I need a favor. Please don't hang up until you hear me out."

With a sigh, Phaedra slid behind the wheel of the Mini Cooper, phone pressed to her ear. After two lectures, a staff meeting, and two sets of papers waiting to be graded, she had no desire to prolong her day. "What's up, Han? I'm just heading home."

"Glad I caught you. Please tell me you can swing by early to Delaford and help me set up. Liv can't make it, and I'm here alone and I really need an extra pair of hands."

"Oh. Of course. I promised Rachel I'd be back this afternoon anyway. Why'd Liv bail? She knows tonight's important."

As chairperson of the local historical society, their mother had recommended Hannah provide pastries for the Historic Holiday Home tour. Tonight, locals would get their first taste of her French confectionary treats. And a little pre-publicity for Tout de Sweet's grand opening tomorrow couldn't hurt, either.

"Family emergency. She's profusely sorry and promised to be at the patisserie tomorrow, bright and early. I baked another tray of cupcakes, and once they cool, I need to glaze and decorate." Her sister, normally calm under pressure, sounded frazzled.

"All right, I'm on my way. See you soon."

"Thanks. I owe you."

At least the roads, like the skies, were clear, and traffic was light as Phaedra headed up Afton Mountain again. She arrived at Delaford forty minutes later and turned into the parking lot. Unlike that morning, the lot was nearly full.

After slotting the Mini into one of the few empty spots, she waited to be admitted. A volunteer appeared and led her across the entrance hall to the kitchen. The towering tree she'd glimpsed earlier glistened now with handblown glass ornaments and miniature white lights. The scent of pine and cedar filled the air, along with the tantalizing fragrance of Hannah's apple-walnut cupcakes.

As she followed the volunteer through a baize door that led into the kitchen, Phaedra heard raised voices.

"I prefer you keep the decoration to a minimum, please." Rachel Brandon's voice was clipped.

"I see," Hannah said, her own voice deceptively calm. "Perhaps I'll leave off the caramel glaze, as well. Just serve naked apple cupcakes. Is that plain enough?"

Uh-oh. Her sister had the exaggeratedly polite tone that meant her temper was on the rise.

"You're the pastry chef," Rachel shot back as Phaedra rounded the corner. "I'm not questioning your expertise. But *I* make the rules. And I don't want gold leaf on the cupcakes."

"Why, for heaven's sake? It's beautiful. Festive. Elegant."

"It's tacky," Rachel snapped. "No. Gold. Leaf."

Phaedra hurried forward to the marble-topped island where the two women faced off over a tray of freshly baked cupcakes as several members of Rachel's staff looked on. "Hannah," she began, "I think maybe Rachel has a point."

Her sister glared at her, hands resting on her hips. "Et tu, Phaedra?"

"Your caramel glaze is perfect as it is," she assured Hannah. "It really doesn't need decoration. Just plate the cupcakes on an eye-catching holiday platter."

"Thank you, Professor Brighton." Rachel cast Hannah a self-satisfied glance and marched toward the door. "At least one of you is capable of compromise."

"That woman!" Hannah scowled as she tipped cupcakes from the tin and onto the counter. "Trying to tell me—a trained pastry chef—how to decorate!"

"It's her house, Han. Her rules. The customer is always right, remember? Especially when the customer is as famous as Rachel Brandon."

"I know, I know," her sister grumbled. "But I don't have to like it."

Two

If I were an Austen character," Phaedra said the next morning as her mother steered yet another single man in her direction, "I'd be seriously vexed right now."

It was Saturday, the grand opening of Tout de Sweet, Hannah's patisserie and Laurel Springs' first French pastry shop. Eager customers crowded the counter, ordering bûche de Noël and sipping espresso as they studied the chalked offerings scrawled on the blackboard behind the counter.

Others bent forward to ogle the mouthwatering array of macarons, éclairs, raspberry tarts, and buttery sablé cookies arranged behind the glass display case.

"But you're not a Jane Austen character," Lucy pointed out. "You're an educated woman with agency who doesn't need to bow to the patriarchy. Hello, Mrs. Brighton," she added as Phaedra's mother approached with a man in tow.

"Hello, Lucy." Nan turned to her daughter. "Phaedra, I'd like you to meet Hector Kranz, an accountant at Webley and Wright. Hector, this is my daughter, Professor Phaedra Brighton."

He extended his hand. He was tall and thin, and a pair of trendy, black-framed glasses rested on the narrow bridge of his nose. He looked like a hipster Ichabod Crane. "Hello, Professor."

"Phaedra, please." She smiled. "I see you're stuck with a name from Greek mythology, too."

"Unfortunately. Hector was a Trojan prince and a fierce warrior. Until Achilles did away with him."

"At least he died a hero. Phaedra was half sister to the Minotaur."

"Let me guess. You're a professor of classical studies."

"English literature. I'm also a Jane Austen scholar."

"Ah." He wrinkled his nose. "Not my thing. Sorry."

She swallowed a sigh as her mother slipped away. "So. You're an accountant?"

"CPA. And a financial forensic consultant."

Intrigued, she asked, "And what does a financial forensic consultant do, exactly?"

"I investigate allegations pertaining to financial fraud and related monetary improprieties." He rocked back on his heels. "I also prepare proof of loss reports for the insurance company . . ."

Phaedra nodded, already wondering how to politely extricate herself, when the bell jangled over the front door and Rachel Brandon arrived with her entourage.

A flurry of excitement rippled through the shop as the Home Network channel star entered. Dressed in a burnt-orange pantsuit with a Kelly bag slung over her arm, her hair pulled back in a chignon, Rachel commanded attention. Heads craned and cameras clicked as customers pressed forward to take photos with their cell phones.

Local reporter Clark Mullinax, Nikon held to his face, snapped a series of rapid-fire photos for the *Laurel Springs Clarion*.

"Ms. Brandon," someone called out, "can I get a selfie?" There was a chorus of requests for autographs and pictures as customers crowded around her.

"Later," Rachel said politely but firmly. "Today belongs to Hannah Brighton and her new patisserie, Tout de Sweet."

She moved forward through the throng as Anna Steele cleared the way. "I highly recommend the dark chocolate cupcakes with salted dark chocolate ganache. They're nothing short of sublime."

A caramel-skinned woman with cropped platinum blond hair and a well-dressed older man, his age anywhere from fifty to sixty, followed Rachel to the front counter.

Hannah, wearing a crisp white chef's jacket with her name embroidered on the breast pocket, nodded to Rachel as she brought out a tray of just-baked financiers—almond cakes—and arranged them behind the case.

Customers swarmed the counter, and in a matter of minutes the chocolate cupcakes sold out. Everyone loved the rich flavor and dark, bittersweet glaze.

"Hello, Phaedra." Her father eased through the crowd and pecked her on the cheek. "I see our local celebrity Rachel Brandon is here. Is that your mother's doing?"

"Not this time. She asked me to deliver Hannah's cupcakes to Delaford yesterday for the Historic Holiday Homes tour. Rachel loved them. Now, here she is. Quite a coup for Hannah." She paused. "Well, well."

He followed her gaze. Rachel leaned over the pastry counter, conversing animatedly with Hannah. The platinum-haired woman reached out to shake Hannah's hand, the oversize gold hoops in her ears gleaming with the motion. The man offered a brief nod. A moment later the four vanished into the kitchen.

"Wonder what that's about," Phaedra mused.

"Hopefully something good." Malcolm glimpsed his wife steaming toward them. "Here comes your mother. I'll head her off at the pass, shall I?"

She grinned. "Thanks, Dad. I owe you one."

He left, and her attention returned to the crowded front counter. What were the three women discussing? An interview? A collaboration? The possibilities were tantalizing, and Phaedra fully intended to grill her sister at the first opportunity.

"What should I choose, Rebecca?" an elderly woman nearby asked. "One of these financiers or a madeleine?"

"Neither." The answer was quick and decisive. "Your *sugar*, Biddy."

Phaedra glanced over. Rebecca Bondurant was tall and thin, her younger sister, Biddy, petite and rounded. Together they owned Scents and Sensibility Apothecary and sold holistic tinctures, ointments, and tisanes.

"Excuse me," Phaedra said. "I couldn't help but overhear. May I suggest Hannah's pinwheel sablés? They're sugar- and gluten-free, and they're to die for."

"Not literally, one hopes," Rebecca sniffed.

"One hundred percent safe. And delicious."

"I'll try one," Biddy decided. Her face crinkled into a warm smile. "Thank you, Professor Brighton."

"My pleasure." Phaedra turned away. Good thing Hannah's pastries were displayed behind a glass case. Local shop owners knew Biddy Bondurant liked to slip small items into her pocket now and then, items her sister, Rebecca, quietly returned. No charges were ever filed, and nothing was said. Biddy had regrettably light fingers, but she was elderly and sweet. And essentially harmless.

"Phaedra!"

Elaine Alexander, proprietor of Stage Door Costumes and a close friend since they'd met at the University of Virginia, waved from her seat at one of the café tables, an espresso and a small lemon tart in front of her.

"Elaine, hi. Where've you been? How's business?"

"Good. Busy. But not like this. The place is rocking!"

"It really is." Phaedra's glance strayed to Patsy Fortune, one of the famous-for-being-famous Fortune sisters and a former social media influencer, now the manager of Woofgang's Gourmet Doggy Bakery and Clark Mullinax's girlfriend.

Patsy nudged Clark and murmured something in his ear.

"Oh, hey, Professor," Clark called out as he held up his camera and pointed it at her. "Say 'fromage.'"

Phaedra produced a polite smile as he snapped a couple of photos.

With a sigh, she turned back to Elaine. "Sorry. Doing my bit for publicity, not that Hannah needs it. I'm free in two weeks. Winter break. We should get together."

"Yes, definitely. I'll hold you to it."

As she moved away, Phaedra noticed a man standing near the front door, hunched into a dingy white parka. He shifted from one foot to the other, his gray brows drawn together as he stared fixedly at something. His hands were jammed in his pockets, and a scar marred one cheek.

It wasn't the scar that disturbed her. The stranger, whoever he was, focused his glare on her father.

What was *that* all about?

"Sorry I'm late," Marisol breathed as she pushed her way through the door, her cheeks rosy from the cold. "The lock on my car door was frozen solid." She loosened her scarf and eyed the pink-and-white-striped walls. "Oh, I love this interior! It's like stepping inside a candy box."

"A very elegant candy box," Phaedra agreed.

"Pink flatters the complexion," Lucy said as she joined them. "Plus, pale green was already taken." Seeing Marisol's blank expression, she added, "Ladurée? Paris?"

"Oh, right." Marisol shrugged. "I knew that."

Lucy grinned. "Sure, you did. Where's Mark?" she asked Phaedra. "Is he coming?"

"As of yesterday, yes. But it's pretty crowded, and"—she peered outside—"there's no place to park. Maybe he decided to give it a miss." She could hardly blame him.

"Professor Selden? I saw him just now," Marisol said. "He's parking his car."

As if on cue the door opened, and Mark Selden entered in a blast of cold air and firm British resolve.

"Over here," Phaedra called out.

He edged through the crowd until he reached them. "Hello, everyone. Bit blustery out there today." He glanced at Phaedra. "Told you I'd make it."

Instead of his usual business-casual teaching attire, he wore jeans, running shoes—he called them trainers—and a navy wool peacoat. His dark brown hair was windblown and a blue-and-yellow scarf hung down the front of his coat.

"I'm glad you did." She added, "Just a reminder, Professor. A scarf doesn't do much good if you don't wrap it around your neck."

"I like to live dangerously."

His eyes met hers. Despite the babble of voices around them, the hiss of the espresso machine, and the incessant beeping of the cash register, they might've been the only two in the shop.

"I'll keep that in mind," Phaedra said lightly.

"A table just became available." Lucy was already arrowing toward it. "Let's grab it."

"I can't stay," Mark said, drawing Phaedra aside as she moved to follow her friends. "But I wanted to congratulate your sister before I go. Where is she?"

"In the kitchen. With Rachel Brandon." Seeing his hesitation, she added, "Go ahead. You'll make her day."

"Okay. Sorry to rush off." He reached out and caught her hand. "Rain check? A real, honest-to-goodness date next week, just the two of us?"

"I'd like that. As long as you don't take me to the Dog 'n Draft again."

"You have to admit, the half-smoke was seriously good." He grinned at her upraised brow. "But yes, I promise, no hot dogs or beer in plastic cups this time."

"In that case, you're on."

He gave her hand a squeeze, released it, and threaded his way through the throng to the kitchen. As she watched him go, Phaedra felt a tingle all the way down to her toes.

The bell jangled as more people came in, and she felt a rush of pride for her sister. Hannah had worked hard for the past two years, saving her money and making valuable contacts in her previous position as a pastry chef at the British embassy, and now her efforts had paid off.

Tout de Sweet was a smashing success.

As Phaedra joined Lucy and Marisol at their table near the display counter, Hannah hurried up, her face flushed and her eyes sparkling. She handed Phaedra a single plated cupcake and two plastic forks.

"For you and Dad to share," she said, casting an apologetic glance at Lucy and Marisol. "Sorry, guys, but it's the last dark chocolate. And Dad's favorite."

"I'll remember that," Lucy retorted. "Next time you want more of that Chinese milk candy you love so much."

"I'll make it up to you. I promise."

"Did Mark find you?" Phaedra asked her sister, setting the cupcake and forks on the table.

"He did. He's so thoughtful. And British. And so . . . Darcy-esque."

"Is that even a word?" Lucy said.

"It is now." Hannah's eyes danced with barely contained excitement. "I've been talking with Rachel and her producer, Vanessa Cole."

"The woman with the short platinum hair?"

She nodded. "That's her. And I have news. Big news." Seeing Clark hovering nearby, she lowered her voice. "Talk later?"

"You bet. I want all the juicy details."

"So do I," Marisol added.

Hannah promised to fill them in later and excused herself. As she rushed back to the kitchen, Lucy eyed Phaedra's cupcake. "Well? Aren't you going to dig in? Because if you don't want it—"

"I do. But I'll wait for Dad."

She scanned the room in search of her father, pleased by the steady stream of customers entering the patisserie. "There's not a single unoccupied table," Phaedra marveled. "I'd be surprised if they don't run out of pastries soon."

The words had barely left her lips when the fire alarm erupted, loud and insistent.

Conversation ceased as Hannah raised her voice above

the shrilling alarm. "It's okay, everyone. Stay calm. Please vacate the shop in an orderly fashion."

"Is there a fire?" a woman asked anxiously.

"No. At least, not that we know of. Please wait outside until the fire department arrives."

Everyone streamed toward the front door. "I guess that means us, too," Lucy said, and stood up with a sigh. Phaedra and Marisol followed suit, grabbing their purses and coats as they joined the customers headed for the door.

"It's too cold for a fire drill," Marisol grumbled as the wind whipped at her scarf. "Hope this doesn't take long."

"It may not be a drill." Phaedra thrust her ungloved hands in her coat pockets. "Could be the real thing."

They waited outside, huddled together in groups, noses turning red and voices filled with speculation as they wondered what was going on. Rachel, Anna, and Vanessa Cole were the last to emerge.

Lucy shivered. "I should've brought my espresso with me. At least my fingers would stay warm."

The distant shriek of a siren heralded the arrival of the fire department. Everyone craned their necks as the truck came to a stop at the curb and four firefighters emerged.

"Everyone, stay back," one of the men ordered. "Keep the area in front of the building clear."

As they all edged away, two of the crew circled around back while two entered through the front door. After what seemed like an eternity but was probably only twenty minutes, the incident commander gave the all clear and everyone filed back inside the patisserie, relieved the alarm had proven false.

"Who do you suppose pulled the fire alarm?" Lucy asked as they followed Rachel Brandon and her crew inside and headed back to their table.

"No idea." Phaedra took out her phone. "I just hope whoever did it is caught. You guys go ahead. I need to check my messages."

As Lucy and Marisol returned to the table, she glanced

at her screen. There was one message, from Mark. I heard there's a fire truck outside Hannah's?? Are you okay?

Fine, she texted back. False alarm.

Returning her phone to her purse—thankfully, she'd worn slacks and a sweater instead of her usual Empire gown and reticule—Phaedra joined the others. She glanced at the table with a frown. Espressos, check. Lucy and Marisol, check. But something was missing.

"Where's my cupcake?" she asked suddenly. "The one Hannah brought out for me and Dad. It's gone."

"It was here when we left," Lucy said.

"Looks like Rachel's assistant grabbed it," Marisol remarked, and they followed her gaze.

Sure enough, Anna Steele held the dark chocolate cupcake aloft on its plate as she made a beeline for Ms. Brandon on the other side of the shop. She caught Rachel's eye and called out, "I got you the last dark chocolate."

Rachel gave her assistant a dismissive wave. "Not now, I'm interviewing Hannah."

Anna visibly deflated. "Oh. Okay. Sorry."

"I can't believe she stole your cupcake!" Lucy glared at Anna. "And Rachel doesn't even want it. Want me to get it back? Because you know I will."

"No. It's okay. Dad will be disappointed, but he'll get over it."

"You're too nice," Lucy grumbled. "And way too understanding."

Phaedra shrugged. "It's a cupcake, Lu." She watched as Anna turned away, plainly disappointed her offering had been rejected, and licked a dab of ganache from her finger. "Let her have it. It's not the end of the world—"

Before she could finish the sentence, the plate tilted and slid out of Anna's hands onto the floor, sending the cupcake rolling. Perspiration broke out on her forehead, and her face went deathly pale.

"Something's wrong," Phaedra breathed, and shot to her feet in alarm. "Anna? What is it? Are you okay?"

But Rachel's assistant didn't respond, didn't even seem to hear her. "Dizzy," she panted, her breath coming in short gasps as she clutched her chest. "Heart beating . . . really fast . . ."

As everyone looked on in horror, Anna staggered forward, teetered unsteadily, and collapsed face-first onto the nearest table.

Three

Phaedra rushed over. “Anna? Anna, can you hear me?”

There was no response. She bent down and pressed two fingers against the young woman’s neck.

“Is she . . .” Hannah eyed her fearfully. “Dead?”

“She has a pulse, barely. Call 911. Hurry.”

After telling the dispatcher a woman had collapsed after consuming a small amount of salted chocolate ganache, Hannah provided the address and stayed on the line.

“Do you think she had an allergic reaction?” she asked Phaedra.

“Hard to say. It’s certainly possible.”

Rachel and her producer, their faces stricken as they stared at Anna’s sprawled form, joined them. “What just happened?” Vanessa turned to Phaedra. “Is she unconscious?”

“She’s breathing, but she needs medical attention. An ambulance is on the way. Does she have any food allergies that either of you know about?” Phaedra asked.

Rachel shook her head. “None.”

“She loves dark chocolate,” Vanessa added. “Eats it all

the time. That's why this"—she glanced down at the smashed remnants of plate and the untouched chocolate cupcake—"makes no sense."

In a matter of minutes, a Somerset County fire department ambulance pulled up in front of the patisserie and two EMTs rushed inside. Phaedra directed them to Anna and told them what had happened.

"Did she inhale anything? Ingest anything?" one of the men asked as he checked her vital signs.

"Only a little of the salted chocolate ganache from that cupcake," Phaedra said as she indicated the lone chocolate cupcake on the floor. "Some got on her finger."

"Any allergies?"

"No." Rachel stepped forward. "Anna Steele is my personal assistant. She was fine. Until she collapsed."

"Based on the symptoms you described on the phone," the EMT told Hannah, "dizziness, elevated heart rate, shortness of breath, loss of consciousness . . . she may have been poisoned."

"Poisoned!" Hannah exclaimed. All the color fled her already pale face. "How?"

"This." The other medic held up the dark chocolate cupcake in one latex-gloved hand. "The ganache has a distinctive bitter almond scent. I can't be positive until the tox report comes back, but the scent indicates the salt granules may be tainted with cyanide."

A shocked silence met his words.

"Cyanide?" Hannah squeaked, and sank down onto one of the chairs. "How did *cyanide* end up on one of my cupcakes?"

"That's a question for the police, ma'am. We've notified the sheriff's department, and they're sending someone out to investigate."

They waited as the EMT administered an injection into Anna's arm. "Hydroxocobalamin," he explained. "It's the first-line treatment in a cyanide poisoning."

"An antidote," Phaedra murmured.

He nodded and turned away as he and the other EMT transferred Anna onto a gurney.

"Will she be all right?" Rachel asked anxiously.

"We'll do everything we can," one of the paramedics assured her as they rolled the gurney toward the exit. "Please, everyone, let us through."

The ambulance had barely left, siren wailing, when a county sheriff's car arrived, closely followed by a white, slightly battered Honda Civic.

Homicide detective Matteo Morelli.

Tall, dark, and disheveled, he thrust his way through the door, looking as if he'd been up half the night. "What've we got?"

"Possible poisoning," one of the deputies replied. "Granules of either sodium or potassium cyanide, not yet confirmed. The EMT believes the granules were sprinkled on the cupcake's salted ganache."

His glance went to the offending cupcake. "Get it tested right away. We need to know what we're dealing with." He turned to face the anxious customers. "Everyone, remain on the premises until we get your names and phone numbers. We'll be questioning each of you."

As one deputy knelt down to carefully bag the cupcake and another stationed himself by the door with a clipboard to take down names and numbers, Morelli withdrew a notepad and pen and approached Hannah and Phaedra.

"I'm Detective Matt Morelli," he told Hannah, and glanced at Phaedra. "You and I met, what? Two murders ago?"

Phaedra shrugged. "What can I say? I have a talent for being in the wrong place at the wrong time."

He turned to Hannah. "What can you tell me? Take me through what happened."

"We sold out of dark chocolate cupcakes," she began, and returned her phone to her pocket. "I brought the last one to Phaedra on a plate with two plastic forks, to share with our dad. He loves dark chocolate," she added.

Morelli nodded. "Okay. So how did . . ."

"Anna Steele," Phaedra supplied.

"How did Anna Steele end up with it?"

"Right after Hannah brought the cupcake out," Phaedra said, "maybe five minutes? The fire alarm sounded. We all went outside to wait for the fire department to arrive."

"It was a false alarm," Marisol piped up. "I'm Marisol," she added as he shot her a cursory glance. "Dubois. D-U-B-O-I—"

"Got it. Thanks." He turned back to Hannah. "Where's the alarm located?"

"The back entrance. Next to the fire exit."

"And is the back entrance normally kept locked?"

She hesitated. "Normally, yes. Today we propped the door open because we had several morning deliveries."

"Which means anyone could have slipped in and pulled the fire alarm."

"Well . . . yes, I suppose so."

"Did anyone stay behind after the alarm sounded?" Morelli asked.

"No. Everyone left," Hannah said. "Including me."

"Who was in the kitchen when the alarm went off?"

"I was," she said. "Along with my assistant, Liv Bianco, and Rachel Brandon. Rachel and her producer, Vanessa Cole, wanted to discuss featuring my shop in an upcoming issue of the *Home Channel* magazine. Oh," she added, "and Jared Harper. He makes our croissants."

"And who made the chocolate cupcakes?" Morelli asked, his eyes still fixed on Hannah. "You?"

"Yes. I mixed the batter and filled the trays. Liv made the ganache and put it on the cooled cupcakes." She returned an Arctic gaze. "I can assure you my ingredients are all carefully sourced. And definitely nonlethal."

"Did anyone else experience an adverse reaction from those cupcakes? Or from anything else you sold today?"

Hannah shook her head firmly. "No. No one."

"When we came back, after the false alarm," Phaedra

said, "Anna must've seen the cupcake on our table and took it."

"Why would she do that?"

"It was the last dark chocolate. She offered it to Rachel. Her boss."

"I take it Ms. Brandon didn't want it?"

Phaedra shook her head. "She was interviewing my sister. Anna must've decided to eat it herself. She licked a dab of ganache from her finger, and . . ." She drew in a steadying breath. "She started perspiring and mentioned feeling dizzy. Said her heart was racing. Then she collapsed onto a table."

"Detective?" One of the deputies appeared. "We found something. In the kitchen."

Hannah exchanged a startled glance with Phaedra. What could the police have found? Her heartbeat quickening, Phaedra squeezed her sister's hand in a gesture of mingled reassurance and solidarity and followed Morelli and the deputy into the kitchen.

"Take a look. We found it in one of the cabinets."

It was a small green box of salt.

"That's Maldon salt," Hannah said. "Chefs sometimes use a few flakes to finish a dish and enhance flavor. It has a briny taste and adds a crunchy texture."

"But this isn't a restaurant," Morelli pointed out. "It's a bakery."

"Yes. But here at the *patisserie*"—she crossed her arms as corrected him—"we often sprinkle it on caramel, chocolate ganache, even our salted chocolate chip cookies."

"Smells odd," the deputy said, and frowned. "Bitter. A little like . . . almonds."

Morelli pulled on a pair of latex gloves and took the box. "You have a discerning nose, Officer Scott. I don't smell a thing. Guess it's true what they say. Not everyone can pick up the scent of cyanide."

"Cyanide?" As she appeared in the doorway, Phaedra's mother, Nan Brighton, let out a horrified gasp. "You can't be serious!"

Morelli turned around. "Mrs. Brighton, I need you to wait out front with the others. Take your daughters and Ms. Dubois with you. I'll question everyone in a few minutes."

"Let's go back to our table, Nan." Malcolm Brighton joined them in the doorway and cast the detective an apologetic glance as he drew his wife away.

Phaedra caught Hannah's hand in hers. It was ice-cold. "Detective—"

"Out front, please, Professor." His words were firm. "Thank you."

Wordlessly she nodded and followed her sister out.

"Forensics is on the way," she heard the deputy say.

"I want that salt tested, along with the cupcake. Take it to a private lab. We'll get a quicker turnaround. Dust the fire alarm and the emergency exit for prints . . ."

Phaedra glanced at the front door. Customers dutifully gave their names and phone numbers to the deputy stationed there. She heard grumbling and the angry scrape of chairs as they returned to their tables to wait.

"They're not happy campers," Lucy said as Phaedra and Hannah returned to the table.

"Who can blame them?" Marisol laid her phone down. "It's Saturday. People have things to do. Places to be."

"I'll offer everyone coffee," Hannah decided. "On the house. And maybe some sablés—"

Phaedra laid her hand atop her sister's and shook her head. "That's thoughtful, but I doubt anyone will want anything to eat or drink until that cupcake is tested."

"Oh." Like a sail deprived of wind, Hannah deflated. "I guess you're right." Her gaze grew anxious. "This could really hurt my business. Do you think . . ."

"What?"

"Maybe someone did this out of spite. A jealous rival, someone who wants to see my business fail."

Instead of dismissing the idea, Phaedra considered it. "Do you have anyone in particular in mind?"

Hannah didn't hesitate. "Kate Brennan. The owner of Brennan's bakery."

"Kate?" She shook her head. "No way. She's quick with a catty remark, and she's not exactly warm and fuzzy, but I can't see her poisoning anyone. And Brennan's has been around for twenty years."

"Exactly. And for all of those years, they were the only bakery in town. Now they have competition. Me."

"I suppose it's possible," Phaedra conceded. "But unlikely."

"The poisoning probably has nothing to do with the patisserie," Lucy said. "Maybe someone has it in for Anna Steele. Someone who wants her out of the way."

"That's a stretch, Lu." Phaedra lowered her voice and leaned forward. "And you're forgetting one very important fact."

"What's that?"

"Hannah brought the cupcake out for me to share with Dad. Which means," Phaedra finished slowly, "the cyanide on the salted ganache might have been meant for me. Or Dad." She drew in a halting breath. "Or both of us."

"This is crazy." Tears of frustration welled in her sister's eyes. "No one in my kitchen would do such a thing. I've known Liv forever. We were in Brownies together! We shared a locker in high school. And Jared loves to play practical jokes, but he'd never do something like this."

"I could use a coffee. Anyone else?" Hannah and Lucy nodded as Phaedra stood. Removing three takeout cups from the stack behind the counter, she poured in French roast coffee and added plenty of cream and sugar. She snapped on lids and carried the cups on a tray back to the table.

"What do you think?" Hannah asked as Phaedra resumed her seat. "I know you must have a theory or two."

"I do." She took a cautious sip. Not because she feared poison, but because the coffee was strong and piping hot.

And French Roast wasn't her favorite. "I think whoever pulled that fire alarm probably poisoned the ganache."

Lucy wrapped her fingers around the cup. "A diversionary tactic, you mean?"

"Exactly. It got everyone out of the shop with ten minutes to spare before the fire department arrived. Plenty of time to tamper with the cupcake and sprinkle the ganache with cyanide granules."

"Makes sense," Marisol agreed.

"I imagine Morelli's thinking along the same lines," Phaedra said. "He asked a lot of questions about the fire alarm." She frowned. "We need to know who was here before the alarm went off, and who was here after."

"How do we figure that out?" Hannah asked.

"The deputy." Phaedra indicated the officer by the door, reviewing the list of customers' names and phone numbers on his clipboard. "If I can get a copy of that list, we can look it over, compare it to everyone who was here earlier, and figure out who's missing."

"He won't give it to you," Lucy said dismissively.

"No." Phaedra pushed her chair back. "But for a cup of coffee and one of Hannah's lemon poppy seed doughnuts? He might."

"True," Lucy agreed. "Although he might take a pass on the doughnut." She cast Hannah a quick, apologetic glance. "Sorry."

Hannah shrugged. "It's okay."

Phaedra persuaded Officer Scott to take a coffee break while she took up his post by the door. As Hannah moved behind the counter to pour his coffee—Lucy was right, he declined the doughnut—Phaedra snapped a quick photo of the list of names with her phone and slipped it back in her pocket just before he returned.

"Thanks, Professor." He lifted his cup in a salute. "I don't care what Morelli says. In my book, you're okay."

"You're welcome. Are you sure you wouldn't like a little something to go with that coffee?"

Detective Morelli emerged from the kitchen and came toward them, his expression flatlining as he saw Phaedra. "Professor Brighton. What are you doing over here?"

"Just making sure this deputy gets a well-deserved coffee break."

He seemed about to challenge her but let it go. "Those the names and phone numbers?" he asked the deputy.

Scott nodded and handed over the list.

"Okay, everyone," Morelli called out. "You're free to go." He swung around to face Phaedra and Hannah as customers gathered up their purses and coats. "Except for you two. I'm detaining your staff, Ms. Brighton, along with Ms. Brandon and Ms. Cole, for further questioning."

Hannah crossed her arms. "Why? You can't seriously think my staff had anything to do with the poisoning—"

"This is a crime scene. No one is above suspicion."

"But Anna's fine," Phaedra pointed out. "She's okay."

"She was, until her arrival at Somerset General. I just had a call from the attending physician." With a weary motion, Morelli thrust his notepad into his pocket. "Unfortunately, Anna Steele didn't make it. She's dead."

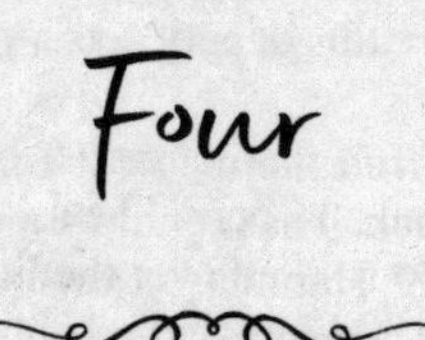

Four

Dead?" Hannah gaped at him. She groped blindly for a chair and sank down, her expression dazed. "She was just here! Joking with Vanessa. Discussing today's schedule with Rachel. I can't . . . that poor girl!"

"This is terrible." Rachel, who'd joined them just in time to hear the grim news, clutched her clipboard to her chest. "What . . . what happens now?"

"The medical examiner is on his way to the hospital," Detective Morelli said. "He'll want an autopsy as soon as possible." He looked up as Phaedra returned from behind the counter and handed him a takeout cup of coffee.

"With a shot of espresso," she said.

"Thanks." He turned back to Rachel. "We'll know more then."

"Why the rush to conduct an autopsy?" Phaedra asked.

"Cyanide has a short half-life. Detection is conclusive only if it's confirmed within the first few hours of exposure."

"I can't believe Tout de Sweet is a crime scene." Hannah shook her head in dismay. "What happens next?"

"We wait for the toxicology and autopsy reports. We conduct an investigation. We ask questions. During that time, your bakery will have to close—and remain closed—until our investigation is finished."

Hannah straightened. "How long will that take?"

"Good question," Rachel said, glancing pointedly at her watch.

"Until we hear from the medical examiner and get the toxicology report back. That could be a week or two."

"A week or two?" Hannah echoed, her eyes widening. "But what about my business? This is my livelihood! Today was our grand opening."

"I'm sorry." Morelli paused. "We'll try to wrap things up as quickly as we can."

Phaedra laid her hand on Hannah's shoulder. "It's okay. We'll figure it out." In an attempt at humor, she added, "It's not like you have to pay rent or anything."

Her sister's face crumpled. "Not only is my business in jeopardy, I don't even have a place to call my own."

After quitting her job as a pastry chef at the British embassy in Washington, D.C., Hannah moved straight into Phaedra's carriage house. The apartment over the patisserie needed new plumbing, an expense she couldn't afford at the moment. Every penny had gone into Tout de Sweet.

"Imagine we're Elinor and Marianne Dashwood," Phaedra suggested.

"Who?"

"The Dashwood sisters in *Sense and Sensibility.* We've lost our home and moved into Barton Cottage—in our case, the carriage house—and anything might happen."

"Yes, anything," Hannah echoed grimly. "Like losing my patisserie. Or being accused of poisoning a customer and going to prison."

"My place is yours for as long as you need it," Phaedra assured her, regretting her ill-timed attempt at literary distraction. "You know that."

Hannah lifted a watery gaze. "I do. Thanks."

"And speaking of 'I do,' you'll have your own place soon, when you and Charles get married and buy a house."

Charles Dalton, her sister's fiancé, worked at the British embassy in Washington, D.C.

"*If* he ever decides to set a wedding date."

"I need to start questioning everyone," Detective Morelli said.

"Everyone?" Rachel huffed. "I hope you don't mean me."

"Everyone." His voice was even. "Including you, Ms. Brandon."

"This is unacceptable! My time is valuable, and every minute is scheduled down to the last nanosecond." Her eyes narrowed. "I insist you put myself and my producer, Ms. Cole, first on your list."

"I assure you, we'll get to you, Ms. Brandon," Morelli said.

She glared at him and stalked away, cell phone pressed to her ear.

"Wow," Marisol said in a low voice. "Entitled, much?"

Phaedra studied Rachel. "She seems more concerned with the inconvenience than the reality of her assistant's death."

"Death hits different people in different ways," Morelli said. He glanced at Hannah. "Is there somewhere I can conduct the interviews? Somewhere private?"

With a sigh, Hannah stood. "My office. In the back."

"Lead the way. We'll start with you."

With nothing to do but wait, Phaedra brewed a fresh pot of coffee and took out her phone. She pulled up the photo she'd snapped of Officer Scott's list of names and numbers and leaned against the counter to study them.

She skimmed the list. Some of the names she recognized, some she didn't. A few names were missing: the Bondurant sisters, Clark Mullinax, Patsy Fortune. Hector Kranz left before the fire alarm, as had Mark Selden. But the first name on the list surprised her.

"Kate *Brennan* was here?" Phaedra returned to the table, a mug of coffee in hand.

"She was?" Marisol barely looked up from her phone. "I didn't see her."

"I did." Lucy closed out of her app. "She wandered over when we were waiting outside. Asked me what was going on. When we went back inside, she came, too, and took a couple of photos of the menu board with her phone."

"Sizing up the competition?" Phaedra frowned. "Why didn't I notice her?"

"Probably because she had on a down jacket and a wool scarf. And sunglasses. I didn't pay her much attention until she started taking photos." Lucy paused. "Now that I think about it, she was the first to give Officer Scott her name." She tilted her head to one side. "And the first out the door."

"Maybe she disguised herself in a bulky coat and sunglasses deliberately," Phaedra said. "Easier to check out her competition and do a little snooping undercover."

"Entirely possible," Lucy agreed.

"What if there isn't any poison in the ganache?" Marisol said with a frown. "What if Anna died from some kind of food allergy? Like anaphylaxis."

"Maybe, but I doubt it," Phaedra replied. "The EMT said the ganache had a bitter almond scent. He treated her for potential poisoning. And Rachel and Vanessa both said that Anna didn't have any food allergies."

"That they knew of," Lucy pointed out.

Phaedra reached for the coffeepot. "If the ganache really was poisoned, then someone obviously intended harm."

"Mens rea," her father said as he joined them.

At Marisol's questioning glance, Phaedra explained, "It's a legal term. It means criminal intent."

"The question is, whose?" Malcolm wondered. "And why would anyone want to poison the poor girl?"

"Maybe they didn't." Phaedra frowned. "Maybe the cyanide was meant for someone else."

"It's possible, I suppose," he agreed.

"So, if the poisoner poisoned the wrong person," Lucy said slowly, "does that mean the culprit gets a pass?"

Malcolm shook his head. "Not at all. Regardless of who's harmed, the intent to harm remains the same."

The door to Hannah's office opened and her sister emerged, her manner subdued. Before Phaedra could question her, Detective Morelli called her back. She brushed past him into her sister's tiny office. Cartons of recycled coffee cups and boxes of wooden stirrers and snap-on lids were stacked nearby. He closed the door and indicated a Bentwood chair wedged in front of the desk. "Have a seat."

Wordlessly she complied.

"Hannah said you were in and out of the kitchen several times."

She nodded. "The staff was busy, so I pitched in. Mostly, I refilled coffee cups." She paused. "At UVA, I waited tables part-time at the College Inn. It's gone now. They had the best gyros. And they stayed open late."

"In Chicago it's Mr. Greek." He tapped a pencil against his notepad. "Did you notice anything when you were in the kitchen? Anything unusual?"

"Not really. Jared was making croissants, and Liv was helping Hannah crank out financiers and cupcakes."

"Any idea who might've tampered with the salt?"

Phaedra shook her head. "Between the fire alarm going off and the place being so crowded, it's hard to say. It was controlled chaos all morning."

"Was anyone in the kitchen who shouldn't have been?"

"That I know of? Only Rachel and Vanessa Cole, and they were here in the office, discussing a possible magazine article with Hannah."

"Did Anna Steele have any enemies that you're aware of? Did she and her boss, Rachel, get along?"

"I didn't know Anna, so I can't be sure, but I don't think she had any enemies. Ms. Brandon struck me as demanding but fair. I don't know if the two got along or not. And as I said, I don't think Anna was the target. Hannah brought the cupcake out for Dad and me to share."

"Right." He sipped his coffee and set it back down with a grimace. "Cold. What about your sister? Can you think of anyone who'd want Hannah's business to fail?"

Phaedra thought of Kate Brennan. "Possibly."

His gaze sharpened. "Who?"

She repeated what Lucy had said. "According to Professor Liang, Mrs. Brennan didn't stay long and she didn't buy anything. Just took photos of the menu board. I've heard rumors that she's more bothered by Tout de Sweet than she admits. She doesn't like competition."

"Where'd you hear this?"

"From a member of her bakery staff. Her daughter, Moira."

He made a note. "I'll check it out." He glanced back up at her. "You stated the fire alarm went off after your sister brought you the cupcake, correct?"

"Yes. She asked everyone to exit the building and wait for the fire department to arrive."

He leaned back in his chair and studied her. "I find the timing of the alarm interesting. I wonder—"

"If whoever pulled the alarm also poisoned the ganache?" She leaned forward. "I wondered the same thing. Maybe the alarm was a diversionary tactic to get everyone out of the shop."

"Seems likely. Although a bit risky." Morelli rubbed the bridge of his nose and dropped his pencil. "I have one more question before I let you go."

She waited.

"Can you tell me who left before the alarm went off?"

Phaedra eyed him doubtfully. "I'm not really sure."

"Give it your best shot."

"Well," she ventured, frowning, "Clark Mullinax took a few pictures for the *Clarion*, but he left right after, along with his girlfriend, Patsy. Patsy Fortune." She crinkled her brow in concentration. "Aunt Wendy popped in for a minute, but she didn't stay. Business at the B and B is booming."

Her mother's sister owned the Laurel Springs Inn. When she'd recently threatened to sell the place, Phaedra convinced her to host a Jane Austen–themed murder mystery week . . . which led, ironically enough, to a real murder.

The resulting notoriety put the bed-and-breakfast on the map. With the case solved and the murderer safely behind bars, everyone wanted to book a stay at the "real murder" house.

"Anyone else?" Morelli asked.

"Well . . . the Bondurant sisters, Rebecca and Biddy. Elaine Alexander. Hector Kranz—he's a friend of my mother's." Phaedra hesitated. "And . . . Mark Selden."

"Professor Selden?"

She nodded. "He stopped by to congratulate Hannah. He didn't stay long. Oh!" she added suddenly, sitting up straight in her chair. "I nearly forgot. There was a man standing by the door. A strange man."

"Why do you refer to him as strange?"

"He was middle-aged, maybe forty. He wore a dirty white parka, with his hands stuffed in his pockets, and he had bushy gray brows."

"That hardly makes him strange. You just described any number of middle-aged men."

"He had a pronounced scar on one cheek." Phaedra met his gaze. "And he was staring at my father across the room. Fixedly. With an expression I can only describe as ill-intentioned."

"Oh, so you can read minds now?"

"It doesn't take a mind reader to see dislike on someone's face."

"Okay. I'll speak to your father. See if he has any idea who the mysterious stranger might've been." He stood up. "Speaking of which, I'm questioning Mr. Brighton next."

"Not Rachel Brandon?" she asked, one brow raised.

"She moved to the bottom of the list right after her outburst."

"Good for you." A trace of a smile curved her lips. "I'll send Dad back."

With Tout de Sweet officially closed and Hannah and her staff still undergoing questioning, Phaedra left. The sky was gray and banked with clouds, and the wind had sharpened. She shoved her hands into her coat pockets and returned to her car. Might as well head to the IGA and pick up a few ingredients for dinner.

The Mini didn't want to start. After a few coughs the engine finally caught, and she breathed a sigh of relief.

"You don't like the cold any more than I do," she soothed as she switched on the heater and patted the dashboard. "I get it."

The air that blew out was barely warm.

She made her way down Main Street. The Poison Pen, her father's bookstore, bustled with business as she drove past. Everyone must be stocking up on books in anticipation of the predicted snow. Just as they'd be stocking up on milk and beer and toilet paper at the IGA.

She slowed to wait for a Volkswagen to back out of a parking space in front of the bookstore, and noticed Brennan's bakery next door. Impulsively, she pulled into the newly vacated spot.

Questions swirled through her mind like flakes in a snow flurry. Why had Kate Brennan shown up at Hannah's patisserie? Was she checking out her competition, as Lucy suggested? Or was her appearance merely coincidental? The timing was certainly odd.

One way to find out.

Phaedra shut off the ignition and dropped the keys in her purse. Lucy said Kate showed up after the alarm was pulled and followed everyone back inside. She was in the patisserie when Anna collapsed and was the first to give her name to the police.

She was also the first to leave.

Like the Poison Pen, the bakery boasted a brisk business as Phaedra swung the front door open. The sugary scents of buttercream frosting and birthday cake assaulted her. Vanilla, sweet cream butter, almond . . .

Almond. Like the cyanide in Hannah's dark chocolate ganache.

Ducking her head down, she scanned the glass display counter. No French pastries here; no madeleines or macarons, no fancy financiers. Just typical bakery fare like cake, cookies, brownies, and pies. Nicely decorated and conventionally appealing, to be sure, but nothing to compare with Hannah's Parisian-inspired confections.

"May I help you?"

With a start, Phaedra looked up, straight into Kate Brennan's expectant face. She forced a smile.

"I'd like a half dozen cinnamon rolls, please."

The creases along either side of Mrs. Brennan's mouth deepened as her eyes narrowed in recognition. "Professor Brighton."

She nodded politely. "Hello, Mrs. Brennan."

"What are you doing in here? Slumming?"

"Mom," Moira Brennan warned, and cast her mother a quick glance as she finished creating a buttercream rose. *Sorry*, she mouthed to Phaedra.

"Just getting a head start on tomorrow's breakfast." Phaedra gave the girl a reassuring smile. She refused to let the older woman rattle her. "In case it snows."

"No croissants, no brioche?" Kate grabbed a pair of tongs and picked up a cinnamon roll, dropping it into a white bakery box. Five more followed in quick succession. "I'm surprised. Cinnamon rolls don't seem fancy enough for you or your sister. What with her new patisserie and all."

Don't respond. "How much do I owe you?" Phaedra asked as she reached for her purse.

"On the house," Kate said expansively, a dark glint of humor in her eye. "Poison's extra, of course."

Despite her determination not to react, anger fizzled through her. "It's not clear at this point if Ms. Steele was poisoned or not. We won't know until the toxicology report comes back."

"Oh, it was poison, no question." Kate laid the tongs aside with a deliberation motion. "I was there. Poor gal took one taste of your sister's frosting and, bam! Dead."

By now, hearing Kate's raised voice, a hush fell over the nearby customers as they listened to the exchange.

"It was ganache," Phaedra pointed out evenly, "not frosting. And how can you be so sure it was poisoned? Do you know something I don't?"

Kate sucked in a breath, her eyes widening. "Are you suggesting *I* had something to do with that girl's death?"

"I'm saying no such thing." Phaedra tossed a ten-dollar bill on the counter. "But if the oven mitt fits . . ." She grabbed the box of cinnamon rolls and headed for the door. "Thanks. You can keep the change."

Five

When Phaedra let herself into the carriage house a short time later, she set the box of cinnamon rolls on the hall table and shrugged out of her coat. The temperature had dropped steadily all morning, and the house was borderline chilly. She nudged the thermostat up several degrees and surveyed the place she called home.

The exposed brick walls and fireplace were original to the house, along with a pair of arched doorways that led out to a slate patio. To one side of the stairs leading up to her loft bedroom was the kitchen. The area was compact but functional.

And right now? Unwashed coffee cups, cookbooks, and a trail of crumpled napkins covered every surface.

Phaedra sighed and decided, for the moment, to ignore Hannah's mess. Her gaze went instead to the living area.

A six-foot tree stood in one corner, its branches fragrant but bare, and her sister had propped a few Christmas cards on the fireplace mantel. Seasonal CDs and a lone pillar candle were scattered on the coffee table.

That was the extent of their holiday decor.

"Wickham?" she called up the stairs. "Are you hungry?"

A rolling purr heralded the arrival of her Himalayan cat. He loped downstairs and meandered over, submitting to a brief scratch behind the ears before he padded into the kitchen to investigate his newly filled kibble bowl.

With Wickham busily devouring his seafood grill, she put the cinnamon rolls away and tackled the stack of dirty dishes in the sink. While she didn't mind sharing the carriage house with Hannah for as long as she needed to stay, as a roommate her sister was less than ideal.

"How," she complained to Wickham as she filled the sink and squirted in dishwashing soap, "can someone color-code her clothes and shoes, yet never wash a single dirty dish or make her bed?"

He lifted his head and regarded her with a disinterested blue gaze. *How should I know? She's* your *sister. Got any more of this seafood grill?*

With a sigh, Phaedra switched on the portable radio on the island and turned back to the sink, plunging her hands into the warm, soapy water.

Next Saturday was her father's annual open house at the Poison Pen. She'd been drafted to bring spiced cider, and Hannah had promised to provide an assortment of festively decorated cookies.

Her mood lifted at the thought of the approaching holidays and three glorious weeks off. As she rinsed a dinner plate, "Silver Bells" wafted out over the airwaves. She never tired of the classic Bing Crosby song and always sang along.

She'd make French onion soup for dinner, and pop one of Hannah's baguettes in the oven later. Han would be tired and hungry after answering questions all day. And what was better than a hot bowl of soup and a slice of warm, lavishly buttered bread on a cold winter's day?

After washing up the last dish she glanced at the clock. Too late to start a proper onion soup, but she could whip up a shortcut version. She dried her hands on a dish towel and reached for a carton of beef stock and a couple of onions.

Singing along to "All I Want for Christmas Is You," she tied an apron around her waist and set to work.

It was nearly five o'clock, and onion soup simmered on the stove, when Phaedra heard a key turn in the front door.

"In here," she called out from the kitchen. "Perfect timing. Dinner's almost ready."

As she reached up to grab a couple of earthenware bowls from the cupboard, she heard voices, and a rich, contralto laugh. She set the bowls down and untied the apron at her waist. "Hannah?"

Standing just inside the door, the first few flakes of snow melting on her coat collar, was her sister . . . and Vanessa Cole, Rachel Brandon's producer.

"Hey." Hannah waited as Vanessa shrugged out of her coat and took it, draping it over her arm. "I asked Vanessa to join us for dinner. Rachel had other plans."

"Hope you don't mind," Rachel's producer said quickly.

"Of course not. Welcome. Would you like a glass of wine? I was just about to open a bottle of merlot."

"I'd love a glass, thanks." She followed Hannah into the living area, her dark eyes sweeping over the exposed brick and arched doorways and coming to settle on the fireplace, where a cozy fire crackled away. "Wow. This is perfect. Cozy and impressive, all at once."

"Thanks," Phaedra called out. "Make yourself at home. How's the snow?"

"Just started," Vanessa replied. "But it's not sticking yet." She wandered into the kitchen. "Need help?"

"You can pour the wine. I hope you like French onion soup. I made plenty."

"I do. It smells fantastic." She filled three glasses with a generous measure of wine.

Hannah came in and lifted the pot's lid. "I planned to order a couple of pizzas, but this is better." She breathed in the rich, oniony scent. "Much better."

A few minutes later they settled around the dining room table with earthenware bowls of soup, each topped with a thick slice of baguette oozing with melted Gruyère.

"This is delicious," Vanessa declared as she lifted a spoonful of caramelized onions to her lips.

"I cheated a little with store-bought beef stock," Phaedra admitted. "Much quicker. I'm glad you like it. Where are you staying while you're here in Laurel Springs?"

"A hotel in Crozet. I tried to get a reservation at the local B and B, but it's booked through spring."

Hannah nodded. "That's our aunt Wendy's place. Business really picked up after last summer's mur—" She cleared her throat. "Murderously busy season."

"How long have you worked with Rachel Brandon?" Phaedra asked as she topped up the producer's glass.

"Too long."

"Oh? Is she difficult to work with?"

"Difficult?" Vanessa rolled her eyes. "She can be downright poisonous at times." She paused. "Sorry. Poor choice of words."

"Why do you put up with her, then?"

She lifted one cashmere-clad shoulder. "Why do any of us put up with her? The money, of course."

"Did she and Anna Steele have any issues?"

"Just the usual stuff. Rachel has high expectations." Her spoon stilled. "You know, I'm starting to feel like I'm sitting in front of that detective again. Why do you ask?"

"No reason. I just noticed a certain . . . tension between Anna and Rachel when I was up at Delaford."

"Oh, Rachel's a full-on diva," Vanessa allowed, "no question. But she's not capable of murder, if that's what you're suggesting." She picked up her wineglass. "Her husband, Kyle, now? He's another matter altogether."

Phaedra's interest quickened. "Why do you say that?"

Vanessa hesitated, then shook her head firmly. "No. Not going there. I can't. Forget I said anything."

"If you know something that might have a bearing on

what happened," Phaedra urged, "please, tell us. Hannah opened Tout de Sweet today, and now it's closed because of Anna's death. We need to get to the bottom of this."

"I understand. But I signed a nondisclosure agreement when Rachel hired me. I can't discuss her personal business."

"It's important, or I wouldn't ask. Whatever you tell us goes no further," Phaedra promised. "You have our word."

"Absolutely," Hannah agreed.

Vanessa hesitated. "Well . . . under the circumstances, I suppose I could make an exception." She took a piece of bread from the basket and buttered it. "Kyle Middleton is husband number two. Alan, the first, owned Brandon Advertising. He was much older than Rachel."

"I take it he died?"

She nodded. "Heart attack. He left everything to Rachel, a fact that did *not* sit well with his son. Or Alan's brother, Max."

"Was that the older man I saw with Rachel?" Phaedra asked. "Her brother-in-law?"

"Yes. He threatened to contest the will but settled out of court. Now he's her business adviser. And a good one, too. Thanks to Max she's worth a bundle now."

"So they made their peace."

"More or less." Vanessa took another sip of wine. "She met husband number two on a shoot for organic dog food, fell in love, and married him a couple of years ago."

"I didn't even know she was married," Hannah said.

"She keeps her personal stuff locked down."

"Was Kyle there?" Phaedra asked. "At the patisserie?"

"He was there." She touched a napkin to her lips. "He brought in Rachel's cinnamon soy latte, coconut milk, no sugar, like the good little lapdog he is. Came in through the back. Left that way, too. He didn't stay long. Said he had errands to run, pecked her on the cheek, and took off."

"I think I remember seeing him." Hannah pushed her bowl aside. "Youngish? Dark hair? Man bun?"

"That's him."

"He seemed pretty devoted to Rachel. He carried in her latte, wished her a great day, kissed her goodbye—"

"It's all for show." Vanessa leaned forward. "Kyle wants a divorce. Badly. He resents the fact that he's a shadow husband. Rachel calls the shots. Always has, always will. She refused to take his name when they got married, told him the Brandon name is her identity. Her brand. And she won't give him a divorce."

"He can still file, though," Hannah said.

"Sure, he can. But he hasn't. My guess? He's hoping to talk Rachel around." She chuckled. "Good luck with that."

"Is he after her money, do you think?" Phaedra asked.

Vanessa shook her head. "He signed a prenup, so he only gets what he brought into the marriage. What he wants is his freedom." She studied each of them in turn. "You didn't hear any of this from me."

"Our lips are sealed," Phaedra promised.

"I should get going." She took out her phone to call an Uber. "Before this snow starts to accumulate."

"What about coffee?" Hannah nodded at the lemon tart on the counter. "And dessert?"

"After two sablés, a mini raspberry tart, and half a croissant at your shop today, you've done enough damage to my diet." She added, "And I enjoyed every bite."

"I can take you home. No need to call someone."

"Thanks, but you and your sister fed me a delicious meal and gave me a break from Rachel. That's more than enough." Vanessa stood and carried her bowl and plate into the kitchen with leonine grace.

"Glad you enjoyed yourself."

Vanessa turned as Phaedra followed her in. "Professor Brighton—"

"Phaedra, please."

"Phaedra." Her voice was low but firm. "I spent every minute at Tout de Sweet with Rachel. She was never out of my sight. Unless she can be in two places at once, there's no way she could've poisoned that cupcake."

* * *

"Okay, so Rachel didn't poison Anna." Phaedra closed the front door behind her as Vanessa's Uber pulled away twenty minutes later. She settled on the sofa and tucked her feet under her. "Maybe Anna tried to poison Rachel."

She listened to the pop and sputter of flames in the fireplace and watched snowflakes drift past the windows. It was mesmerizing, she reflected. And beautiful.

As long as you didn't have to drive in it.

"Why would she do that?" Hannah scoffed as she joined Phaedra in the living room.

"You heard Vanessa. Rachel isn't the easiest person to work for. High expectations, demanding. Could be Anna had enough of being treated poorly. Or maybe it was Max," she added thoughtfully. "Rachel's brother-in-law. He threatened to contest the will. Maybe he poisoned the cupcake and asked Anna to bring it to Rachel."

"What's his motive?"

"Payback. He lost out on his brother's inheritance when it all went to Rachel. I'd say that's a good motive."

"But he works for her now. He's her business adviser. And aren't you forgetting something? That cupcake wasn't meant for Anna, or Rachel. It was meant for you. And Dad."

"True." Phaedra kept her voice light as she pushed the unwelcome thought aside. "Which means *you* did it."

"It's all part of my insidious plan," Hannah agreed as she took the other end of the sofa. Wickham leaped up to settle on her lap, and she stroked his soft white fur. "Isn't it, Wicks?"

Phaedra drew her knees up and regarded her sister somberly. "Seriously, though, I just can't wrap my head around all this. Poor Anna! It shouldn't have happened."

"No." She frowned. "Who'd do such a thing? And why?"

"Wish I knew. But I'm sure the culprit will be found."

"What if they aren't found?" Hannah persisted. "What if that detective of yours thinks *I* did it? Or one of my staff? My business will be over before it's begun."

"He's not 'my' detective. And you didn't do it, so you have nothing to worry about. Just cooperate. Tell the truth."

"How long before word gets out, do you think?" Hannah chewed on her thumbnail. "The news of Anna Steele's death?"

"A day or two. Her family has to be notified."

"At least no one from the press was around when it happened. Clark left right after he took those photos."

"I'm sure he'll kick himself when he learns he missed out on a big news story." Phaedra frowned. "I wonder . . ."

"What?"

"He took a *lot* of photos. Maybe he snapped a picture of something that could help the investigation."

"Like what?"

"I don't know." Phaedra shrugged. "He might've photographed someone in the crowd. Someone who left early, someone we didn't notice."

"Someone who might be the murderer, you mean?" Hannah made no secret of her skepticism. "Please."

"You never know. Call him tomorrow, ask him to email you the photos he took. See if he'll let you choose a few to post on social media."

"Okay, I'll call Clark. Tomorrow." She yawned and nudged Wickham gently off her lap. "Right now, I'm heading up to take a bath and then I'm going to bed. It's been a *really* long day."

Phaedra peered out into the darkness. "The grass is covered, and it's sticking to the street. I hope Vanessa makes it back to her hotel with no problems."

"She should be okay. It'll be a mess by morning, though."

Snow removal in Somerset County was dicey at best. Sometimes it took hours before the county trucks reached Laurel Springs. Privately owned snowplows and neighbors equipped with plows on their trucks and farm vehicles kept the main roads clear. Rural side roads were another matter.

Recalling the series of hairpin turns and twists on the

road leading up Afton Mountain to Delaford, Phaedra turned away from the window with a shiver.

As she said good night and headed upstairs to bed, she felt a chill settle in her bones that had nothing to do with the falling temperatures.

Six

Fresh snow covered the ground the next morning. Phaedra, a mug of Earl Grey in hand, gazed out one of the arched doors to admire the pristine beauty of ice-glazed branches, the mailboxes and bushes capped with snow. Although forecasters had predicted six to eight inches, accumulation had fallen short by a couple of inches.

Just enough to create a slushy, slippery mess when the temperatures rose.

But for now, it made for a picture-postcard view. She watched as a pair of male cardinals swooped over to the bird feeder. Their bright red plumage stood out against the white, silent background.

"Is the street clear?" Hannah mumbled as she sat up on the sofa bed.

"Of traffic? Yes. Of snow? No."

"Arghh." She flopped back down and tugged the blankets over her shoulder. "Wake me when it's over."

"Slacker."

"It's Sunday." Hannah emitted a long, muffled sigh. "And it's not like I have anywhere to go."

“The shop won’t be closed forever.” Phaedra tried to sound upbeat. “A week from now it’ll be business as usual.”

Hannah didn’t answer. Swallowing a sigh of her own, Phaedra carried her mug to the dining room table and set it aside, then reached for her laptop to check on the latest weather report.

She slid onto a seat and navigated to the *Laurel Springs Clarion*’s homepage. A low groan escaped her lips as she saw the headline.

DEATH DISRUPTS BAKERY’S GRAND OPENING

With a sinking sensation she began to read. After a brief recap of Tout de Sweet’s inaugural opening, Clark—*of course* the story was written by Clark Mullinax—launched into the details of Anna Steele’s collapse, her emergency transport to the hospital, and her subsequent death.

MS. STEELE’S DEATH IS CURRENTLY UNDER POLICE INVESTIGATION. SHORTLY AFTER CONSUMING A SMALL AMOUNT OF DARK CHOCOLATE GANACHE FROM ONE OF PASTRY CHEF AND OWNER HANNAH BRIGHTON’S CUPCAKES, MS. STEELE COLLAPSED AFTER COMPLAINING OF DIZZINESS AND A RACING HEARTBEAT. NO OTHER CUSTOMERS SUFFERED ILL EFFECTS FROM CHEF HANNAH BRIGHTON’S PASTRIES.

THE GANACHE IS CURRENTLY BEING TESTED. WHILE NOT CONFIRMED, AN ANONYMOUS SOURCE BELIEVES THE GANACHE MAY HAVE BEEN TAINTED WITH SODIUM CYANIDE.

What anonymous source? Phaedra wondered. *One of the EMTs? Someone at the grand opening? Kate Brennan?*

She studied a photo of Anna Steele with Rachel Brandon, and another of Hannah standing in front of the patisserie in her chef’s whites. She’d worked so hard to realize her dream and open Tout de Sweet.

Casting a quick glance at the sofa, she closed the laptop. She didn't want Hannah to see this. Not yet.

Not ever.

If the story was out, that meant the police must have notified Anna's family of her death. *Poor girl. Her life had been cut short for no reason. Was her death accidental, or deliberate?* Phaedra puckered her brow. So many questions, so many things that didn't make sense.

If Anna hadn't tasted that ganache . . . if everyone hadn't left the patisserie when the fire alarm sounded . . . if Phaedra or her father had taken a bite of that cupcake when Hannah first brought it out . . .

She carried her mug to the sink and set it down with an unsteady hand. As she stared out the kitchen window, she firmed her resolve to dig around—discreetly, of course—until she could figure out who'd done this terrible thing. Not only did the poisoned cupcake threaten to end Hannah's fledgling business . . .

. . . it had ended Anna Steele's life. Which meant that someone in Laurel Springs was a cold-blooded killer.

Wickham had just finished his breakfast of kibble topped with a half can of salmon when the doorbell rang. Phaedra washed and dried her hands and headed for the door. Even before she glanced outside and saw the aging white Honda, she knew who she'd find standing outside.

"Detective Morelli." She swung the door wider and ushered him in. "You're up early. Come in."

"Thanks." He knocked the snow from his boots and wiped his feet on the doormat. "Is your sister up? I understand she's staying here."

"Temporarily." Her gaze flicked to the stairs leading up to the loft. "She's taking a shower, but she'll be down soon. Would you like some coffee?"

He nodded. "I have a few questions for both of you."

"I thought you might." She invited him to take off his

boots and headed into the kitchen to brew a pot of coffee. "I just saw the story in this morning's *Clarion*," she said over her shoulder as he followed her in.

"Mullinax didn't lose any time."

"I assume you've notified Anna's family?"

"Late yesterday. Never an easy task." He removed his coat and draped it over a chair. "Her parents are dead, just a stepsister and an aunt left."

"I still can't quite believe it. So awful. And so senseless." She pressed the brew button and folded her arms loosely together. "Any leads so far?"

"No. But even if I did, I wouldn't tell you. This is a—"

"Police investigation," she finished. "I know. But Anna's death directly affects Hannah. Her business is closed because of it, and once word gets out about the poisoning . . ." She turned back to the cupboard and took down a cup. "Her reputation could be seriously damaged."

"We'll do everything we can to move things along. It all depends on how long it takes to gather evidence at the scene. In this case, your sister's bakery."

"Patisserie. There's a difference." She set his cup down and followed it with a carton of cream. "I'd offer you a doughnut, but I don't have any."

"Just as well. I don't like doughnuts."

She lifted her brow in mock surprise. "A cop who doesn't like doughnuts? Isn't that illegal?"

"Only in three states." He poured in a splash of cream and stirred it a few times. "You're not joining me?"

"More than two cups of tea and I get jittery."

"I'll have a cup."

Hannah padded down the stairs in a pair of woolly socks, wearing jeans and one of Phaedra's old UVA sweatshirts. She gave Morelli a wary nod. "Hello, Detective."

"Ms. Brighton."

She took the mug of coffee Phaedra handed her. Faint smudges under her eyes indicated she hadn't slept well. "I suppose you have more questions." She slid onto a seat at the island.

"A few." Setting his mug aside, he withdrew a pad and pencil. "I spoke with Rachel Brandon's staff. They told me they overheard you and Ms. Brandon get into a heated argument at Delaford on Friday afternoon."

"It wasn't an argument." She pressed her lips together. "And it was hardly 'heated.' We had words, that's all. A professional disagreement. It was nothing."

"It was enough to catch the notice of Rachel's photographer and producer." He poised his pencil over the pad. "Can you tell me about it, please?"

With a sigh, Hannah relayed her attempt to put gold leaf on her apple-caramel glazed cupcakes. "I'd decorated maybe three cupcakes, and they looked perfect. Elegant. But Rachel was adamant. She insisted on keeping things simple. She wanted"—she curved her fingers into quotes—"'No. Gold. Leaf.'"

"And that's what you argued about? Nothing more?"

"That was it. We agreed to disagree, I left off the gold leaf, and Rachel got what she wanted." She glanced at Phaedra. "As a wise woman once said, the customer's always right."

Morelli jotted a quick note and nodded his thanks as Phaedra topped off his coffee. "Did you notice anything while you were at Delaford during the Historic Holiday Homes tour, Hannah? Anything unusual? Any tension?"

"To be honest, I was too busy to notice much of anything. We were crushed all evening. We ran out of cupcakes and spiced cider well before the tour ended."

"Did you bring other flavors besides apple caramel?"

"Of course. The dark chocolate cupcakes were the most popular; we ran out of those first." Her brows furrowed. "Now that I think about it, Kyle really liked them. He had one, and a few minutes later, he came back and grabbed another one. He said it was for Rachel but I saw him walk right past her with it."

Morelli's pencil paused in its scratching. "Kyle?"

"Middleton. Husband number two. Tallish. Man bun."

"He was at the grand opening," Phaedra said. "He came in through the back. He left that way, too."

"I don't recall seeing him," Morelli said. "His name wasn't on the list."

"He didn't stay long. He took off before the fire alarm sounded."

More scratching as he noted Kyle's name. "Hannah, did you notice if any of the guests at Delaford showed up at the bakery's grand opening?"

"Patisserie," Hannah corrected him automatically. She frowned into her coffee cup. "Most of the guests on the tour were strangers." Her face brightened. "But I do remember seeing the Bondurant sisters. Rebecca and Biddy," she added. "They own Scents and Sensibility."

"The apothecary shop in town." He nodded. "I know the place. Crystals and incense and holistic medicines."

"They have a small but loyal following," Phaedra said. "They even have a physic garden behind the shop. Their feverfew tisane is actually very effective."

"I'll stick with the pharmacist at Getty's Drugs." Morelli leaned back in his chair. "If these sisters grow herbs, I presume they're familiar with plant properties. Poisonous and otherwise."

"Cyanide isn't an herb," Hannah said with a shrug. "If that's where you're going. It's a chemical compound."

"True. But it can also be derived from crushing peach or apricot pits. Or apple seeds." He paused. "I noticed several apple trees on their property."

"I don't know a lot about cyanide," Phaedra said, "but I do know you'd need an awful lot of seeds—or pits—to make enough to kill someone. And I can't see Rebecca or Biddy doing something like that. They wouldn't have the time, for one thing. The shop keeps them busy."

"Just entertaining every possibility."

"What about that strange man I saw by the door at the grand opening?" she asked him.

Hannah straightened. "What strange man?"

"Professor Brighton noticed someone loitering near the front door of your shop yesterday," Morelli said. "A man in a parka, glaring at Mr. Brighton."

Alarm chased over Hannah's face as she rounded on her sister. "Why is this the first I'm hearing about it?"

"There was a lot going on. And I didn't want to worry you." She reached across and squeezed her sister's hand. "You have enough to deal with right now."

"When I questioned Mr. Brighton yesterday," Morelli said, "he didn't recall seeing the man you described." He studied Phaedra. "Would you recognize him if you saw him again?"

"Absolutely. I'll talk to Dad today. Maybe if I describe him, he'll be able to come up with a name."

"It's worth a shot." Morelli took a last, lingering sip of coffee and pushed himself to his feet. "It's time I got going. Thank you both for your cooperation."

"Has the ganache been tested?" Phaedra asked him in a low voice as she walked with him to the front door. "Was it cyanide? It was, wasn't it?"

"We don't know yet. Still waiting on the toxicology report. And you know I can't share that information."

She folded her arms against her chest. "This is my sister we're talking about. This isn't some random case involving a complete stranger."

"I understand that. But your relationship to Hannah doesn't change the fact that I can't discuss details of the case with you."

"You have to clear her name. And if you won't," she added, shooting him a determined look, "you know I will."

"If she's innocent, she has nothing to fear."

"*If* she's innocent?" Phaedra pressed her lips together. "Of course she's innocent!"

"Look." His voice was low but firm. "I'll do everything I can to expedite the process, but we need to be thorough. We have to follow the evidence. In the meantime, stay out of it. Whoever poisoned that cupcake knew exactly what they were doing. And they could do it again."

"Fine, point taken. Warning heeded. I'll stay out of it and let the police do their job."

"That's what I like to hear . . . even though I don't believe it for a second. Thanks for the coffee, Professor." He shrugged into his coat and tugged on his boots. "I'll be in touch."

As the door closed behind him, Hannah carried her coffee into the living room and curled up on the sofa. She set her mug on the coffee table and picked up her phone.

"Who are you texting?" Phaedra asked as her sister's fingers began flying over the virtual keypad.

"Clark. Asking him to send me yesterday's photos."

A moment later, a notification dinged on her phone, and she clicked on the link.

"That was fast." She opened a thumbnail folder of photographs Clark had taken at the grand opening of Tout de Sweet. "Let's have a look."

Phaedra perched beside her on the sofa's arm and peered down at the screen as her sister swiped through the photos. He'd captured the excitement of opening day, from Hannah's glowing face to customers thronging the display case, as well as mouthwatering shots of French pastries, a close-up of the artistically hand-scrawled menu board, and Jared, wreathed in steam as he pulled an espresso on the commercial Italian espresso machine.

"There's Elaine," Phaedra said, pointing, "and Mom and Dad. And Hector, the CPA." She rolled her eyes. "And there's . . ."

"There's who?"

A frown settled on her brow as Phaedra studied the snapshot of a man, intently studying a cupcake behind the display case.

But not just any cupcake. This was a dark chocolate cupcake, with chocolate salted ganache.

And the man studying it was Max Brandon. Rachel's brother-in-law.

"Why are you being weird?" Hannah lifted her gaze from the picture. "It's just a photo of a random customer trying to decide what to buy."

"That's not a random customer. It's Max Brandon, Rachel's business adviser. And isn't that the last dark chocolate cupcake he's eyeing?"

"No." Hannah shook her head firmly. "Clark took this picture before the alarm went off, remember? There were a couple dozen more in the kitchen, cooling on baker's racks. I hadn't put them out yet."

With a sigh, Phaedra leaned back. "Sorry. I'm jumping to conclusions based on absolutely nothing."

"You want to solve this. I get it. We both do."

They skimmed through the rest of the photos, all twenty-seven of them, until Phaedra touched Hannah's shoulder. "Wait. Go back. I saw something."

Obediently, she clicked on the previous photo, and a picture of someone standing by the entrance filled the screen. "What are we looking at?"

"Not what," Phaedra said excitedly, "who. That's him."

He wore the same dirty white parka, with his hands jammed in his pockets as he glared at someone out of range of the photo.

"Him, who?"

"The guy who gave Dad the stink eye yesterday. Clark got a picture of him." She pushed herself to her feet. "Send a copy of that photo to my phone, please?"

"Sure," Hannah said as she went about forwarding the picture to her sister. "But why—"

But she was talking to the air. Phaedra was already grabbing her coat and heading out the front door.

Seven

The sidewalks along Main Street were cleared of snow as Phaedra headed out in her boots and coat and walked to the Poison Pen bookstore. A snowplow rumbled past and she waved at the driver. Hank Hawkins had kept local roads clear of snow and ice for fifteen years, a boon when the state plows couldn't keep up.

"Good thing it's Sunday," he called out as he lowered his window. "Most folks are staying off the roads. Makes my job a lot easier. Where're you headed, Professor?"

"The bookstore, to see Dad." She'd promised Detective Morelli she'd stay out of the investigation, and she would. But that didn't mean she wouldn't ask a few questions.

Like learning who the scowling man was at Hannah's grand opening.

"Well, tell Malcolm I said hello," Hank said. "Mrs. H. has a blackberry pie with his name on it in the freezer, waiting for his next visit."

"I'll tell him. He's a sucker for a good blackberry pie. And hers is the best." She paused. "Just don't tell Mom I said that."

"Our secret." With a wave and a grin, he drove on.

A few minutes later, she spotted the Victorian row house

with its turreted windows and pair of potted topiaries standing guard on either side of the narrow front doors. Snow frosted the hedges and the edge of the front porch, but the sidewalk and steps were clear.

A white flag, with a black quill pen superimposed over a splotch of blood, denoted the house as the Poison Pen bookstore. Her parents lived upstairs with Fitz, her mother's elderly pug.

After a lot of begging, pleading, and persuading, Bella the cat had also joined the family. The white Persian, a former Instagram star, had settled into a far quieter lifestyle with Phaedra's parents after her owner's death. While Fitz wasn't happy with the interloper, the elderly pug wisely steered clear of her and gave Bella a wide berth.

Ignoring the "CLOSED" sign on the door, Phaedra let herself inside. The scent of freshly ground coffee wafted down the hallway, and she realized she was ravenous.

"Mom? Dad?" she called out as she took off her coat. "Anyone here?"

"In the back," her mother, Nan, called out. "Get yourself a cup of tea and join us. We're in the reading room with the Sunday papers."

The sunporch, glassed in on three sides, functioned as a year-round reading room for customers and, on Sundays when the bookstore closed, for family. The library table from her father's former law office served as a reading surface, desktop, and dining table.

"Be right there." After going upstairs to the recently renovated kitchen, Phaedra poured a cup of green tea with lemon and helped herself to a couple of cranberry walnut cookies. Thus fortified, she returned downstairs.

Her father glanced up over the top of his black reading glasses as she came in. "Hello, pumpkin."

"Hey, Dad. Mom." She set her tea down and bit into a cookie. "Sorry," she apologized around a mouthful of walnuts, white chocolate, and tart dried cranberries, "but I didn't have breakfast. Mom, these are *amazing*."

"I can't take credit, unfortunately." She pushed her cup aside. "They're from Brennan's." A guilty expression skimmed her face. "Don't tell your sister, but I stop in from time to time to see Kate. She insisted I take them home rather than throwing them away unsold."

"Oh? Is their business down?"

"Quite a bit, evidently. Kate's more than a little worried." She sighed deeply. "And now Hannah may face the same predicament, after . . ." She added, "After everything that's happened."

Phaedra sank down on a chair. "I know. What a nightmare. I feel so awful for poor Anna Steele. Not to mention Han. We've already had a visit from Detective Morelli this morning."

"Instead of questioning you and Hannah," her mother huffed, "he should figure out who poisoned that cupcake. This could ruin your sister's business before it's even begun."

"I'm sure Morelli is doing his level best to solve the crime." Malcolm lowered his copy of the *Richmond Times Dispatch* and regarded his wife with a stern gaze. "Let's not forget, Nan, that a young woman has lost her life. In the greater scheme of things, Hannah's business troubles pale by comparison." He reached for his coffee. "What brings you here, Phaedra?"

"Two things, actually. I saw Hank plowing Main Street just now, and he said to tell you there's a blackberry pie with your name on it in Mrs. Hawkins's freezer."

Nan sniffed. "Ramona thinks her pies are the best, just because she won a blue ribbon at the county fair last August. They're good, I'll grant you. But they can't compare to mine."

Phaedra and her father wisely said nothing.

"And the other thing?" Malcolm asked.

"I have a question," Phaedra said. "About someone I saw at Hannah's grand opening yesterday."

"Who? The man Detective Morelli asked me about yesterday? I already told him I don't remember him."

"I was hoping this might jog your memory." She took out her phone and opened the photo Hannah had sent, then held it up. "Clark Mullinax took it. Recognize him?"

He frowned at the photograph on the screen. "No. Can't say I do. Should I?"

"I hoped you might. Do you see how he's scowling?"

Malcolm nodded slowly. "Hard to miss."

"He was scowling at *you*," Phaedra said. "Pretty intensely. And I wondered why."

"I have no earthly idea. I've never seen the man before."

Disappointment deflated her hopes of identifying the stranger. "He stared at you with such—such blatant dislike, I thought you might recognize him."

"Afraid not." He shook his head. "Why is it so important?"

"Because," she answered as she returned her phone to her pocket, "someone tampered with Anna's cupcake, and she died. He looked at you with such intense dislike, it made me wonder if maybe this man"—she tapped the phone's screen—"if he was responsible for poisoning that cupcake."

"It's possible," Malcolm agreed, "but unlikely. Why would he do such a thing? I don't even recognize him. Send me the photo and let me think on it."

She forwarded Clark's photo to him and set her phone aside. "How did things go at Delaford, Mom? Hannah said so many people showed up for the historical homes tour, they ran out of cupcakes and spiced cider."

"It was a huge success," Nan confirmed. "The Historical Society exceeded its goal, and now we have enough funds to begin restoration on the Morland estate."

"That's great. I know that's a pet project of yours."

"Why don't you join us for dinner," her mother offered, "and we can discuss it in more detail. You can bring that charming Professor Selden along. I'm sure he'd be interested." She set her teacup down with a clink. "And I'd welcome the chance to get to know him better."

Inwardly, Phaedra groaned. This wasn't the first time her

mother had suggested she invite Mark to dinner. Twice before she'd extended an invitation, and both times Phaedra managed to sidestep with a quick, facile excuse. This time, however, she was running low on excuses.

"Can't, sorry. I'm meeting Lucy and Mari tonight." She took a last, guilty sip of tea. She planned to ask her friends for help on the fundraiser for this year's Coats 'n Caps drive, a Regency-themed Jane Austen Christmas tea.

"A Tea Society meeting?" Nan eyed her in suspicion. "But it's not the first Monday of the month."

"No, just a get-together. An excuse for the three of us to drink tea and discuss our sad, unmarried status."

Malcolm disguised his chuckle behind a cough.

"Mock me if you will, Phaedra, but you and your sister will thank me one day, when you're both happily married."

"I'm sure we will."

Mollified, Nan sipped her tea. "I hope you're not putting yourself in the middle of the investigation of that young woman's poisoning."

Phaedra gave a noncommittal shrug of her shoulders.

"It's a murder investigation, Phaedra!" Nan exclaimed. "Stay out of it."

"You know I can't do that. Hannah's shop is closed indefinitely. I need to do whatever I can to help her."

"And that's admirable," her father said. "But misguided. I have to agree with your mother on this. Let the police handle it."

"I'm not getting involved. Not officially," she amended. "I'll ask a few questions. Compare notes with Lucy and Mari. Observe. Nothing more."

"Anything more is *dangerous*." Nan pushed her teacup and saucer away. "Even asking questions is a risk. Suppose you question the wrong person. For instance, whoever actually poisoned that ganache. How would you know? Please, darling. Promise me you won't do anything to put yourself or your father in jeopardy."

"Fine. I promise." Phaedra stood to leave. "I should go. I have errands to run. A Christmas tea to plan."

"And a murderer to find, I suppose," her mother added darkly.

"Bye, sweetie." Her father was already reaching for his paper. "My advice? Leave the investigating to Detective Morelli. And try to stay out of trouble."

"And tell your young man I said hello when you see him tomorrow," Nan called after her.

Phaedra bit back a retort as she retraced her steps to the front door and shrugged into her coat. Mark was hardly her 'young man.' He was a coworker, an esteemed Shakespearean scholar. A member of the Somerset University faculty and, yes, a friend. They were still navigating their relationship—or whatever existed between them at the moment—and she didn't want to label it. Not yet, anyway.

She opened the front door and stepped out into the brisk, wintry air. Things were still new between the two of them, like freshly fallen snow, and she wanted to keep the footprints of coworkers, friends, and family at bay for a while. She wanted to solidify her relationship with Mark before sharing it with the world.

Or, God forbid, with her mother.

She took her phone out and called Lucy. After several rings, she heard a clunk, a muttered expletive, and a fumbling sound. "Phaedra?"

"Lu? Did I wake you?"

"No. I dropped my phone in my cereal bowl. Luckily it was empty. I'm sitting at my laptop catching up on local news, and I saw Anna Steele's story in the *Clarion*."

"Good old Clark."

"How's Hannah holding up? She must be devastated."

"She's still numb. Worrying about how long Tout de Sweet will be shut down."

"Have the police questioned anyone else? Do they have any leads, any idea who might've done this?"

"No idea. Detective Morelli won't share any official information with me. No surprise there."

Lucy sucked in a sharp breath. "I still can't believe someone did this. And on Hannah's opening day."

Phaedra refrained from reminding her that there'd been a murder in Laurel Springs only last summer, at aunt Wendy's bed-and-breakfast. "Crime can happen anywhere. Even right here in Laurel Springs."

As she waited on the corner for the light to change, Phaedra glanced at her watch. "Any plans for lunch?"

"Mom invited me to dim sum, but I'm not feeling it. This is a stay-on-the-sofa-and-watch-Netflix kind of day."

"How's that going?"

"Great," Lucy answered, deliberately misunderstanding. "I have my blanket, my jammies, and I'm stocked up on popcorn and Pocky."

"That wasn't what I meant and you know it."

Lucy's mother abandoned her and her sister, Leah, when they were eleven and six, respectively. Her reasons for leaving were myriad, but now Anhe was back and determined to build a relationship with her estranged daughters.

"It's going." Lucy's voice was measured. "After she disappeared for twenty years, I'm not exactly ready to go shopping with her or get mani-pedis together. It takes time, Phae. And I'm not there yet."

"Fair enough. Sorry."

"I'll get there." Lucy sighed. "But not today."

"Does that mean I can't lure you out for a burger? Or maybe a glass of wine at Josie's later?"

"Nope, sorry. It's just me and the sofa and junk food today."

"What about our meeting tonight?" Phaedra asked. "We need to discuss our plans for the Coats 'n Caps fundraiser. It's only a few weeks away."

"Oh, right. The coat-drive thing."

"I'm thinking we could host a Regency-themed Christmas tea. We need to plan the menu."

"But it's cold outside," Lucy protested. "And my couch is warm and comfy."

"We can talk about the case . . ." Phaedra knew she wasn't playing fair, but dangling an unsolved mystery in front of Lucy was like offering catnip to Wickham. It couldn't fail.

"There's nothing to talk about," Lucy said. "We don't know much at this point. No more than we did yesterday, anyway."

"True. But we can compare notes. Maybe one of us noticed something the others didn't." Phaedra paused. "It'll just be a quick get-together. If Marisol's free, that is."

"Oh, I'm sure she's free. If her love life is as arid and nonexistent as mine right now, anyway."

Phaedra chuckled. "I'll call her. If you don't hear back, meet us at seven at the Poison Pen. I'll let Dad know."

"Why not your place?"

"Because, Hannah." Phaedra sighed. "Better to leave her out of any discussion about the poisoning. It'll only upset her more than she already is."

"Point taken. Okay, then. See you at seven."

Phaedra arrived back at the carriage house just before noon to find Hannah hunched over her laptop, a length of blond hair twisted around one finger and an expression of disbelief on her face.

Removing her coat, Phaedra hung it up and hurried into the dining room. "Han? What is it? What's wrong?"

"Tout de Sweet is trending on social media!" she cried. "And not in a good way. You should see it. Post after post, talking about #killercupcake and #poisonpastry. It's over, Phae. I might as well rack up my losses and move back to D.C. See if the embassy will take me back. Maybe they'll hire me to w-wash dishes."

"You're overreacting. It can't be that bad," Phaedra reassured her as she joined her. "You know how these things are. It'll blow over. It's all just a tempest in a . . ."

Her eyes widened as she saw posts about Hannah's patisserie trending with hashtags like #DeadlyDelight and #cyanidecupcake. Even the national news media had picked up on the story.

"Teapot," she finished weakly.

Hannah snapped her laptop shut. "This is awful. Catastrophic. My career is over before it's even begun. It's collapsed like an overbeaten soufflé." She thrust herself away from the table and began to pace from the dining room to the living room and back again.

"Don't let it get to you. The police are investigating and they'll get to the bottom of this. They'll figure out who put that cyanide on your ganache."

"But when, Phaedra? You heard what Detective Morelli said. It could be days. Weeks!" Hannah flung herself on the sofa as tears spilled down her cheeks. "In the meantime, my reputation is in tatters, and I can't show my face in town. I'm ruined. Finished."

After fixing Hannah a cup of calming chamomile tea with plenty of sugar and settling beside her to binge on cookies and romantic comedies all afternoon, Phaedra was relieved when her sister rallied enough to put on her coat and hat to go outside for a walk.

"Want some company?" Phaedra offered.

Hannah shook her head. "I need to be alone for a while. Clear my thoughts. Thanks, though."

"Things will look better in the morning," Phaedra promised.

Han nodded. But neither of them really believed it.

Eight

"Are we all agreed on the menu?"

That evening, Phaedra scrawled the last item on the reading room's whiteboard under "Regency Christmas Tea fundraiser" and turned to face Lucy and Marisol.

They'd gathered at the Poison Pen as agreed and quickly decided on a menu of jam tartlets, miniature Christmas puddings, Shrewsbury cakes, and an assortment of tea sandwiches—shrimp salad, roast beef, and cucumber avocado.

Lucy nodded. "Now all we need to do is pair the courses with teas. And convince Hannah to make everything."

Marisol eyed Phaedra doubtfully. "Do you think she'll agree? With everything that's going on right now?"

"I do. It'll give her something to do besides brood, along with an excuse to do what she loves best—bake. Plus, it's for a good cause. Han loves a good cause."

"The only potential glitch," Lucy said, "is location. You wanted to hold this tea at Tout de Sweet, right?"

"Ideally." Phaedra put her black marker aside. "If the police are done with the crime scene by then. If not, we'll have to choose an alternate location."

"What about here?" Marisol suggested. "At the Poison Pen? The tea takes place on a Sunday, and the bookstore will be closed. With your parents' permission, of course. We can set up in the reading room and people can help themselves."

"Like a buffet." Lucy nodded. "Good idea. Tickets?"

"Mari, will you handle that?" Phaedra asked. "Buy a roll of raffle tickets. We'll charge twenty dollars each and every ticket holder gets a chance at a raffle prize."

Marisol tapped in a note on her phone. "On it. What'll the raffle prize be?"

"A basket," she decided. "With an assortment of holiday tea blends and a couple of festive teacups and saucers. Maybe some shortbread cookies and a jar of lemon curd. And maybe Hannah can whip up some cranberry-almond scones."

"Perfect." Lucy glanced at Phaedra. "What about games? Charades was popular back then."

"We won't have room." She tapped a finger against her chin. "Snap-dragon was popular, too, but it's a fire hazard. And bullet pudding is too messy."

"Snap-dragon?" Marisol's eyebrows rose. "What's that? And why was it a fire hazard?"

"A silver punch bowl of brandy was set alight. The object was to grab a raisin out of the bowl without burning your fingers."

"Good grief," Lucy muttered. "*That* was their idea of entertainment?"

"And bullet pudding?" Marisol prompted.

"Everyone gathered around a dish piled with flour to resemble a sort of pudding, with a bullet or a coin on top," Phaedra explained, "and each player cut a slice. Whoever made the bullet fall had to dive face-first into the flour and retrieve it using only their chin and nose."

"Sounds like fun." Lucy leaned back. "But you're right—it also sounds messy."

"Let's skip the games," Phaedra said. "We'll offer acoustic guitar music. Or maybe a chamber quartet." She picked up the marker and added "music?" and "tea basket" to the listed items. "I think we're all set."

"There's one thing we haven't discussed," Lucy pointed out. "Comparing notes on Anna's poisoning."

Marisol laid her phone aside. "I have nothing to report. But I did get a glimpse of the new art gallery's owner. All I can say is, he's seriously gorgeous."

"Oh?" Lucy didn't sound convinced. "On a scale of one to ten . . ."

"A fifteen. Dark blond hair, strong jaw, Italian suit, but he'd *rock* a pair of board shorts—"

"We're getting off track," Phaedra said. "Lucy? Anything new to report since yesterday?"

"Not really. Only that Hannah's patisserie is trending on social right now. In the worst possible way."

"I know." Phaedra sank onto a chair. "She's devastated. I wish there was something I could do, some way to make this whole thing disappear."

"Did she get those photos back from Clark yet?" Marisol asked. "The ones he took for the grand opening?"

"This morning. Which reminds me," Phaedra added. "Remember the guy I mentioned to Detective Morelli? The one hanging by the door, scowling at my dad?"

They nodded.

"He's in one of Clark's photos. I showed it to dad to see if he recognized him, but he didn't."

"That's disappointing," Lucy said. "Who knows, though? Maybe it'll come to him eventually. He'll remember in the middle of the night. That's how it usually works for me."

"Happy Monday."

Phaedra, ensconced behind her desk at Somerset University the following morning, looked over the rim of her reading glasses to see Mark Selden resting one shoulder against the doorframe. He wore a dark blue suit, a pale blue collared shirt, and a disgustingly cheery smile.

"You're the only person I know," Phaedra grumbled as she removed her glasses, "who actually likes Mondays."

"We've had this conversation before," he reminded her. "What's not to like? It's a new week. A new start." He cocked an eyebrow. "And winter break starts soon."

"I can't argue with that logic."

"Any plans for your three weeks of freedom?"

She glanced out her office window. The snow was already a memory, reduced to piles of dirty gray slush in the wake of the university's snowplow and the steadily rising temperatures.

She'd stayed up late to finish preparing her notes. The incident at the patisserie eclipsed everything else, and she'd focused her energies on pampering her sister as she made them a dinner of baked chicken and Caesar salad. Hannah's contribution was an apple tart.

She'd barely touched her food.

"No plans," she answered Mark truthfully as she gathered up her lecture notes. "Aside from organizing a Regency-themed Christmas tea we're holding for the annual winter clothing charity drive."

"Sounds ambitious."

"Lucy and Mari and I hope a holiday tea will drum up donations for the coat drive. Tickets are twenty dollars each, and Hannah's providing the baked goods."

He withdrew his wallet and held out two twenties. "Here you go. My contribution toward a worthy cause."

"Thank you." With a smile she tucked the bills into her desk drawer. Although she didn't say it, she hoped the patisserie reopened in time for the planned tea . . . and that Anna's death didn't give anyone second thoughts about purchasing tickets. "Right now, Hannah's my priority. The patisserie is closed until the police finish their investigation."

"I heard. I'm sorry. Is there anything I can do?"

She reached for her briefcase and thrust her notes inside. "No, not really. But thanks for offering. This whole thing is surreal. And so sad."

"Have the police determined a cause of death yet?"

"They'll know more after the autopsy. But in the meantime—" She thrust her chair back and stood. "I have a lecture to give in ten minutes. Will you be at the staff meeting this afternoon?"

"Alas, yes." He straightened and turned to go. "By the way—are we still on for our date this week?"

"Absolutely." Her heart quickened from a foxtrot to a tango. "Which night?"

"Thursday?"

"Perfect."

"I'll text you the details." He paused and gave her a crooked grin. "Just as soon as I figure out what they are. Cheers."

"Cheers. And thanks," she added impulsively.

He turned back, surprise on his face. "For what?"

"For making Monday a little better."

His gaze softened. "Try not to worry, Phaedra. Everything will work out. It always does, in the end."

She nodded, unable to answer, and gave him a tremulous smile instead.

A short time later she arrived at the second-floor lecture room, her thoughts preoccupied and her briefcase in hand. A knot of students huddled together at one end of the dais and buzzed with excited conversation. As she drew nearer, Phaedra caught the words "poison" and "killer cupcake," along with "French bakery" and "police."

"Good morning," she called out as she breezed past in her Regency walking dress of maroon figured silk. "Are we ready to discuss Jane Austen's *Sense and Sensibility*? I hope so, because there *will* be a test afterward."

They fell into a guilty silence and drew apart to take their seats. Retrieving her notes, Phaedra took her place behind the lectern to gather her thoughts.

Anna Steele's death was the talk of Laurel Springs. How could it be otherwise? Her death, and the circumstances surrounding it, were upsetting, to say the least. Phaedra only wished she could shield her sister from the fallout.

"Let's get started," she said, her eyes sweeping the faces of the students before her. "The story of the Dashwood sisters, Elinor and Marianne, begins in Norland Park . . ."

Halfway through a late lunch at her desk, with twenty minutes to spare before the staff meeting began, the phone rang. "Professor Brighton, Somerset University," she said as she set her salad aside.

"Hector Kranz here. We met at your sister's grand opening on Saturday?"

Ah, yes. The CPA-slash-financial-forensic-consultant and Ichabod Crane look-alike. "I remember. How are you?"

"Doing well. I wondered if you were free for lunch one day this week."

Phaedra hesitated. She had no interest in going out with her mother's most recent husband candidate. He was perfectly nice, obviously intelligent, and attractive in an offbeat, hipster way, but as far as sparks? There were none.

"I'm sorry," she began, "but I'm afraid I have a lot on my plate just at the moment—"

"Oh, I'm not asking you out on a *date*." He chuckled. "Sorry. I'm actually seeing someone."

"You are?" How had her mother, with her finely honed, unattached-single-male radar, made such an error?

"Startling as it may seem, yes."

Warmth crept up her face. "Now it's my turn to apologize. I'm sorry. I didn't mean . . . It's just that my mother . . . she . . ."

"Tried to hook us up because she thought I was single?"

She let out a rueful breath. "Yes. Exactly."

"If I were—single, that is—I'd definitely be interested. And although I can certainly empathize, my mother is much, much worse than yours when it comes to the whole matchmaking thing. Trust me. No, I called because I'd like to talk to you."

Her curiosity was piqued. "About?"

"I'd rather not go into it over the phone." He paused. "It's . . . sensitive. It has to do with something I saw at your sister's grand opening. Something odd."

"Well. I'll admit, I'm intrigued. Does tomorrow at noon work?"

"Great. Dog 'n Draft?"

"I'll be there."

When Phaedra arrived home that evening, Detective Morelli's Honda sat in the driveway. Her surprise gave way to unease as she shut off the engine and grabbed her briefcase and reticule.

What was going on? Was there a new development in the case? Was her sister about to be arrested?

She unlocked the front door and let herself in. Hannah and the detective looked up as she came in, coffee on the kitchen island in front of them, their faces unreadable.

"Is anyone hungry?" Phaedra asked as she lifted a large brown takeout bag containing Chinese food. "I brought dinner. I hope you like veggie lo mein or moo goo gai pan, Detective. There's plenty of both."

When no one moved, she shrugged out of her coat and carried the bag into the kitchen. As she placed it on the island, her glance darted from her sister to Morelli. "I'll get plates."

"Phaedra." Hannah cleared her throat. "The toxicology report came back today."

Dread settled over her, making it difficult to form words. "And?"

"Anna Steele was poisoned," Detective Morelli said. "The ganache on her cupcake contained potassium cyanide. Even though she consumed only a trace amount, the concentration was high enough to prove lethal."

Phaedra groped for one of the high-backed seats at the

island and sank down. The mouthwatering scents emanating from the takeout bag, so appetizing only a few moments ago, now made her queasy.

"And . . . the autopsy?" she asked.

"Confirmed the toxicology report. The pathologist ruled it as death by poisoning." Morelli stood and reached for a glass from the cupboard. "Water?"

"Yes, please. Thanks."

"The inside of Anna's nose exhibited sores," he explained as he filled the glass at the sink and handed it to Phaedra, "indicating exposure to potassium cyanide. The autopsy also revealed damage to her esophagus and stomach lining.

"The good news, if you want to call it that," he went on, "is that nothing else in the display case or on the cooling racks at the patisserie was tampered with. Only the dark chocolate cupcake Anna consumed."

"It doesn't matter," Hannah said, and lifted a resolute expression to the detective. "Never mind the work that went into making those pastries, or the expense. It's all going in the garbage. Every last tart, macaron, éclair, and financier. Every last crumb."

Phaedra's fingers tightened around the glass of water. "At least now we know the cupcake was definitely poisoned." Her eyes locked with Morelli's. "We have to find whoever did this, Detective."

"I agree. And we will. *We*," he added, "meaning the police. I hope I don't need to remind you again, Professor, to stay out of this investigation."

She nodded, but she wasn't really listening. Why bother, when she'd heard it all before? Still, she knew Morelli was right. Finding the killer was the responsibility of sheriff's department and the homicide detective assigned to the case, namely, Matteo Morelli.

But this wasn't just any case. Anna Steele's death was senseless and tragic, no question. But it also directly impacted Hannah. After only one day—and not even a full one!—her business was shut down, and would remain so until the police went over every square inch of the patisserie. Her reputation hung in the balance.

In the meantime, Phaedra would do whatever she could to clear her sister's name from even a whisper of wrongdoing. Hannah hadn't done this.

Who had?

Who harbored enough hate to sprinkle potassium cyanide granules on the ganache? Did the perpetrator know that particular cupcake was intended for Phaedra and her father? Or was the poisoning random?

So many questions. And as of now, she had no answers. Just a list of possible suspects, most of whom she'd never met before Saturday. Swallowing a rising sense of frustration, Phaedra reached for the brown carryout bag and began unloading the Styrofoam containers of food.

"So," she said brightly. "Who's up for moo goo gai pan?"

The Dog 'n Draft, typically crowded with locals and tourists throughout the summer, was quiet as Phaedra stepped inside the next day. A scattering of patrons noshed on hot dogs and half-smokes or sipped craft beer. The thwack of darts hitting a board in the back punctuated the hum of conversation.

Removing her sunglasses and thrusting them atop her head, her gaze came to rest on Hector. His long legs were folded under a two-top in the back and he was hunched over his phone, a bottle of beer at his elbow.

He spotted her and waved her over.

"Hello, Hector."

"Professor Brighton, hello." He half rose as she took a seat across from him. "Glad you could make it. Can I get you an IPA?"

She shook her head. "Much as I'd love that, I have one more lecture this afternoon, so I'm afraid I have to pass. I'll have an iced tea," she told the waitress when she arrived and handed them menus.

"What looks good?" he asked as they consulted their

laminated list of choices. "They have plenty of options." He lifted a brow. "As long as you like hot dogs, half-smokes, or fried cheese, that is."

They settled on two Dog House Specials and the waitress left with the menus to put in the order.

"So, you've been here before," Hector ventured.

"Once. With a colleague."

"Not a date, then?"

"No. Not a date." She paused as the server brought out her iced tea along with a small dish of lemon slices and set them down. "I admit, your call left me curious. You said you saw something during my sister's grand opening. Something odd."

He tilted the bottle of beer and poured the pale ale into a plastic cup. "I did. Not sure what to make of it. Not sure if I should even mention it. But in view of what happened to Ms. Steele . . ." He frowned. "I'm not sure I shouldn't, either."

"If something struck you as odd, then please, tell me. Sometimes nothing turns out to be something."

Hector set his emptied bottle aside. "I saw an elderly woman slip something into her purse."

Phaedra's interest, piqued only a moment ago, waned. "What did she look like?" she asked, although she already knew the answer.

"Petite. Small, like a wren. White-gray hair, sweet, a little flustered."

"That sounds like Biddy Bondurant." Phaedra squeezed lemon into her tea. "She and her sister, Rebecca, own the apothecary shop down the street."

He nodded. "Is the tall, gray-haired woman Rebecca? She came up to the shorter woman, took her by the arm, and basically frog-marched her out the door." Hector eyed her. "You don't seem bothered by any of this. Like I said, probably nothing. I shouldn't have mentioned it."

"No, I'm glad you did. It's just that everyone knows about Biddy. She helps herself to small items now and then," she explained. "All the local shopkeepers know, and tend to look the other way. Rebecca always brings the items back, with apologies."

"The stolen items, you mean."

"Well . . . yes. But Biddy is elderly, and sweet, and she means no harm. It's just a little—personality quirk."

Hector leaned forward. "What she snuck into her purse wasn't a cookie wrapped in a napkin, or a handful of sugar packets, or a tip she swiped from a table."

"I don't understand. What did she take, then?"

"It's probably nothing."

"Hector," Phaedra warned. "What did Biddy take?"

"Okay, okay. Sorry." He lowered his voice. "Your light-fingered friend stole a dark chocolate cupcake."

"Oh." She regarded him in surprise. "When was this?"

"Not long before the fire alarm went off. I was just saying goodbye to your mother—charming lady, by the way—when one of the staff called out a ticket order and set the cupcake on a plate on the counter. Miss Biddy grabbed that cupcake so fast I'd have missed it if I hadn't happened to glance over."

"Are you sure she took it? Are you sure it wasn't *her* cupcake?"

"No. This was someone's eat-in order, on a plate, with a fork. She scooped that cupcake up and tucked it in her bakery bag faster than you could say 'takeout.'"

Nine

That is a little strange," Phaedra agreed. "Especially since Biddy already bought a half dozen of Hannah's gluten-free pinwheel sablés on my recommendation. She's not supposed to have too much sugar at her age."

The waitress arrived with their food and set two sauerkraut-topped half-smokes and a red plastic basket of fries on the table. "Anything else I can get you folks?"

"Antacids?" Hector said. "Kidding. It looks great."

Gingerly, Phaedra picked up her half-smoke and bit into it. An explosion of sweet and savory flavors burst in her mouth.

"Outstanding," Hector pronounced after he'd swallowed his first bite. "Nice crust on the half-smoke. And I love the sauerkraut. It's got that sweet-sour thing going on, and then the mustard takes it to a whole other level."

Phaedra smiled. "So, you'd come here again?"

"Definitely."

They ate, conversing about everything and nothing, until finally, after sampling a couple of the seasoned fries, she nudged the basket his way. "You'll have to finish these. I'll be lucky to polish off my half-smoke."

"Same. I'll get a couple of to-go boxes."

"None for me, thanks. In my experience fries rarely reheat well." She reached for her reticule. "I appreciate your meeting me and sharing your concerns about Biddy."

Hector grabbed the check and withdrew a twenty. "No problem. And lunch is on me." He glanced down at a mustard splotch on his tie. "Literally."

"I'll talk to Biddy the next time I see her."

He hesitated. "You won't rat me out, will you?"

"No, of course not. I promise I'll be the soul of discretion." She looped the reticule over her wrist and stood. "I'm sure it's nothing. But I'm glad you told me. Now, I really have to get going or I'll be late for my own lecture."

On her way home that evening, Phaedra slowed the car as she passed Tout de Sweet. It was dusk, and up and down Main Street, street lights blinked on. Christmas lights glowed around shop windows and homes.

But Hannah's patisserie remained dark.

There was no sign of activity outside her sister's shop, no police cars or news vans or curiosity seekers; the only decoration was a length of yellow crime scene tape stretched across the front entrance, fluttering half-heartedly in the chilly evening air.

The sight filled her with a mix of feelings. Regret that Anna had died such a horrible, pointless death. Anger that someone had deliberately ended the young woman's life . . . and for no discernable reason.

But mostly, Phaedra felt a fierce desire to protect Hannah, who certainly didn't deserve to have her business sidelined like this.

When would the police finish their investigation and give her sister the go-ahead to reopen Tout de Sweet? Every day that it remained closed cost Hannah money, fueled the local rumor mill, and exacerbated her own fears that Han's fledgling business might not survive the fallout from Anna Steele's poisoning.

They were both in serious need of comfort food.

She turned into the IGA parking lot and shut off the engine. She'd get the ingredients to make something delicious, but quick. Pasta puttanesca and a fresh green salad came to mind. Then, she'd pop next door to the florist for a basket of colorful poinsettias.

Twenty minutes later she emerged from the IGA, grocery bag balanced in one arm, and turned down the sidewalk until she reached Millie's Florist. She was about to enter when the glass door flew open and nearly knocked the bag from her arm.

"Oh, I'm terribly sorry! My fault entirely! I'm such a lummox. Are you all right?"

Phaedra had a brief impression of reddish-blond hair, a flushed but genial face, and an impeccable English accent as she tightened her grip on the grocery bag. "Charles?"

"Phaedra?" The surprise on his face was almost comical. "Well, this is one for the books!" His flush grew deeper as he glanced down at the bouquet of roses in his hand. "I just popped in to get flowers for Hannah. Owe her a bit of an apology. I couldn't make it out for her grand opening on Saturday, so—" He brandished the bouquet with a sheepish grin and a crinkle of cellophane.

"They're beautiful. She'll be thrilled. You heard about what happened, I suppose?"

"I did." A troubled expression chased away his smile. "We talked yesterday, and she assured me she's fine, but I need to see for myself. She sounded a bit shaky."

"It's all been a shock, to say the least. Her shop's closed while the police investigate."

"Yes, well, crime scene and all that. Hopefully it won't take too long. Poor girl."

Phaedra wondered if he referred to Anna, or Hannah. Or both.

"I bought the ingredients for supper," she offered as she readjusted the bag on her hip. "Why not join us? You're sticking around for a while, aren't you?"

"A couple of days. And yes, I'd love to stay for dinner, provided it's no trouble. In view of me arriving on your doorstep unannounced, that is."

"No trouble at all." She wondered briefly where she could put Charles tonight if he didn't have a hotel room. The carriage house was small and already bursting at the seams since her sister's arrival.

"I'm parked over there." He indicated a dark gray Audi nearby. "Rental. Shall I follow you over?"

She nodded. "See you in a few."

When she arrived at the carriage house, Phaedra slid her reticule over her wrist, gathered up the bag of groceries, and unlocked the front door as Charles pulled into the driveway behind her.

"Hannah," she called up the stairs to the loft as she made her way to the kitchen, "I'm home. And I brought a visitor." An enticing, chocolaty scent wafted on the air.

"Good thing I made a batch of double-fudge brownies earlier. Be right down."

"I would've helped with that, you know," Charles protested as he followed Phaedra inside and shut the door. "Least I can do—"

At the sound of feet treading lightly down the stairs, he paused. "Hannah?"

She froze in momentary surprise, then bolted down the remaining steps and flung herself straight into his arms. "Charles," she breathed, laughing and drawing back to look at him. "It really is you!"

"Yes, of course it's me. You didn't think I wouldn't come straight out to see you, did you?" He pulled her close, his arms wrapped tightly around her waist. "Sorry I couldn't come sooner. Had a meeting I couldn't get out of. I've been worried sick in light of everything that's happened. How are you?" he asked as he drew back to study her face. "The truth."

"I'm fine, honestly. Trying to make sense of it all. It's so horrible it hardly feels real." She took the roses he held out and breathed in the delicate perfume. "They're gorgeous. Thank you."

As Hannah followed her into the kitchen to find a vase, Phaedra unloaded the groceries. "Open up a bottle of wine, Han. There's cheese in the fridge. Why don't you plate it along with some olives and crackers while I start the water for our pasta? I'm sure Charles is famished."

"On it." She took down three glasses, opened a bottle of red, and poured a glass for Charles. "Sorry, but it's a recent vintage."

"Last week, to be exact," Phaedra put in, smiling. "It was on special."

He took a healthy sip. "Plonk or Pouilly-Fuissé, it's all the same to me." He took a seat at the kitchen island as Hannah retrieved a block of cheddar and muenster and began slicing them into squares. "Now, bring me up to speed on what's going on at the patisserie. Any suspects?"

"Too many." Hannah set down a plate of cheese and crackers and a bowl of olives. "Everyone who was at the grand opening before"—she took a steadying sip of wine—"before the poisoning. What I can't figure out is how they did it."

He popped an olive in his mouth. "Perhaps the culprit dusted the cupcake with cyanide before the event. Set it aside somewhere out of sight until just the right moment."

"How?" She shook her head. "I would've noticed."

"Would you, though? With so much going on?"

"Maybe not," Hannah admitted. "But I think it's highly unlikely. I mean, no one on my staff and certainly no one in my family would do such a thing. And they were the only ones around before we opened."

"There was a fire alarm," Phaedra told him as she turned the heat up under a pot of water. "About an hour after the opening. It turned out to be false. We all went outside to wait for the fire department, and—"

"And you think that's when the killer struck." Charles nodded. "Makes sense."

"That's my theory. The back door was propped open for deliveries. It would've been easy for the killer to pull the alarm, wait for the place to empty out, slip back in through the service entrance, and poison the ganache."

"They'd have to work fast. And they'd have to know the back door was open," he pointed out. He glanced at Hannah. "Were the doors normally kept open? Before Saturday, I mean?"

"Sometimes. We had a lot of deliveries last week."

"Someone must've known." He leaned forward and rested his forearms on the island. "Someone who knew your routine and saw a way to use it to their advantage."

"But why?" Phaedra lifted the lid on the pot and dumped a box of linguine into the boiling salted water. "And why poison Anna, a random stranger? Who'd have a motive to do such a thing? Who even knew she'd be there?"

"A business rival, possibly? Hannah—didn't you tell me there's another bakery in town, one that's been around for years?" Charles asked her. "You had misgivings about competing with them."

"Brennan's. But Kate Brennan would never do something like this." Hannah sipped her wine. "She'd never poison a customer."

"Maybe not one of hers. But if the customer was yours?"

"I still can't see it." She swirled the wine around in her glass with a doubtful expression. "And where would Kate get potassium cyanide?"

"Online. Or from any place that sells insecticides and rat poison. It's not that difficult to obtain."

Phaedra took a head of lettuce and a couple of carrots out of the vegetable bin. "Okay, guys. Can we please table this discussion, at least until after dinner?"

"Sorry." Charles straightened. "Just following my thoughts. I had a Sherlock moment, but I'm over it now. Hand me a carrot, Phaedra, and a vegetable peeler, and let's get on with that salad."

* * *

After entertaining them over dinner with anecdotes from the British embassy, Charles reluctantly pushed the remains of his double-fudge brownie à la mode aside.

"Much as I hate to leave you two lovely ladies, it's time I got going. Thank you for dinner and for giving me a home-cooked meal. It's been ages since I had a decent plate of pasta, Phaedra."

"I'd hardly call it home-cooked," she said, and shrugged. "I boiled water and opened a jar."

"After a week of airplane food and trail mix bars, believe me, this was a treat."

"Do you have a place to stay, Chaz?" Hannah asked. She glanced at her sister. "If not, I can bunk with Phae and you can have the sofa."

"Much as I appreciate the offer," he said as he stood, "I booked a hotel room in Crozet." He suppressed a yawn. "Speaking of which, I'm a bit knackered. Think I'll check in, unpack, take a shower, and fall into bed."

"I'll walk you out." Hannah rose and reached out to link her arm through his. "Be back to help you clear up in a minute, Phae."

She made a dismissive motion. "I've got this. Go and say good night to your fiancé."

Charles Dalton made Hannah happy, and right now, that was exactly what her sister needed.

Phaedra had just put the last dish in the dishwasher when Hannah returned, her face flushed and her lip gloss mostly gone. Although her teenaged self would've teased Han mercilessly, Phaedra said nothing as she put the last dish in the dishwasher and started it up.

"Thanks for doing that, Phae. I'll unload the dishes in the morning," Hannah said. "Promise."

"I'll hold you to it." Phaedra dried her hands on the dish towel. "I think I'll stop by the Poison Pen. Take Mom some of those brownies you made. Otherwise . . ." She patted her stomach. "I'll eat them all myself."

Hannah nodded distractedly and reached for her phone. "Yeah, okay. See you later."

The bookstore had just closed when Phaedra arrived and made her way up the front steps. As she paused at the top of the porch steps to dig out her key, she glanced up Main Street.

Most of the shops had closed, leaving a number of parking places empty, but a few vehicles were still parallel parked at the curb. The Farrar Gallery, Laurel Springs' newest—and only—art gallery, was dark, as was Millie's Florist, Bascom's Jewelers, and the costume shop.

Only Brennan's bakery remained open.

As the bakery's front door opened, Phaedra's fingers tightened around the brownie-laden plate she held. Several customers entered as one left. Kate Brennan was plainly making the most of Hannah's misfortune, extending her normal business hours to capitalize on the patisserie's temporary closing.

She heard a car pull up and park nearby. It was a dark gray Audi, and it looked suspiciously like Charles's rental car. It *was* his car. She recognized the Illinois tag.

Her brow furrowed in puzzlement. Why was Charles here? Why was he parked on Main Street and not on his way to his hotel room in Crozet? Where was he going?

She climbed the porch steps and kept to the shadows, grateful her parents hadn't switched on the outside light yet. Her gaze followed Charles as he emerged from the car, dropped his keys in his jacket pocket, and headed down the sidewalk to the entrance to Brennan's.

The sound of the electronic door chime carried clearly on the cold night air.

Phaedra crept to the edge of the porch. Charles stood in front of the display case, talking to Kate's daughter, Moira, smiling and gesturing at something in the case. Sugar cookies.

Why in the world would he buy cookies when he'd indulged in not one, but two of Hannah's double-fudge brownies? With ice cream?

She'd just decided to set the plate down and head for Brennan's to ask him herself when the porch light snapped on and the front door flew open.

"Phaedra!" Her mother exclaimed, plainly put out. "What are you doing, loitering out here in the dark? I was about to call the police!"

Ten

Hi, Mom. Sorry, I didn't mean to alarm you. Just digging out my key to let myself in." She thrust the plastic-wrapped plate at Nan. "Hannah sent these."

"Double-fudge brownies? My favorite! They smell divine. And they're still warm." She ushered her daughter inside and shut the door with her free hand. "Well, don't dawdle. Come in."

"I can't stay. I have a morning lecture tomorrow—"

"Nonsense. You can spare a few minutes." Her mother sat the plate aside and lowered her voice. "Your timing's impeccable. There's someone in the reading room I'd very much like you to meet."

"Not another introduction to another single man, I hope." Phaedra remained by the door. "Speaking of which, your last attempt at matchmaking? Hector Kranz, the CPA? He's seeing someone. You're losing your touch, Mother."

"If you'd find your own eligible young men, I wouldn't have to bother."

"I don't *want* you to bother. I'd prefer you not to bother. Please, don't bother."

"A source told me you two had lunch together, so, not a total loss."

"'A source'?" Phaedra repeated. "You're not a journalist, Mom. Hector had something to tell me, that's all. Something he noticed at Hannah's grand opening."

"Oh?" Nan, her eyes bright with curiosity, leaned forward. "What was it?"

"Nothing important."

"It must've been, if you met him for lunch."

She lowered her voice. "He saw Biddy Bondurant slip a cupcake into her bag. During the grand opening."

"Well. That's hardly news, is it?"

"That's what I told him. I should go."

"Not until you come back and meet our visitor." She took Phaedra firmly by the arm.

There was nothing for it but to let herself be led down the hallway, past the stairs, and through the French doors that opened into the reading room. By day it was a place for customers to browse through a book, take notes, or sit and enjoy a cup of complimentary coffee or tea.

After hours, Malcolm Brighton often settled in the tufted leather wing chair in the corner to read or, Phaedra suspected, to escape from his wife.

Now, however, instead of sun streaming through the tall glass windows, lamplight warmed the room. The reading table was scattered with books and cups of tea.

Her father glanced up. "Phaedra? This is a pleasant surprise. Come and meet our new neighbor, Michael Farrar. Michael, this is my daughter, Professor Phaedra Brighton."

As she entered, the visitor thrust his chair back. Six feet, side-parted dark blond hair. Blue eyes, clean-shaven, with a dimpled smile that revealed teeth worthy of a toothpaste commercial.

If not for the dark blue Brioni suit, she would've pegged him as a game show host, or maybe a surfer.

Marisol was right. He was made for a pair of swim trunks. Or maybe a wetsuit . . .

"Hello, Professor." He reached across the table to shake her hand. His grip was firm. "It's a pleasure."

"Nice to meet you, Mr. Farrar." She thrust her wayward thoughts aside. "And, please, call me Phaedra. Are you the man behind our new art gallery?"

"Michael, please. Yes. I opened the Farrar Gallery last month, so it's still a work in progress."

"I've been meaning to stop by."

"Please do. As a matter of fact," he said, reaching into his breast pocket and withdrawing a card, "we're sponsoring a showing on Saturday evening. A promising new artist who deserves a wider audience." He held it out. "I hope you'll come. Invite your friends."

She took the card. It was of high quality, obviously expensive, yet understated. Rather like its owner.

"Thank you." Phaedra tucked it into her purse. "It's great to finally have a gallery here in Laurel Springs."

"I was just telling Michael about my grandfather, James Brighton," Malcolm said. "He was an artist. During his honeymoon in Italy, he painted the Piazza del Campo in Siena and presented it to his wife as a wedding present."

"Such a romantic gesture." Nan poured herself more tea. "Practical, too. He knew the painting would only increase in value over time."

"Unfortunately, she died giving birth to their first and only child," Malcolm continued. "My father. He eventually inherited the painting and gifted it to my mother, Rose, as a wedding present."

"I'd love to see it," Michael said. "Although he's not as well known today as he was at the turn of the twentieth century, he was highly regarded in his day. He utilized light and shadow with breathtaking realism."

"It's in decent shape," Nan said, "but the frame is tarnished, and it could do with a cleaning. Right now, it looks like one of those old sepia photographs. Dreary tones of beige and brown."

"Sounds as if it's in need of restoration."

"Can you recommend someone?" Malcolm asked.

"I can do better than that. I do a bit of restoration work, now and again. I'd be happy to take a look at it."

"That would be lovely!" Nan exclaimed.

"I hope you'll excuse me for running off," Phaedra said, "but I have an eight o'clock lecture in the morning, and I need to go. It was lovely to meet you, Mr. Farrar."

"Michael. And I assure you, the pleasure was mine. I hope to see you at the gallery on Saturday."

With a polite smile she turned to go.

"I'll see you out," Nan offered.

At the front door, Phaedra paused. "You're not fooling anyone, you know."

"What do you mean?"

"It's obvious, at least to me, that you 'saw me out' so you could extoll Michael Farrar's virtues."

"And why not? He's single." She added, "His suit's Italian, you know."

"Good night, Mom."

"You should take him up on his invitation to the showing," Nan added as she followed Phaedra onto the porch.

Because a man in possession of a Brioni suit and his own art gallery must *be in need of a wife.* "I'll think about it."

"And be sure to dress appropriately. No Empire gowns or ballet slippers allowed."

"I'm closing the door, Mom."

"Did I mention he's unattached?"

"You did. Goodbye, Mother."

As she retraced her steps and returned to the Mini, Phaedra glanced up the street. Brennan's was dark and a "CLOSED" sign hung at the door. Charles's rental car was gone.

She slid behind the wheel and started the engine. Asking Charles about his visit to Brennan's would have to wait until the next time she saw him. Before dinner, he'd asked if Hannah had any business rivals, and she'd mentioned the bakery. Which probably explained his visit.

The drive back to the carriage house was short; she should have left the car behind and walked. On impulse, she drove past the house and continued around the block. The extra time would give her an excuse, not only to admire the Christmas lights decorating the shops and houses, and the wreaths hung on every lamppost, but to allow her thoughts free rein.

Charles was right about one thing. Whoever poisoned Anna Steele's cupcake—and pulled the fire alarm—must have known Tout de Sweet's back door was open. Which meant he or she knew of the previous week's delivery routine.

She slowed at the corner and waited for the light to change. No one could've known the back door to the patisserie had remained open, except for the staff . . . or perhaps one of the other shop owners along Main Street.

As for Hector's account of Biddy stealing the cupcake, Phaedra decided there was no point in pursuing the matter. Her questions would only embarrass the elderly woman. And knowing how closely Rebecca monitored her sister's diet, Biddy probably often resorted to subterfuge to get her sugar fix.

No mystery there.

She'd just turned into the carriage house driveway when her cell phone rang. She scrabbled in her purse and pulled it out. "Dad? What's up? Did I forget something?"

"No. I remembered something." He paused. "I know who the man in Clark's photograph is."

"You do?" Her fingers tightened on the key fob as she shut off the engine. "Who is he? What jogged your memory?"

"All that talk about my grandfather did the trick," he said. "When Michael Farrar was here earlier."

"I don't understand."

He chuckled. "The mind is a mysterious thing. You remember I mentioned the painting? The one he gave to my grandmother as a wedding present?"

"Yes, of course. You asked Michael about restoring it."

"He wanted to see it, so I went upstairs after you left and brought it down. I hadn't thought about that picture in years. It hung in my law office in Charlottesville."

"I remember. But I still don't see what your painting has to do with the man in the photo."

"Eight years ago, I defended a client charged with vehicular manslaughter. He'd been drinking. He crossed a double yellow and hit a car head-on, killed the driver instantly. The victim was a twenty-year-old UVA student, home for spring break."

"How awful." Phaedra could only imagine the family's anguish. "And I suppose your client didn't have a scratch. Was he convicted?"

"Yes. He was sentenced to ten years in state prison."

"I'm sure you were glad he went to prison. Even if it meant you lost the case."

"Rouse was guilty. I knew he was guilty. But as his defense attorney it was my job to defend his right to a fair trial. And that's what I did."

"Rouse?" She paused. "That's his name? You're sure?"

"Positive. Arthur Rouse. Seeing that painting again . . . it all came rushing back. I used to study it when I was reviewing documentation for the case. And I remembered his expression when the state found him guilty."

"I saw him, Dad. Which means he's out. He's been released." Her fingers groped for the car door handle.

"Yes."

"Aren't you the least bit bothered? You defended him and lost the case. Now he's out and shows up at Hannah's grand opening, the same day that cupcake was poisoned. Don't you find the timing just a little . . . unsettling?"

"Phaedra." He switched the phone from one ear to the other. "I was a trial attorney for many years. In all that time I've never had a former client come after me seeking revenge."

"There's a first time for everything."

He chuckled. "You watch too many crime shows on TV, pumpkin."

"You need to tell the police about this, Dad." Her voice was firm. "Give Detective Morelli a call, tell him you've identified Rouse. Let him decide what to do with the information. At the very least, he'll want to question him. Your former client is a suspect. He had the opportunity. And he has a motive."

"All right." Malcolm released a sigh. "I think you're overreacting. But if it makes you feel better, I'll call Morelli first thing in the morning."

"Good. Be sure you and Mom lock up tight. And set the security alarm before you go to bed."

"I always do. You and Hannah do the same. Good night, Phaedra."

"Good night, Dad. I love you."

"Love you, too."

As she returned her phone to her purse and slid out of the car, Phaedra's glance darted across the shadowy lawn. Snow made the familiar front yard look like an alien moonscape. Bare tree limbs reached bony fingers up to the sky and a chill wind stirred the bushes.

Halfway up the sidewalk to the front door, a sound froze her steps. A slithery, heaving sound. Like a heavy boot dragging through the snow. But it came from overhead.

Was someone hiding on the roof? Her gaze lifted to the snow-frosted eaves. Was Rouse up there, waiting until she opened the door to leap down and force his way into the house? Was he crouching behind one of those bushes?

What to do? Call the police, or run back to the car and lock the door?

A chunk of ice slid down the roof and crashed onto the front steps.

Ice, she realized, and released a shaky, held breath. *The perfect murder weapon. You could stab someone with an icicle, and the evidence would eventually melt away.*

She could almost hear her father's voice. *You watch too many crime shows on TV, pumpkin.*

Maybe Dad was right. She was being ridiculous. Jumping to conclusions.

Phaedra cast one last uneasy glance over her shoulder, inserted her key in the lock, and opened the front door.

"I'm home, Han," she called out.

"Be right down."

Once inside, as the comforting scent of bayberry and cinnamon candles flickering on the hall table enveloped her, she breathed a sigh of relief.

And triple-locked the door.

Eleven

The next day, Phaedra took advantage of her free morning—Wednesday meant only one afternoon lecture to give—and headed for the Coffee Stop.

"One matcha latte, one Americano," she told the girl behind the counter. "Oh. And one of those, please." She pointed to a monster cookie in the display case.

A moment later, with her drink tray and cookie stowed on the passenger seat, Phaedra headed for the Laurel Springs police station.

Nothing like a little bribery in the form of fresh-brewed coffee and a cookie, she reasoned, to sweeten up an intractable detective and finagle a little information.

As she retrieved her purse from security, she heard voices approaching the lobby, growing closer.

"Professor Brighton." Detective Morelli paused as he rounded the corner and caught sight of her. He wore his customary jeans and a black Henley with the sleeves pushed to his elbows. "This is a surprise."

"A good surprise, or a bad surprise?"

"Depends." He eyed the tray. "Is one of those for me?"

"It is. I have a cookie with your name on it, too."

"Definitely a good surprise. Hold my calls, please," he said to the desk sergeant.

"You got it, Detective."

He led Phaedra down the opposite hall to the last office on the right and gestured her inside. "Have a seat."

She set the tray down on his desk and handed him the Americano and the cookie.

"Ah," he approved as he peeked inside the brown wrapper. "Monster. My favorite. Thank you."

"Sorry to stop by unannounced," she said as she perched on the end of the chair in front of his desk.

"I'm glad you did."

She suppressed a smile. "Because of the cookie."

"Well, yeah," he admitted. "And the coffee." He took a lengthy sip. "But also, because I have some good news."

"You've caught the poisoner?"

"Let's not get ahead of ourselves." He took a seat behind the desk. "We're still questioning everyone at the grand opening on Saturday."

"Half the town was there."

"Exactly. And not knowing if our poisoner targeted Anna, or Rachel, or possibly you or your father, makes finding the culprit a lot more complicated. Good news is, forensics finished with the crime scene late yesterday. Hannah can reopen the bakery."

"Patisserie."

"Whichever. Either way, she's back in business."

"She'll be happy to hear it." She glanced at the phone on his desk. "Did Dad give you a call this morning?"

"About the release of his former client?" He set his cup aside. "He did. We'll question Mr. Rouse as soon as we track down his current address."

"He has a motive. A grudge against my father. Maybe he wants payback after losing eight years of his life."

"*If* your father was the intended target. He wasn't the

prosecuting attorney or the judge in Rouse's case. And *if* Rouse was at the grand opening."

"He was definitely there."

"For how long? And what about after the fire alarm sounded, when everyone came back inside? Do you remember seeing him?"

"No." Her fingers tightened briefly around her cup. "It was crowded, there was a lot going on . . . and like I said before, I worked the counter for a while, so I was busy. But he'd hardly stick around if he poisoned that cupcake. Would he?"

"He might. If he wanted to make sure he succeeded."

She felt a chill chase up her spine.

"But I doubt it," Morelli added. "Honestly? I don't think he's our guy. He'd probably use a handgun or a knife rather than plan out an elaborate poisoning scenario."

"Why do you say that?"

"I don't think Rouse is smart enough or connected enough to pull off something like this. He just got out of prison. Some criminals are logical. Methodical. They plan every move before they act. Rationality drives their every movement. But your average criminal is unpredictable. Violent. And not terribly astute."

"Meaning, Rouse isn't our guy."

"I didn't say that. I said he could be, but in my professional opinion, I think it's unlikely."

"What about the list?" Phaedra asked suddenly. "The list of names Officer Scott took down."

He leaned back in his chair. "Rouse wasn't on it. Doesn't mean he didn't use a bogus name. Or he might have left before that point. I'll have Scott check again. See if any of the names fail to show up online in the usual places."

"Like the DMV database?"

He nodded. His phone rang, and he reached for it. "If that's all, Professor?"

She stood. "That's all. Thanks for the info."

"Thanks for the coffee. I'll be in touch."

As she made her way to the door, he added, "Whoever poisoned that cupcake planned it well in advance. My guess? They're playing a long game. Which means whoever did it is smart. Patient. And extremely dangerous."

"Is this the part where you tell me to stay out of it?"

"Do I need to tell you?"

Reluctantly, she shook her head. "No."

"Good. Thanks for stopping by." He answered the phone. "Detective Morelli here. What've you got?"

The rest of the day passed in a flurry of lectures, student consultations, grading papers, and preparation for Friday evening's staff holiday party.

"'Party' is a complete misnomer," Lucy groused as she joined Phaedra and Marisol in the faculty lounge on Thursday morning. "Watered-down punch and a conference room full of people competing for tenure, pretending to make nice over a plate of cookies? Not my idea of fun."

"At least it's only Thursday. You still have time to come up with a valid excuse by then," Marisol said.

"Like what?" She sighed heavily. "Maybe someone will drink too much and behave inappropriately."

Thursday, Phaedra suddenly remembered. *Tonight is my date night with Mark.* And she still didn't know what they were doing or where they were going.

"Who's behaving inappropriately?" Mark asked as he sauntered in, briefcase in hand.

"Not me," Marisol sighed. She rose and shouldered her book bag. "No time. I'm off to the library to tutor an undergrad. I'll see you later, Professor B."

"Wait." Lucy finished her coffee and tossed the cup in the recycle bin. "I'll go with you."

Mark nodded goodbye as they left and set his briefcase on the table. "Are you ready for tonight, Professor?"

"That depends."

"On what?"

"On you." Phaedra eyed him. "You still haven't told me where we're going or what we're doing. I don't know what to expect. Or what to wear."

"It's a surprise." He turned away to pour himself a cup of coffee.

"Are we going to a restaurant? Haute cuisine, Asian fusion, or pizza and beer? Can you give me a hint?"

"None of the above. Not this time, anyway. This is more of an . . . activity date. It'll be fun, I promise."

In Phaedra's experience, a promise that something would be fun usually wasn't. "Okay. So . . . jeans and boots? Tennis whites? Snowshoes?"

"Eat something beforehand and dress warmly," he added as he reached for the creamer, "and I'll see you at eight."

"Dress warmly?" She eyed him suspiciously. "Why?"

"Just trust me." His green eyes were amused as he turned and met her gaze. "You can manage that, can't you?"

Eight o'clock arrived and Phaedra heard singing outside, growing closer. Christmas carolers!

She abandoned her makeup mirror and forgot her first-date jitters as she hurried downstairs to open the front door. Hannah had left earlier to have dinner with Charles; the two had been inseparable since his return.

The singing provided a welcome distraction.

"Good King Wenceslas" segued into "I Saw Three Ships" as the carolers filled the frosty air with song. Mark Selden, yellow-and-blue-striped scarf wound at his neck, his face flushed with cold and high spirits, stood in the midst of the group and held a lantern aloft.

"Are you ready to come and join us?" he called out.

She nodded. "Let me get my coat and hat."

A moment later, clad in a down coat and woolen cap with earflaps, Phaedra pulled on her warmest gloves and joined them as they resumed their stroll along Main Street.

"I hope you don't mind," Mark said as he fell into step alongside her.

"Mind? I love it. I haven't gone caroling since I was a kid. But I'll warn you now—I'm not much of a singer."

"Doesn't matter. We're loud. We'll drown you out."

They sang "Silent Night," "It Came Upon a Midnight Clear," and "Winter Wonderland," one of the women jingling sleigh bells as the men provided counterpoint harmony. They lingered outside shops and houses, greeted everywhere they went with smiles and enthusiastic clapping.

When they sang their last song, they trooped to the community center, where volunteers waited to serve them cookies and cups of hot chocolate or mulled wine.

"Where'd you learn to sing like that, anyway?" Phaedra asked as they thawed out on a pair of folding chairs.

"I belonged to a madrigal group in college. It started out as a lark, but I found I quite enjoyed it."

"Why did you stop? Why don't you sing any longer?"

He shrugged, his smile remaining but his eyes inscrutable. "Time. As in, I don't have much of it to spare these days. Tutoring, peer-review input, research and lecture preparation . . . not to mention, papers to grade. You know how all-consuming it can be."

"I do. But if you really enjoy doing it, if you have a passion, you owe it to yourself to fit it in."

"This is enough, for now." He took a swallow of mulled wine.

A smile curved her lips. He was so earnest, so full of enthusiasm. The cold had turned his cheeks ruddy and ruffled his dark hair, and she could almost imagine him as a rosy-cheeked student, equally at ease studying Shakespeare's sonnets in the Bodleian or chucking snowballs at an unsuspecting friend across the quad.

"I see you listened to me," she added, and glanced at his scarf.

"This?" He fingered the fine cashmere wool. "A very smart woman once told me it was useless hanging down my front."

"Not totally useless." Phaedra brushed her fingers against his and took the scarf gently in her hands. It was soft. Warmed by the heat of his body. Her heart beating wildly, she drew him forward until their foreheads touched and their lips were inches apart. "Kiss me, Professor Selden," she whispered.

The surprise in his green eyes darkened to something more. He drew her closer and, slanting his lips over hers, he kissed her, warmly and thoroughly. He tasted of mint and mulled wine.

After a moment, her heart still thundering in her ears, Phaedra drew reluctantly back. "I'm sorry."

"I'm not."

"I don't usually . . ."

"You should. I like this side of you." His eyes crinkled in a smile.

Heat burned her cheeks. She felt, suddenly, like a self-conscious teen, overwhelmed with angst and embarrassment even as her hopes soared.

"I've wanted to do that for a long time," he admitted. "Since I walked into your office that first day, twenty minutes late."

"Twenty-five."

Mark laughed. "Fair enough. You were seriously annoyed with me. For two semesters, as I recall."

"Three. But I got over it. Eventually."

"I'm glad you did." He reached out for her gloved hand. "Your opinion means a lot to me, Phaedra. Even if I don't always agree with it."

"'My good opinion once lost . . .'" She laughed. "Healthy disagreement is a good thing, now and then."

Why are we here again?" Lucy popped a stuffed olive in her mouth and glanced around the room. "Wasting a perfectly good Friday night at the staff holiday party? Is it too early to leave yet?"

"Much too early," Phaedra said. "Sorry."

"Professor Brighton! So glad you and Professor Liang could make it."

"Dean Carmichael." Phaedra affixed a smile to her lips and inclined her head. "We wouldn't miss it."

Her gaze wandered past him, to the conference room crowded with faculty and a table groaning with chips and dip, crackers and cheese, a veggie tray, several pizzas, and every festively decorated cake and cookie known to man.

"Good turnout." Already his gaze moved past them, seeking better prospects. "Well. Enjoy yourselves, ladies." With a vague, insincere smile, he drifted away.

She watched him go with equal parts resignation and relief—mostly relief—and wished Mark would turn up. He hated these things as much as she did, but he'd promised to put in an appearance. It wasn't like him to go back on his word. And he rarely passed up a food buffet.

How he and Marisol remained so slim was a mystery.

"How's the case going?" Lucy asked, reaching for another olive. "Have the police narrowed the suspect list?"

"They're still questioning everyone who was at the grand opening." She risked a sip of punch and grimaced. "But Dad remembered who the guy in Clark's photo is."

"That's great. Who is it?"

"A client he defended eight years ago. Arthur Rouse. He was found guilty and convicted of vehicular manslaughter."

"I'm guessing this Arthur Rouse served his time, and now he's out."

"Early release for good behavior."

"What was he doing at Hannah's grand opening, giving your dad the stink eye? Seems a little suspicious to me."

"Exactly what I told Detective Morelli. Rouse certainly has a motive. A personal grudge and a desire for payback."

"And did Morelli agree?"

"Not really. He thinks a small-time criminal like Rouse would've used a weapon if he wanted to harm Dad. A gun or a knife. Not poison. Whoever tampered with the cupcake planned it out meticulously."

"He has a point," Lucy said. "You hear about bungled burglaries and getaway cars that run out of gas all the time. Your average criminal isn't very bright. But this poisoner is smart. Smart enough to dust a cupcake with cyanide without being seen. And get away with it."

"For now." Phaedra refused to believe that the perpetrator wouldn't be caught.

Lucy touched her arm. "There's Professor Cleland. I need to speak with her. Is our Tea Society meeting still happening on Monday night?"

"Yes. Sorry I had to reschedule. See you then."

As her friend left and wove her way through the crowd, Phaedra's gaze wandered past the familiar faculty faces. Where was Marisol? It wasn't like her to miss a party.

And where, she wondered suddenly as she moved away from the buffet table, was Mark Selden? Had a student consultation run late? Had he decided to dodge the holiday party altogether this year?

Was he avoiding her?

Even as the thought occurred, she dismissed it as unworthy. And ridiculous. Why would he avoid her? Just because they shared a brief kiss, a momentary brushing of lips? Just because she'd initiated it and not him?

Ah, that was the crux of the matter, wasn't it? That's what troubled her. Men liked to take the lead on such things. Didn't they?

She could almost hear Lucy's words on the subject. "Phaedra, women seize the initiative all the time. There *are* no rules. The patriarchy is dead. You decide what you want, and then you go out and get it."

Problem was, Phaedra found a certain level of comfort in rules. Expectations could sometimes be burdensome, no question; but there was also reassurance to be found in knowing what was expected. To rely on the tried-and-true.

Mark was reserved. A traditionalist, like herself. It wasn't far-fetched to imagine he'd been taken aback by her boldness. Even though he'd professed otherwise.

She took a last sip of punch and tossed the cup into the plastic-lined bin. No use second-guessing her actions now. It was too late. What was done, was done.

And it was only a kiss.

Saturday meant no classes to teach. No hurry, no need to get up. Jeans and a sweater instead of a chemise, silk gown, and pinned-up hair. Phaedra stretched luxuriously and snuggled deeper under the blankets.

No need to do anything but go back to sleep.

Wickham, annoyed by her movements, leaped down from the bed and stalked to the door with a plaintive meow.

"You want breakfast, I suppose." She sat up and yawned, glanced at the clock. Nearly eight.

Wickham meowed again. *I don't ask much*, his glare

seemed to say. *Just breakfast, second breakfast, lunch, dinner. With an occasional catnip* amuse-bouche, *and perhaps a sardine. Is that really too much to expect?*

"I'm coming, you demanding little feline."

As she drew on a robe, Phaedra sighed. It was the day of the Poison Pen's semiannual open house. She'd promised to bring spiced cider, and Hannah had baked an assortment of festively decorated sugar cookies.

"Rise and shine," she sang out as she descended the stairs and headed for the kitchen. Her sister stirred under the sofa bed's blankets but didn't sit up.

"We're due at the bookstore in forty-five minutes," Phaedra added over her shoulder. "Open house. Remember?"

"How can I forget?" Hannah sat up, scowling. "With you and Mom constantly reminding me?"

"At least your cookies are done and decorated." Phaedra emptied half a can of Mixed Seafood Grill into Wickham's dish and set it down by the refrigerator. He began to devour his breakfast with a customary blend of greedy fervor and delicacy. "They look pretty enough for a magazine cover."

"Maybe," Hannah said glumly, "but looks can be deceiving."

"Meaning?"

"What if no one eats them? After what happened to Anna Steele . . ."

"Han, you're being ridiculous." Phaedra put the kettle on and reached for a mug. "Remember what Grandma Rose always said? 'Don't borrow trouble'? Now, get dressed and help me load the car."

Wreaths of fresh greenery greeted Hannah and Phaedra as they arrived at the Poison Pen an hour later, cookies and apple cider in hand. The place was crowded as they edged their way inside. Conversations hummed, and holiday jazz played unobtrusively in the background.

"There you are," Nan exclaimed as she spotted them and

swooped over to take the platter of cookies from Hannah. "Welcome. Oh, these look divine! Phaedra, put the cider in a slow cooker. Is it heated through?"

"No."

"No matter, it's early. We'll keep the Crock-Pot in the kitchen on high for an hour or so and then we'll bring it out."

By "we," she meant Phaedra. With a sigh she lugged the jugs of cider upstairs to the kitchen and set them down on the counter. Now, to find the slow cooker.

"Hello, Phaedra." Her father, a mug of coffee in hand, greeted her with a guilty smile. "I should be downstairs mingling and jingling, but I refuse to waste a perfectly good cup of coffee."

"Your secret's safe with me. Love the hat." An elf's hat of green felt trimmed in red rested atop his head, and a jingle bell hung down one side.

"Your mother's idea."

"At least she didn't make you wear the elf shoes." Phaedra opened and closed cabinets until she found what she was looking for. "Ah, here it is." She unearthed the Crock-Pot and plugged it in. "How's the book biz?"

"Hectic. You know how it is during the holidays."

"I do. I worked behind the counter enough to remember the long lines and short tempers." She poured cider carefully into the slow cooker. "I just hope things improve for Hannah once everything settles down."

"By 'everything,' you mean the poisoning."

She nodded. "The police are doing all they can to find the culprit, but it takes time. Han's discouraged. Which is why," Phaedra added as she tied cinnamon sticks and star anise into a cheesecloth and added it to the cider, "I'm asking her to provide the menu for our Regency Christmas tea. I'm not sure she'll do it, though."

"Why wouldn't I do it?" Hannah entered the kitchen with Charles. "I love planning menus."

"Because your fiancé's back." She nodded to Charles. "You have a wedding to organize. And the Tout de Sweet thing isn't over. I wasn't sure if you'd be willing to take on the tea or not."

"We've put our wedding plans on hold. Just until all of this blows over," Charles said, and reached out to take his fiancée's hand.

Hannah nodded. "*If* it blows over. Either way, I refuse to hide in the house any longer. I miss baking, and I need to get back out there. Show my face. Defy the haters."

"That's the Han I know and love." Phaedra put the lid on the slow cooker and switched it on.

"At least the patisserie is cleared to open again." A frown shadowed her sister's face as she slid into a seat at the kitchen island. "Now, if only the police can figure out who poisoned Anna, my troubles will be over."

"That would definitely be welcome news," Charles agreed. "The Christmas tea is, what? Two weeks away? I'm sure they'll have the culprit under arrest by then."

Phaedra cast Hannah a curious glance. "Have you heard anything more from Detective Morelli?"

"Not a word since Wednesday, when he told me the crime scene investigators were finished."

"Maybe no news is good news?"

"You don't believe that any more than I do," her sister said. "My involvement in this Christmas tea may not be the best idea. Once people realize I baked the scones and tea cakes and tartlets, they'll stay away in droves."

"No one in town who knows you believes for one nanosecond that you had anything to do with Anna's poisoning. It was a horrible accident. It wasn't your fault."

"Your sister's right, Han," Charles agreed. "The people who matter—your friends, your family, your very wise, very handsome fiancé—will stick by you. Another story will come along to fuel the news machine. And a lot can happen in a couple of weeks. The investigation might be over by then, and the poisoner behind bars."

Although she'd never admit it, Phaedra wasn't quite so optimistic. This was a puzzling case, and she feared it wouldn't be solved easily or quickly. Detective Morelli's words came back to her.

"Not knowing if our poisoner targeted Anna, or Rachel, or possibly you or your father, makes finding the culprit a lot more complicated."

"Malcolm!" Nan called up the stairs. "Where are you?"

"Uh-oh, my cover's blown." He sighed and set his cup down. "Back to elf duty."

"Did you learn anything the other night?" Phaedra asked Charles as her father trudged back downstairs. "During your recon at Brennan's?"

"My . . ." He wrinkled his brows. "What *are* you talking about?"

"I saw you, Charles. I stopped by the bookstore to drop off a plate of Hannah's brownies, and there you were, chatting away with Moira Brennan."

"Oh. Yes. That." He cast an uncomfortable glance at his fiancée.

"And don't tell me you 'fancied something sweet,'" Phaedra added, "because you'd just eaten two double-fudge brownies. With ice cream."

"You're right." He let out a sulky sigh. "I thought I'd do a bit of investigating. Ask a few casual questions. That's all."

"And what did you learn?"

"Absolutely nothing. I might've done, only Mrs. Brennan arrived and told me quite unequivocally that they were closed. End of."

"But the bakery was open when you arrived, at a quarter past nine, wasn't it?"

"Yes." He shrugged. "I suppose as the owner, Mrs. Brennan can change the hours on a whim."

"She recognized you and decided to shut you down," Hannah said. "Your Sherlock act needs some work."

"I thought I did rather well."

"At least you tried." Phaedra patted his hand. "Thanks." She headed for the stairs. "I'll make the rounds downstairs, and then I have errands to run. See you later."

"Actually, we need to get going, too," Charles said. "There's a matinee at the Bijou, a double feature. *It's a Wonderful Life* and *Holiday Inn*. Why don't you go with us?"

Phaedra shook her head. "I'd love to, but I can't."

"Why not?" Hannah asked. "Date?"

"Michael Farrar invited me to a showing at his new art gallery tonight."

"On Saturday night? It *is* a date."

"Believe me, it isn't." Phaedra lifted her brow. "You sound more like Mom every day."

"You could do a lot worse. According to the *Clarion*, Michael Farrar is the most eligible bachelor in Laurel Springs."

"Sorry to disappoint, but I'm going with Lucy and Marisol. Lucy wants to check out the artwork."

"And Marisol?"

"Wants to check out the new owner."

At ten to seven, Phaedra pulled into a parking spot at the far end of Main Street and cut the Mini's engine. Couples and families crowded the sidewalks as they headed to restaurants, shopping, or lingered to admire the colorful holiday decorations.

"Look at this place!" Marisol eyed the couples passing by, some holding hands, while shoppers laden with packages and bags rushed in and out of the shops. "I know it's Saturday night, but this is insane."

"Christmas is only a few weeks away," Lucy reminded her. "Wait till Christmas Eve. That's when the male of the species emerges from his winter cave to forage for last-minute gifts at the drugstore."

"Last year my boyfriend bought me a stuffed animal and one of those generic cheese boards with summer sausage."

"But you're allergic," Lucy pointed out. "And vegetarian."

"Exactly why he's not my boyfriend any longer."

"At least he got you something." Phaedra opened her door and slid out. "Isn't it the thought that counts?"

"No," Lucy and Marisol said at the same time.

As they neared the Farrar Gallery, their footsteps slowed.

The entrance was flanked by a pair of lollipop-shaped topiary trees, and a wreath of Frasier fir decorated the glossy black door.

"Wow," Marisol murmured. "This looks like the entrance to Number Ten Downing Street."

Inside, white walls and pale gray carpet provided an unobtrusive backdrop for the artwork. The paintings ranged from huge, color-splashed canvases to small, thoughtfully grouped studies. Interspersed with modern pieces were works from the early twentieth century.

"Impressive," Lucy whispered to Phaedra. "I can almost smell the money."

Marisol hovered at Phaedra's elbow. "That landscape over there?" She pointed at a six-by-twelve painting. "It's six thousand dollars!"

"Good evening, Professor Brighton." Michael Farrar approached them, a smile warming his face. "Welcome to my gallery." From his polished Italian shoes to his tailored suit, his style was as striking as it was understated.

"Introduce us," Marisol whispered. "Please. He's even better looking than I remember."

"Hello, Michael." Phaedra took his outstretched hand. "And it's Phaedra, please. This is Professor Lucy Liang, and my teaching assistant, Ms. Marisol Dubois."

"Professor Liang, Ms. Dubois. I'm honored to welcome you both to our showing tonight." His eyes lingered on Marisol. "Our featured artist, Colette Parrish, hails from Charlottesville. She's known for her vibrant use of color in her landscapes."

"I don't know much about art," Marisol admitted. "Other than knowing what I like and what I don't."

"That's a good place to start. Always trust your instincts." He held out his arm. "May I give you a tour?"

"I'd love that."

He drew her away, nodding now and again at people studying the artists' work, as Marisol, her expression rapt, hung on his arm and drank in his every word.

"Should I be insulted?" Lucy asked, amused. "He literally didn't even notice me. Or you, for that matter."

"Gives us time to check out the paintings on our own."

"And avoid small talk," Lucy added. "Win-win."

They wandered from one work to the next, pausing to admire the artist's local settings and bold brushstrokes, some places recognizable and some more impressionistic, as jazz played softly in the background.

"Look." Lucy stopped before a small oil and gouache painting of Main Street on a rainy day. "It's your aunt's B and B, and the Poison Pen." She pointed. "And the Bijou."

"It's charming," Phaedra agreed. Her glance went to the white card tucked discreetly in one corner. "Fifteen hundred."

"Too rich for my blood," Lucy sighed. "Maybe someday I can afford an original artwork. But today isn't the day."

"You're here! I'm so glad you showed up."

Nan Brighton bore down on them, a flute of champagne in one hand and a gallery brochure in the other. She nodded to Lucy. "Michael's giving Marisol a tour." She tapped her daughter's arm playfully with the brochure. "He should be giving *you* a tour. Missed opportunity there, darling."

Phaedra swallowed her irritation along with the last of her champagne. "I have no interest in Michael Farrar. Mark and I are seeing each other."

"Oh?" Her eyebrow lifted. "I thought the two of you were 'just colleagues.'"

"Things change." The only way to derail her matchmaking mother was a change of subject. "Where's Dad?"

"He stayed behind to close up. As excuses go, I couldn't argue with that one." Nan sipped her champagne and eyed the door. "Well, well. Look who just arrived."

An electronic chime sounded as a pair of newcomers entered the gallery. The woman wore a bone-white wool coat with sleek black boots; her male companion sported a bomber jacket and jeans.

"It's Rachel and Man Bun," Lucy observed. "I thought they were getting a divorce."

"So did I." Nan frowned. "Yet they go everywhere together. Like a pair of newlyweds."

They pretended not to watch as Rachel's soon-to-be ex-husband, Kyle Middleton, grabbed a flute of champagne from a passing tray and knocked it back in one swallow.

"Happy now?" he said, his voice a low growl as he returned the empty glass to the tray and fixed Rachel with a glare. "I came. I saw. I'm out of here."

"Kyle, please. If you'd only wait—"

"Pretend to be the happy hubby for your adoring public? Sorry, but no. I kept my end of the bargain." He brushed past her and headed for the door. "See you later."

"But how will I get back to Delaford?" Rachel hissed.

"Call an Uber. If you can manage it without Anna or one of your minions to do it for you."

With that, he flung the front door open and left.

"That poor woman," Nan murmured as Rachel's cheeks flushed in embarrassment, no doubt aware that they'd witnessed Kyle's desertion. "I think I'll go over and offer her a ride home."

Phaedra laid a hand on her arm. "Leave it. It's none of our business. And Michael's coming back with Marisol."

"If you have any further questions, Ms. Dubois, don't hesitate to reach out. Here's my card." He paused and scribbled a number on the back. "And my personal number." He handed it to her. "I look forward to seeing you again."

"Same," she echoed, plainly dazzled. "Thanks."

"I see you found your daughter, Mrs. Brighton." He smiled and signaled to a waiter. "More champagne, ladies?"

"None for me, thanks," Phaedra said. "I'm driving."

"I'm good," Lucy seconded.

The waiter arrived, and Michael took two glasses. "Well, enjoy the rest of your evening. Now, if you'll excuse me . . . one of my guests requires attention." He held up one of the champagne glasses in a brief salute and headed toward Rachel.

"Did you enjoy the private tour as much as he did?" Phaedra asked Marisol.

Her cheeks turned as pink as her angora sweater. "I did. He's very knowledgeable. Especially about early-twentieth-century art."

"Did he invite you upstairs to look at his etchings?" Lucy teased.

"No." Marisol snagged a glass of bubbly from a passing tray. "But he did ask me out." She took a sip. "To dinner, next Tuesday night. And I said yes."

Nan congratulated Marisol as Phaedra glanced over at Michael. He handed Rachel a flute of champagne. After a few quiet words, he led her through the knots of people and toward the back of the gallery.

"She looks upset." Phaedra set her own glass aside.

"Kyle ditched her two seconds after they got here," Lucy pointed out. "That's enough to upset anyone. And everyone keeps sneaking glances at her, like they want to approach but don't quite dare."

"They're too sophisticated to fangirl over Rachel in a place like this."

"You're right, Mari." Lucy suppressed a yawn. "I know it's barely nine thirty, and it's Saturday night, but it's been a long day. Can we please head out soon?"

"I need to do laundry," Marisol agreed. "And go through my closet to figure out what to wear on Tuesday."

"What a couple of lightweights." Phaedra sighed. "Okay. Let me visit the ladies' first and then we'll go."

"I'll come with you," Nan decided. "That champagne's gone right through me."

They wove their way through knots of people—the volume of conversation had increased—to the restrooms in the back, and Nan pushed the door open. "Oh. It's a single stall."

"Go ahead. I'll wait."

Phaedra studied a nearby painting, admiring the vivid

oranges and yellows of the tree-lined Blue Ridge Parkway in autumn, when her phone dinged. A text, from Mark.

Are you free tomorrow evening?

Possibly, she texted back. Why?

Ice skating? Town square?

She smiled. Sounds fun. What time?

They arranged to meet at seven o'clock. She tucked her phone away and peered around the corner. Michael's office door was partly ajar. He and Rachel were talking in low but intense voices inside.

Michael was no doubt offering comfort to his celebrity guest following Kyle's surly behavior. Commendable of him. But, to her ears at least, their conversation sounded almost . . . contentious.

Perhaps he had designs on Rachel? An alliance with the media star, romantic or otherwise, would certainly benefit his gallery. Curious, Phaedra edged closer until she could see Rachel's side profile.

Michael had his back to the door as he spoke to her in a low voice.

Her voice rose. "What . . . what did you say?"

He murmured something Phaedra couldn't make out.

She hesitated, not sure if she should interrupt or retreat, when the champagne flute slipped out of Rachel's hand and shattered on the floor.

The bathroom door opened behind her, and Phaedra turned and fled her post before Michael or Rachel saw her.

"All done," her mother said. "Your turn."

"I can wait. Let's go." Phaedra took her elbow and hurried her toward the front. Had the two in Michael's office heard Nan? Probably. Their voices had gone quiet.

"Phaedra, for heaven's sake," her mother protested, drawing back in irritation. "Why the sudden rush to leave?"

"Wickham, Mom. He needs to go outside. Now."

As she led her mother through the gallery in search of Lucy and Marisol, she realized they'd already left. She spotted them standing in front of Bascom's Jewelers, admiring the Christmas display in the front window. Phaedra risked a quick glance over her shoulder.

Just in time to glimpse Rachel, slipping out the back exit in a flash of white coat and a black bootheel as Michael closed his office door. He smiled at Phaedra and returned to the gallery floor.

"Professor Brighton. Are you and your charming mother leaving so soon?"

"I'm afraid so. I have . . ." She groped for an excuse. "An early-morning lecture. I need to get home."

"I see. That's too bad. And on a Sunday, too."

Although his expression was sympathetic, Phaedra sensed amusement behind his words. He didn't buy it. Not for a minute.

"I'm sorry we can't stay longer," she added. "I hope we're not the first to leave."

"No, unfortunately, you're not." Regret tinged his smile. "Ms. Brandon had to leave early as well."

"I do hope she's all right," Nan said. "We couldn't help but overhear the conversation."

His gaze sharpened. "What do you mean?"

"Why, her husband's rude behavior. Storming off like that and leaving her stranded."

"The man's a cretin." He shrugged. "I didn't wish to invite him, but there was no way around it. Ms. Brandon was understandably upset," he added. "I did my best to calm her down and called a car service. You needn't worry."

"How gallant of you." Nan turned to her daughter. "Mr. Farrar is a true gentleman, don't you think?"

"Yes. I also think it's time we left." Phaedra bestowed a smile on him and took his outstretched hand. "Your gallery is impressive. I wish you every success."

"Thank you. That means a great deal. And thank you both for coming. Good night, ladies."

"Good night," they echoed.

He inclined his head, and as she followed her mother out of the gallery, Phaedra sensed his gaze following them.

She closed the door firmly after her, relieved to depart the confines of the gallery and escape back into the cold night air.

Last time I skated I was twelve," Phaedra told Mark when they met at the ice rink early Sunday evening.

"It's like riding a bike." Mark took her hand. "You never forget."

They rented skates and joined the throng, circling the rink to the strains of Christmas music until, laughing and breathless, they left the ice.

"I was a little wobbly," Phaedra confessed as they found a bench and sat down.

"You did great. Mum would say skating put 'the roses in your cheeks.'"

"Your scarf's crooked." She reached to straighten it.

He caught her hand in his. "I remember the last time you straightened my scarf."

A blush warmed her cheeks. "You're not falling for my feminine wiles again?"

"On the contrary," he said, leaning nearer. "I've already fallen."

Several glorious, head-spinning moments later, he lifted his mouth from hers. Phaedra's lips tingled, and she was far too dazzled to speak.

"What magic is this?" she whispered.

"'Lady, as you are mine, I am yours.'"

She felt a giggle bubble up. "You're quoting Shakespeare at me? Seriously?"

"'Better three hours too soon than a minute too late.'"

"Stop," she warned, "or I swear, I'll start spouting Austen back."

Reluctantly, he drew away. "Let's turn in our skates. We could both do with a hot chocolate."

Afterward, they walked side by side through the brisk night air. Mark slipped his hand in hers as they passed a tall Victorian house trimmed in tiny white lights, and the gesture felt natural. Right.

"We missed you at the faculty holiday party," she ventured as they paused on the corner for a stoplight.

The flashing message changed from "DON'T WALK" to "WALK," and he squeezed her hand briefly as they crossed the street. "Sorry. I meant to go. Was it awful?"

"You tell me. Green mystery punch and a roomful of people who didn't want to be there."

"It was awful."

"It would've been better if you were there."

As they reached the other side, Phaedra waited for him to say more, to elaborate on why he'd skipped out, but he didn't. They stopped in front of Bascom's Jewelers to study its bay window, decorated with a detailed recreation of an old-fashioned Christmas village. Sledders raced down a snowy hill, a train chugged over a trestle bridge, and skaters performed figure eights on a mirrored surface.

"Amazing." Mark watched as the train engine, its tiny headlight shining, led the freight cars across the bridge and disappeared into a snowy tunnel, then circled back to do it all over again. "Do they do this every year?"

Phaedra nodded. "It's a local tradition to come and see Bascom's window during the holidays." She slowed her steps as they rounded the corner. "Here we are."

The Mini was just where she'd left it, parked under a streetlight.

"Guess I'll see you tomorrow." He waited as she unlocked the door and slid behind the wheel, then leaned in to kiss her goodbye. "I'm glad you came."

"So am I. See you tomorrow."

He stepped back from the curb as she started the engine and lifted his hand as she pulled away.

And it occurred to her, as she drove away, that he never actually told her where he'd been on Friday night.

As the holidays drew closer, the students grew more distracted. With midwinter break only a week away and midterms behind them, the halls echoed with travel plans and excited chatter.

Phaedra nodded hellos as she strode down the hall to her office. Christmas parties, ride shares, and invitations to hang out over the holidays. Last-minute plans to get together. Sign-up sheets for the faculty cookie exchange.

"Are you participating in the cookie exchange this year?" Marisol asked as she entered the office.

"I'm hosting the Regency Christmas Tea on Sunday, remember?" Phaedra dropped a pile of folders on Mari's desk. "Speaking of which—have you sold any tickets?"

"Only a few left. People are curious, I guess."

"Curious? About what?"

"Well, now that Tout de Sweet's open again, it's all anyone's talking about. Not just the opening. But the . . ." She hesitated. "The poisoning."

Phaedra sank down in her chair. "I thought everyone had moved on to new gossip by now."

"They have, but Anna's death is still a hot topic. The police haven't arrested anyone yet. I heard that a group of students in criminology started a suspect bracket."

"Maybe this Christmas tea is a bad idea." Phaedra rested

her forearms on the blotter. "I don't want to subject Hannah to whispers and speculation all over again."

"Honestly? I think holding the Regency tea is smart," Marisol assured her. "Confront the naysayers head-on. Prove that Hannah is an excellent baker with amazing French pastry skills who'd never poison anyone. She deserves a chance to put the kibosh on all of these crazy rumors."

"You're right," Phaedra agreed. "Full steam ahead and damn the torpedoes."

Marisol straightened the folders and tidied them into a neat stack on one corner of her desk. "Did you see Mark this weekend?"

"We went skating last night. It was fun." Although it wasn't Mark's skill on the ice she remembered as much as his thoroughly dazzling, head-spinning kiss . . .

"I heard he didn't make it to the faculty party."

"He wasn't the only one. What's *your* excuse for ditching us? Lu and I looked for you."

"I had a flat tire. A nail, if you can believe it. Luckily, I was near a garage. By the time it was fixed, the party was almost over."

"Convenient."

"It kind of was," she admitted. "How was the party?"

"Painful, as always. You didn't miss anything."

"Oh, I almost forgot," Marisol blurted. "When I left, I saw Mark."

"Where?" Phaedra frowned. "At the garage?"

"No. He was coming out of Orsini's with a—" Her face paled and she began to stammer. "With someone."

"With who, Mari?"

"I—I don't know who she was."

"Was she a faculty member?"

"Um . . . no."

"A teaching assistant? A student?"

"I've never seen her before. She was about my age.

Maybe younger. Cute. In an Alicia Silverstone, *Clueless* kind of way."

Even as her heart plummeted like a capsized ship going under, Phaedra grasped for a lifeline. "Were they there together, together? Maybe they left at the same time."

"They were definitely together. They stood out front talking, and it looked kind of intense. I only got a glimpse, but it seemed like they . . . like they knew each other pretty well. I'm sorry," Marisol finished in a rush. "I shouldn't have mentioned it. Forget I said anything."

Phaedra shrugged, even as a thousand questions filled her brain. "No, it's okay. I'm glad you told me."

No wonder Mark hadn't told her why he'd missed the faculty party, or where he'd been. He didn't want her to know the truth—that he'd had another engagement.

He'd taken "Alicia" out to dinner. To Orsini's. Easily the nicest, most expensive restaurant in Laurel Springs.

Marisol balanced a stack of folders on her arm and stood. "I'll be at the copier. Be back in a few. Unless it jams on me again."

Phaedra gave her a distracted nod and reached for her lecture notes. "Try the copier upstairs." She picked up her pen and wrote a couple of lines.

But her thoughts intruded. *It's your own fault. You scared Mark away.* She never should have kissed him.

And yet, everything seemed fine on their date. He'd been genuinely glad to see her; he'd walked her back to her car; he'd even kissed her. Twice.

But she couldn't forget that he'd also evaded her attempt to question him about missing the faculty party. If the mystery companion with him outside Orsini's was merely an acquaintance, or even a friend, why had he failed to mention it?

Fifteen

Just before seven on Monday evening, Malcolm rang up the last sale of the day, waited until his customer left, and locked the front doors.

"The reading room is all yours," he told Phaedra and her friends as he flipped the sign in the door to "CLOSED."

"Thanks, Dad. I'll lock up when we're done."

As he nodded and headed upstairs, Phaedra led Lucy and Marisol down the hall to the reading room.

"Hannah sent a plate of macarons," she said over her shoulder. "Mom's steeping a pot of tea."

"Speaking of macarons, how are things going at Tout de Sweet?" Marisol asked as she slid into a seat at the table. "They reopened today. I didn't get a chance to stop by."

"Business is slow," Phaedra admitted. "It'll take time to recover. Like I told Han, it won't happen overnight."

"But it *will* happen." Lucy looked up as Nan arrived with the tea tray. "What smells so good?"

"Orange and spice black tea," Nan answered. "My favorite holiday brew."

Once everyone poured themselves tea and helped themselves to a few macarons, the monthly meeting of the Jane Austen Tea Society got underway.

"First order of business," Phaedra said as she set her cup down and went to the whiteboard, "is this month's book discussion."

She wrote "*Sense and Sensibility*" on the board. "The novel was published in 1811, 'By a Lady.'" She put her marker aside. "Initial thoughts?"

"Actually," Lucy admitted, "I haven't read it yet."

"You know the story," Marisol prodded. "Don't you?"

"Of course. Two sisters lose their home, move to a small cottage, and fall in love with two different men."

"How would you say the two suitors differed?" Phaedra asked. "Aside from their occupations."

Marisol leaned forward. "Edward Ferrars was a clergyman. He was disinherited for honoring his promise to marry Lucy Steele, a woman his mother considered beneath him. His integrity basically cost him his inheritance. And nearly cost him Elinor Dashwood, the woman he loved."

"The other suitor, John Willoughby," Lucy said, "expected to inherit a fortune. He was handsome and charming, and he fell madly in love with Marianne Dashwood, but in the end, he valued money and status more."

Phaedra picked up the marker and wrote two names on the board. "Elinor and Marianne were sisters, but like their suitors, they were very different. In what ways?"

"Elinor was sensible," Marisol said. "Dependable. Just like Edward. Marianne was ruled by her emotions."

"Elinor personified 'Sense,'" Phaedra said, "and Marianne represented 'Sensibility.'"

"Yes. Not unlike the Bondurant sisters." Lucy took a thoughtful sip of tea. "Rebecca is the businesswoman; Biddy, not so much. She wears her heart on her sleeve."

"Maybe that's why they named their shop Scents and Sensibility," Marisol said.

"You're probably right." Phaedra erased the board. "Okay, Janeites, what's next on our agenda?"

"Anna's poisoning," Lucy said. "We haven't really discussed it since it happened."

"Okay." Phaedra turned back to the board. "Let's recap what we know so far."

"Whoever pulled the fire alarm probably poisoned the cupcake," Marisol said. "Which means it was a diversionary tactic by someone who knew the back door was open."

"We also know the culprit likely targeted either Hannah, Phaedra, or Mr. Brighton," Lucy added. "I think we should focus on anyone who might have reason to try to harm them."

"Let's make a suspect list," Phaedra suggested. "And a list of the shopkeepers on Main Street."

Marisol frowned. "You think one of the shop owners might've done it? Why?"

"Could be that someone took issue with a new business popping up nearby. Maybe they resented the competition, or worried it would affect their sales. Kate Brennan, for instance." She put Kate's name at the top of the list.

"Might as well add Josie's wine bar to the list," Lucy said, "and Bascom's Jewelers. And don't forget the apothecary shop. We can't leave anyone out."

"Even though we've known these people for years?" Marisol asked. "You can't seriously think Mr. Bascom or Josie would do something like this."

"No, of course I don't." Phaedra added their names to the board. "But we have to consider the possibility that someone in one of the shops along Main Street noticed Hannah's daily routine. Maybe they saw the back door standing open when they took the trash out to the dumpster or the recycle bins in the morning. Maybe they have a grudge against Hannah and saw her grand opening as an opportunity."

"Maybe," Marisol said doubtfully. "I'd hate to think that's the case, though." She frowned. "What about the shops on the other side of Main? Orsini's, and Millie's Florist, and the Dog 'n Draft?"

"Let's stick to this side of the street for now."

Their final list included Harper's pub, the Farrar Gallery, the Coffee Stop, and Woofgang's Gourmet Doggy Bakery, along with Bascom's, Scents and Sensibility, the wine bar, and the costume shop.

"We need to talk to the owners." Phaedra studied the list. "Marisol, after the meeting, leave the unsold tickets with me. I'll visit a few of these shops on Wednesday morning, see if I can glean any information."

"Under the guise of selling tickets," Lucy approved. "Sneaky. I love it."

"Okay, back to suspects." Phaedra scrawled Rachel's name on the board, followed by Hannah and Malcolm. "When I talked to Detective Morelli last week, he made a good point. The police haven't determined if the poisoning was random or intended for a particular individual. If the poisoner *did* target someone, was it Anna? Doubtful; the cupcake wasn't meant for her. Rachel? Or me? Possibly, but again, doubtful. Where's the motive? Which leaves Hannah, who has a jealous business rival." She paused. "And then there's Dad."

Marisol drew in a sharp breath. "Who'd want to harm Mr. Brighton?"

"He was a prosecuting attorney for a number of years. He put plenty of people behind bars. Maybe someone he put away is out and wants payback."

"Someone like Arthur Rouse," Lucy said.

"Wait." Marisol looked at Lucy in confusion. "Who's Arthur Rouse?"

"He was one of my father's clients," Phaedra said. "Dad defended him years ago, before he became a prosecuting attorney," Phaedra said. "He lost the case, and Rouse did time in state prison. He's out now."

"And," Lucy added, "he was at the grand opening."

"Well, then, he's our guy," Marisol exclaimed. "He had motive and opportunity. He's obviously the poisoner."

"Not so fast." Phaedra crossed her arms loosely against her chest. "Whoever poisoned that cupcake planned out every detail in advance. Which means premeditation. Malice aforethought. According to Detective Morelli, the average criminal, like Rouse, is unpredictable. Impulsive. And they're not always smart."

"The opposite of our culprit," Lucy ventured.

"Exactly. Plus, he just got out of prison." Phaedra's cell phone rang. She went to the table and picked it up. "Sorry." She glanced down at the incoming number. "Speak of the devil. It's Detective Morelli."

"You'd better answer it," Marisol advised. "It might be important."

With a nod, Phaedra answered. "Hello, Detective."

"Professor Brighton. Not interrupting anything, am I?"

"No, not at all. What's up?"

"I thought you might like to know we're questioning a couple of suspects in the morning."

"Oh? I'm surprised you're telling me. You don't usually share information."

"Ordinarily I wouldn't. But if it pans out, this may be important, and I want to keep you and Hannah in the loop. I hope I don't need to add that this stays between you and me and your sister."

"Absolutely. Understood." She held her index finger up to Lucy and Marisol, both shamelessly eavesdropping.

"I spoke with Vanessa Cole earlier today. Rachel Brandon's producer. She told me something interesting about Anna Steele. Something she failed to mention before."

Phaedra's pulse quickened. "Oh?"

"It seems Ms. Steele and Kyle Middleton were having an affair."

"Anna and Rachel's husband?" Surprise colored her voice. "Wow. Had it been going on very long?"

"For a month or so. Vanessa suspects that Rachel recently found out about the affair. She overheard a heated exchange between the two women last week."

"Which gives Rachel a motive," Phaedra said slowly.

"Kyle's not off the hook, either."

"Why do you say that?"

"Because Anna's the one who told Rachel about the affair."

Phaedra's frown deepened. "That's crazy. Why would she do that?"

"According to Vanessa, Anna was insecure and clingy. Kyle got tired of the drama pretty quickly and ended the relationship. His jilted girlfriend wasn't a happy camper." He paused. "My theory? Anna wanted payback. What better way to do that than by throwing Kyle under the bus to Rachel?"

"Which also gives him a motive to poison Anna."

"I'm paying Mr. Middleton and Ms. Brandon a visit first thing tomorrow. I called Hannah but got her voice mail. Will you let her know?"

"Of course," Phaedra said.

She couldn't wait to tell her sister that Anna's accidental death may have been no accident at all.

Lucy and Marisol eyed Phaedra expectantly as she ended the call. She sighed. "How much did you two hear?"

"Enough to know that Anna Steele and Kyle Middleton were having an affair," Lucy said.

"Which gives Rachel Brandon a motive for murder." Marisol glanced at Phaedra. "*If* she knew about the affair."

"She did. At least, according to Vanessa Cole."

"Who's the 'him' you referred to?" Lucy asked.

"Kyle. Anna threw him under the bus after he dumped her. She went to Rachel and told her everything."

"Seriously? Why would she do that?"

Phaedra shrugged. "You know what they say. 'Heaven has no rage like love to hatred turned,'" she quoted, "'nor hell a fury like a woman scorned.'"

"Shakespeare?" Marisol asked.

"William Congreve. *The Mourning Bride*."

"Whatever the reason, it wasn't the smartest move. Rachel could've fired her." Lucy leaned forward. "Is Kyle a suspect, too? Is that why Morelli called you?"

"He's a person of interest," Phaedra confirmed. "Along with Rachel. They're being questioned tomorrow." She reached for the eraser and cleared the whiteboard, wiping away their suspect list, and glanced at the clock. "If you're all agreed, let's adjourn."

Lucy and Marisol nodded and began gathering cups and paper plates. "An affair between Kyle and Anna changes everything," Marisol said. "Maybe you and your dad weren't the targets. Maybe Anna was the intended victim all along."

"It's beginning to look that way." Phaedra put everything onto the tea tray. "I can't help but feel a measure of relief at the possibility." The thought of someone hating her or her father enough to attempt to poison them was unsettling, to say the least.

"Nice of Morelli to keep you in the loop," Lucy said. "And very unlike him."

"He's keeping me informed only because it directly affects Hannah. And you both know the drill," she added. "This stays between the three of us."

"Our lips are zipped." Marisol grabbed her legal pad and copy of *Sense and Sensibility* and shoved both into her shoulder bag. "Sorry if I was a little distracted tonight. I don't know how I'll get through the day tomorrow."

"That's right." Phaedra lifted her brow. "You have dinner plans with Michael Farrar." She switched off the light and picked up the tea tray. "Where's he taking you?"

"Somewhere *très chic*, no doubt." Lucy slung her bag over her shoulder. "Orsini's?"

"Even better," Marisol said. "The Ivy Inn."

Lucy and Phaedra exchanged an approving glance.

"Respect," Lucy said. "If he's taking you to Charlottesville for dinner, I hope you're leaving early."

"We are. The gallery closes at noon on Tuesday." Marisol turned to Phaedra. "You don't mind if I leave a couple of hours early tomorrow, do you?"

"No problem. There's not much going on this week anyway. Did you copy and bind those presentations?"

"Every last one. Now all I have to do is figure out what to wear for my date tomorrow night. And get rid of these butterflies swooping around in my stomach. See you later." With a distracted nod, Marisol departed.

"Will you still canvass the shops on Main Street?" Lucy asked as she followed Phaedra down the hall. "Now that we know Kyle or Rachel might be behind it?"

"It can't hurt. A few discreet questions might turn up a tidbit or two. Maybe a shop owner or staff member saw something when they were out back, taking a smoke break. Or taking the trash out."

"Good possibility. And Rachel and Man Bun might turn out to have alibis."

"I need to tell Hannah. Maybe knowing that Anna's poisoning was part of a love triangle gone wrong will ease her mind a little."

"Having Charles around probably helps."

"No question," Phaedra agreed. "He's keeping her company at the patisserie until closing tonight. He worries about her safety."

"When are they tying the knot? Have they set a date?"

"Not yet. But soon, I think."

Lucy reached for the doorknob. "Speaking of lovebirds, I haven't seen Mari so excited about a date since she went out with that guy with the tats."

"Apparently, he didn't live up to expectations."

"Let's hope Michael Farrar does. She deserves a decent guy. For that matter, so do I." She sighed. "See you tomorrow. And don't forget to lock up."

The bell over the apothecary door chimed softly as Phaedra entered Scents and Sensibility on Wednesday morning. Bayberry, lemon verbena, lavender, and cinnamon mingled in a subtle, earthy perfume as she stepped inside.

Tiny white lights crisscrossed the pressed-tin ceiling, lending the shop a festive air. Wreaths fashioned of glossy magnolia and bay leaves hung in the front windows. Shelves stocked with tinctures, salves, and handmade soaps lined the walls, and baskets filled with sachets of custom tea blends or dried herbs sat atop display tables.

Phaedra looped her reticule over her wrist. She was the first customer through the door. Perfect.

"Professor Brighton! Hello." Rebecca Bondurant emerged from the back—she and her sister, Biddy, lived upstairs—with a carton in hand. "Just arrived," she added as she set the box down and began removing tins of echinacea cough drops. "It's that time of year. Cold and flu season."

"I'm on my way to Somerset," Phaedra said in answer to Rebecca's curious regard.

"Well, I'm no amateur sleuth, Professor," Rebecca replied,

"but I deduced that much. Our customers don't normally wear Regency gowns or carry drawstring purses."

"My students expect it. I teach in period clothing because . . ." She searched for a suitable explanation. "It's a kind of literary cosplay."

"Cosplay?"

"Dressing up in costume as a book or movie character." Phaedra brushed her fingers against a crystal pendant hanging nearby. "I'm hosting a Regency Christmas Tea this Sunday at the patisserie. I hope you and Biddy might be interested in coming?"

"We already bought tickets."

"Great! Let your sister know we'll have plenty of cupcakes on hand. And those gluten-free pinwheel sablés she likes."

Rebecca's mouth puckered in disapproval as she arranged tins of cough drops in front of the cash register. "I hope you offer a few savory items as well. Too many sweets aren't good for her, you know. Her sugar."

"I understand. Hannah's menu should please every palate." Phaedra wandered over to a basket stuffed with tea blends. "We're holding a raffle, with a prize to the winning ticket holder, so hang on to your stubs."

"No need to worry about Biddy tossing it out," Rebecca sniffed. "She saves everything. What's the prize?"

"A Christmas-themed tea basket. Any suggestions?"

The eldest Bondurant sister came around the counter. With her starchy black slacks and pinned-up gray hair, she reminded Phaedra of an officious blackbird.

"These are our premium custom tea blends," she said as she withdrew a flat basket from one of the shelves. "I mix them myself. I'd recommend something spiced, with a citrusy note. Oh, and a tea infuser. Perhaps a pair of Christmas mugs." She rounded the counter and plucked two cups, each decorated with bright red cardinals, from a table top, along with a rose gold infuser. "And those shortbread cookies on the counter are made right here in Virginia."

"Sold." Phaedra studied a display of handmade soaps in on the counter. "Where's Miss Biddy today?"

"She's not feeling well." Rebecca began ringing up the items. "I caught her sneaking sweets. Again. Sent her glucose levels soaring."

"I'm sorry to hear that. I hope Hannah's dark chocolate cupcake didn't have anything to do with it."

She paused. "Why on earth would you think that?"

"No reason. It's just . . ." She hesitated. "Biddy slipped a cupcake into her purse. At the grand opening. I didn't mention it, but I couldn't help but notice. No harm done," she hastened to add. "I know she loves her sweets."

"Then why mention it now?" Rebecca jabbed at the keys on the cash register. Her fingers stilled and her eyes narrowed in suspicion. "Wait. Dark chocolate . . . The cupcake that killed that poor Steele girl was dark chocolate." She bristled. "Are you suggesting my sister—"

"No, of course not. I only just remembered the incident. I'm sorry she's not feeling well but I'm relieved it wasn't due to something Hannah baked."

"It's nothing to do with your sister." Rebecca resumed ringing up Phaedra's purchases. "It's those shortbread cookies. That's why I'm persuading customers to buy them. Not that they aren't delicious," she added. "But Biddy sneaks a pack every chance she gets. Just between you and me and the cash register, my sister has a bigger problem than her addiction to sugar."

"Oh?"

"She's a trifle light-fingered." The elderly woman leaned closer as the door opened and two customers entered the shop. "Clinical kleptomania, to be precise. Diagnosed when she was nineteen. She's been that way ever since—"

"Excuse me," one of the customers said, "but do you carry lemongrass oil?"

"Yes. I'll show you where it is when I ring up this customer." The woman thanked her and wandered off to browse, and Rebecca turned back to Phaedra. "Is there anything else I can help you with today, Professor?"

"I'll need a basket to hold all these goodies."

"I have a few in the back, now you mention it. I'll put them aside and you can pick them up in a day or two. No charge," she added, her lips creaking into a smile. "That'll be fifty-seven dollars and sixty-three cents."

After paying for her purchases and stashing everything in the car, Phaedra paused. Most of the shops had opened for business. People filled the sidewalks, shopping, stopping to chat with neighbors, some running or walking dogs. A snap of winter chill lingered in the air but the sun was bright in a flawless blue sky.

Where to next? Her gaze settled on the blue-and-white-striped awnings of Woofgang's Gourmet Doggy Bakery. Like Bascom's Jewelers, it stood at the far end of Main Street, alongside Harper's pub. None of which had close proximity to Hannah's patisserie. So probably a waste of time to question anyone at either of those places.

Which left Elaine's costume shop, the Farrar Gallery, and the Coffee Stop.

And Brennan's bakery.

Phaedra closed the car door and hesitated. Did she dare enter Kate Brennan's shop again? Things hadn't gone too well the last time. As she hesitated, a man exited with a bakery box of doughnuts, giving her an idea.

She'd buy a dozen doughnuts at Brennan's, a couple of coffees at the Coffee Stop, and after making discreet inquiries at both, head for the Farrar Gallery. Hopefully a doughnut and a cup of fragrant Jamaica Blue Mountain would help jog Michael's memory. Perhaps he'd noticed something out of the ordinary behind Tout de Sweet that day. Something that didn't seem important at the time.

Something that might help her identify the killer.

And thanks to her father, she had a plausible cover story—she'd ask Michael if he'd begun work on restoring the James Brighton painting.

Her phone pinged with a text message from Mark. Where are you?

Took AM off. Back at 11.

The message was delivered, and a few ellipses appeared, but he didn't respond. His text reminded her that she hadn't heard from Detective Morelli yet. Had he interviewed Kyle Middleton and Rachel Brandon yesterday? Had Kyle admitted that he'd had an affair with Anna Steele?

Patience is a virtue, Phaedra told herself. *Or so they say.* She put her phone away and headed to Brennan's bakery.

Luckily, there was no sign of Kate at the counter, only her pretty, red-haired daughter.

"Good morning, Moira," Phaedra said.

"Hi, Professor. What can I get you today?" If she thought it odd that Phaedra was patronizing the bakery instead of Tout de Sweet, she gave no sign.

"Two coffees and a dozen doughnuts, please. Half glazed, half . . . whatever."

Moira grinned. "You're easy. Most people take forever deciding what they want. Choosing between chocolate frosted or maple nut shouldn't be that hard." She picked up tongs, unfolded a box, and began placing doughnuts inside.

"It smells amazing in here." Phaedra breathed in the scents of cinnamon and vanilla. "Nice and warm, too."

"In the afternoon it gets a little *too* warm in here."

"Sometimes Hannah props the patisserie's back door open. Even when it's cold outside."

"Absolutely," Moira agreed. "We do, too. Especially in the summer." She rang up the sale. "Ten dollars, please."

Phaedra handed over her card. "Where's your mom?"

"Out back. Smoking." She ran the card and returned it. "She thinks I don't know. But I do."

"I imagine it's a hard habit to break." Phaedra tucked the card away and took the box of doughnuts. "Does she often sneak a cigarette?"

"Only when we're not too busy."

Phaedra opened the box and breathed in the scent of sugary sweetness. "I can't wait to try the maple nut."

"It's our most popular cake doughnut. They always sell out." Moira frowned. "Except for last Saturday."

"Oh?" Phaedra closed the lid. "Why was that?"

"We had maybe three customers all morning. Everyone was at . . ." She lowered her voice. "Your sister's bakery. Mom wasn't too happy."

Interesting. Kate Brennan was out back the morning the fire alarm went off, smoking a cigarette and seething over her lack of customers. Meaning she had not only opportunity—easy access to the back entrance to Tout de Sweet—but a motive, as well . . . smoldering resentment of Hannah's success. A success that affected her bakery's bottom line, and her family's livelihood.

Had Kate Brennan been angry enough to slip in behind the patisserie and set off the alarm?

More important, had she poisoned that cupcake?

As Phaedra left Brennan's, she glanced at her wristwatch. Nearly ten o'clock. Almost time to return to Somerset. Walking past the Poison Pen, she saw it was doing brisk business. She headed for the Farrar Gallery.

Balancing her tray of coffees atop the bakery box, she opened the gallery's door and stepped inside. The space was empty and quiet. Quite a change from Friday night.

A young woman in a gray pencil skirt, a black cowl-neck sweater, and sleek black boots rose from a desk in the back and strode forward. Even her bobbed hair was black. "Hello. May I help you?"

"Is Mr. Farrar available?"

"Let me check. Please, have a seat." She indicated one of two chairs with a brief smile. "I'll be right back."

Phaedra sat down and set the coffee and doughnuts on a small round table between the chairs.

A few minutes later, Michael appeared. "Professor Brighton! I'm sorry, Phaedra." His smile was warm even as curiosity gleamed in his eye. "What a pleasant surprise."

She indicated the coffees and the bakery box. "I brought coffee. Cream and sugar in the bag. And doughnuts."

"Brennan's. How thoughtful." He took the lidded cup she handed him. "Thank you. I can't manage without coffee. Although I'll pass on the doughnuts. I'm not one for sweets. I'll put them in the back for the staff.

"Amelie," he called out, "take these to the break room for everyone to enjoy, please."

His assistant nodded, rose from her desk, and spirited the box away without comment.

As she disappeared into the back, he returned his attention to Phaedra. "I hope you enjoyed the showing."

"I did. Ms. Parrish's works are striking. Modern, but approachable. Lots of color and movement. Lucy and I were both quite taken with her painting of Main Street."

"Oh, yes. That's one of my favorites as well. We've had a lot of interest, but no sale. What can I do for you?"

"I wondered if you'd had a chance to take a look at my father's painting. The one you offered to restore."

"I have. In fact, it's in my office right now. I haven't begun work on it yet. The showing occupied a lot of my time."

"Believe me, I understand. I'm hosting a Regency Christmas Tea at my sister's patisserie on Sunday. There's so much to do." She smiled at him. "You should join us."

"Unfortunately, I won't be here on Sunday." He sipped his coffee. "Perhaps I can contribute to the cause in absentia." He reached for his billfold and withdrew a crisp, fifty-dollar bill. "A clothing drive, isn't it?"

"The Coats 'n Caps drive," she affirmed. "Thank you for your generosity. This will help ensure that everyone in Laurel Springs have coats and hats to keep them warm." She tucked the bill into her reticule and stood. "I should go. My duties—and my students—wait for no one."

"Indeed. The never-ending demands of academia." He

accompanied her to the door. "Your pupils are fortunate to have such an accomplished and dedicated professor. And one so attuned to the needs of the community."

And Marisol is fortunate to have such a handsome and generous admirer. Phaedra smiled demurely. She couldn't wait to hear the details of her dinner with Michael.

"You're very kind. Your donation will go a long way toward helping realize our goal." Although she longed to ask if he'd noticed anything out of the ordinary on Saturday, and to inquire about his date with Marisol, she refrained.

Michael Farrar was astute. She sensed that any casual-but-pointed question she might ask would rouse his suspicion. Very little escaped his notice. The clothing drive, for instance. He'd known all about it.

Which only proved that Marisol told him about it. Or he saw one of the flyers they'd posted all over town.

"Is there anything else I can help you with?" Although the question was polite enough, she sensed the merest trace of impatience behind his words.

"Not a thing. I've taken up enough of your time. And I should go." She reached the door. "Have a good day."

"You as well, Professor. Tell your father I'll begin work on the restoration tomorrow. I look forward to it."

"I will. Thank you." Before she could thank him for the donation, or assure him that there was no hurry, he closed the door softly but firmly behind her.

Seventeen

As she dug into a salad at her desk, Phaedra reviewed her notes, reading glasses perched on the end of her nose. Just a couple of changes . . .

"The prodigal professor returns."

"Mark." She glanced up. "Yes, I'm back."

He rested one shoulder against the door and crossed his arms. "Not like you to skive off."

"I wasn't skiving off."

He raised his brow. "So you *do* know what that means."

"Yes, I do. And I wasn't shirking my responsibilities. I was . . ." She pressed her lips together. Honestly, she didn't owe him an explanation. Had he explained his mysterious companion last Friday night? Or told her why he'd ditched the faculty holiday party to take his cute *Clueless* look-alike to dinner? No, he had not.

"It doesn't matter." She removed her glasses, folded them carefully, and set them aside. "I have a lecture in a few minutes. Is there anything in particular you need?"

"Is there . . ." He straightened. "Are you annoyed with me?"

She thrust her notes into a folder. "Why would I be annoyed with you?"

"An excellent question." His amused disbelief gave way to perplexity as she remained silent. "Phaedra," he added, lowering his voice, "seriously. What's wrong?"

"Nothing's wrong. I'm just busy." She stood and tucked the folder into her briefcase. "Now, if you'll excuse me . . ."

"Okay. Sorry. We'll talk later?"

"Of course." With a smile as insincere as it was vague, she grabbed her briefcase, brushed past him—uncomfortably aware of his subtle, soap-and-balsam scent—and headed for Lecture Room 3.

"Oh, Phaedra—I think I'm in love."

Phaedra had returned to her office that afternoon to finish grading midterms. She looked up as Marisol floated in and dropped her shoulder bag onto her desk.

"After one date? You're kidding, right?"

"I'm totally serious." She opened her bag and took out her phone. "Dinner was amazing, and incredibly romantic, and we talked. About everything. We have a lot in common."

"Such as?"

"Well, like art, for one thing. He knows so much about the subject—history, restoration. What sells and what doesn't. And we both love Ingres."

"Ingres? He was a neoclassicist. Doesn't Michael sell modern art?"

"Primarily, yes. But he doesn't limit the gallery to one specific style or period. He's eclectic."

Holy chamomile, Phaedra mused. *She's got it bad.*

"He's so funny," Marisol went on, "and attentive. Most of the guys I go out with spend the entire time checking out other women. And talking about themselves."

"I can see where Michael would offer a welcome change," Phaedra admitted.

"*So* welcome. He's charming, intelligent, sophisticated . . . everything I'm looking for in a man." She hesitated. "Maybe even in a husband. Someday."

"Well. That's great. I'm happy for you, of course."

"There's a 'but' coming, isn't there?" Marisol sank into her chair. "Go ahead. Let me have it. I may not agree with you, but I'll listen. I value your opinion. Usually."

"No lecture, I promise. I'm glad you enjoyed yourself. And I agree, Michael is all of those things you mentioned. But . . ." Phaedra held her finger up as Marisol rolled her eyes. "Hear me out. You've only just met the guy, Mari. And you've been on one date. One. Don't you think your lovestruck reaction is a little premature?"

"I don't think so. No. Love at first sight is a thing, Phaedra." She leaned forward. "I've never felt this way about anyone else I've dated. Not even close." She blushed and added earnestly, "I think he might even be The One."

Phaedra swallowed a retort. Although she very much doubted Michael was in the market for a wife—she suspected he enjoyed his bachelor status too much—who was she to say? Like Marisol, she didn't know him well.

"Just take it slow," she advised. "Rushing into romance didn't turn out so well for Marianne Dashwood."

"That's hardly a fair comparison." Marisol bristled. "Michael Farrar is nothing like John Willoughby. And I'm no starry-eyed Regency miss with cotton wool for brains."

"No, of course you're not. You're smart. Far too smart to rush into anything. Get to know each other better, take your time. If it's meant to be, and if he returns your feelings, then there's no rush, is there?"

"I hate it when you're right." Marisol's smile was grudging. "He wants to see me again."

"That's great. Sounds like he's as taken with you as you are with him. I'll invite you both to dinner at the carriage house. After the holidays."

"I'd love that. Then you can get to know him a little better, too." She glanced at Phaedra. "How'd your recon go this morning? Did you learn anything?"

"Not much. Rebecca admitted Biddy is light-fingered. No surprise there; everyone in town knows." She jotted a reminder to research kleptomania. "I also found out Kate Brennan sometimes sneaks a cigarette behind the bakery. Like last Saturday morning. Her daughter told me."

"Interesting. Same time as the grand opening. Maybe she saw something."

"Or maybe," Phaedra mused, "she did something. As in, snuck over to Hannah's and pulled the fire alarm."

Marisol's eyes widened. "Do you really think she'd do that?"

"Moira admitted her mother resents Hannah's success. They've lost customers. It's affected their bottom line. Which gives Kate opportunity. And motive."

"But would she *poison* someone? Just to cause trouble for Hannah? Wouldn't she just—I don't know. Put a cockroach in the buttercream, or something?"

"You make a good point." Phaedra sighed. "I'm so focused on proving Hannah didn't do it that I'm ready to throw anyone under the bus. Especially Kate Brennan."

"Who can blame you? After all, her own daughter told you Kate is jealous of Hannah's success. Maybe she pulled the alarm to throw a wrench into the grand opening. Maybe it was her idea of a malicious joke. But I don't think she's jealous enough to poison someone. That's next level."

After grading the last paper, Phaedra dropped her pen onto the desk blotter and leaned back in her chair. Her fingers were cramped and her eyes ached. Marisol had long since gone home, along with most of the departmental staff.

She glanced down at the note she'd scribbled earlier. Rebecca had said Biddy was diagnosed as a kleptomaniac. Phaedra knew the term referred to an impulse-control disorder, one that led to a compulsion to steal. Perhaps it was time to delve a little deeper into the particulars of the condition.

Opening her laptop browser, she typed "kleptomania."

"Kleptomania indicates an individual's attempt to seek compensation for a real or imagined loss. The stolen items often hold symbolic meaning and may offer a key to understanding the origin of the patient's behavior."

Poor Biddy. Had she lost something, or someone? What sort of things did the elderly woman typically take? Small items, from what she'd heard; nothing anyone would miss. Nothing of value. But as to specifics, she had no idea.

Phaedra closed the laptop. The halls were quiet, and darkness pressed against the windows.

Time to gather her things and head home.

As she reached for her coat, wondering what to do for dinner, her cell phone rang. "Han, hi. What's up?"

"Tell me you're not still sitting at your desk."

"Just leaving. I had midterms to finish grading." She shrugged her arm into a sleeve. "Are you staying till six?"

Hannah sighed. "Yes. Not sure why, though. No one's here. Customers, I mean. We've had three sales all day."

"Oh, sweetie . . . I'm sorry. It'll get better. Give it time." Not unlike her advice to Marisol about her latest romantic infatuation. "Is Charles there?"

"He was, but he left a few minutes ago."

"Any ideas for dinner? I'll pick something up."

"Not really hungry."

"You have to eat," Phaedra reminded her. "Did you have lunch?"

"Jared brought us subs around eleven. After he finished the morning delivery run."

"Hannah, that was *hours* ago. So, what are you in the mood for? Chinese? Pizza? Tacos?"

She hesitated. "Maybe an enchilada? And some chips and cheese. And a side of black beans."

Phaedra's lips curved upward as she shrugged her other arm into the coat and reached for her reticule. "I thought you weren't hungry."

"I can look at French pastries all day and not be the least

bit tempted. But if you say 'taco,' I'm starving." She added, "I'll close up. No point sitting around any longer. See you soon. Oh—and don't forget the hot sauce."

The parking lot was empty as Phaedra walked out to her car. She'd arrived late, and the spaces reserved for faculty had been taken. She pointed her key fob at the Mini, and with a flash of the headlights, unlocked the car. After stowing her briefcase on the back seat, she slid behind the wheel and closed the door.

She paused. There was something on the passenger seat. Frowning, she leaned closer. It was a small white bakery box with a cellophane window, like those used at Tout de Sweet. She switched on the interior light to get a better look.

Inside was a single cupcake. Topped with a thick swirl of buttercream frosting, and colorful sprinkles.

"Hannah." She smiled. Her sister must've asked Jared to drop the cupcake off during his morning deliveries.

Why hadn't she mentioned it earlier, though? And she distinctly remembered Hannah saying they'd taken cupcakes off the menu. "They just aren't selling," she'd admitted. "Not after what happened."

Which meant she must've made this confection especially for her.

A yellow sticky note was stuck to the top of the box, one word scrawled across it in cursive.

Phaedra

She lifted the lid. Rainbow sprinkles decorated the frosting, and she breathed in the enticing scents of vanilla bean and sugary, buttery deliciousness.

She noticed another odor as well. This one was more subtle. Harder to define. Maybe . . . a hint of almond?

Phaedra remembered Detective Morelli's comment after Anna's poisoning, when they found the box of tainted Maldon salt in Hannah's kitchen. Officer Scott said the salt had an odd smell. Like bitter almond.

She let the lid fall and shrank away.

"You have a discerning nose, Officer Scott," Morelli had replied. *"Guess it's true what they say. Not everyone can pick up the scent of cyanide."*

Could this unassuming cupcake, with its buttercream swirl and colorful sprinkles, be poisoned with cyanide?

Eighteen

Phaedra stared at the box, scarcely daring to breathe. Who had left this in her car? Who would do such a thing?

If it was meant to be a joke, it wasn't funny.

Only one way to find out, she reasoned. She'd approach this logically. Rationally.

She'd call Hannah.

Phaedra fumbled in her reticule for her phone and withdrew it with unsteady fingers.

"Pick up, pick up," she muttered as the phone rang several times on Hannah's end. She was just about to end the call when her sister answered.

"Phae? Tell me my enchilada is on the way."

"Did you leave a cupcake in my car?" Phaedra asked without preamble. "Vanilla buttercream, rainbow sprinkles?"

"A cupcake? No. Why would I do that? We're not even making cupcakes right now. Not until this whole poisoning thing goes away. If it ever does."

"Somebody did. It's sitting on the front seat. It's in one of your bakery boxes, the kind that holds a single cupcake."

"Mark, maybe?"

Phaedra thought of her earlier exchange with Professor

Selden, how he'd teased her about "skiving off." Her less-than-receptive reaction.

"Could be," she admitted. "Things are a little strained between us at the moment."

"Why? What happened?"

She released a sigh. "Marisol told me she saw him leaving Orsini's on Friday night with someone."

"A female someone?"

"Not only female, but young, blond, and cute."

"Did you ask him about it?" When Phaedra hesitated, Hannah sighed. "You didn't, did you?"

"I'm calling him now. About the cupcake."

"Do that. And ask him about young blond cutie while you're at it. I'm sure there's an explanation. I'll pick up dinner in the meantime. I'm leaving Tout de Sweet now."

"Would you?" Phaedra glanced at the box. "That'd be great. Because if Mark didn't leave this cupcake here, my next call is Detective Morelli."

"Keep me posted."

She promised to call back and found Mark's name in her contacts. He didn't answer. She left a quick message—Did you leave a cupcake on my front seat? If so, thanks—and drummed her fingers against the steering wheel. What to do?

If Mark *had* left it, wouldn't he have scrawled a quick note, or at least signed his name? Unless he was in a hurry when he left. Or unless he truly wanted to surprise her. If that was his goal—mission accomplished.

Her fingers stilled. No point in calling Morelli. No point wasting police time on what was probably nothing.

But what if Mark hadn't left it?

As she debated whether to put a call through to the police, her cell phone rang.

"Mark." Relief coursed through her. "Thanks for returning my call."

"Sorry I didn't pick up before," he said. "I just got home. And to answer your question, I didn't leave a cupcake on your front seat. Although I gather someone did?"

"Vanilla, with almond buttercream. And sprinkles."

"Is that why you were annoyed with me before?" he asked suddenly. "Is it your birthday?"

"No." Her laugh was shaky. "It's not my birthday."

"You sound flustered. What's wrong? Are you okay?"

The sight of the cupcake box, and the knowledge that he hadn't left it for her, brought a tremor to her voice. "I'm a little spooked," she admitted. "I don't know who left it here. It's just a cupcake, but . . ."

"No, I get it," he said grimly. "In view of what happened to Anna Steele, it's disturbing, to say the least. Someone's idea of a joke, maybe? A not-so-funny joke."

"It's possible." While his theory was plausible, considering Anna's poisoning had been trumpeted all over the local news and social media, she didn't want to believe it. "Who'd do something like that?"

"The locals know you drive a bright blue Mini Cooper."

"And that I teach at Somerset." Which meant anyone could've left that cupcake on her front seat. A student, a faculty member. A stranger.

Anyone.

"There's no note?" he asked. "No indication who might've left it there?"

"Just a sticky note with my name written on it."

"Where are you right now?" he asked, concern undercutting the question. "Are you still at Somerset?"

"Yes. In the parking lot. I stayed late to finish grading midterms, and when I returned to my car . . ." She paused. "It's not from Hannah, or you, and now I'm seriously unnerved."

"I'm on my way." His voice brooked no argument. "Lock the doors and call the police. Call your detective friend."

"Morelli."

"Right. And stay put. I'll be there soon."

She thanked him and called to tell Hannah that Mark and Detective Morelli were on the way and she'd be home as soon as she could.

Now all she could do was wait. And try to keep her spiraling fears at bay.

Mark arrived twenty minutes later, just as Detective Morelli parked his battered Honda next to the Mini.

"Professor Brighton," Morelli said, his expression concerned as she got out of the car. "Are you okay?"

"Fine. Just a little unsettled." She pointed to the passenger seat. "It's right there. I touched it, to lift the lid. That's when I noticed a distinct almond smell."

"Okay." He reached in his pocket and drew on a pair of blue latex gloves. "Let's take a look."

As he rounded the car to the passenger door, Mark joined them. "I got here as quickly as I could."

"I'm glad you're here. Thanks."

He followed her gaze to Morelli, who'd opened the car door and knelt down to study the boxed cupcake.

"Did you lock your car when you arrived today?" the detective asked her.

"Yes." She hesitated, frowned. "I think? I came in late this morning. I was in bit of a hurry."

"So you're not sure if you locked the doors or not."

"No, I guess not."

Morelli motioned to Officer Scott, who'd just arrived. "Dust the doors for prints. And take this cupcake back to the lab and have it tested."

With a nod, the officer returned to his car to grab a pair of gloves and retrieve an evidence bag.

"Did you notice anyone when you left the building?" Morelli asked her. "Someone sitting in a car or parked nearby? Loitering by the doors?"

Phaedra shook her head. "The lot was empty. It's the last Wednesday before winter break. Everyone was gone."

"Everyone except you."

"I had midterms to finish grading." She added, "I've never had reason to doubt my safety here."

Morelli studied the pavement outside the passenger door. "I don't want to alarm you, but whoever did this intended, at the very least, to frighten you."

"Could this be connected to Anna's poisoning?"

"We won't know until the tox report comes back. In the meantime, I recommend you buddy up if you stay late. Ask a colleague you trust to walk with you to the car. Speak to the administration about increasing campus security."

"I will."

"You need to determine who did this." Mark thrust his hands deep in his overcoat pockets and met Morelli's eyes, and there was no mistaking the challenge behind his words.

"We'll do our best," Detective Morelli replied evenly. "I'll question local bakery owners. See if anyone recalls someone ordering a cupcake, to go. We might get lucky."

"But you don't think so." Phaedra's hopes deflated.

"Whoever did this probably paid with cash. Or ordered it through one of those online delivery services."

"So there's no way of knowing who's behind it."

"Only if someone remembers the customer who bought the cupcake, and only if their description matches someone you know. Otherwise, it's a long shot. I'll keep you posted."

"Hannah said it didn't come from Tout de Sweet. They've taken cupcakes off the menu."

"Probably a wise decision in view of what happened to Ms. Steele."

Phaedra turned to Mark. "Will you excuse me for a minute? I need to ask Morelli a question. About the case."

"Of course. I'll wait here."

As Morelli and Officer Scott returned to their cars, Phaedra caught up to the detective. "Is there any news? Any developments? Did you question Rachel and Kyle?"

"I did. They both have alibis."

Again, her hope that they might be closer to learning who poisoned Anna was dashed. "Do you believe them?"

"They claim they were both in your sister's office, arguing. They provided each other with an alibi. And they have witnesses."

"Who?"

"Vanessa. And Hannah."

Disappointment swept through her. "Meaning Kyle and Rachel are off the hook. And we're back to square one."

"Welcome to my world."

Phaedra pushed aside a strand of hair with an impatient gesture. Frustration furrowed her brow. "I want to catch whoever did this. Hannah's reputation is on the line, and she can't move ahead until this case is solved."

"And it will be, in time. Even the smartest criminal eventually trips up."

She sighed. "Patience isn't one of my virtues."

"I noticed." He canted his lips in a half smile. "I'll let you know if anything useful turns up. Good night, Professor."

"Good night. And thank you."

As he left, she returned to her car, where Mark waited. He dropped his phone in his pocket and withdrew his keys. "I'll follow you home."

He didn't ask what they'd talked about, didn't try to insert himself into the investigation. He was there. And that was enough.

"Thanks," Phaedra said, and meant it. "Ordinarily I'd say there's no need. But after everything that's happened, I appreciate it." She added, "Have you eaten? Hannah's picking up dinner. She always orders way too much food."

"I'll stop and get something on the way home."

"Okay. No problem." Maybe he had other plans. With the *Clueless* cutie.

He hesitated. "Phaedra, I hope you're not still annoyed with me. If so, please tell me what I've done. We can discuss it."

"There's nothing to discuss. I'm good." She slid behind the wheel and started the engine. He was a free agent, after all. They weren't a couple. They weren't even dating. She didn't know what they were to each other.

"Did you ask him about it?"

Hannah's question echoed in her thoughts.

"Right. See you tomorrow." Disappointment skimmed his face as he turned to go. "I'll follow you out."

"Mark. Wait." She searched the shadowed planes of his face, indistinct in the pale glow from a nearby sodium light. "Before you go, I have a question. You can tell me if it's none of my business. But I have to ask."

"Okay." He eyed her warily. "I'm listening."

She told him about Marisol, and her flat tire on Friday night, and how she saw him leaving Orsini's with a cute young blond woman on his arm.

"I assume she's the reason you skipped the faculty party," Phaedra went on. "And honestly, I'm fine with that, but . . . it bothers me that you didn't tell me when I asked why you weren't at the party. Is she . . . this girl . . . is she special, to you?"

For a long, excruciating moment, he didn't answer.

"Yes," he said finally. "She is."

Before she could process the twist of pain his words brought, or summon words to respond, he cleared his throat.

"But not for the reasons you might imagine. Ivy was a close friend of my sister."

"Oh. I didn't know you had a sibling. I assumed you were an only child." Why had he never mentioned a sister?

"I was six when Georgiana was born." His voice was low and measured. "She was as much of a surprise to my parents as she was to me. I was the textbook overprotective older brother. She drove me crazy, but . . . I loved her."

Was. Loved. He'd referred to his sister—and his relationship to her—in the past tense.

"She died nine years ago. In a car crash. On her eighteenth birthday."

Phaedra's throat tightened. "I'm so sorry. That must have been . . . I can't even imagine."

"She spotted a car in a sales lot two weeks before her birthday and fell in love with it. A bright red Fiat. I bought it for her." He studied his key fob. "When the lorry—sorry, tractor trailer—drifted into her lane coming home that night, she didn't stand a chance."

"Oh, Mark." She reached out to lay her hand atop his. "How awful."

"If I hadn't bought her that damned car . . ." Pain undercut every word. "I blamed myself. Still do. Which is why I don't talk about it." He drew his hand away, plainly done with the subject. "Now, let's get you home."

Nineteen

Friday afternoon arrived, and with it, the beginning of winter break. And the end of lecture planning, grading papers, and student consultations. The long-awaited holiday season had officially begun.

Three glorious weeks of freedom, Phaedra thought. And only two days before the Regency Christmas tea fundraiser on Sunday.

She changed the sheets on the sofa bed and thrust them into the washing machine. Hannah hadn't made up the bed, but she'd finalized a menu of savory and sweet courses and had all the necessary ingredients in readiness for a baking marathon on Saturday.

"It's not as if I won't have time," she'd added. "Our customers have dwindled to a handful. If things don't improve soon, I'll have to start letting staff go."

Although Phaedra assured her that things would get better, she no longer believed her own assurances. A cloud of uncertainty hung over the patisserie's future, leaving her sister's professional reputation in the balance, and it wouldn't lift until the culprit was put behind bars.

And who knew when—or if—that might happen?

Rachel and Kyle had alibis. As did everyone else who'd been at the grand opening. No word from Morelli yet on who might've left the cupcake in her car or whether it contained poison or not.

And she knew what he'd say if asked. Toxicology reports took time. There were other cases. Be patient and trust the process.

Which left them with no new suspects. No clues. No certainty as to who the poisoner had even targeted. Was it Anna? Herself? Or Rachel?

And what about Arthur Rouse? Had her father's former client been located? Would he have an alibi? She still believed he was the most likely perpetrator. His defense attorney, Malcolm Brighton, had let him down, leading to a ten-year prison sentence and leaving Rouse with a grudge and a motive for retribution.

Phaedra thrust her thoughts aside. She'd have to put her theories on hold until the next Tea Society meeting.

Besides, speculation was getting her nowhere. She had errands to run. A holiday basket to put together. Tea pairings to choose. She grabbed her coat, wondering as she did if Lucy and Marisol might agree to meet up at Josie's for a glass of wine later that evening.

Wickham looked up from his spot atop the sofa back as she retrieved her keys and purse and headed for the door.

"See you later, Wicks."

He slanted his ears forward, unimpressed. *Just be back in time for dinner. Mine, not yours.*

She thrust her hands deep in her coat pockets and decided to walk. Her first stop was Tout de Sweet. As she pushed the front door open, Phaedra's buoyant good mood dipped a little. Hannah wasn't exaggerating.

The patisserie was—no pun intended—dead. Not a single customer waited at the cash register or lingered in front of the glass display case. Jared, usually busy pulling espressos and filling the air with the hiss of steam and the delectable scent of coffee, sat atop a stool reading a magazine.

"The decorations look great," Phaedra called out as she saw Hannah behind the counter.

"Thanks." Her sister's glance swept over the swathes of tiny white lights and garlands of greenery pinned up with gold bows. "Now all we need are customers."

"Oh, Han," she sighed as she set her purse down on the counter, "you can't just give up."

"Please don't tell me things will get better," Hannah retorted. "Things won't get better until the police find whoever poisoned that cupcake."

"Is there anything I can do to help out for the tea? Grate cheese for the savory scones? Crumb coat the cake?"

"You can finalize the tea pairings. And you can make a playlist."

The bell jangled over the door behind them.

"Have you found someone to provide musical entertainment?"

"No. I haven't had any luck," Phaedra admitted.

"Did I hear someone say 'musical entertainment'?"

Phaedra glanced up as Detective Morelli, wearing jeans and a brown leather bomber jacket, joined them.

"Don't tell me you play an instrument."

"I don't. But Lucas does."

"Lucas?"

"Officer Scott. He plays guitar and sings in a folk duo. They play at the Vineyard Inn now and then."

"Really." Skepticism was plain in her voice. "Officer Scott is a musician?"

"Good one, too. When's the gig?"

"Sunday afternoon. Right here," Hannah said warily. "Three hours, one break between sittings. He'll need to audition first. Can he stop by tomorrow?"

"I'll have him give you a call tonight. You can set something up." Morelli glanced at the menu board. "How's the coffee in this place?"

"Excellent," she replied, and turned away to start a fresh pot. "And for you? It's free."

"Thanks." He turned to Phaedra. "No classes today, Professor?"

"No. Like you, I'm off duty."

"How do you know I'm off duty?" he asked, brow lifted.

"Desert boots." She pointed to his feet. "And no shoulder holster."

"I'll make a detective of you yet." He eyed the paper and pen she was scribbling on. "What's that?"

"A list of tea pairings for each course. I'm thinking ginger chai, peppermint rooibos, and plum tea." Phaedra regarded her sister thoughtfully. "Should we call it 'Sugar Plum Tea'? For the name card?"

"I like that. A nod to *The Nutcracker*."

"We'll offer a savory course first," Phaedra explained in answer to Morelli's quizzical glance. "With scones, either cranberry orange or maple walnut, and a selection of tea sandwiches. Followed by a dessert course. Each course is accompanied by an assortment of teas."

"Sounds good."

"You should come. The tickets are sold out, but I'll put a plate aside for you if you like."

"Bribery, Professor?"

"If that's what it takes."

"Tea isn't really my thing." He shrugged. "But if it's information you want, I might have something of interest."

Phaedra waited as Hannah set two coffees in front of them, along with two spoons and a pitcher of cream.

Morelli lifted his cup and took a cautious sip. "We located Arthur Rouse."

She poured cream into her coffee, watching as it swirled, turning the liquid from dark brown to taupe to almond, and ignored the quickening of her pulse. "Where?"

"He's living in a motel just outside of Crozet. I'm paying him a visit tomorrow."

"He seems like the most likely suspect. He was Dad's client. And he was sentenced to ten years in prison."

"He definitely has a motive," Morelli agreed. "He was

paroled after serving eight. I'm curious to hear what he has to say."

"Maybe you'll learn something useful. Something incriminating."

"It's a lead, and we'll follow it. Whether it pans out or not? Hard to say."

"What about fingerprints? Were any found in my car?"

"Mostly yours, which we've excluded. And one partial we haven't identified."

"And the toxicology report on the cupcake?"

"Not back yet. I'd tell you if it was," he reminded her. "You have to be patient—"

"And trust the process." Phaedra sighed. "I know."

"We still don't know who the killer targeted. It wasn't Anna; there's no motive. Rachel and Kyle appeared to have motives, but they both have alibis. Which means you and Hannah and your dad remain the most likely targets."

"I know this much," she said. "Someone poisoned Anna. They've compromised Hannah's business, and they left me a calling card in the form of another potentially poisoned cupcake. If I'd eaten it, I'd probably be dead right now."

A chill chased through her.

"But you didn't." He laid his hand, warm and strong, atop hers. "You didn't, because you're too smart for that."

"Thanks." She cast him a quick smile. "Good thing I wasn't hungry at the time. My willpower isn't the best.

"And I think you're right about the killer," she went on as he lifted his cup. "One of us—me, or dad, or Hannah—is the real target. Anna Steele was just . . ." Her fingers tensed around her own cup. "Collateral damage."

"Which is why," Morelli said as he took a last sip of coffee, "it's imperative you stay out of this case." His expression was grim. "No investigating. No Nancy Drew derring-do from you and your Tea Society ladies."

"'Nancy Drew derring-do'?" she echoed. "Seriously?"

He leaned forward and fixed his dark eyes on hers. "This person is clever, Professor. Focused. I'm no profiler, but it's possible we're dealing with someone on the sociopathic spectrum. Someone familiar with poisons and not afraid to use them. In the perpetrator's mind, the end justifies the means. And until we know what the endgame is," he finished, "I need you to stay safe and stay out of it. Will you do that? For me?"

She managed a nod. "Okay. Of course."

"Good. I'll let you know if anything turns up."

With a nod and a thumbs-up to Hannah for the coffee, Detective Morelli left.

"He likes you." Hannah deposited his cup and spoon in a plastic tub and eyed Phaedra.

"Oh, please. We're friends. Barely even that."

"Bull hockey. When he talks to you, he's focused, like there's no one else in the room."

"He's a cop, Hannah."

"So?"

"So, he's focused by nature. He listens. It's part of his job. It's what he does."

"With perps, maybe. You're not a perp. You're a college professor. And what about Mark?"

"This conversation is giving me whiplash," Phaedra said, exasperated. "What about Mark?"

"I thought you two were getting closer."

She'd thought so, too. Just when it seemed they'd moved forward in their relationship—sharing a head-spinning kiss, for instance—Mark's reluctance to tell her about his sister gave her pause.

Why had he not mentioned Georgiana before? What else was he keeping from her? Why couldn't they trust each other?

"We're a work in progress." Phaedra tucked her list of tea pairings into her coat pocket. "I'm off. Rebecca promised to give me a basket to use for our Christmas raffle prize and I need to go over there and pick it up. Let me know how the audition goes tomorrow."

"I will." Hannah toyed with the bracelet at her wrist. "I hope this lead of yours pans out."

"Arthur Rouse? He's the only suspect with a motive. Fingers crossed he's the killer and Detective Morelli can arrest him and close the case."

"Who knows?" Her sister glanced out at the empty tables. "Maybe this nightmare is almost over."

A brisk wind kicked up the few remaining dead leaves along the curb, sending them whirling, and quickened Phaedra's steps as she approached the apothecary shop.

"More snow coming," Rebecca announced from her perch atop a stool behind the counter as the door opened.

Phaedra regarded her in dismay. Snow might spell disaster for their Regency Christmas tea. "Is that what the weather forecast says?"

"That's what my bursitis says. Are you here for your basket?"

She nodded. "Did you find one?"

"You can take your pick. I'll be glad to get rid of 'em, to tell you the truth. Wait here. I'll be right back. Biddy," she called up the stairs that led to their apartment over the shop, "come down and watch the counter."

"Coming," she warbled.

A moment later, Biddy descended the stairs and slipped behind the counter. "Well, hello, Phaedra. I haven't seen you or your sister since the grand opening. How are you?"

"We're fine, thanks." She eyed the shawl around the elderly woman's shoulders. "Are you cold?"

She drew the shawl closer. "A trifle chilly. Every time the front door opens, a draft comes up the stairs."

"It's the same at the bookstore. Mom always wears a sweater."

"Very sensible," Biddy approved. "And how is your father? I enjoy talking to him. I've been meaning to stop in and look for a new book. But the store keeps me busy."

"He's doing well. Busy, like you. He's decided to have one of his old paintings restored."

"Oh? Which one?"

"A scene of Siena, the Piazza del Campo. His grandfather painted it. It hung in Dad's law office for years. I don't know if you ever saw it."

"I most certainly did. I remember it well."

Phaedra eyed her in surprise. "You do?"

Biddy glanced over her shoulder to make sure Rebecca hadn't returned, and leaned forward. "My sister doesn't like me to talk about it. Says it's better forgotten."

"I see." She added carefully, "Perhaps she's right."

"No. No, she isn't." She pressed her lips together. "When I was a young woman, I fell in love. Oh, he was such a wonderful, handsome man. Kind, too." Her expression softened. "He loved me to distraction. It was expected we'd marry. We were promised to each other, you see."

Knowing that Bridget Bondurant had never married, Phaedra's curiosity was piqued. "How romantic. What happened? Why didn't you marry him?"

Her face clouded. "He fell in love with someone else." She lifted her eyes to Phaedra's. "Your grandmother."

"My—"

"Yes. He married Rose," she went on, "and gave her that painting as a wedding gift." She tugged at her shawl with birdlike fingers. "I accused her of stealing it, just like she stole my fiancé. Because he'd promised it to me when we married, you see."

"I never knew." Phaedra could scarcely comprehend it. Why had no one ever told her this? "You . . . you must've been heartbroken."

"I was devastated. We made a promise to each other, we had an understanding. But he broke his promise. He didn't marry me. He married *her* instead." Her eyes glittered with remembered emotion. "And I've never forgiven him."

Biddy! You're not plaguing the professor with one of your maudlin tales of woe, are you?"

Rebecca, several baskets looped over her arm, marched up to the counter and set them down.

"It isn't a tale," Biddy said with a defiant quaver. "It happened, and it broke my heart."

"Oh, for pity's sake, Bridget. That was a lifetime ago. Give it up. And please don't bother our customer with your troubles."

"It's all right," Phaedra said, placing a comforting hand on Biddy's sleeve. "I don't mind. I'm sorry things didn't work out for you, Ms. Bondurant."

Biddy laid her own hand, gnarled and misshapen, atop Phaedra's. "Thank you, dear. Forgive me for burdening you. Now, if you'll excuse me," she added, suddenly looking every bit of her eighty-one years, "I'm feeling a little fatigued. I think I'll go back upstairs and rest."

"An excellent idea," Rebecca concurred. "I'll be up in a moment to make you a cup of tea."

As her sister trudged upstairs, she turned back to Phaedra.

"I'm sorry. My sister has no right to dredge up the past, and to you, of all people."

"I never knew my grandfather was engaged to Biddy."

"He wasn't."

"But she said—"

"They had an understanding for a short time. But they were never officially engaged. He married Rose, and that was that."

"Is that when Biddy began taking things?" Phaedra recalled her previous conversation with Rebecca. "After my grandfather married Rose?"

The bell jingled as a customer entered the shop.

"Yes," Rebecca said, her voice low. "The psychologist spouted a lot of mumbo jumbo about the loss manifesting itself in the form of a desire to take random objects. Things that symbolized her loss."

"And taking those things is a way of, what?" Phaedra asked. "Regaining a sense of control? Rewriting her past?"

"I've no idea," Rebecca said with a trace of impatience. "I'm not a psychologist. It's all a lot of nonsense."

"Have you any bayberry candles?" the customer, a middle-aged woman, inquired behind them.

"Yes. I'll be right with you." Rebecca straightened. "Choose a basket, Professor Brighton. Take as many as you like. Now, if you'll excuse me," she added firmly, "I have a customer to see to and a shop to run."

Okay. I can take a hint. Phaedra chose a large, oval-bottomed basket with a pretty woven handle, tucked it over her arm, and thanked Rebecca as she left the shop.

She made her way down the street to the Poison Pen bookstore, her thoughts consumed with what she'd just learned.

Her grandfather had nearly married Biddy Bondurant. Why had no one in her family ever mentioned it?

She bounded up the steps to the front doors, pleased to see a flyer for the Regency Christmas Tea prominently displayed, and went inside. Late-afternoon sun slanted across the floors and for once, the bookstore was quiet.

Fitz, curled up on a rug in front of the counter, lifted his head and wagged his curly tail.

Phaedra bent down to ruffle his ears and chucked him under his little pug chin. "How's my boy?"

"Phaedra?" Her father rounded one of the shelves, a stack of new Agatha Raisin cozy mysteries in hand.

"Hi, Dad. Need some help?"

He set the stack down at one end of the counter. "Just finishing up. What brings you here?"

"Can't I stop by to say hello?"

"Certainly. I'm always glad to see you." He slid onto a stool behind the cash register. "But you usually have an ulterior motive. Speaking of which—any news from Detective Morelli?"

"They've located Arthur Rouse and they're questioning him tomorrow."

They talked briefly about the case and her hopes that Rouse would prove to be guilty of Anna's death.

"The police eliminated Kyle as a suspect," she added.

"I didn't even know he was a suspect. You're referring to Rachel Brandon's husband?"

Phaedra nodded and told him about Kyle's affair and subsequent breakup with Anna Steele. "Anna was furious, so she told Rachel everything. Which gives Rachel and Kyle a motive. But they both have alibis."

She didn't mention the cupcake left on the front seat of her car; she and Hannah decided there was no point in upsetting either of their parents unnecessarily.

"Not to change the subject, but how's the restoration going?" She straightened and set her basket down on the counter.

"It's going well." He reached for his coffee. "Michael's begun work on the painting."

"I can't wait to see it when he's finished."

"According to him, the painting is noteworthy, or it will

be once it's restored, but it isn't well known. It's regarded in artistic circles as a minor work."

"Meaning it's of no great value."

He shook his head. "It doesn't matter; I have no intention of selling it. Your mother's asking someone at the historical society about the painting to see what she can find out."

"Good idea. Can't hurt to ask."

"Any value it has is strictly sentimental because it belonged to my father. It's a family heirloom. And that makes it priceless."

"About that." Phaedra drew in a breath and rested her forearms on the countertop. "Why did you never mention that grandfather nearly married Bridget Bondurant?"

He set his mug down so quickly that coffee sloshed over the rim. "Who told you that?"

"Miss Biddy, at the apothecary just now. We were talking, and I mentioned your painting, how it used to hang in your law office. I told her Michael was restoring it. She said she remembered it very well, which surprised me. I didn't think she'd ever seen it."

He grabbed a paper towel and mopped up the spill. "It's true that she and my father were sweethearts for a time, before he met your grandmother." A frown creased his brow. "But to my knowledge, they were never engaged. I recall my father once saying that things were one-sided between them. Biddy's feelings were far stronger than his. He was fond of her, mind you. Very fond. But he never loved her."

"No promises were made?"

"Not as far as I know. But then again," he added, "my father was a deeply private person. Perhaps at some point he *did* have an understanding with Ms. Bondurant. If so, he never mentioned it to me."

Phaedra returned to the carriage house a short time later. She shrugged off her coat and checked the mail, then headed into the kitchen.

The padding of four small paws sounded on the stairs, and a moment later, Wickham sauntered in to rub himself against her legs.

She knelt to stroke his silky fur and smiled as he purred his approval. "Want to go out while I get dinner?"

He shot to the door and disappeared into the yard the minute she opened it. She opened a can of Seafood Grill and spooned half into his bowl, then refilled his water dish.

As she set the dishes down, a number of questions troubled her. Rachel Brandon had disappeared of late. Had she left town? Returned to New York after being questioned by Detective Morelli? And what of her promise to run a piece about Hannah in her magazine? To date, no one had appeared to interview her sister.

And what had Michael said to Rachel at the gallery showing last week? Whatever it was upset her so much she'd dropped her champagne flute. Was she distraught because Kyle ditched her, as Farrar claimed? Or was something else going on? What was her connection to Michael?

Seeing her laptop on the dining room table, Phaedra sat down and opened it. Michael Farrar claimed her father's painting wasn't worth much. That it was a little-known piece, and therefore without a great deal of value.

Was it, though?

She typed James Brighton's name into the search engine. The browser returned a respectable number of hits, mostly links to biographical information or the artist's better-known works. There were gallery listings, and places to purchase prints; but there was no mention of the Siena painting.

His rendition of the Piazza del Campo, while hardly a masterpiece, had always struck her as a charming glimpse into the past. The women in their wide-brimmed hats and Edwardian tea dresses; the men, sporting walking sticks and mustaches. The way sunlight shadowed a building or warmed the side of an upturned face . . . she never tired of studying it and always noted something new.

With a sigh, she closed the laptop. Michael was right.

The painting her father had inherited was a minor work, so minor that it didn't appear anywhere online.

At least it would be restored to its former glory. If nothing else, it made for a charming conversation piece.

"Let's move a few of these tables back," Phaedra suggested. "Clear some space for our guitarist."

It was Sunday morning and there were a million things to do before the Regency Christmas Tea kicked off at Tout de Sweet at two o'clock. At least dealing with last-minute cancellations due to snow wasn't one of them.

With two sittings scheduled, the first at two o'clock and the second at four, this shindig had to go off without a hitch.

The scents of orange and cranberry scones and fresh-brewed coffee wafted on the air in a delicious perfume. As Marisol and Lucy rearranged tables, Phaedra set out plates, teapots, cups, and saucers. She frowned. Festive, but something was missing.

"Don't forget the centerpieces," Hannah reminded her.

"Ah. That's what we need." She placed a crystal bowl nestled with greenery and gold ornaments on each table.

"Going out with Michael tonight?" Lucy asked Marisol.

"No."

"Why? No, don't tell me." Lucy paused. "His voice is hoarse from reading you romantic poetry."

"I hate poetry." Marisol bristled. "And please stop comparing him to John Willoughby."

Lucy regarded her in mild surprise. "Sorry. Just kidding, I swear. Did you two go out yesterday?"

"Michael was busy. The gallery. Today, he's out of town."

Noting the disappointment in Marisol's voice, Phaedra sent Lucy a warning glance and changed the subject. "There's always next week, Mari. Right now, let's all focus on getting everything ready for the Christmas tea."

"You mentioned a guitarist earlier," Marisol said as she set down a plate. "Who'd you find?"

"I didn't find anyone. Detective Morelli did. He says Lucas is really good."

"Lucas?"

"Oh, sorry. I meant Officer Scott."

"The cop who took everyone's statements after Anna's poisoning?" Skepticism lifted her brow. "I'll believe it when I see it."

The morning passed in a blur of baking, decorating, joking, second-guessing, and rearranging, until it was nearly time to open.

"Do you think Rachel will show up?" Phaedra readjusted the centerpiece on a table and stood back to study it with a critical eye.

"No idea." Hannah shrugged. "No one's seen her. It's like she's fallen off the face of the earth. Vanessa, too."

"Do you think they went back to New York? Now that Rachel and Kyle are officially cleared as suspects?"

"Could be. She has a magazine to run, after all."

Hannah cast an anxious glance through the window. "People are lining up outside. Should I let them in?"

"In a minute." She laid a hand on her sister's arm. "Have you heard anything more from Rachel? About your magazine interview?"

"Not a word. It's obvious she's decided against it." Hannah sighed. "After all, who wants to run a feature on an alleged cupcake killer? Rachel publishes an upscale lifestyles magazine, not a tabloid."

"You're not a killer, 'alleged' or otherwise." Phaedra gave Hannah's hand a reassuring squeeze. "Innocent until proven guilty, remember?"

"Either way, no one's buying my baked goods. Every morning the three of us come in and make croissants and mille-feuille, and every evening, most of it goes to the homeless shelter or Aunt Wendy's B and B, and the rest gets tossed. It's costing me a fortune." Her voice wavered. "As far as everyone's concerned, I'm guilty."

"You're wrong. Look outside." Phaedra turned her toward the large plate glass window, where a crowd of people had gathered outside the door. "Half of Laurel Springs is out there, our neighbors and friends, waiting to sample your tarts and mini plum puddings. To sip peppermint rooibos and ginger chai while they devour your scones and listen to Lucas play acoustic versions of their favorite holiday songs."

Hannah pressed her lips together. "They're just nosy, that's all. They want a closer look at the crazy cupcake poisoner."

"No. Those are your *customers*, Hannah. They're here because they know your pastries are the best, just like they know, deep down, that you'd never willfully harm anyone. It's up to you," Phaedra finished, her words firm, "to prove once and for all that you're the best baker in Laurel Springs. This is your chance to silence the naysayers and win them back over. And wow their socks off."

Hannah sighed. "Nothing like a little pressure." But she managed to produce a smile and straightened her chef-coat-clad shoulders.

"If everyone's ready," she called out to Jared and Liv and the extra help she'd hired for the event, "let's get our game faces on and get this party started."

Twenty-One

The Regency Christmas Tea fundraiser was a success beyond even Hannah's wildest dreams.

The menu was a hit, so much so that they ran out of plum tea and barely had enough Devonshire cream to dollop alongside each scone. They raised fifteen hundred dollars for the Coats 'n Caps fund and donated two boxes brimming with enough parkas, car coats, hats, and down jackets to keep dozens of underserved children and adults warm through the course of a cold Blue Ridge winter.

"I got a few side-eyes early on," Hannah admitted as Jared pulled her a cup of espresso afterward, "and I fielded some pointed questions about the ingredients in the cranberry-almond scones. But after a few bites, when no one fell over dead, it was business as usual."

"Everyone loved your music, Officer Scott," Marisol said as Lucas joined them, his guitar case in hand. "You're really good."

"Don't sound so surprised." He grinned. "And please, it's Lucas. I'm off duty."

"Marisol." She thrust a plastic tray under her arm. "Now, if you'll excuse me, I'm still on duty. I have tables to clear."

He flashed her a quick smile. "You should stop by the Vineyard one night when we're playing. Bring your friends."

"I might just do that."

Phaedra looked up as Detective Morelli pushed through the front door as the last of the guests departed. "How'd the tea party go?" he asked her.

"It went very well. We raised almost fifteen hundred dollars for the Coats 'n Caps fund and, I hope, shored up Hannah's confidence. She's cleaning up the kitchen with Liv and Jared. Did you need to talk to her?"

"No. I wanted to speak with you, actually."

"Oh." Surprise colored her words. "Okay. We can talk here." She indicated the table Marisol had just cleared.

"I went out to Crozet yesterday and spoke to Arthur Rouse." He waited until she was seated in the chair opposite. "Your father's former client."

Her pulse picked up. "And?"

"I'm afraid the break you hoped for didn't pan out."

Disappointment swept over her. "But he has a motive."

"Murderers don't always have a motive."

"Maybe not. But we're not talking about a serial killer, or a psychopath. We're talking about Rouse. I'm convinced he poisoned that cupcake. Nothing else makes sense." She frowned. "I wouldn't be surprised if he left the cupcake on my front seat, too."

"There's no evidence linking him to either incident. We found a partial print on the cupcake wrapper in your car, but it's inconclusive."

"I still think he's the culprit."

"We can agree on one thing. Your father isn't Rouse's favorite person," Morelli said. "He admitted as much. He also admitted he went to your sister's grand opening."

"Which indicates he intended to do harm. Why else would he show up? To thank my dad for taking away eight years of his life?"

"He was angry, no question, and he fully intended to give

Malcolm a piece of his mind. But he realized it would only lead to trouble, changed his mind, and left."

"And you believe him? Why?"

"Because he's on parole. I spoke with his probation officer over the phone. She confirmed that Rouse was released early on good behavior. He was a model prisoner."

"A model prisoner? Isn't that an oxymoron?"

He leaned forward, his arms resting on the table, and met her eyes. "Arthur Rouse has the best motivation in the world to stay clean. He's terrified of going back inside." He drew back. "And he has an alibi."

"But I saw him at Hannah's grand opening."

"Yes, you did. But he didn't hang around. He said he went to Harper's for a beer after he left. Several beers. I checked it out, and the bartender backed up his story."

"A beer? But it was barely ten a.m."

"Which is why," Morelli said patiently, "the bartender remembered him. He was parked on the same barstool all morning."

"What about the cupcake in my car? Was it poisoned?"

"No. It was a vanilla cupcake with vanilla buttercream frosting. No toxins were found."

"Then why?" Phaedra said, frustration undercutting her question. "Why go to the trouble of leaving it in my car? What was the point?"

"Maybe it was nothing more than a gesture of appreciation from a student," he suggested. "Or a faculty member. Someone who thought it was your birthday."

"Or maybe," she said as she scraped her chair back and stood, "someone wanted to frighten me. Now, if you'll excuse me, I need to help Hannah clean up."

"I'm not the bad guy here, Professor." Detective Morelli stood as well.

"Evidently, neither is Arthur Rouse. Thanks for stopping by."

He seemed about to say something more, changed his mind, and left.

* * *

That night, Phaedra slept like Rip Van Winkle. No tossing, no turning, and thankfully, no dreams. She woke refreshed and bounded out of bed early on Monday morning.

Drawing on a robe and a pair of thick, woolly socks, she headed downstairs to be greeted by the scent of coffee. Hannah had not only left her half a carafe of Kona, she'd also dropped off a couple of freshly made croissants.

"Hannah, you're an angel," Phaedra said as she poured a coffee and reached for one of the soft, buttery treats. She glanced at the sofa. "You even made up the bed."

She was glad things were back to normal for her sister, relieved her business had picked up. And thrilled that their holiday tea had raised money for a worthy cause.

Today she planned to drive out to Delaford to find Rachel Brandon and ask her—discreetly, of course—if Hannah's interview was still on. Maybe hit her up for a donation, too. Why not? Rachel could certainly afford it.

She was also curious to learn what prompted Rachel to drop her champagne flute at the Farrar Gallery, shattering the delicate glass on Michael's office floor. What had he said to her to cause such a reaction?

Phaedra frowned. What would her cover story be?

Her glance went to the bottle of glühwein sitting on the counter, a German mulled wine one of her students had gifted her with on Friday.

Wine! Of course. She'd take a tour of the Delaford Winery. Tours ran hourly every day, giving her a perfect excuse to drop by. After the tour ended, she'd figure out a way to gain admittance to the house. But how?

She'd just have to wing it.

Wickham padded into the kitchen, his tail twitching and ears flattened.

"You smell Hannah's croissants, don't you?" She reached for his food dish. "Sorry, but it's kibble and Tuna Supreme for you this morning."

He settled on his haunches and regarded her with haughty contempt. *I'll have you know my culinary tastes stretch further than the occasional inferior can of tuna.*

She set the dish in front of him and straightened. "There you go. Bon appétit."

Bon appétit? He eyed the dish with distain. *As if.*

But he settled in to his breakfast, eschewing his kibble in favor of the canned stuff.

Phaedra took a seat at the kitchen island and spread a layer of raspberry jam atop a halved croissant and let out an indulgent sigh.

No lectures to give or papers to grade, nowhere to go and not a single commitment. She'd be busy nonetheless. It was nearly Christmas and she'd barely made a dent in her gift shopping.

Hannah was easy; anything related to personal grooming, from that fancy cordless hair dryer she coveted to a gift certificate for a day of pampering at the spa, would be a hit. Maybe a first edition of Mickey Spillane's *I, the Jury* for Dad, along with a copy of the latest Patricia Cornwell novel. Wendy loved scarves and chunky costume jewelry.

That left her mother.

Nan didn't spend much time in the kitchen, beyond assembling a casserole or salad for two, or producing a Sunday roast with potatoes, onions, and overcooked carrots after church once a month. She preferred audiobooks to print books. The things she liked—art, clothing, travel, jewelry—Phaedra couldn't afford to give her.

She texted Hannah. What are you getting Mom for Christmas?

Perfume, she texted back. After a pause, she added, Chiles Chocolates! She loves. Too much $ 4 me.

Phaedra sighed and laid the phone aside. She'd given her mother a bottle of perfume last Christmas, and again for her birthday. A box of chocolates, no matter how good or how pricey, wasn't very personal. She had to come up with something else. Something unique.

But what?

* * *

The sky was clear as Phaedra navigated the twists and turns of Afton Mountain Road on her way to the Delaford Winery a short time later. A brisk wind had scrubbed the clouds away, and there was no snow in the forecast.

But it was frigid enough to make her glad she'd worn her down coat and driving gloves. With the heater still acting up, driving required layers of non-Regency clothing and a pair of thick woolly socks.

In the fall, a riot of reds, oranges, and yellows blanketed the mountainside, drawing spectators from all over the country, and in spring, redbuds and dogwoods flowered alongside tulip trees and jacarandas.

But now only bare branches scraped the sky. Aside from the brilliant blue arching overhead, the winter landscape consisted of blacks and browns and mottled grays.

Thirty minutes later she arrived and turned into the winery parking lot. Only a handful of cars occupied the space. Surprised by the lack of visitors, she parked and headed toward the entrance, wondering where everyone was.

Christmas shopping, she thought with a twinge of guilt. *Which is what I should be doing.*

As she neared the front doors, her steps slowed. A sign was taped to the glass door.

WINERY TOURS CLOSED FOR THE HOLIDAYS
REOPENING ON JANUARY 2

She read the notice in dismay. Now what?

As she hesitated, debating whether to try her luck at the house or just turn around and head back to Laurel Springs, a familiar voice called out to her.

"Professor Brighton! Did you want a tour?" Rachel asked as she emerged from the building. Her hair was tucked under a tweed bucket cap, and her cheeks were ruddy with cold. A folder of papers was nestled under one arm.

"I did, but it seems I've chosen a bad time."

Rachel locked the door behind her and returned her attention to Phaedra. "I'd take you through myself, but I'm pressed for time this morning. The gift shop is open, though. If you're looking for a unique holiday present."

She thought of her mother. "I am, actually."

"Just go around the corner and you'll see the sign." She pointed to the left. "Can't miss it."

"Thank you." Phaedra clapped her hand on her hat as a gust of wind nearly snatched it from her head. "This wind is something else."

"At least it isn't snowing." Rachel's smile was wry.

"I didn't expect to see you. Hannah and I thought perhaps you'd returned to New York."

"I am going back, and soon, but there's been a . . . change of plans."

"Perhaps we might talk," Phaedra suggested. "About your interview with Hannah."

Rachel paused, studying her for a moment. "Why don't you stop by the house when you're done? We can talk privately over tea."

"I look forward to it."

With a polite, practiced nod, Rachel strode across the parking lot to return to the Delaford residence as Phaedra rounded the corner and entered the gift shop.

Rough brick walls lined with oak racks housed dozens of bottles of wines. A Persian rug silenced her steps as she ventured inside. Tables displayed a variety of wine paraphernalia—bottle openers, corkscrews, aerators, charms, stoppers—and gift baskets stuffed with wine, cheeses, and chocolates sat on the checkout counter.

Surely, she'd find the perfect gift for her mother here.

"May I help you?" a woman in a teal shirtdress inquired as she emerged from behind the counter.

"I need to find something for my mother. Do you make up custom baskets?"

"We do. What type of wine does she prefer? Let's start there."

"Viognier is her favorite."

"Excellent. I'd suggest pairing it with milk chocolate—we have some lovely options—and a couple of soft cheeses. Brie or Gouda are both good choices."

"Perfect. I'll just look around in the meantime."

Phaedra chose a set of white-wine glasses and charms for Lucy and a wine cookbook for Marisol, who'd expressed interest in cooking a gourmet meal for Michael.

She carried her purchases to the counter and watched as the shop assistant put the final touches on her mother's gift basket.

"Will this do?" The woman nestled a bottle of Viognier in the center of the basket and tied it with a red bow.

"Cheese, chocolate, and wine? Mom will love it."

"You'll need to refrigerate the cheeses for a few days, then allow them to ripen at room temperature in the basket," she said as she rang up Phaedra's purchases.

"That's just what I'll do. Thank you." She gathered up the pair of paper-handled bags and returned to the Mini, where she stowed the gifts on the passenger seat.

Her phone rang. "Under Pressure," her mother's ringtone.

With a sigh, and knowing she'd probably regret it, Phaedra answered. "Hi, Mom. What's up?"

"I spoke with the lead historian at the Historical Society on the phone yesterday. I meant to tell you at the fundraiser, but you were so busy, I never got the chance."

"I barely had time to say hello to you and Dad. I'm pleased we had such a great turnout. It was a huge success." Phaedra closed the passenger door. "What did you want to tell me?"

"Mrs. Bavier says the painting your father inherited is unknown in art circles. There's no record of it, but rumors of its existence resurface from time to time. It's known as the 'honeymoon painting.' The art world has largely dismissed the rumors as nonsense. A sort of urban legend, if you will. Mrs. B said it would prove a rare find if its provenance could be authenticated."

"A rare find," Phaedra repeated. "As in, valuable?"

"Quite valuable. Upwards of six figures," she added, "if the painting truly is an undiscovered work by James Brighton and if it can be authenticated."

Her thoughts whirling, she thanked her and ended the call.

Michael had lied. The painting her father had inherited wasn't minor; far from it. It might be an unknown work by a highly regarded, late-nineteenth-century artist. And if its authenticity was confirmed, it might be worth half a million or more.

She unlocked the car, her expression thoughtful, and headed for Delaford house.

"Please leave the tea tray on the coffee table, Mrs. Leeson."

Rachel Brandon waited as the housekeeper departed and invited Phaedra to join her on the drawing room sofa. "How do you take your tea, Professor?"

"Lemon, no sugar." She took the cup and saucer Rachel held out. "Thank you. And thank you for taking the time to talk to me. I'm sure you're busy."

"Always, unfortunately. What can I do for you? I understand you're here to discuss your sister's situation."

Phaedra took a sip of Earl Grey and nodded. "She's reopened her shop, and things are back on track after a rather unsettling couple of weeks."

"I can imagine," Rachel agreed. "An unfortunate circumstance for all concerned."

"The thing is, before the—" Phaedra cleared her throat and set her cup down. "Before Anna's poisoning, you and Ms. Cole discussed publishing a piece about Hannah in your magazine. You were both quite enthusiastic about it. Hannah hopes that, despite everything that's happened, you might still consider—"

"I'm sorry, but no." She, too, set her cup down and regarded Phaedra with a mixture of regret and resolve. "We can't possibly go ahead with the article in view of what took place. My assistant is dead, Professor Brighton, after consuming a trace amount of cyanide on one of your sister's cupcakes. I can hardly ignore that."

"But surely you understand," Phaedra said, angling herself to face the woman as she struggled to keep her voice calm, "that Hannah had nothing to do with it."

"I do. But unfortunately, it happened in her patisserie, in front of dozens of customers. The story was picked up by the wire services and social media. It even made a couple of national newspapers. Surely you understand my position," Rachel added reasonably. "I can't feature Hannah in the pages of my magazine now. It's impossible."

"She hasn't been charged." Steel undercut her words. "There's not one shred of evidence linking Hannah to the crime. Because she didn't do it."

"I'm not questioning your sister's veracity, or her innocence. But I have my own reputation to protect. Perhaps," she added, in an attempt to placate her guest, "we can revisit the idea later, when things have settled down." She smiled at Phaedra and reached once again for the pot. "More tea, Professor?"

Twenty-Two

After finishing her tea and accepting a generous check from Rachel for the Coats 'n Caps fundraiser, Phaedra thanked her for the tea and the donation and left. Poor Hannah, Phaedra thought as she descended the front steps. She'd be disappointed to learn her interview wasn't happening.

She suspected there'd be no swaying Rachel into changing her decision. And under the circumstances, Phaedra could hardly blame her.

But she still felt badly for her sister.

She tugged the woolen cap back on her head as she headed to her car. At least she'd found a gift for her mother, and something for Lucy and Marisol. The morning hadn't been a total loss.

As she unlocked the Mini, she glanced at the house and noticed a late-model black Jaguar parked to one side.

Nice wheels, she mused. Rachel's? Or maybe it belonged to her brother-in-law, Max?

She glanced with satisfaction at the gift bags on the passenger seat. Three presents off her list, and only two—Dad's and Hannah's—left to go.

And Mark, she thought suddenly. What on earth would she get Mark?

As she pulled out of the parking lot, her phone rang. The number was unfamiliar, but she decided to answer it. "Hello?"

"Professor Brighton?"

"Yes?"

"This is Lucy's mother."

"Mrs. Liang?" Her brows arched upwards. "Hello. How . . . how did you get my number?"

"I saw it on Lucy's phone. You're her friend, yes? I wrote your number down so we could talk." Her voice brooked no argument. "You can talk now?"

"Of course. How can I help you?"

"I'm most upset. I've tried everything to win over my daughter, but nothing works. She is very stubborn. I don't know what to do."

Phaedra's heart sank. What on earth was she meant to say?

"I'm sure the two of you will work things out," she began, "if you just give it a little more time—"

"No. No more time." Mrs. Liang's words were firm. "I'm leaving next week. I already have my plane ticket. No point staying for the holiday if my daughter does not wish to see me."

"Perhaps I can talk to her." She really didn't want to get in the middle of her friend's personal life; she knew Lucy wouldn't appreciate it. "But I doubt she'll listen."

"No, of course she won't." Her words were impatient. "She never listens to anything I say. All we do is quarrel. Argue. I had hopes that our visits would help things between us, but they are no better. They're only getting worse, in fact. I grow weary of bickering. I . . . I feel I am wasting my time. Lucy won't ever forgive me."

"You need to try again," Phaedra said. "For your sake, and Leah's. And Lucy's."

"Perhaps you're right." Mrs. Liang let out a long, defeated sigh. "I will try one more time. But I need your help. You're her friend, she will listen to you."

"What is it you want me to do, exactly?"

"Convince her to meet me for dim sum on Sunday. Eleven o'clock. If she fails to show up, I will consider that her answer and return to Shanghai on Monday. For good."

Phaedra promised to relay the message and do her best to convince Lucy to be there. Which, she reflected as she headed back to Laurel Springs, was a pretty tall order.

After all, no one understood more than her just how fraught the relationship between a mother and daughter could be.

Halfway down Main Street, Phaedra slowed for a stop sign and called Hannah. It was nearly twelve, and she was starving. "Are you free for lunch?" she asked when her sister answered. "My treat."

"Only if we make it quick."

"On my way."

After picking Hannah up from Tout de Sweet, Phaedra headed to the Coffee Stop—the only place that wasn't jam-packed with holiday shoppers—and let her sister out.

"Go grab us a table," she said, and left to find somewhere to park.

When their orders were called fifteen minutes later, Hannah went up to retrieve them. "One ham, one tuna salad on rye," she announced as she deposited their respective sandwiches on the table. "Dibs on your pickle," she added, eyeing the garlic dill.

Phaedra offered her the plate. "Help yourself."

"So," Hannah asked several bites later, wiping her mouth with a napkin, "what have you been up to?"

"I went to the Delaford Winery." She eyed her sandwich. "I thought I'd take a tour, but they're closed for the holidays. The gift shop was open, though."

"Did you find a present for Mom?"

"I did. A custom wine, cheese, and chocolate basket."

"She'll love that."

"I ran into Rachel. She invited me up to the house for tea.

And I asked her about the status of your interview." Phaedra squeezed lemon into her cup of oolong.

Hannah lowered her ham sandwich. "What did she say?"

With a sigh, she met her sister's quizzical gaze. "It's not happening. She insists it isn't because she believes you did anything wrong," she hastened to add as she registered Hannah's crestfallen expression. "It's because of all the negative publicity."

"In other words, she can't feature a possible murderer in the pages of her glossy magazine."

"Well . . . yes. I'm sorry, Han."

"It's okay." Hannah shrugged. "At least business has picked up since the tea fundraiser. I have two orders for a wedding cake and a referral for a catering job next month."

"Good. I told you it'll all work out eventually."

She nodded. "I know you and Detective Morelli will figure it out, and catch whoever really poisoned poor Anna Steele. Now"—she pushed her chair back—"I have to run. We're finally busy. And thanks for lunch."

After returning her sister to the patisserie, Phaedra deposited the Coats 'n Caps money—she'd write a check and officially present it to the charity with Lucy and Marisol the next day—and headed to the Poison Pen. Hannah's faith in her ability to find Anna's killer was a bit optimistic. She had a plethora of suspects and even more questions, but no answers. And no evidence.

At least, not yet.

As she neared the Farrar Gallery, she slowed as a sleek black sports car ahead of her pulled over to take the reserved spot in front.

And it wasn't just any sports car. It was a black, late-model Jaguar. Exactly like the one she'd just seen at Delaford. A moment later, a well-dressed man emerged from the driver's side, pointed his key fob at the car, and strode inside the gallery.

Michael Farrar.

Phaedra drew her brows together in puzzlement.

The winery was closed, and Farrar definitely hadn't been

present at her tea with Rachel, nor had Ms. Brandon made mention of him. Yet it was his car she'd seen parked by the side of Delaford house.

Which made her wonder: What was Michael doing at Delaford in the middle of a workday morning?

Holiday shoppers filled the aisles of the Poison Pen when Phaedra arrived a short time later.

"Wow. Busy much?" she asked her harried father as he rang up the last of a line of customers.

"It's been like this all day. We're offering free gift wrapping in the reading room, and your mother's been inundated. And the new girl didn't show up. I haven't had a break since we opened the doors."

"I'll take over." She rounded the counter and tucked her purse into one of the cubbies underneath. "Go."

"Well . . . if I'm not keeping you from anything?"

"Not a thing. I'm off this week, remember? Take a break," she insisted, shooing him away. "Before I change my mind."

He thanked her, answered a question from a customer, and disappeared upstairs. Another line began to form, and she busied herself ringing up one purchase after another.

She drew the next stack of paperbacks toward her. On top was Homer's *Iliad*. "Will this be all for you today?"

"Unless you have a Dog House Special stashed away behind the counter, then yes, that's all."

"Hector!" Phaedra glanced up, surprised. "No Dog House Specials today, sorry. Just books. What brings you here?"

"Presents for my nephews. And new business," he added as she rang up a copy of the *Odyssey* and the *Aeneid*. "Your mother just hired me to do your father's books."

"As in accounting?" She paused, scanner in hand. "That's great. But I thought you worked at that big accounting firm in Charlottesville. Webley and Wright."

"I did, until last Friday. I decided to go freelance. Hang out my shingle. I already do a lot of side work preparing tax returns. And I keep the books for the Bondurant sisters."

"The apothecary? Scents and Sensibility?"

He nodded and handed her a card. "Tell your friends."

"I will." She slid his books forward. "I wish you every success. And I hope your nephews like their books."

"Oh, they won't even crack the covers. My sister frowns on gifts that aren't educational." He dropped the books into a canvas tote. "That's why they're signed up for a paintball session with Uncle Hector on New Year's Day."

Phaedra laughed. "Sounds like a lot more fun than reading Homer. Enjoy, and happy holidays."

She closed the cash drawer as he left and glanced up to see her father returning. He lifted a box of expensive candies, beautifully wrapped in green and red tartan paper and tied with a gold bow, and eyed her inquiringly.

"Chiles Chocolates," she exclaimed as she glimpsed the embossed gold emblem. "Nice. Where'd they come from?"

"I thought you brought them."

"No."

He shrugged. "Someone must've left them on the counter, then. Customers often bring in cookies or small gifts this time of year, to show their appreciation."

"Probably. I've been so busy behind the cash register, I didn't notice."

"Well, whoever left them, I can't wait to try one." He untied the bow and lifted the lid, breathing in the heady scent of chocolate, and studied the selection. His fingers hovered over the tray.

"Wait." She stopped him from popping a dark chocolate square into his mouth, a strange feeling of foreboding settling over her. "Is there a card? Who's it from?"

He lowered the square with a frown. "I think so. Yes, here it is." He picked up a small card and opened it. "Ah. It's from your sister. See?" He handed it over.

Phaedra stared at the handwritten signature. "From Hannah? But that's impossible. They can't be from her."

"Why not?"

She frowned. "Was this box here when you opened the bookstore?"

"No. We've been busier than Santa's workshop all morning, but I would've noticed this."

Phaedra gave a slow shake of her head. "Then the chocolates aren't from Hannah."

"But the note says—"

"That's not her handwriting. Here, look at this." She took out her phone and showed him Hannah's earlier text about buying a gift for their mother.

Chiles Chocolates! She loves. Too much $ 4 me.

"Well, there you have it," he said. "They're from Hannah, just as her text says. Mystery solved."

"No, Dad. She can't afford them. She suggested I give a box to Mom for Christmas. They're not from her."

"But . . . who sent them, then? And why would someone lie about such a thing?"

"I don't know. But it can't be anything good."

"They were sealed, Phaedra," he pointed out. "Gift-wrapped and tied with a bow. A very elegant bow, I might add." He dropped the chocolate in his hand back into the tray and chose another. Hazelnut crunch.

"No!" she cried, knocking the candy from his fingers and snatching the box away. "It might be poisoned!"

"Phaedra." Malcolm regarded her in surprise. "Don't you think you're overreacting just a tad?"

"In view of what happened to Anna Steele? No, I don't. I just had lunch with Hannah. Afterward, I dropped her off at the patisserie, so I know for a fact that she didn't leave these here. She couldn't have."

He stared at the beautifully wrapped lid before lifting a troubled gaze to hers. "Then who? Who left them?"

"I have no idea." She sank down onto the high stool behind the counter, her legs as wobbly as gelatin. "But I'm betting it was the same person who poisoned Anna Steele's cupcake."

Twenty-Three

The police arrived a short time later.

"Are those the chocolates?" Detective Morelli indicated the gift-wrapped lid and the box lying nearby.

Phaedra nodded. "Someone left them on the front counter. We don't know when, and we don't know who. The note says they're from Hannah. But they're not."

He lifted his eyes to hers. "What makes you so sure?"

"We had lunch at the Coffee Stop before I came here, to discuss gift ideas for my mother. She mentioned Chiles Chocolates, which Mom loves, but said she can't afford to buy them. They're very expensive. And that's not her handwriting on the card."

Morelli pulled on a pair of blue latex gloves and glanced at the box. "And these are Chiles Chocolates?"

"Yes."

"Strange coincidence." He picked up the lid and studied it. "Did anyone overhear you and your sister? At the Coffee Stop?"

"No."

"You seem very sure of that."

"I am." Phaedra suppressed a flicker of exasperation.

"Because we didn't talk about the chocolates at lunch. We texted each other about gift ideas beforehand."

"I see. And what did you talk about at lunch?"

"Nothing relevant."

"Let me be the judge of that, Professor Brighton."

She sighed. "I told Han that I saw Rachel Brandon this morning. I went up to Delaford Winery to take a tour, but they're closed for the holidays. I ran into Rachel as I was leaving, and she invited me up to the house for tea."

"And you told your sister about it? Why?"

"When she came to Hannah's grand opening, Rachel mentioned she wanted to run a feature about the patisserie in her *Home Channel* magazine. But then the poisoning happened, and . . ."

"And Rachel changed her mind."

"It wasn't a surprise, really. At least not to me. But Hannah's pretty disappointed all the same."

"Who's been in the bookstore this morning?"

"Who hasn't? Half of Laurel Springs, judging by how busy it's been."

"Does anyone come to mind? A neighbor? A friend?"

Phaedra hesitated. "No one. Except . . ." She thought of Hector, buying volumes of Homer for his nephews. And Rebecca Bondurant, who'd purchased *Monk's Hood*, an Ellis Peters mystery, for her sister. "A couple of people. I only remember them because I know them personally."

"Names?"

"Hector Kranz. He's an accountant, he works—worked—at Webley and Wright until last week. And Rebecca Bondurant, she owns the apothecary shop. But neither of them would do something like this," she hastened to add.

"Where does Mr. Kranz work now?"

"He's gone into business for himself. The apothecary shop is one of his accounts. And Mom just hired him to do Dad's books."

"How well do you know him?"

"Not well. My mother introduced us at Hannah's grand

opening. He's nice, in a nerdy way." A flush crept up her neck. "Mom hoped there'd be sparks between us."

Detective Morelli paused. "I take it there weren't."

"No."

He turned to Officer Scott. "Have these chocolates tested. No one leaves the premises until we have everyone's name and phone number. As well as the names of anyone who came through those doors this morning."

"I can help you with that, Officer," Malcolm said. "I've been behind the front counter since we opened."

As her father led Officer Scott to the reading room, Phaedra turned back to Morelli. "If it turns out those chocolates aren't poisoned, I apologize in advance for wasting your time."

"But if they *are*," he pointed out, "you just saved your father's life." He turned to an officer. "Lock the front door and close up. I don't want the scene contaminated by new arrivals any more than it already is."

"Phaedra? Phaedra, what's happened?"

Mark, grim-faced and determined, thrust his way through the doors. His gaze landed on her.

Phaedra, always calm and clearheaded, at least on the surface, felt her composure dissolve when she saw him. He rushed forward and swept her into his arms.

"Someone . . . I think someone may have tried to poison my father just now," she choked out as she drew back.

Shock and confusion registered on his face. "Is Malcolm all right?"

"Yes, he's fine. He's . . . fine." Deeply shaken by the knowledge someone had tried—and nearly succeeded—to kill her father, she couldn't stifle a series of dry, shuddery sobs.

Mark enfolded her gently into his arms. "It's okay," he said into her hair. "Your father's all right. Everything's going to be fine."

She leaned into him, feeling his arms around her, and allowed herself to relax. The soft cashmere of his scarf and the warm, aftershave-and-soap smell of him enveloped her and made her feel safe. Protected.

"I thought I was okay," she admitted, "until I saw you. Then, I don't know. It hit me all at once. If I hadn't been here, if Dad had opened those chocolates, thinking they were from Hannah, and popped one in his mouth, he'd . . ." She swallowed. "My father would be dead right now."

"But you *were* here," he said firmly. "You saved him."

"I'm sorry," she mumbled, and lifted her head.

"For what?"

"I'm not usually . . . weepy. I got your scarf wet."

"My scarf will dry. It's you I'm concerned about."

"I'm okay, now. Thanks to you." She drew back and squeezed his hand. "What brings you here? Aside from"—she gestured at the police and Detective Morelli, who were questioning customers—"all this."

"I need to pick up a few paperbacks." He rubbed the back of his neck. "For my, ah . . . flight tomorrow evening."

"Flight?" She said when she'd regained her composure. "What flight? Where are you going?"

"England. To spend the holidays with Mum."

"What about your father?" she asked. *And what about me?* she almost added. "Doesn't he live in Charlottesville?"

"He does. Health much improved, enjoying every minute of his divorce from my mother and his retirement from the bench. But when it comes to Christmas, he's a full-on Grinch. He detests the holidays, always has, and prefers to spend them alone with a bottle of single malt."

"We should invite him over for Christmas dinner," Nan suggested as she returned and slipped behind the counter.

Mark shrugged. "That's kind of you. But I'd spare yourself the trouble. I very much doubt that he'll accept."

"Perhaps he'd join us for a drink," Malcolm said, reappearing from the reading room with Officer Scott. "I'll extend an invitation. The Honorable Judge Selden and I go way back."

"He ruled on one of your cases?"

"Several." Malcolm shrugged. "He presided over my first big case." He frowned. "I defended a man charged with armed robbery. I knew he was guilty, and I only had a fifty-fifty chance of winning the case, but my client went free on a technicality. The arresting officer failed to read him his Miranda rights, and the judge tossed the case out."

"My father?" Mark asked.

He nodded. "Two days later the same guy was in a high-speed police chase following a bank robbery. He lost control of the car and struck and killed a young single mother. She had two kids, four and six." His gaze remained focused on the road ahead. "No other family. They both went into foster care."

"That's so sad." Phaedra's heart went out to those poor kids.

"I've had a lot of cases over the years," Malcolm added, "but that one? It still haunts me."

"I didn't realize you and my father knew each other," Mark said. "In a professional capacity."

"Every trial attorney knows Judge Selden." Malcolm's smile faded. "Never been overturned on appeal. He's something of a legend hereabouts."

"And that," Mark confided to Phaedra as he drew her aside, out of Malcolm's earshot, "can be a good thing, or bad. Knowing my father? I'm guessing bad."

"It's true Judge Selden has—had—a reputation for following the letter of the law. 'Harsh, but fair,'" she quoted her dad. "He can't be *that* bad."

"Believe me, he can." Mark's gaze drifted past her to the shelves of paperback thrillers. "Now, Professor Brighton, tell me. Which of these books do you recommend to keep me absorbed for a seven-and-a-half-hour flight?"

Later, when she'd sent Mark on his way with several paperbacks, after a brief but memorable kiss behind the shelves, and his promise they'd do something special when he returned, Phaedra realized it was nearly three o'clock.

Everyone had been cleared to leave, and the Poison Pen was closed until further notice.

"How long will that be?" Nan demanded. "This is our busiest time of year, Detective."

"Until the crime scene's been processed," Morelli had answered her. "A day. Two, at most."

Here we go again, Phaedra thought. First Hannah's new business was shut down, now the Poison Pen was closed—

A series of loud thumps erupted on the front door. "Phaedra? Phaedra, are you in there?" More banging. "I know you are. Your car's parked out front. Let me in!"

"Lucy," she muttered, and hurried to the entrance. She cracked the door open and peered out. "Sorry, Lu, but you can't come in."

"I saw the yellow tape. Is this a crime scene? Has someone been *murdered*?"

"Yes, it's a crime scene. And no, no one's been murdered. Not yet, anyway."

"Phaedra, if you don't tell me what's going on right now," Lucy warned, "I'll—"

"Meet me at the carriage house in ten minutes. I'll explain then."

"Fine. See you in ten. I want to know *everything*."

"Professor Brighton!" Clark Mullinax called out, already heading across the street with his microphone. "Is it true there's been another poisoning incident? Who's the victim? Has a suspect been identified? Can I get a quote?"

She slammed the door, called upstairs to tell her parents she was leaving, and grabbed her coat and purse. She'd promised Mrs. Liang to try to talk Lucy into giving her another chance.

Now she had the perfect opportunity. She headed down the hall to the back door and let herself out.

After unlocking the carriage house door and turning on a lamp, Phaedra shrugged off her coat, greeted Wickham, and went into the kitchen to open a bottle of pinot gris.

Forgetting something? He settled on his haunches and eyed her with sphinxlike regard as she took down glasses.

"The basket!" she exclaimed, remembering her mother's gift from the winery, sitting on the front seat of the Mini.

Wickham followed her to the door and watched her go outside with a baleful expression. *That wasn't what I had in mind. I'm thinking about dinner.* My *dinner, to be exact.*

She darted out to the car and retrieved the basket. Where to put it? The carriage house was out. Her mother often popped in and out, and she wasn't above a little snooping. And there wasn't room in the refrigerator for such an unwieldy gift.

The trunk would have to do. Goodness knew it was cold enough outside. She lifted the rear door, wrestled the basket inside, and tossed a blanket over it. Perfect.

"I know what you want, Wicks," Phaedra said as she returned and bent down to ruffle the Himalayan's ears. "Mixed Seafood Grill."

You got it in one. Very good.

A moment later, as Wickham fastidiously nibbled at his early dinner, the doorbell sounded.

She let Lucy in and gestured at the sofa. "Have a seat while I pour us a glass."

"Hurry. I'm dying to know what's going on."

Phaedra returned to the living room a moment later and handed Lucy a glass. "How'd you spend your day off?"

"I treated Leah to a mani-pedi and a facial at the new spa. She loved it."

"Isn't your sister more the nose ring and torn T-shirt type?"

"She is. All those gorgeous nail colors, and she chose black. But at least she agreed to go. Baby steps."

As Phaedra curled up on the sofa, she wondered how to broach the subject of Mrs. Liang's dim sum invitation—or more truthfully, her summons—to Lucy.

As prickly as Lu was about her past, she wouldn't welcome

a conversation about her mother. Phaedra had to tread carefully. Where to begin?

"Enough small talk." Lucy eyed her over the rim of her wineglass. "What happened at the bookstore? Spill."

"Someone left a box of gift-wrapped chocolates for Mom and Dad. The note said they were from Hannah."

"But they weren't?"

She shook her head. "Han was at Tout de Sweet all morning. Then we had lunch at the Coffee Stop. Afterward she went straight back to work. Unless she can be in two places at once, she couldn't possibly have left that box."

"Any idea who did?"

"None. Dad said it was busy all morning, and the new girl never showed up, so I helped out. I'd been there for an hour or so when he noticed the chocolates on the counter. Chiles," she added.

"At least whoever left them has good taste."

"A tasteful murderer?" Phaedra lifted her brow. "Somehow that isn't very reassuring."

"Murderer? Wait—what? Were they—" She set her drink down with a thump. "Were the chocolates poisoned? Like Anna's cupcake?"

"We don't know yet. They're being tested."

"No wonder the place was crawling with cops and covered in crime scene tape. Good thing you knew that box wasn't from Hannah. Otherwise . . ."

"I don't even want to think about 'otherwise.' About what might have happened."

"And I'm making jokes." Lucy let out a sigh. "Sorry. I'm just glad that particular gift stayed in the box."

"Me, too." Phaedra swirled the wine in her glass. "I hope the lab test shows that the chocolates are nothing more than chocolates. That they were left on the counter by one of Dad's customers."

"Oh, please, Phae." Lucy eyed her accusingly. "You don't believe that any more than I do."

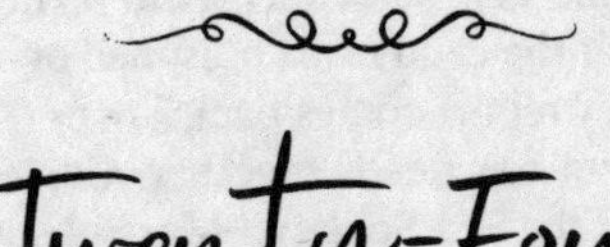

Twenty-Four

The doorbell rang twice in succession, and Phaedra frowned. "Who could that be? I'm not expecting anyone."

"Let's hope it's not a candy-gram."

She parted the curtains and peered out the window. "It's Marisol."

Setting her glass down, she answered the door. A blast of chilly air greeted her. "Mari, Come in. What's up?"

Marisol's cheeks were flushed pink with cold as she stepped inside and tugged off her gloves. "I saw your lights on, and Lucy's car out front." She yanked her zipper down. "I also saw the crime scene tape across the front doors of the Poison Pen." She thrust her parka—bright pink, like her cheeks—into Phaedra's hands with an accusatory glare. "Care to tell me what's going on?"

"Sure." She sighed. "We're in the living room."

Once Marisol was seated with a glass of pinot gris in hand, Phaedra returned to the sofa and filled her in on the latest developments in the case.

Shock parted her lips. "Someone tried to poison your dad?"

"Or whoever was unlucky enough to try one of those chocolates," Lucy said.

"Luckily, no one did." Phaedra picked up her glass again. "We don't know if the candy was poisoned or not. We won't know until the tox report comes back."

"We should put our heads together. Convene an emergency meeting of the Tea Society," Marisol suggested.

"What's the point?" Lucy asked. "We don't know any more now than we did the last time we met. Which was a week ago. We have no evidence, no real suspects. Everyone who might've done it has an alibi. All we have is another potential poisoning attempt to add to the list."

"The killer is getting bolder." A delicate shiver traced visibly up Marisol's spine.

"And you're getting overly dramatic," Lucy retorted. "We don't even know if those chocolates were poisoned."

"Why else would someone sneak in and leave them on the counter, with Hannah's forged signature on the card, and sneak back out, unless they were tampered with?"

"You make a good point," Phaedra agreed. "But so does Lucy. We don't have any new information."

"At least we're unencumbered by academia for the next three weeks," Lucy said. "Leaving us free to do some digging and figure out who's behind the poisoning. Or poisonings."

Everyone agreed that was the most sensible plan.

Marisol's phone bleated. She reached into her purse and pulled it out. Her surprise turned to a blush when she saw the caller's name, and she jumped to her feet.

"Excuse me, I have to take this," she said in a rush as she headed to the door.

"One guess who that is," Lucy said as she left.

"I'll go top up our wine." Phaedra got up and headed for the kitchen.

But Marisol wasn't there. As Phaedra retrieved the bottle of pinot, the motion detector behind the house sprang on. Her teaching assistant was outside, pacing the terrace, phone pressed to one ear.

She'd just refilled Lucy's glass and settled on the sofa with her own when Marisol returned, her face radiant.

"That was Michael. He apologized for being so busy lately and asked me to spend the day with him tomorrow. He's closing the gallery down. For me."

"Wow." Lucy exchanged a quick glance with Phaedra. "Sounds like he's really into you." She paused to sip her wine. "Kind of last minute, though."

"He has a gallery to run, Lucy." A note of defensiveness crept into her voice.

"Still. He could've called sooner, couldn't he?"

"Any plans for the day?" Phaedra asked, hoping to head off an argument between the two.

Marisol leveled a glare at Lucy before turning away. "He wants to spend the day in Charlottesville. That's all I know."

"Well, whatever you end up doing," Lucy said in a conciliatory tone, "I'm sure you'll have a good time."

"Let's drink to that." Phaedra raised her glass and smiled at Marisol. "Okay?"

"Okay," she relented. "Cheers."

"Cheers," the others echoed.

"This is *so* wrong," she admitted, leaning forward to set her glass down, "after all that talk about poison earlier. But I'm really, really hungry. What about you guys?"

"How does pizza sound?" Phaedra asked.

Lucy and Marisol agreed that pizza on such a frigid night sounded perfect. As she picked up her phone to call in the order, Phaedra bit back a sigh. So much for having a quiet word with Lu about her mother's dim sum invitation.

The matter was far too personal to discuss in front of Marisol. And Hannah would be back from the patisserie soon.

She'd just have to leave it for another time.

"I know you'll both be busy today," Phaedra said on Wednesday morning as she entered her parents' kitchen above the Poison Pen. "After being closed yesterday. Now that you've been cleared to reopen, I'm here to offer my help."

"That's thoughtful of you." Malcolm took a lengthy sip

of coffee and set his mug down. "But we've got it covered. The new hire promised she'd be here today."

"I certainly hope so," Nan said. "Because I have every intention of putting her on gift-wrapping duty."

As her mother went downstairs to start the coffee brewing in the reading room for their soon-to-arrive customers, Phaedra took a seat at the island.

Malcolm glanced up from his newspaper. "Something on your mind?"

"I need to talk to you."

He reached for the carafe and poured more coffee into his mug. "No time like the present."

"It's about your grandfather's painting. The one that Michael Farrar is restoring."

"He started work on it last week."

"Yes, I know." She tapped a finger against the countertop. "Mom spoke to Mrs. Bavier at the Historical Society about it."

"Yes, your mother mentioned it. And no one knows more about local history than Mrs. B." He glanced at the clock. "I don't mean to rush you, Phaedra, but we open in seven minutes."

"Right. Sorry." She leaned forward. "Did Mom tell you that the painting you inherited may be an *unknown* work by James Brighton? If so—and if its authenticity is confirmed—it could also be extremely valuable."

"Which is all well and good," he said patiently, "but as I said before, I have no interest in selling it. I'm restoring it purely for sentimental reasons."

"I understand. But the thing is, Michael told you your painting is regarded in the art world as a minor work of little or no value. And the fact that I couldn't find it mentioned anywhere online seems to corroborate his claim."

"Then I don't see the problem."

"The problem," she went on, tamping down a flicker of impatience, "is the painting's provenance. According to Mrs. Bavier, it's possible you own an undiscovered work by a highly regarded, late-nineteenth-century artist."

"'Possible'? 'Could? Those words indicate uncertainty. Supposition, not fact."

"True." She paused. "Even so, Michael should have disclosed its potential value to you. And he didn't."

"Perhaps he didn't know."

"How could he not know? He's an art conservator and a gallery owner. It's his business to know." Phaedra gave a slow shake of her head. "It means he lied to you, Dad."

"Even if you're right," Malcolm said, folding his arms against his chest with a frown, "and Michael *did* lie, it doesn't make him a criminal. He's a businessman, Phaedra. He's hoping to convince me to sell the painting to him at a rock-bottom price. That's the way the art business—any business—works," he pointed out. "Profit is the name of the game."

"What about ethics? Fair disclosure?"

"Oh, honey . . . you're overthinking this whole thing. Michael is in business to make money, like anyone else. And as I said before, I'm not selling the painting. Its provenance is a moot point. Which means there's nothing for you to worry about."

Not completely convinced, but knowing there was no use arguing with her father once he'd made up his mind, Phaedra kissed him goodbye and returned downstairs. She resolved to learn a bit more about Mr. Farrar. Do a deep online dive.

"Are you sure you don't need my help?" she asked her mother as she returned downstairs and headed for the door.

"Positive. The new hire will be here any minute. Go, relax. Enjoy your time off."

"How dare you!"

Startled, Phaedra came to an abrupt stop on the sidewalk in front of Brennan's bakery. Several shopping bags dangled from her wrists after a morning spent hunting down Christmas presents.

She'd found a gift for everyone on her list but Mark. Her feet ached and she was hungry.

And now this.

"Excuse me?" Her words were measured, polite.

Kate Brennan, hair scraped back and a scowl on her face, rested her hands on her generous hips. "Don't play innocent with me, Professor Brighton. Moira says you've been asking questions about me. Insinuating I had something to do with that poor girl's death. I repeat: How. Dare. You!"

Passersby slowed their steps and a few necks craned as people glanced over their shoulders, avidly curious. Phaedra drew in a calming breath before she spoke.

"Mrs. Brennan, I assure you, I questioned several other shop owners. I only want to figure out who might've poisoned that cupcake."

She snorted. "By hinting that *I* had something to do with it? Because I have a cigarette out back now and then?"

"I'm just examining every possibility—"

"You're not a police officer! You have no right poking your nose into my affairs, questioning my daughter. Any questions you have, you ask *me*, do you understand?"

"Mrs. Brennan—"

"I came over when I saw everyone outside, to see what all the fuss was. I was curious. Then the fire trucks came, and I left. That's all."

"But that's not all," Phaedra countered. "One of my colleagues saw you come in afterward and take a couple of photos of the menu board with your phone."

"Maybe your *colleague* is mistaken."

"Your name is first on the list that Officer Scott drew up. You were there, Mrs. Brennan. Shall I pull up the photo of the list I took and stored on my phone?"

"Even if I was there," Kate challenged, her face turning red, "there's no law against taking a picture."

"What seems to be the problem here?"

Phaedra looked up to see Detective Morelli approaching. He was wearing jeans, boots, and a gray sweater under his army-green jacket. His manner was relaxed, but his eyes were watchful as he glanced between the two women.

"Okay. Who wants to go first?" he asked.

"I will. This woman," Kate spat as she glared at Phaedra, "acts like she's wearing a badge. She came into my place of business and asked a lot of nosy questions."

Morelli sighed. "That true?" he asked Phaedra.

"I asked her daughter a couple of questions last week, yes. But they were general questions."

"About what?"

Before she could answer, Kate jumped in. "Moira—that's my daughter—told her I go out back to have a cigarette now and then."

"Moira volunteered that information," Phaedra pointed out. "I asked her where you were, and if the bakery was busy last Saturday. That's all."

"You were fishing for information." Kate turned back to Morelli. "The professor wanted to know if I was out back smoking on the morning her sister's customer was poisoned. As if she thinks I'm a suspect. Or a common criminal."

"I can assure you, Mrs. Brennan, you're not a suspect." He scrubbed a hand through his hair and turned to Phaedra. "Professor Brighton, as a civilian, you have no authority to question this woman. Or anyone. That's my job. Got it?"

"I was only gathering information."

"On what? My smoking habits?" Kate snapped.

"Professor," the detective said, his words patient but firm, "I think you should apologize to Mrs. Brennan and assure her that this won't happen again."

"What? But I was only . . ."

His eyes narrowed.

"Fine," she said, and squared her shoulders. "I apologize if I overstepped my bounds, Mrs. Brennan. I certainly didn't mean to upset you. I hope you can forgive me."

In answer, Kate Brennan shot her a venomous glare, marched back inside the bakery, and slammed the door.

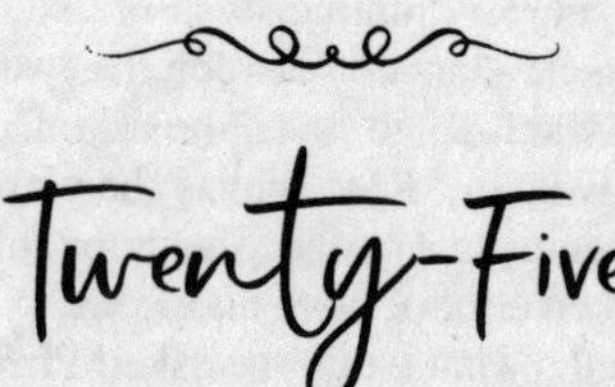

Twenty-Five

That went well," Morelli observed.

Phaedra sighed. "Sorry you had to get involved."

"I am, too. A good way to keep me from getting involved in future is to steer clear of Mrs. Brennan and her daughter."

"Trust me, I will. I try to avoid that woman at all costs." Her fingers tightened on the handles of her shopping bags as she resumed walking. "Although, just for the record, she accosted me. Not the other way around."

"Noted." He fell into step beside her and eyed her assortment of bags. "Christmas shopping?"

"All morning. I'm nearly finished." All except for one present—Mark's. Which was proving far more difficult to choose than she'd ever imagined.

"Buy you a coffee? I have a feeling you could use it."

She nodded. As they made their way to the Coffee Stop, passing kids and holiday shoppers laden with bags, she slanted him a glance. "Do you have information? Has the toxicology report come back?"

"Not yet. Sometimes," he added, lifting his brow, "a cup of coffee is just a cup of coffee. You in?"

"I'm in."

When they were seated by the window with two thick white cups of coffee in front of them, she shrugged off her coat. "At least the Poison Pen is open again. Which is a relief. I take it the police didn't find anything?"

"Not a thing. Nobody noticed anything unusual, no prints, no clue who might've left those chocolates."

Phaedra stirred a packet of sweetener into her coffee. "I'm afraid for my family," she admitted, the calmness of her words belying her unease. "This person, this poisoner, is like a ghost. A very clever ghost. Floating in and out, leaving no trace. No clues. No apparent motive."

"This is no ghost. We're dealing with a real flesh-and-blood person. Which means that whoever it is, no matter how clever they are—or *think* they are—they'll make a mistake." His jaw tensed, eased. "In the meantime, we need evidence. And sooner or later, we'll get it."

"What do you know about Michael Farrar?"

He poured cream into his cup. "The art gallery owner? Not much. Why?"

She told him about her father's painting, and Michael's assertion that it was a minor work of little value. "He's restoring it for Dad. But according to a local historian, if it proves to be a previously unknown work by James Brighton, it could be worth a great deal."

"You're talking to the wrong guy. I don't know much—correction, anything—about art. Have you researched its provenance online?"

"I have." She tapped her fingernail against the saucer. "There's no mention of Dad's painting anywhere. Which seems to confirm Michael's opinion that it's a minor work of no importance."

"But you don't believe it. Because now you have reason to doubt his word."

"Well, yes. Even if the painting was minor, wouldn't it be referenced somewhere? Mentioned in an old letter or a bill of sale, or displayed in a gallery, once upon a time?"

"Maybe. Maybe not. You're talking about, what? Over a hundred years ago?"

"Late nineteenth century so, yes, a hundred and twenty-five years ago, give or take. Even so, James Brighton was a well-known artist," she pointed out. "There would've been a record, a reference to the work somewhere."

"Seems likely," he agreed.

"According to Mrs. Bavier, it's rumored that he completed the work during his honeymoon in Siena. But no one's ever seen it. Dad's painting is a view of the Piazza del Campo, in Siena. Signed by the artist."

"Her information certainly throws an interesting light on things." He signaled the waitress for the check. "Have you mentioned any of this to your father?"

"He brushed it off. Says Michael is a savvy businessman looking to make a profit—which I believe—and he may not realize the painting's worth. Which I don't believe." She took a last sip of her coffee. "It makes me wonder what else he might be lying about."

After promising to keep Phaedra apprised of the toxicology findings on the chocolates, the detective left. She reached her car and began thrusting shopping bags onto the back seat when she heard her name called.

Marisol emerged from the Farrar Gallery and hurried over. Under her white faux-fur coat, she wore a vintage Pucci print dress and knee-high black boots. Her eyes sparkled, and her face glowed with happiness.

"I won't ask how your day with Michael went yesterday," Phaedra said as she closed the car door. "I can see it written all over your face."

"It was perfect. Absolutely perfect." Her blush deepened. "We had the best time. Michael's nothing like the guys I usually date. He's intelligent and well-spoken. Thoughtful. He even knows how to read a wine list."

"I'm glad you had a good time. He sounds like a keeper." Which made Phaedra feel all the more guilty for suspecting him of . . . what, exactly? Deceiving her father? Lying about the value of a painting that might—or might not—be worth anything?

In the face of Marisol's exuberant happiness, she wondered if perhaps she wasn't overreacting. Doing Michael a disservice.

After all, the painting wasn't yet confirmed to be a work by James Brighton. Maybe her father's family lore—the artist's honeymoon in Siena, the painting of the Plaza del Campo he gave to his wife, his father's eventual inheritance of the work—was nothing more than a story. Family folklore, embellished and exaggerated over the years.

Maybe Michael truly believed the work was of little value. And perhaps he was right.

"He's been working on your dad's painting," Marisol was saying. "In his studio at the gallery. I wanted to take a peek, but he won't let me. He's very protective of his restoration work. His work space is strictly off-limits."

"Even to you?" she teased. "His main squeeze?"

She blushed. "I'm hardly that."

Phaedra shoved the last bag onto the back seat and locked the car. "Have you had lunch yet?"

"No. We're having a late dinner. After the gallery closes."

"How about a glass of chilled white Burgundy and a portobello mushroom burger at Harper's Pub in the meantime? My treat."

"Ooh, that sounds amazing. You're on."

An hour later, Phaedra touched the heavy cloth napkin to her lips and leaned back in their booth overlooking Main Street. "I can't eat one more bite."

She wasn't a vegetarian, Marisol was, and she'd suggested Harper's because of their meatless options. But after trying the portobello burger, Phaedra had to admit it was delicious. Meaty, juicy, a little salty . . . heaven on a bun. And she'd eaten nearly all of it.

"Another glass, ladies?" the waiter, Jared's older brother, asked.

"Yes, please," Marisol piped up.

Phaedra hesitated. "I really shouldn't."

"Oh, come on, live a little. You've got all of your Christmas shopping done, which is more than I can say."

"Everyone except for Mark."

"You'll figure out what to get him. I know you will."

"It's tricky," Phaedra admitted. "Choosing a gift for someone you're seeing is a thorny prospect. I mean, we like each other. A lot. But I'm not sure what we are to each other yet. If that makes any sense."

"It makes perfect sense. You don't want to give him something too personal," she said with a knowing nod, "but you don't want to give him something impersonal, either."

"Exactly."

As they finished their wine, the waiter appeared and left the check. "No hurry," he assured them as he departed.

Phaedra reached for the leather folder, but Marisol grabbed it first. "I've got this," she said as she slid her credit card into the slot. "After all, I practically forced you to try a meatless burger."

"And I'm glad I did. It was delicious. But lunch is supposed to be my treat."

"Next time. And you can bet I'll make sure we go somewhere much more expensive." Marisol excused herself to go and visit the restroom.

Phaedra took out her phone and decided to do a quick online reconnaissance on Michael Farrar.

She located the Farrar Gallery website and clicked on the link, revealing a photo of the gallery's exterior, several interior shots, as well as a listing of current works for sale. There were recent photos of Michael and his staff, each photograph accompanied by a potted biography.

Although she searched further, she found nothing else. Only an Instagram account for @FarrarArt with a few photos of the recent showing for Colette Parrish.

"Hashtag, zilch," Phaedra muttered, and put her phone away. Either Michael was publicity shy or he was determined to live his life off the social media grid.

Hard to do this day and age.

She drew her brows together. What did she know about him? He was handsome, a successful business owner, and knowledgeable about art. He'd charmed Marisol and lied to her father. Yet he didn't exist. At least, not online.

Who *was* Michael Farrar, exactly?

Twenty-Six

As she pondered the question, Phaedra rested her chin on her hand and gazed out the window. The sky, so clear and windswept this morning, had given way to clouds. Across the street, a gust of wind ruffled the apothecary shop's awnings. She heard the short, sharp blast of a car horn.

The light on the corner changed from yellow to red, and the traffic slowed. And that's when she saw it. A dark green convertible Triumph TR5, license "ET2BRUT," idling at the light. Mark's car.

A smile warmed her face. He must be on his way to the airport for his evening flight back to London.

Just as well, she supposed, that she hadn't yet chosen a gift for him. They couldn't exchange presents until he returned.

With a pang as sharp as it was unexpected, she realized how much she'd miss him. She'd grown used to his boyish grin and the Shakespearean quotes that peppered his conversation like a sort of Elizabethan spice. She'd even grown accustomed to his striped scarf.

The stoplight changed, and the Triumph surged forward

and rounded the corner, headed for 250 East, and Charlottesville. Her smile faded.

She pressed her palm against the window in an unseen goodbye and wished she was going with him to England.

"Ready?" Marisol returned and paid the bill.

Phaedra nodded and slid out of the booth. "Thanks for lunch. I'll never make fun of meatless burgers again."

Returning to the Mini after Marisol departed, she slid behind the wheel and started the engine. Wreaths hung on most of the shop doors, and shoppers crowded the sidewalks. Woofgang's Gourmet Doggy Bakery, Bascom's Jewelers, Brennan's bakery, and the Poison Pen were all inundated with shoppers.

Looked like she wasn't the only one who'd left her holiday shopping to the last minute.

As she waited for an opening to ease out into the stream of traffic, her gaze strayed across the street to the Poison Pen.

A shiver chased through her. And not just because the car hadn't yet warmed up. Someone had left a box of candy on the counter for her parents and signed the card with Hannah's name. Someone who definitely wasn't her sister.

Who, then? Had whoever put cyanide on the cupcake at Hannah's grand opening also poisoned those chocolates? Why else would they leave a gift under such mysterious circumstances?

And if the candy was poisoned, did that mean the cupcake was intended for her father, not Anna?

Stop, she admonished herself. Maybe the chocolates were just . . . chocolates. But she couldn't help worrying, just a little.

She wouldn't stop worrying until Anna Steele's killer was caught.

The door opened, and a young woman emerged, thrusting a pair of oversize sunglasses on her face as she hurried down the steps to the sidewalk. Dark pixie haircut. Slim.

Although she wore jeans, flats, and a bomber jacket, not the pencil skirt and boots she remembered from the gallery, Phaedra recognized her at once.

Michael Farrar's assistant. Amelie.

She carried no bags, held no books pressed against her chest. Window-shopping, probably. Taking a break before she returned to the gallery.

A minivan stopped behind her and gave a short toot of its horn. The driver waved her out. Parking was at a premium, and he wanted her spot. Phaedra waved back and eased out, more than ready to head home and call it a day.

It was late afternoon when she arrived at the carriage house. Hannah wasn't home from the patisserie, and Phaedra took advantage of her absence to stash the gifts—including her sister's—on the top shelf of her closet.

Wickham jumped down from his spot on her bed and followed her downstairs, meowing impatiently to be let out. *What to make for dinner?* she wondered as she opened the back door and watched him dart outside.

Something easy, she decided, and took a box of lasagna out of the freezer. She'd just opened the fridge to forage for salad ingredients when her phone rang.

"Mark," she said, her lips relaxing into a smile. "Hi. Are you at the airport?"

"I arrived an hour ago. Total madness," he grumbled.

"I saw you. I was having lunch at Harper's when your car stopped at the light."

"I wish I was there. Better yet, I wish you were here. Not waiting in line to get through security, of course," he added, and sighed. "But here. With me." He lowered his voice. "I miss you."

"I miss you, too." This should've been their first Christmas together. She swallowed the sharp taste of disappointment. "Is your flight leaving on time?"

"According to the board, yes. Phaedra . . . I'm sorry for taking off so suddenly. My mother's been feeling a bit down. It's her first—*our* first—Christmas without Gram."

"It's okay. Please don't apologize. I'm glad you're spending the holidays with her. She needs you."

"Thanks for understanding. I'll be back in three weeks. Perhaps then—" He muttered under his breath. "Sorry, I have to go. I'm about to head through security. Promise me you won't get into any trouble while I'm away."

"Trouble?" she asked, feigning ignorance.

"You know what I mean. Leave it to the police."

"I'll stay home and drink hot chocolate," she promised. "Watch *Holiday Inn* on TV."

"Good. It's just . . ." His voice softened. "I worry about you, Phaedra. I couldn't bear it if you got hurt. Take care."

"You, too. Have a safe trip."

Her heart sank to her toes as he ended the call. She felt his absence keenly and his plane hadn't even left the runway yet.

The phone rang again. Mark!

"I miss you like blazes," she said, her words a breathless rush as she answered the call.

But it wasn't Mark on the other end. She knew, because there was a long pause.

"Professor Brighton? This is Detective Morelli. I have the results of the toxicology report for the chocolates left at the Poison Pen."

She groped for one of the high-backed seats at the island and sat down. "Oh. Sorry. Go on."

"The pathologist, Dr. Kessler, found a small puncture in the lid of the box. Like one left by a syringe."

"A syringe." Her knees began to tremble and she pressed them together. "Are you saying someone injected those chocolates?"

"Someone injected *one* chocolate. A piece in the middle of the box, to be exact. Hazelnut crunch. None of the other chocolates were tampered with."

Hazelnut crunch. Her father's favorite. The piece he'd been about to pop in his mouth before she stopped him.

"What . . . what was it injected with?" she asked, both wanting and dreading the answer.

"Aconite. A substance derived from wolfsbane, also known as monkshood. It's—"

"A perennial herb native to mountainous areas," Phaedra said slowly. "And a highly toxic poison."

"You're familiar with it?" Morelli couldn't quite keep a note of surprise from his voice.

"Only from a scholarly standpoint. Some historians theorize that Socrates wasn't poisoned with hemlock, but an extract of *Aconitum nappellus.* The Greeks used it to poison arrowheads. The flowers are a beautiful purple-blue. But the roots and leaves are highly toxic if ingested."

"Resulting in heart arrythmia and, if untreated, respiratory paralysis. And there's no specific antidote." He paused. "Your father's very, very lucky you were there when he opened those chocolates."

"You know what doesn't make any sense, though?"

He waited.

"Why poison only one chocolate? Why not poison the entire box?"

"Your guess is as good as mine. Maybe there wasn't enough time. Or maybe there wasn't enough of the toxin."

"It's just so . . . random." Phaedra got up and began to pace around the kitchen island. "Almost like someone's playing a kind of sick game." She came to an abrupt stop. "And why inject that particular piece? How could the killer have known that hazelnut crunch is Dad's favorite?"

"Either he or she knows your father pretty well," Morelli said, "or they found out some other way. Is it common knowledge, his fondness for that particular type of candy?"

"No, not really. I mean, I know about it, and Hannah and Mom do, and Wendy. No one else."

"None of his customers? A neighbor, maybe?"

"No. No one that I know of."

"Okay." His chair creaked as he leaned forward. "I'll let you know if I learn anything else."

She thanked him and ended the call. And gripped her hands together to keep them from trembling.

Someone had tried to kill her father using the same method they'd used to kill Anna Steele. Poison. This time, thankfully, they didn't succeed.

But the next time, her dad might not be so lucky.

Twenty-Seven

I'm calling an emergency meeting of the Tea Society," Phaedra said as she ushered Marisol and Lucy inside the carriage house the next morning and took their coats.

"Is that why we're here?" Lucy asked as she handed over her quilted parka. "You said it was urgent."

"It is. Come into the kitchen and I'll explain. Tea or coffee? I have both. And croissants."

Everyone agreed that coffee was definitely required.

They followed her and slid onto seats at the island as she took down mugs and poured the coffee.

"Hannah's?" Marisol asked as she eyed the plate of flaky, buttery pastries.

"Baked this morning," Phaedra confirmed. "She dropped them off a few minutes ago. Dig in."

"Why the sudden urgency for a meeting?" Lucy asked as she chose a croissant and dropped it onto her plate. "Is there a new development in the case?"

"There is." She sat down across from them and reached for her mug. "Detective Morelli called yesterday afternoon. The toxicology report came back on the chocolates left at the bookstore."

"And?" Marisol leaned forward. "Were they poisoned?"

"Yes. But only one piece was tampered with."

"Only one?" Lucy frowned. "How'd they manage that? I thought the box was gift-wrapped. Unopened."

"It was. This is where it gets weird."

"*Gets* weird?" Marisol echoed. "This whole thing is weird."

"The pathologist noticed a tiny puncture in the lid of the box, under the ribbon. Someone injected the box—and one of the chocolates—with Aconitum. A deadly toxin."

"Monkshood," Lucy said slowly, and nodded. "It's used in Chinese herbal preparations to treat joint or muscle pain. In small amounts it's considered therapeutic. Too much, though, and you die." She grimaced. "The line between therapeutic and lethal is razor-thin."

"Strange that only one chocolate was poisoned," Marisol ventured.

"I thought so, too," Phaedra said. "Why not open the box and inject every piece? I guess they didn't want anyone to suspect the box had been tampered with."

"It's obvious, to me, at least. Whoever did this is the same person who poisoned Anna's cupcake," Marisol said.

"Not necessarily," Lucy replied. "It's been written about in the papers and bandied around on social media enough. Could be a copycat. Someone who decided to emulate the poisoner."

Phaedra shook her head. "Why would anyone do that?"

"For attention? Notoriety? Who knows?"

"Both culprits used poison," Marisol pointed out.

"Two different kinds, though," Phaedra said. "Potassium cyanide and Aconitum. Granules in the first instance, and a liquid extraction in the second."

"Either way, one culprit or two," Lucy said, "we're dealing with someone who knows their poisons."

"Okay. Let's write down what we know." Phaedra grabbed a legal pad and a pen.

For several moments they were silent, wiping buttery crumbs from their fingers as she listed the facts on paper.

"Only one chocolate was poisoned," Phaedra said as she wrote. "No one saw the culprit leave the box on the counter. Whoever left it signed Hannah's name on the card. And we know Hannah did *not* leave those chocolates. Just like we know she didn't tamper with Anna's cupcake."

"You mean, *your* cupcake," Marisol pointed out. "She brought it out to you."

"She brought it out for me and Dad to share."

"Okay," Lucy stated, "we're dealing with someone who's knowledgeable about cyanide and Aconitum. Someone with access to those poisons. Who would have access?"

"A florist?" Marisol suggested. "Monkshood, wolfsbane, blue rocket—whatever name you call it, it's a flower, right? Maybe it's used in flower arrangements."

"Why would a florist use a highly toxic plant in a floral arrangement?" Lucy scoffed.

"It's still worth checking into," Phaedra said. "I agree, it's unlikely, but we could ask about recent local bouquet orders. Find out what specific flowers were used in each one."

"I'll check with Millie's Florists," Marisol offered. "Maybe they can give us a list. And they sell Chiles Chocolates, too."

"I doubt they'll give out customers' names," Lucy said.

Marisol glared at her. "Do you have a better idea?"

"I hate to even suggest this," Phaedra admitted as she laid her pen aside, "because I don't for a minute suspect them, but . . . the Bondurant sisters sell herbal remedies and tinctures. They also sell gardening stuff. Weed killers and rat poison. And they carry Chiles Chocolates.

"There's one more thing," she added, her expression troubled. "Rebecca stopped by the Poison Pen the other day. She bought a book by Ellis Peters."

"So?" Marisol asked.

"Ellis Peters," Lucy said. "Pen name Edith Pargeter. She wrote a bunch of murder mysteries with that twelfth-century monk. What's his name—"

"Brother Cadfael." Phaedra nodded. "The book Rebecca bought was *Monk's Hood*."

"I haven't read it, but I'm assuming it must be a play on words, if it's a murder mystery."

"Right. Brother Cadfael is an herbalist as well as a monk, and he makes monkshood oil to relieve joint pain. In the book, it's stolen from his stores and used to poison someone."

"Kind of an odd coincidence that Rebecca checked that particular book out and right before the second poisoning," Marisol agreed. "Unless it really *is* just a coincidence."

"If you're right," Lucy said, "Rebecca would have to know how to extract the poison. She'd need a syringe, and a rudimentary knowledge of chemistry. Wouldn't she?"

"I'd think so." Phaedra added, "She may or may not have access to syringes. I know Biddy has to watch her sugar intake, but as far as I know she isn't diabetic."

"I'll stop by the florist's and talk to Millie later," Marisol said. "I need to order flowers for someone."

"Oh?" Lucy's eyebrow shot skyward. "Who, I wonder?"

Marisol's cheeks turned pink, but she didn't answer.

"And I'll stop by the apothecary," Phaedra decided, "and talk to Rebecca. See what I can find out. Discreetly, of course."

Heaven knew, she didn't want to get on the wrong side of Rebecca Bondurant again. Or Detective Morelli, for that matter. He'd made no secret of his feelings on her involvement in the investigation.

"Thanks for breakfast." Lucy stood up and put her mug in the sink. "My compliments to Hannah. I'll head over to the bookstore, see if anyone noticed anything."

"Detective Morelli and Officer Scott have already questioned everyone who was there," Phaedra pointed out. "Nobody—including Mom and Dad—saw anything."

She shrugged and reached for her coat. "You never know. Maybe someone will remember something. Can't hurt to ask around."

"I suppose not."

"See you both later." And she was gone.

Marisol grabbed her coat and shrugged it on, tucking her long hair under a woolen cap. "Thanks for the coffee."

"You're welcome. And thanks for your help."

"What help? I haven't done anything."

"Don't be so modest. Suggesting we visit the florist to find out who ordered bouquets lately was good thinking."

"Lucy's right, it's probably a waste of time. Toxic flowers in a floral arrangement? But I'll let you know what I find out," Marisol promised. At the door, she put her hand on the knob and hesitated.

"Is there something else?" Phaedra asked.

"I didn't want to say anything in front of Lucy," she admitted, "because it doesn't really concern her. But it concerns you. And your dad's painting."

"Oh?"

"I had dinner at Michael's last night. He has a really nice apartment upstairs."

"I bet. Is he a good cook? Or did you skip dinner?"

Marisol blushed. "He made steak and baked potatoes, and when I told him I'm a vegetarian, he was super apologetic. I said it was no big deal and ate the salad and a potato."

"Well, you're still getting to know each other. These things take time."

"True. But I've mentioned it before, and we've been to dinner a few times now. I guess he didn't remember. Or he wasn't listening."

"He's a guy," Phaedra said, and shrugged. "You just have to be patient."

"I guess." She didn't look convinced. "I asked him how the restoration work was coming along on the painting. He said it's going well, and then he asked me if I wanted more wine." She knitted her brows together. "Whenever I bring up the subject, he becomes evasive. Or changes it altogether."

"Maybe he's not comfortable discussing it."

"Why, though? Why won't he let me see it? It's almost like he's being secretive. Like he's hiding something."

"That *is* a little strange," Phaedra admitted. "I think I'll stop by and ask him to let me take a look. Maybe he's waiting until it's finished . . . or maybe he hasn't even started to work on it yet."

"You know what? Leave it to me." Marisol opened the door. "Next time I'm at the gallery, I'll have a quick snoop around his workroom. The painting is on an easel, covered up. I'll take a little peek."

"Not a good idea. What if he catches you?"

"Oh, you know me," she said airily. "I'll just sweet-talk my way out of it." She reshouldered her purse. "See you later. I'll let you know what I find out at Millie's Florist."

Watch. Purse. Phone. Keys.

Phaedra placed each item into the small plastic bin an hour later and watched it move down the conveyor and through the courthouse complex's screening equipment.

No reticule this time, no historically correct gown or cloak; she wore jeans and a sweater under a wool overcoat, and low-heeled boots.

This time, she meant business.

Stepping through the metal detector and receiving the all-clear, she retrieved her personal items and headed across the lobby, and turned right at the elevators.

Her phone rang. "Marisol? Hi. What's up?"

"I just left the florist's. I won't have time this afternoon, since Michael and I have plans later, so—"

"Did you learn anything?" Phaedra interjected.

"Not really. Lucy was right. They don't use monkshood in floral arrangements. Too toxic to handle. And they wouldn't give out any customer information. Sorry."

"It's okay. Thanks for trying."

"I'll see if I can take a look around Michael's workroom

later. He's closing early, and I'm meeting him at the gallery before we go out to dinner. If nothing else, I can update you on his progress on the restoration."

"Sounds good. Just be careful, okay?"

Marisol promised she would and ended the call.

As Phaedra neared Detective Morelli's office at the end of the hall, she slowed her steps. Someone was already paying the detective a visit. And judging from the volume of the visitor's voice, it wasn't a social call.

". . . pressure from my constituents, which means pressure on me," Sheriff Dobbs growled. "And you know how much I love pressure. Almost as much as I love unsolved cases."

"Understood, sir," Morelli replied evenly. "We're getting close to an arrest, but the evidence isn't there yet. At the moment it's all circumstantial. But we'll keep pushing."

"I don't want excuses, Detective. I want a conviction. Sooner, rather than later. Do you understand me?"

"Yes, sir."

Dobbs strode out of the office, red-faced and jowls quivering. He spared Phaedra a tight nod as he brushed past her and stalked down the corridor.

She was about to enter Morelli's office when a female captain hurried in, a folder in hand.

"I need your signature on these, Detective."

Phaedra waited until he'd signed the requested forms and the captain departed before peering inside. "Bad time?"

Morelli glanced up. "It's always a bad time. Come in." He gestured her inside. "What can I do for you, Professor?"

"I have a favor to ask."

"Why am I not surprised? Have a seat." He dropped his pen on the blotter and regarded her wearily. "What can I help you with?"

"I've been doing a little online research," she began. "Nothing major; I'm just looking for some basic information on someone."

"Uh-huh. And who is this lucky someone?"

She hesitated. "Michael Farrar."

"The art gallery guy? The one you suspect of misrepresenting the value of your father's painting."

"Yes. As I said, there's no record of the painting anywhere online. Which may or may not mean anything." She paused and leaned forward. "But there's no record of Mr. Farrar online, either."

"None at all?" Morelli was plainly skeptical.

"Not much. His gallery's represented with a couple of social media accounts. There's plenty of generic information about the paintings for sale, upcoming showings, that sort of thing. But nothing personal."

"No website?"

"There's a gallery website, yes. It has photos of Michael and his staff, with brief bios. Not much else."

He shrugged. "Not everyone lives their lives online."

"I agree. I'm one of them. But this guy . . . he's like a cyber ghost. He doesn't exist."

"And I'm guessing," Morelli said, leaning back in his chair, "that you're about to ask me to use police resources to check into Farrar's background."

"Well . . ."

"Come on, Professor. You know I can't do that. Not without probable cause."

"But there must be a way—"

"I don't even have a reasonable suspicion. Farrar's done nothing to justify an investigation. Other than maybe, possibly, lying about the value of a painting that may, or may not, be worth a decent chunk of change. Which in and of itself isn't a crime. Does that about sum it up?"

Phaedra didn't answer. How could she refute him when he was right?

"Now, if you'll excuse me, Professor Brighton," he added as he reached for a folder, "I have work to do."

She rose and shouldered her purse. "Thank you for your time. Sorry to bother you."

His chair creaked. "Phaedra, wait."

She paused by the door. “Yes?” she asked stiffly.

“It’s not that I don’t want to help you.” He tapped his finger against the blotter. “I’ll do whatever I can for you and your sister and your father, you know that. But I can’t do a deep dive on Farrar without just cause. I won’t put my job at risk. As much as I’d like to pack it in right now and spend my days sitting at a tiki bar in Maui with a drink in my hand, I can’t do that just yet. Bring me something compelling enough to justify a search through NCIC or the DMV database and then we’ll talk.”

“Fine.” She pressed her lips into a determined line. “Then that’s what I’ll do. Thanks, Detective. And have a good day.”

Twenty-Eight

Phaedra left the county courthouse complex and glanced at her watch. It was nearly eleven o'clock and she had one more stop to make before she returned home.

It might be a waste of time, but she wanted to drop by Scents and Sensibility and take a closer look at the Bondurant sisters' herbal concoctions.

She knew most of the items they sold at the apothecary—things like evening primrose oil, ginseng, chamomile, Saint-John's-wort—were available online or in drug or natural food stores. Rebecca also created her own herbal tea blends and infusions.

Did any of those concoctions, she wondered, contain a poisonous ingredient? Aconite, for instance? Lucy had mentioned that Chinese herbal preparations, those created to relieve joint and muscle pain, contained small amounts of the substance.

Phaedra unlocked her car and slid behind the wheel. Did Rebecca and her sister unknowingly carry something similar to those Chinese preparations on their shelves? Something with deadly potential if it fell into an ill-intentioned person's hands?

She backed out of the parking spot and headed to Laurel Springs. First, she decided, she'd read labels. Look for any potentially dangerous or questionable ingredients. Have a chat with a few of the other customers in the shop.

More important, she'd try to find some answers to her growing list of questions.

So far, Phaedra's foray into herbal espionage had yielded nothing useful. Nada. Zilch.

She thrust on her reading glasses and frowned as she studied various herbal remedies, supplements, lozenges, and oils on the Bondurant sisters' apothecary shelves.

All were unremarkable, with not a single poisonous ingredient to be found. Although the labels carried the usual warnings to pregnant women, children, and those taking certain medications, none were inherently dangerous in and of themselves.

As to their actual usefulness, she remained unconvinced. Although Hannah swore by her daily cranberry supplement, and although they both drank herbal tea infusions such as hibiscus and elderberry, Phaedra believed in doing her due diligence before consuming any unregulated or off-the-shelf herbal remedy.

"Are you thinking of trying the gingko biloba?"

She looked up to see a young, pregnant woman in a pale blue parka with a dark auburn braid over one shoulder, eyeing the bottle in her hand. "I'm just reading labels."

"It's good for the memory. Or so I hear."

"Oh? Do you use it?"

"My mom does. That's why I'm here." She brandished a bottle. "I take echinacea sometimes, though. And the zinc lozenges when I have a cold. They really work."

"Good to know. Thanks."

"Can I help either of you ladies?"

Rebecca Bondurant came around the counter, her lips turned up in a smile of polite inquiry.

"I'm good," Phaedra said. "Just checking out your herbal remedies."

"Anything in particular? Herbs can help address a number of issues. Anything from memory loss and sleep issues, to strengthening a weak immune system."

"Just browsing at the moment."

"I'm ready to pay for this, please." The young woman gave Phaedra a nod and followed Rebecca to the register.

When the woman left, Phaedra approached the counter and set down a metal container of zinc lozenges.

Rebecca slid the tin forward. "Will this be all, Professor?"

"That's it." She took out a five-dollar bill and handed it over. As she waited for the elderly woman to make change, she asked, "How are you liking the book? Have you started reading it yet?"

"Book?" She eyed Phaedra in bafflement as she pressed two dollars into her outstretched palm. "What book?"

"The Ellis Peters mystery you bought at the Poison Pen on Monday. *Monk's Hood.* I rang you up. Are you enjoying it?"

"Oh, that. I'd nearly forgotten." She glanced up the stairs. "I bought it for Biddy," she confided in a low voice. "A Christmas present. She loves murder mysteries. I prefer nonfiction, myself."

"Well, you made an excellent choice for your sister. I'm sure she'll love it."

"I certainly hope so. Now, I apologize for rushing you out the door," Rebecca added as she rounded the counter and followed her to the front, sounding not the least bit sorry, "but we're about to close for lunch."

"Oh." Phaedra regarded her in puzzlement. "I thought your shop stayed open all day."

"New hours. We reopen at one. Now, thank you for your purchase. Goodbye."

"Goodbye." She returned her reading glasses to her purse, thanked Rebecca, and went out the door. Ms. Bondurant locked it behind her and flipped the sign from "OPEN" to "CLOSED."

Another dead end.

Thrusting the small bag of lozenges into her coat pocket, she left her car at the curb and decided to walk to the Poison Pen. It wasn't far and the day was bitingly cold, but clear.

Perhaps Lucy had learned something of interest at the bookstore, something the police had overlooked. She could say hello to Mom and Dad and make sure no more mysterious boxes of candy had turned up.

As she drew nearer to Brennan's bakery, Phaedra's steps quickened. She had no wish to cross paths with Kate Brennan again.

Or ever, for that matter.

She risked a quick glance at the bakery's old-fashioned bow window. Fake snow frosted the corners of each pane, and a drift of glistening white "snow" showcased pedestals of varying heights displaying cakes decorated for Christmas. Buttercream poinsettias, fondant holly leaves and berries, and marzipan Santas abounded.

Her steps slowed. Not to admire the cakes or the frosted sugar plum cookies dangling from red and green ribbons above them, but to peer inside.

A police deputy stood at the display counter, questioning Moira. What was going on?

Curiosity won out over her desire to avoid Kate, and Phaedra headed for the entrance. Just as her fingers closed over the door handle, a Somerset County police SUV sped past, light bar flashing, followed closely by a sheriff's car. Both came to a stop in front of the Poison Pen.

Seized with panicked dread, Phaedra abandoned all thoughts of Brennan's and raced down the sidewalk to her father's bookstore. Had something happened? Had another lethal present been left on the counter?

As she drew closer, stomach knotted with worry, her steps slowed and her breathing returned to a semblance of normal. The police activity wasn't at the Poison Pen, but farther down, at the Farrar Gallery.

"What's going on?" she asked the first officer she saw.

"We had a report of an attempted breaking and entering at the art gallery," he replied. "Sorry, but you can't go in," he added, blocking her path as she moved to go around him.

"But my friend might be inside. Marisol Dubois? She's . . . she's the owner's girlfriend. Michael Farrar. Can you at least tell me if she—if they—are all right?"

"There are no reports of any injuries, ma'am. The gallery was closed at the time."

Relief made her shoulders sag. She thanked him and stepped back, craning her neck to peer around the deputy. A "CLOSED" sign hung in the gallery's door. Michael must have decided to lock up at noon and left to spend the rest of the day with Marisol.

She frowned. Mari had said they planned to meet at the gallery later in the afternoon and go out to dinner.

As she reached for her phone to call and check on her teaching assistant's whereabouts, it rang. "Marisol! I was about to call you. Are you okay? Where are you?"

"I'm fine. I'm with Michael. We were on our way to Crozet for lunch when he got a notification from his security system. The police just called and said someone tried to break into the gallery. Are you there now?"

"Yes. When I saw the police out front, I was worried about you. Both," she added.

"We're fine. And we're on our way. I'll see you soon."

A short time later, the Jaguar glided smoothly around the corner and slowed. Michael double-parked in front of the gallery and turned on the flashers.

"What's going on?" he demanded of the nearest officer as he slammed out of the car and strode toward the entrance. "Have you apprehended the thief? Is anything missing?"

"And you are?"

"Michael Farrar," he snapped, and reached for his wallet. "I own the gallery."

The deputy studied the driver's license Farrar gave him, then handed it back. "As far as we can tell, nothing is missing, sir," he replied. "But you'll need to come in with me and take a look."

As the two men disappeared through the front entrance, Michael without a backward glance, Marisol turned to Phaedra. Her face was pale and wan. "So much for our romantic afternoon."

"You must be disappointed. But at least you weren't inside the gallery when the break-in attempt happened."

"That's true." A delicate shiver passed over her. "Michael has a state-of-the-art security system installed. Cameras, motion detectors, the works. We knew the moment it happened. I'm just glad we weren't here."

"Me, too." At the sound of footsteps behind her, Phaedra turned to see Detective Morelli approaching.

He nodded briefly. "Professor."

"Detective." She met his gaze. "I hope everything's all right?"

He glanced at the gallery and back at her, his expression unreadable. "I'm sure you already know about the B and E attempt. Have you solved the case yet?"

"I saw the police cars and flashing lights," she said evenly. "When they stopped in front of the Poison Pen. I thought . . ." She drew in a breath. "I was afraid something had happened."

Understanding softened his expression. "Well, you can rest easy. As you can see, this has nothing to do with the bookstore. I spoke with your father earlier when he called to see if we'd learned anything more about the poisoned chocolate. He's fine."

Relief swept over her. "Thank you."

"You're welcome." He moved toward the door. "And, Professor?"

"Yes?"

"Just this once? Try to stay out of trouble."

Twenty-Nine

Would you like me to take you home?" Phaedra asked Marisol. "My car's just down the street. I imagine Michael will be dealing with the police for a while."

She shook her head. "I should probably stick around. They may want to question me."

While Phaedra doubted that would be the case, she didn't argue. "Let's sit down," she suggested, indicating an empty bench nearby. "I'll keep you company."

"Thanks. I'd like that."

"Any idea who might've tried to break in?" Phaedra asked as they sat down.

"None. Amelie and the rest of the staff are off for the holidays as of close of business yesterday."

"Do any of his staff know the security keypad code?"

"Only Amelie. And she's gone back home for the holidays."

"Where's that?"

"Montana, I think." She shrugged. "If you ask me, this attempt was random. It's nearly Christmas. Doesn't crime normally go up during the holidays?"

"It can," Phaedra agreed. "The thief probably hoped to grab a few paintings and sell them for quick cash."

"Selling stolen art isn't easy, though," Marisol said. "Especially the really valuable stuff. It's nearly impossible. They'd have to go through a fence or sell on the black market."

"Why bother, then?"

"Stolen paintings are portable currency. Criminals trade stolen artwork back and forth like . . . like baseball cards. In exchange for all sorts of unsavory things. Drugs, guns, a new identity—you name it."

"You seem to know a lot about the subject," Phaedra said, surprised by the extent of Marisol's knowledge.

"Only because I listen when Michael talks about that stuff. He has to stay current. That's why he has a top-of-the-line security system in place."

"He doesn't take any chances. I get it."

"Only a fraction of stolen artworks are ever recovered."

"Forgive my ignorance," Phaedra said, frowning, "but are any of the paintings in Michael's gallery actually worth that much? They're not museum-quality works, or priceless antiquities, or anything like that."

"No. But some are worth six figures. Not exactly millions, it's true, but not small potatoes, either."

The gallery's door swung open, and Michael emerged. He shrugged his arms into his coat and strode toward them.

"Professor Brighton. Hello."

"Phaedra, please. I'm sorry about all this." She glanced at the police cars still parked out front. "I hope nothing was stolen."

"Everything seems to be in place. I've provided an inventory list to Detective Morelli."

"That's good to hear. I'm sure you're relieved."

"Luckily, the break-in attempt failed. I've filed a report with the police nonetheless." He turned to Marisol and reached out to take her hand. "If you're still interested, let's go get that lunch I promised you."

She rose eagerly to her feet. "I'd love that."

He glanced at Phaedra. "Would you like to join us? The more the merrier, as they say."

"Thank you, but no. You two go and enjoy yourselves."

I may be many things, she thought, *but a third wheel isn't one of them.*

As she neared the Poison Pen, she glanced up the porch steps. A pair of dwarf blue spruce trees, each wrapped with strands of fake gumdrops and twinkling white lights, flanked the front doors. A steady stream of customers came in and out.

"Phaedra!"

The door opened and her mother, a cashmere sweater over her shoulders, waved her onto the porch. Despite her neatly coiffed hair and the casual elegance of her slacks-and-silk-blouse combo, she looked distraught. She twisted a strand of pearls at her neck with a troubled expression.

Once again, panic bubbled up inside her. "Mom. What is it? Is something wrong? Has something happened?"

"What? No. Other than being insanely busy, we're fine." Her glance went to the gallery. "What's going on over there?"

Relief mingled with annoyance as she realized her mother was being her usual dramatic, and overly nosy, self. "Someone tried to break in."

"Really?" Nan drew her perfectly groomed eyebrows together. "Odd we never heard an alarm go off. We're practically next door."

"It's a silent alarm. State of the art."

"Oh. Well, that's a good thing, I suppose. Still . . . poor Michael. He must be beside himself."

"Actually," Phaedra said, "he and Marisol just left for Crozet. They have lunch plans. He seemed fine. More annoyed than upset."

Which, she realized as she followed her mother inside the bookstore, was a little surprising. Wouldn't Michael want to postpone their lunch plans? Stick close to home, maybe re-inventory everything, just to ensure nothing was taken? Wouldn't he be more rattled?

"Hello, pumpkin," Malcolm greeted her from the display table he was arranging.

"Hi, Dad. Did you hear about the excitement at the gallery?"

"I heard the police were there. What happened?"

After filling him in on the details of the attempted break-in, and buying a few books—a new police procedural for Morelli, and a couple of murder mysteries for herself—she said her goodbyes and headed for the door.

"Phaedra, wait."

Her mother finished ringing up a customer and hurried after her. "We invited Mark's father to stop by for drinks on Christmas Eve. We're having an open house."

"Judge Selden? And did he accept?"

"He did. If you and Hannah want to join us—"

"Not sure if I can," Phaedra hedged. "Lots to do."

"Try to stop by, at least for one drink." Her mother paused. "Don't you want to meet your young man's father?"

"He isn't my young man. He's a colleague. A friend."

"But the two of you are seeing each other."

"Yes, we are. But we're not engaged."

"You're in an exclusive relationship," Nan persisted. "Aren't you?"

"I don't know. I suppose. We haven't really talked about it."

"Have you heard from Mark?"

She thought of the single text he'd sent early that morning. Arrived safely. Miss you already.

"Yes. He landed at Heathrow and said he'd be in touch once he got some sleep."

"Oh, Phaedra." Nan reached out a tentative hand and touched her arm. "You miss him, don't you? You really do care for him."

She nodded mutely. With a mumbled goodbye, she made her excuses and fled.

Once behind the wheel, she started the engine and turned on the radio. She needed music to chase away thoughts of how much she missed Mark. Singing along with Alvin and the Chipmunks or José Feliciano should do the trick.

Instead, "Please Come Home for Christmas" filled the car, not the original, but the plaintive, bluesy version by the Eagles. Normally she loved the song, loved belting out the lyrics.

But not right now.

She switched off the radio. Better silence than a sad Christmas song any day.

She pulled away from the curb and headed for the patisserie. She couldn't face going home to the carriage house yet. The empty rooms and half-decorated tree, the unmade sofa bed and Hannah's breakfast dishes piled in the sink, was more than she could bear right now.

As she rounded the corner opposite Church Street, she caught sight of Tout de Sweet and slowed down. A laurel wreath adorned the front door, glittering with tiny white lights. More lights bordered the front windows and doors.

But the centerpiece was a towering croquembouche in the window—individual choux puffs filled with pastry cream and laced together with spun caramel. Bûches de Noël, opera cakes, and macarons of palest pink, blue, and green, iced with snowflake designs, were scattered underneath the croquembouche like Christmas presents.

Hannah and her staff had outdone themselves.

"*Joyeux Noël*," her sister called out as Phaedra pushed her way thought the front door.

"*Joyeux Noël*, yourself. The window looks amazing. I love the croquembouche. It's stunning."

"It was a lot of work," Hannah admitted, "but worth every bit of effort. Come in the back and have a coffee. Liv? Will you watch the counter, please?"

"Sure thing."

After handing over a demitasse of espresso, Hannah headed to her office and shut the door. "I have news."

Phaedra took a cautious sip. "You and Charles have finally set a wedding date."

"Oh, please. Let's be realistic." She grinned. "Besides, this is even better."

"What could be better than your own wedding?"

"Rachel Brandon," she announced as she sat behind the desk, "asked me to cater her private New Year's Eve party."

"What? That's incredible! Oh, Hannah . . . I'm so happy for you." Phaedra set her cup down on the edge of the desk. "But I thought you were persona non grata with Rachel. The last time we spoke, she told me she'd nixed the interview."

"I know." Excitement bubbled just beneath the surface as Hannah leaned forward in her chair. "She's decided to give me another chance. A chance to prove myself—not to her, because she already believes in me—but to all the naysayers. And that's not all," she added. "If I pass the event with flying colors, she'll rethink my interview and feature me in her magazine."

"I know you'll do a great job. You always do."

Her smile deflated. "Right. Until someone eats one of my dark chocolate cupcakes. And dies."

"Oh, come on, Han," Phaedra reproved. "We've been over this a million times. What happened to Anna Steele was tragic, but it wasn't your fault. Everyone knows that. Including the police."

"They still haven't caught the culprit."

"No. But they will. Detective Morelli won't rest until he has a suspect in custody."

"I know." She lifted a troubled gaze. "But until he makes an arrest, in some people's minds, I'll remain guilty."

Thirty

Maybe it was the espresso, or maybe it was a desire to occupy her thoughts with something other than Mark Selden.

Whatever it was, when she got home, Phaedra buzzed with renewed energy. She refused to sit around and mope.

Wickham eyed her shopping bags from his bird-watching roost on the back of the sofa. *Got any Christmas catnip in those bags, perchance? No? Guess it's every cat for himself.*

He leaped down from the sofa in high dudgeon and made for the kitchen door. She let him out, rolled up her sleeves, and launched a strategic cleaning attack.

With the dirty dishes stashed in the dishwasher, the unmade sofa bed restored to order, and a handful of newly arrived Christmas cards added to the collection on the mantel, the carriage house once again felt like home.

Her phone bleeped with a text message, and her heart soared. Mark?

But it was from Hannah. Taking the staff to dinner at Sans Souci tonight. Probably be back late.

Have fun, Phaedra texted back. You deserve to celebrate! If you need a ride, call me.

Jared's our DD. No worries. x

Perfect, she decided as she put her phone aside. With Hannah out all evening, she could finally wrap presents. After gathering up tape, wrapping paper and scissors, and everything she'd bought, she poured a glass of chardonnay, put on some holiday music, and got to work.

Small things first. She began with the books. As she cut, snipped, taped, and wrapped, her thoughts wandered.

Who tried to break into the Farrar Gallery? Whoever it was, they'd made the attempt in broad daylight. A bold move. But Marisol said Michael's security system included cameras. Finding the culprit should be as simple as checking the footage.

She reached for another gift.

Amelie—she had no idea what her last name was—had an alibi. She'd gone back home to Montana, according to Marisol. Unless she hadn't.

Arthur Rouse, maybe? But she discarded the thought even as it occurred. As a parolee, his movements were closely monitored. He was required to check in regularly with his parole officer. And Morelli had said Rouse was determined to stay out of prison.

Besides, Rouse wasn't a burglar. Or an art thief.

Phaedra stuck a dark green bow on her book for Hannah and added it to the small, but growing, pile of wrapped gifts. She reached for her glass.

Who else?

She could strike Kate and Rebecca from the list of suspects. Both had been in their respective shops. Kate accosted her outside the bakery, and the eldest Bondurant sister rang up her zinc lozenges and mentioned that Biddy was upstairs.

But was she? Or had she crept downstairs and slipped out the back door?

Phaedra paused with the tape dispenser in hand. She hated to think it, to even consider it.

But Biddy Bondurant was the only person with a possible motive for breaking in. The painting.

The James Brighton painting, handed down to her grandfather, had eventually been given to his bride, Rose, as a wedding gift.

"I accused her of stealing it, just like she stole my fiancé," Biddy had told her.

The younger Bondurant sister had a history of kleptomania, stealing things that didn't belong to her, in an effort, according to the psychology books, to gain back something she'd lost.

Had Biddy attempted to break in to the gallery to reclaim her lost painting?

The next morning, as Hannah nursed the devil's own hangover following one too many French 75 cocktails, Phaedra brewed a pot of extra-strong coffee.

"What's in a French Seventy-Five, anyway?" she asked.

"Champagne, gin, um . . . lemon juice, I think? And a little bit of sugar. It's delicious. But deadly."

"Snuck up on you." Kneeling down to scratch Wickham's ears, she bit back a smile. "Glad you didn't drive home."

"I could've walked. If I had to." She watched as her sister opened a can of Mixed Seafood Grill and spooned it in a dish, and turned a shade of chartreuse. "'Scuse me," Hannah mumbled, and decamped to the living room.

When the coffee was ready, Phaedra took down two mugs. After carrying Hannah's out to her, she returned to the kitchen just in time to answer her phone.

"Phaedra?"

The voice on the other end was barely audible.

"Marisol?" Her fingers tightened around the phone. "Hi. I can hardly hear you. Is everything okay?"

"I don't have much time before he realizes I'm not upstairs," she added in a low rush.

"Who? Michael?"

"Yes. I stayed over at his place last night. I know you don't approve of him," she added with just a trace of defiance, "but I have no regrets. None. It was wonderful. Romantic. Perfect."

"I don't understand." She sank down onto a chair at the island. "I mean, of course I do. And I'm happy for you. But if everything is perfect, why do you sound upset?"

"Oh, you know me, always being dramatic. Making mountains out of molehills. Silly Marisol." She let out a rueful sigh. "But this time, I think . . . I really think Michael might be up to something."

"You do?" Phaedra's spoon clinked rapidly against her mug as she added cream. "What, exactly?"

"I snuck downstairs to have a quick look around his workroom while he's in the shower. I found your father's painting propped up on an easel."

"Okay. That's good. At least he's started on it."

"That's just it," she whispered. "He hasn't done any work on it. Not that I can tell, anyway."

Phaedra frowned. "Well, you have to admit, Mari, you're no art expert. This is a restoration, not a new work. You could be mistaken."

"I'm not mistaken about the copy I found. At least that's what I think it is."

Her pulse quickened, and not just from the caffeine. "A copy? What are you talking about?"

"Here. I'll show you." There was a whooshing sound, and a second later, two photos popped up in Phaedra's text app. "Did they come through?"

She studied the shots, both a little blurry, but unmistakably her father's painting . . . in duplicate.

"They did." Shock spiraled through her. "But . . . I don't understand."

"There's a second canvas behind the original. I only got a glimpse, but it looks exactly like your great-grandfather's painting. Right down to the smallest detail. It's not completely finished, and I can't be certain, but I think—" She muttered an exclamation. "The water's stopped running. I have to go."

"Marisol, wait—"

"Sorry. Talk later." There was a click and the line went dead.

"You've got to be kidding me."

An hour later, Detective Matteo Morelli stared across his desk at Phaedra. The bagel with cream cheese and large coffee—black, no sugar—she placed in front of him did little to soften his irritation.

"You told me not to come back until I had something concrete on Michael Farrar," she said. "And now I do."

"What you have is secondhand speculation from your teaching assistant." He pulled the to-go cup of coffee toward him and pried off the lid. "It isn't concrete. It's not even . . . wet cement."

"It's proof that Michael's making a copy of my father's painting. Why else would he have another canvas hidden behind the original? Why else would the second painting be identical to the first?"

"Did you see the painting?" He took a long, much needed, sip of coffee. "I mean, paintings? For yourself? The copy, or the original?"

"Well, no. Not firsthand. How can I see them when they're hidden away in his workroom?"

"Then how can you be sure that what your friend says is true? She could be mistaken."

"She saw the paintings and called me right away. And she sent me these." She reached in her purse and pulled out her phone, showed him the photographs Marisol had taken.

"I don't know much about art," Morelli said, studying the snapshots and handing her phone back, "but copying a work isn't illegal. Selling it as the original is."

"Art students learn by copying paintings by famous artists.

To study technique and hone their skills." She added, "'Good artists copy, great artists steal.'"

"Maybe that's what Farrar's doing. Honing his skills."

"He's not an artist, though. He's a dealer who does restoration work on the side. And why would he copy a work he claims is 'minor'?"

He shrugged. "Could be painting's his hobby."

"I doubt it." Phaedra leaned forward. "Aside from a couple of generic social media accounts," she persisted, "he doesn't exist online. Don't you find that odd?"

"It's not enough." He focused a steely gaze on her. "Here's the deal. Michael Farrar isn't the subject of an investigation. Nor is he a suspect in Anna Steele's murder. Right now, the investigation into Ms. Steele's murder takes precedence over Farrar and your half-baked art forgery theories."

Her fingers tightened on her phone. "And how is the investigation going, by the way? Have you arrested anyone? Figured out who poisoned the cupcake or the box of chocolates? Cleared Hannah's name by finding the real perpetrator?"

"Hannah's never been charged. And that's because," he added evenly, "just like your groundless accusations against Mr. Farrar, there is no evidence."

She let out an exasperated sigh. "I'm not suggesting you drop everything to look into Farrar. But there's something off about him. Something that doesn't add up."

"I don't have enough to go on. Sorry."

She returned her phone to her purse and stood. "Fine. I'll just have to make it my business to find something more damning. And when I do, I'll bring you your proof, all wrapped up and tied with a big red bow."

As parting shots went, Phaedra thought as she reached his door, it wasn't bad.

"You do that, Professor. Thanks for the bagel," Morelli called after her. "And just for the record? I prefer veggie cream cheese."

The midmorning sun shone in Phaedra's eyes as she emerged from the county courthouse complex. As she dug her sunglasses out of her purse, her phone rang.

"It's official. You're invited," Lucy said without preamble when she answered.

"Thanks. What am I invited to, exactly?"

"I'm making egg custard tarts. Aunty Roz's closely guarded recipe. Stop by this afternoon, and I'll brew a pot of tea to go with. We can catch up."

"You know I can't resist your egg custard tarts," Phaedra said, and sighed just thinking about the decadent, vanilla-scented treats. "You always say they were your favorite thing on the dim sum cart—"

"They still are."

"Did you invite Mari?"

"I texted her, but I doubt she'll show up. Said she and Michael probably won't get back until late."

I doubt she'll show up. Phaedra slowed her footsteps as she reached the Mini, and dismay swept through her. "Uh-oh."

Lucy paused. "Phae? What is it?"

"I just remembered something. Something important. With everything else going on, I completely forgot."

"Forgot what?"

Anhe's words came back to her, full force.

"If she fails to show up, I will consider that her answer and return to Shanghai on Monday. For good."

"I'm so sorry," Phaedra said, and came to a stop beside her car. "I meant to tell you sooner, much sooner, but we kept getting interrupted, and with so much happening lately, it slipped my mind, and I never found the right time to tell you—"

"Tell me what?" Lucy demanded. "Are you okay? Is it bad news? Or good news? Please tell me it's good news."

"Good. At least I think so. You may not agree."

"Phaedra," she warned. "Talk. Now."

"It's your mother. She wants to meet for dim sum on Sunday. *This* Sunday. Just the two of you."

Lucy huffed out a breath. "Bad news, then."

"She's tired of the two of you bickering. Her word, not mine," Phaedra added in the wake of the resounding silence on the other end. "She wants a redo."

"Well, that's not happening."

"Why not?"

She sighed. "The reasons are many, and varied. Look, I won't burden you with all the ways she hurt Leah and me, all the times she let us down. She couldn't raise us on her own, so she gave up. And then she gave *us* up."

"Maybe it was the only thing she could do at the time. Maybe she gave you up because it was better that way."

"Better for who?" Anger undercut the question. "All I can say is, thank God for Aunty Roz. Because without her, who knows where we'd be right now."

"This is all my fault." Phaedra tucked her phone between her chin and shoulder and unlocked the car.

"How do you figure that? None of this is your fault."

"It's also none of my business." She slid onto the front seat. "I know how private you are, and I feel uncomfortable inserting myself in the middle of this. But your mother seems to think I might have some influence with you. Since we're friends. She made me promise I'd ask you."

"Right. That's her standard modus operandi. Coercion, with a side of guilt."

"She says if you don't show up, she's leaving for Shanghai on Monday. She already bought a ticket."

Silence greeted her words.

"I waited too long to tell you." Phaedra leaned back against the seat. "I feel like I've ruined everything."

"You can't ruin something that's already damaged."

"At least give your mom's offer some thought, Lu," she entreated. "I think she's sincere. She really wants to broker a truce."

"I'll think about it," Lucy said finally. "And thanks for relaying the message. I'm sorry you got dragged into the middle of my family drama."

"It's okay. What else are friends for?"

"Good artists copy, great artists steal."

For some reason, the quote attributed to Pablo Picasso popped into Phaedra's thoughts as she drove back to Laurel Springs.

Why would Michael Farrar make a copy of her father's painting if, as he claimed, it was a minor work of no value? Answer: he wouldn't.

Which indicated, to her at least, that Farrar believed the painting to be an undiscovered work by a highly respected, late-nineteenth-century artist, one worth quite a bit of money if its provenance checked out.

No wonder he didn't want to show Marisol his progress on the restoration. He intended to copy it first.

Frowning, Phaedra lowered the heat and switched off the radio in an effort to focus her thoughts. Michael wasn't an artist. At least, not to her knowledge. He was a gallery owner. An art dealer, who restored paintings as a sideline.

So why create a copy of Dad's painting? Did he mean to keep the original for himself?

Her fingers tightened on the steering wheel. Or . . . did he intend to give her father the copy and sell the original on the black market?

Could Michael Farrar be an art forger?

She'd already shared her doubts with her father, and Detective Morelli, both of whom had dismissed her concerns. Malcolm believed Michael to be a nothing more than a savvy businessman, deliberately downplaying the value of the painting in order to purchase it at a rock-bottom price.

And Morelli gave little credence to her theories, either. Not without evidence. She had to find proof. Somehow.

The detective was right about one thing, though. She couldn't allow her suspicion of Michael Farrar to eclipse the more immediate issue—finding Anna's killer.

Phaedra turned the corner onto Main Street and glanced over at Tout de Sweet. The patisserie would remain open until two o'clock, when it closed for the holidays. Last-minute customers crowded the shop, picking up bûches de Noël and other French holiday treats. Hard to believe the next day was Christmas Eve.

Where had the time gone?

As she neared the carriage house, she decided to gather the presents she'd wrapped for Lucy, Marisol, and Detective Morelli. She'd deliver Lucy's gift—a delicate jade pendant—that evening. Marisol's present, a gift certificate to her favorite vintage clothing store, would have to wait for another time. Probably during her parents' open house. Mari had promised to be there, with or without Michael.

Which made her think of Mark. *I wonder what he's doing.* Just as well he was in England, Phaedra reflected as she pulled in the driveway, because she hadn't a clue what to give him for Christmas.

Not a book of Shakespeare's sonnets, or plays. He surely had multiples of those. And although she knew he liked fiction, she wasn't sure what authors he preferred. She could get him a gift card; but she'd rather present him with something more personal.

But not *too* personal.

Choosing a gift for a romantic partner was a puzzle fit for Sherlock Holmes.

On impulse, she took out her phone and sent a text. Wish you were here. Miss you. After a moment's hesitation, she pressed send. She waited, but there was no reply.

Immediately she regretted it. Did her message sound needy? Clingy? Desperate?

"I'm not cut out for romance," she said, and sighed as she got out of the car.

There was no sign of Wickham as she unlocked the door and let herself in. She dropped her purse on the hall table and glanced at her wristwatch. It was a few minutes before noon, which meant it was almost five p.m. in the UK. A little early for dinner, too late for lunch. So where was Mark?

Maybe he was in the pub. Chatting up some rosy-cheeked British stunner, no doubt. Buying her a pint as they bonded over cheese-and-onion crisps and the Bard . . .

"Stop," Phaedra muttered. "You're being ridiculous."

Filling a kettle with water, she set it on a burner and clicked it on. She hadn't eaten all morning and realized she was ravenous. A slice of Hannah's lemon tart would pair nicely with a mug of tea.

The soft pad of paws on the floor behind her alerted her to Wickham's presence, and she turned to greet him.

"Ready to go out, Wicks?"

He eyed her balefully. *Why do you insist on asking me that question when you already know the answer?*

She opened the kitchen door and waited as he sauntered outside, pausing on the doorstep to survey his backyard territory. Her phone dinged with a text message.

Picking it up, hoping it was Mark, she saw that it was . . . Clark Mullinax. She groaned.

Running the poisoned Chiles Chocs story tomorrow, morning edition. Quote? Last chance.

"As if," she muttered, her finger hovering over the delete button.

But she was curious. How did he know they were Chiles Chocolates? The police had kept that information quiet.

Who talked? she texted back.

U know I can't reveal a source.

She rolled her eyes and deleted the text.

The kettle began to boil. Taking down a mug, she placed one of Rebecca's herbal tea bags inside and topped it with hot water. She stirred in a touch of honey and breathed in the calming scent of hibiscus.

She'd taken her first sip when Wickham meowed to be let in. With a sigh, she set her cup down and went to the door. "That was fast."

He padded inside and cast her a brief glance. *It's cold out there, if you hadn't noticed. Not a creature is stirring.*

Not even a mouse.

Don't forget to take your custard tarts."

Phaedra paused outside Lucy's apartment door early that evening as her friend ducked back inside. After exchanging presents and agreeing to wait until Christmas day to open them, they'd gorged on egg custard tarts and downed an entire pot of white tea.

"Thanks," she said as Lucy returned and placed an oval platter filled with tarts wrapped in plastic into her hands. "These will disappear in five seconds flat at Mom and Dad's open house tomorrow. You're invited, by the way. Drop in whenever you like between four and seven thirty."

"I'll have Leah," she warned. "In all her Goth glory."

"Bring her. I'd love to meet her. She can give me all the dirt on her older sister." She paused. "And Mark's father said he'd try to drop by."

Lucy's brows rose. "Mark's father? Isn't he a judge, or a peer of the realm, or something?"

"A judge. Former. He ruled on a couple of Dad's cases. He's retired now. But according to Mark, he's still a 'full-on Grinch' and a 'crusty humbug.' Whatever a crusty humbug is." She laughed.

"Doesn't sound too flattering."

"No. But he does sound intriguing."

"If you ask me," Lucy said, "it also sounds like someone's getting serious. Meeting your significant other's father? That's next level. When can I expect to hear wedding bells?"

"Not any time soon. And he's hardly my significant other." Although she kept her tone light, Phaedra's smile slipped as she thanked Lucy and turned to go.

Her earlier text to Mark had gone unanswered. Which could mean something, or nothing.

There were any number of reasons he hadn't responded, she told herself as she returned to her car. He was busy. He couldn't get a signal. His phone was dead, or on the charger. He'd forgotten to take it with him.

Or maybe he just didn't want to talk to her.

Darkness had settled over Laurel Springs as Phaedra left the apartment complex and drove back to the carriage house. In no hurry, she turned off Main and detoured down a side street to check out the Christmas lights decorating the historic homes fronting either side of the avenue.

But lights of a different kind caught her eye on the corner. Police lights.

She slowed as she drew closer, blinking as the blue-and-red lightbar cast garish color over a group of people standing near a vehicle pulled up to the curb.

It was a Jaguar, Phaedra realized as she brought the car to a stop. Black, like Michael Farrar's car. She got out of the Mini and immediately heard the crackle of the two-way radio and the sound of voices, one raised in anger.

"I can't believe this! As you can see, Officer, it's a simple fender bender. The damage is minor. I'll pay for any repairs the other car requires. I'll write a check out to this woman right now."

Michael, she realized.

"No way. This was your fault," the driver of the other car, a middle-aged woman with murder in her eye, shot back. "You rear-ended my car. The bumper is crushed."

"You backed out in front of me!" Anger flared on his face, his fury evident in the vivid flash of red and blue lights. "I'm sure," he said more calmly, "we can settle this between the two of us. There's no need to involve the police."

"Sorry, sir," the officer said as he prepared to call in the accident. "It's too late for that. License and registration, please." He glanced at the woman. "Both of you."

Officer Scott, Phaedra realized belatedly.

Michael scowled and reached for his wallet. "This is ridiculous," he muttered as he handed over his license. "The registration's in my car. In the glove box."

Scott nodded over his clipboard. "Go ahead."

Several people had gathered nearby. Scanning their faces, she spotted Marisol, standing slightly apart from the others, away from Michael. Her cheeks glistened in the faint glow of a streetlight. It was obvious, at least to Phaedra, that she'd been crying.

"Marisol? Are you okay?" She hurried across the street and slipped an arm around the young woman's shoulders and eyed her in concern. "You're shaking."

"I'm fine. Just cold. I've been standing out here for a while now, waiting for the police to arrive. This fake fur looks warm," she said as she eyed the fluffy white fur, "but it isn't."

"At least the police are here now. After he calls it in, Officer Scott will do the paperwork, and you'll both be on your way home before you know it."

"Michael's furious," she choked out. "I've never . . . oh, Phaedra, I've never seen him so angry."

"Why? There's barely any damage to the front of the Jaguar. At least, none that I can see."

"He said it was my fault, that I distracted him." She gave Phaedra a stricken look. "He says I talk too much." She took the tissue Phaedra produced from her coat pocket and dabbed at her eyes. "We had such a great afternoon. We had lunch at this cute Italian restaurant, and we talked, and shared a plate of spaghetti, just like Lady and the Tramp . . . and afterward we walked, and held hands. Then we came back, and Michael turned the corner of Maple, and he wasn't even speeding, because he never speeds, when that woman—" She cast a glare at the other driver. "When she backed out of her driveway right in front of us."

"I'll drive you home," Phaedra suggested. She glanced at Michael. "Unless you'd prefer to stick around."

"No." The word was low, but firm. She lifted a determined, tear-streaked face. "I'm through with Michael Farrar. Take me home, Phae, please."

"Okay. Let me tell Lucas and make sure you're cleared to leave. I'll be right back."

Marisol waited as Phaedra rounded the car, skirted the onlookers, and sought out Officer Scott. "Marisol's a little upset," she explained. "Is it okay if she leaves?"

"Yes, of course. Ms. Dubois can leave whenever she likes." His expression morphed from polite professionalism to guarded concern. "Is she . . . is she okay?"

"She will be. Thanks for asking." Unless she was very much mistaken, there was a more behind his inquiry into Marisol's health than mere politeness.

Officer Lucas Scott was sweet on Marisol Dubois.

With a warm smile, Phaedra thanked him, said good night, and returned to the Jaguar.

"Let's go," she told Marisol, and led her across the street to the Mini. Michael glanced up once, his expression shuttered, but made no move to come after them.

"You were right about him," Marisol said as she slid into the passenger seat next to Phaedra. "You told me to take things slowly. You warned me that he was just a modern-day W-Willoughby. But I didn't believe you. And I didn't listen."

She began, quietly, to cry.

Phaedra popped a packet of tissues out of the glove box and handed them over.

With a sniffle, Marisol took them. "Thanks."

She nodded and switched on the radio. Soon, soothing classical music filled the car, and she drove her weeping friend home without comment.

Sometimes, the kindest thing was to say nothing at all.

After dropping Marisol off and reassuring her everything would be all right, Phaedra returned to the carriage house. With a string of multicolored lights under the eaves and surrounding the front window, the place looked festive and welcoming. The house was dark inside, but the outside lights were on. Hannah must have gone out.

Poor Marisol.

Her heart went out to her teaching assistant. She remembered how she'd rhapsodized about Michael Farrar from the moment she'd met him at the gallery. He was all she talked about.

"I think he might even be The One."

Or not. Phaedra released a long, gusty sigh. There was nothing more painful, or more devastating, than suffering through the first real disappointment in love. It was a crash landing of the heart.

She'd gone through her own share of heartbreak when her high school sweetheart, Donovan Wickes, invited her to the senior prom and then failed to show up.

But that was years ago, she reminded herself. She was a different person then. Now she'd met someone truly wonderful, someone she cared for. A lot.

Maybe, she thought with a surge of hope, Mark had finally texted her back. She hadn't checked since she'd messaged him earlier.

She pulled out her phone. No new text messages.

Why hadn't he responded? Where was he? Could he be . . . ghosting her?

Although she knew she was being paranoid, Phaedra remembered the young, blond mystery woman Marisol saw with Mark outside Orsini's restaurant. When she'd pressed him about it, and asked why he didn't show up at the staff holiday party, he said Ivy was a close friend of his sister's. They'd bonded after Georgie's death.

But she couldn't help wondering—was Ivy, the *Clueless* look-alike, more than a friend?

"You're the one who's clueless," she muttered, and thrust the phone back in her purse. "Get a grip."

There was a logical reason for Mark's failure to respond to her text. Had to be. Time to stop being insecure, grab Lucy's egg custard tarts, and get inside.

Two sharp raps sounded on the driver's side window.

She gave a violent start as a pale face materialized just outside the glass. A man's face.

Instinctively, she fumbled for the key fob hanging in the ignition and hit the panic button.

Then she screamed.

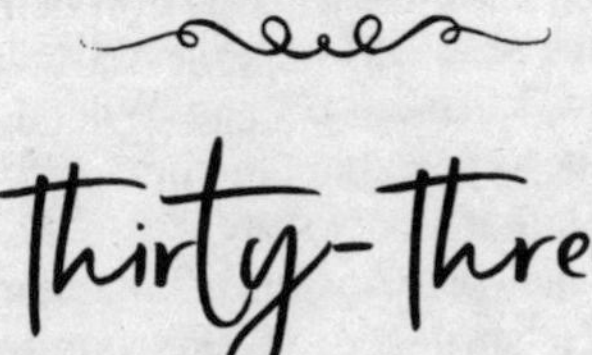

Phaedra!" More banging on the window. "Phaedra, turn that thing off! It's me, Clark!"

Her breath whooshed out. She risked another peek and realized it was, indeed, Clark Mullinax standing by her window, looking almost as unnerved as she felt. As her panic began to recede and her pulse returned to normal, she switched off the shrieking alarm with unsteady fingers and glared at him.

"What were you *thinking*, Mullinax?" she demanded as she flung the car door open. "You scared me half to death!"

"Sorry," he said, holding up his hands in apology. "I didn't mean to startle you."

"Well, you did. Where's your car?" She glanced behind her and saw it in the driveway behind her. "I didn't hear it pull in."

"Prius," he said, and shrugged. "It's electric."

She climbed out of the Mini. "What do you want, Clark? A quote? I don't have one. A life? Can't help you there, either."

"Wow. Someone's in a bad mood tonight."

"Someone," she gritted as she removed the plate of custard tarts from the back seat, "is hungry, and tired. Never a good combination. Now, I'll ask you again. What do you want?"

"I'd like to talk to you about the box of poisoned chocolates left at your father's bookstore."

"Chocolate," she corrected him. "Singular."

"Whatever." He shrugged. "We're running the story tomorrow and I'd really appreciate your input. I'm calling it the 'chocolate box poisoning.' Clever, huh? Very Agatha Christie." He eyed the tarts. "Say, those look good. Did you make them? What are they, exactly?"

"Egg custard tarts. And no, I didn't make them. A friend did." Phaedra shut the car door with her hip and studied him. "I might consider giving you one, along with a cup of tea. Or coffee. Your choice."

"What's the catch?"

"No catch. Just an exchange of information. You tell me what you know, and maybe I'll share what I know."

"I already have all the information I need."

"Fine." She shrugged and headed up the walk to the front door. "Have a good evening, Clark."

"Wait!"

She turned back, house key in hand.

"Okay, okay. It's a deal." His expression remained wary. "But you have to give me something in return. A tidbit, a quote. Something I don't already have."

"We'll see." She unlocked the door and preceded him inside. "Hannah's not back yet, but I expect her at any time. Take a seat while I brew us some tea." She indicated the kitchen island. "And start talking."

"And that's everything I know. I swear." Clark finished his egg custard tart in record time and pressed a few crumbs, all that remained on the plate, onto his fork. "Kudos to your friend. These are addictive."

Phaedra nodded. "More tea?"

"I'm good. What I need now is more information. Insider stuff."

"There's nothing more I can add, insider or otherwise. Your basic facts are right on the money. Where'd you get your info, anyway?"

He smirked. "I have my sources. I also check the police blotter every day."

"Who told you the chocolates were Chiles?" She leaned forward and locked her gaze with his. "That information wasn't released. And don't tell me you can't reveal your source," she warned. "Or I'll show you the door right now."

"Give me a quote, then."

"Give me the name of your source first."

He hesitated. "If I do, it stays between us."

"Fair enough."

"Okay." He toyed with his spoon, then set it aside. "Her name is Amelie. I don't know her last name; she didn't say and I didn't ask. She works at the art gallery."

She nodded slowly. "Michael Farrar's assistant." Her brows puckered. "When did she talk to you?"

"Late yesterday morning. I bumped into her at a coffee shop in Crozet. I was following up on a tip."

"She's gone back home for the holidays." That's what Marisol had told her yesterday evening. *"Montana, I think."* She'd also said that Michael had closed the gallery for the duration of the holidays on Wednesday evening.

Either Amelie had changed her mind about leaving town. Or she'd lied.

"What else did she tell you?" she asked.

"Only that the chocolates were Chiles, very high end." He paused. "She also said she saw the person who left the chocolates on the Poison Pen's counter."

She nearly choked on her tea. "Did she report it to the police?"

"No."

"Why not, for heaven's sake? She saw the poisoner!"

"She's afraid, and she prefers to remain anonymous."

"Well, I can certainly understand that," she agreed. "No one wants to be a killer's next target."

"No. But she also wants to do the right thing."

"And I'm guessing you offered to run the story and keep her name out of it. The police will have a suspect, they'll make an arrest, and we can all eat chocolates and cupcakes again without fear." She glanced at him. "Does that about sum it up?"

"Not quite," he said, frowning into his teacup. "I can't divulge the alleged suspect's name. If I do, as my editor very emphatically pointed out, the *Clarion* could be sued for libel. And I'd be out of a job."

"And we don't want that."

"No."

"Just one more question." Phaedra studied him intently. "Who *is* this mystery person? You may not be able to put his or her name in print, but you can tell me. Better yet, you should tell Detective Morelli. Who left those chocolates on my father's counter?"

"You won't believe me when I tell you."

"Try me."

He dropped his voice to a barely audible whisper. "It was that elderly lady, one of the sisters who owns the apothecary shop. Biddy Bondurant."

"Biddy? You think Biddy is the killer." Despite her quickening heartbeat—after all, she'd suspected the Bondurant sister herself—Phaedra kept her expression neutral. "What makes you think that?"

"I don't think, I know." Clark leaned forward, a gleam in his eye. "Amelie saw her."

"Amelie," she repeated. "As in, Michael Farrar's assistant."

"The very same."

Phaedra took a sip of tea, allowing herself time to gather her thoughts. It wouldn't do to let Clark know how deeply his news unsettled her. She wanted to know who'd poisoned the chocolate, of course she did; but learning Biddy might be the culprit was difficult to accept. "You're saying sweet, kindhearted Biddy left those chocolates on the Poison Pen counter?"

"I'm telling you what Amelie told me."

Phaedra didn't want to believe it. "What if she's mistaken? What if it was Rebecca she saw?" She thought of the Ellis Peters book the elder sister had bought that same day, *Monk's Hood*. "She was in the bookstore that morning. I sold her a book myself."

"She swore it was Biddy."

"Okay." She pushed herself away and got to her feet to carry her cup and saucer to the sink. "Let's say, just for the moment, that Amelie's right, and it was Biddy she saw. Why would either of them want to poison my father? What possible motive could they have?"

But even as she voiced the question, she pondered a possible answer. Biddy claimed that Phaedra's grandmother Rose had stolen her beau, as well as the painting he'd promised to give her, breaking her heart in the process.

Could the painting Phaedra's father had inherited account for Biddy's strange behavior? It might, if she'd decided she wanted it back. But why not offer to buy it outright from Dad, or—with her propensity for theft—why not steal the painting?

Her thoughts quickened. Once again, she wondered if Biddy was behind the recent attempted break-in at the Farrar Gallery. If she'd known Michael was restoring the painting, perhaps she tried to steal it. But how did the poisoned chocolates fit in?

None of it made sense.

"Who knows?" Clark followed her to the sink and handed over his cup and saucer. "Not every murderer has a motive. And motive doesn't always equal guilt. But both of those sisters are a little peculiar, if you ask me. Growing those herbs behind the shop, brewing up tisanes and herbal remedies . . . I think they're both a little batty."

"Rebecca is sharp as a tack, and so is Biddy. Just because

they're elderly doesn't mean they're not in full possession of their faculties."

"I know. Sorry." He reached for his jacket and shrugged it back on. "Now it's your turn, Professor B. Give me a quote. Something you know that I don't."

Twice, he'd referred to the poisoned "chocolates," so Mullinax had no idea that only one of the chocolates had been tampered with. Nor did he know the piece in question was injected with aconite.

That information was between her, and Detective Morelli. And that's where it would stay.

"Here's a quote," she replied as she put a couple of egg custard tarts on a paper plate and covered them with plastic wrap. "'I have every confidence that the Somerset County police department will identify and apprehend the person or persons responsible for this heinous crime.'"

"Hey," he protested as she thrust the paper plate into his hands, "that's not the kind of hard-hitting, insider quote I had in mind."

"Sorry." She led him to the front door. "You got your quote. And you have egg custard tarts to take home. Consider us even."

"But—"

"Good night, Clark." She opened the door and ushered him out. "Enjoy your tarts."

Instead of snow, Saturday morning brought a cold, sleeting rain.

"Not a very festive start to my day off," Hannah complained as she sat slumped over her laptop at the kitchen counter.

"Not a festive start to Christmas Eve, either." Phaedra poured her a cup of coffee. "Are you going to Mom and Dad's open house later?"

"I might put in an appearance to appease Mom." She began tapping at the keyboard. "What about you?"

"Same. Mom invited Mark's dad."

Hannah's fingers paused. "Judge Selden?"

"Former judge. Yes." Phaedra shrugged. "You know Mom. When Mark mentioned his father was spending Christmas alone, she felt sorry for him and extended the invitation, and he accepted."

"Is Mark coming, too?"

She gazed at the sleet tapping against the kitchen window and shook her head. "He's visiting his mother in the UK until after the holidays."

"Oh. Sorry. That must be difficult."

"It's okay. He'll be back in time for New Year's."

"Charles is coming out for a few days. He . . ." A frown settled over her forehead. "Phae, have you seen this?" She turned her laptop around to face her sister.

Phaedra peered at the screen.

POISONED CHOCOLATES LEFT AT POISON PEN

The headline was the lead story on the *Laurel Springs Clarion*'s online site. And the byline, of course, belonged to Clark Mullinax.

While the article hinted that a suspicious person was seen at the bookstore on the day the chocolates were found, the suspect wasn't named.

The story, while full of colorful speculation and innuendo, didn't unveil anything new or surprising. Clark obviously valued his job more than a libel lawsuit and had erred on the side of caution.

"Who do you suppose the suspicious person was?" Hannah asked as she turned the laptop back around.

Before she could answer, Phaedra heard a car pull into the driveway. Footsteps approached, and someone knocked on the front door.

"Who the heck is that at—" Hannah glanced at the clock. "Eight twelve on a Saturday morning?"

"Are you expecting Charles already?"

She shook her head. “Not until later tonight.”

Phaedra made her way into the living room and glanced outside. A white Honda Civic that had seen better days sat in the driveway.

“Detective Morelli,” she said as she opened the door. “Come in.”

“Thanks.” His hands were thrust into his coat pockets, and his dark hair glistened with rain. “Hello, Hannah,” he added as she joined them in the hallway.

“Hello.” She canted her head to one side. “Is this an official visit? Did you catch whoever poisoned my cupcake?”

“The investigation is still ongoing. Right now, I need to speak with Professor Brighton.”

“So, not an official visit, then. Or at least, not one that involves me.” She turned back to the kitchen. “I’ll just grab my coffee and run along upstairs.”

“Thanks, Han.” As her sister retrieved her mug and trudged upstairs, Phaedra eyed Morelli. “Sorry about that. She’s not at her best before nine. Coffee?”

“Sure.” As she handed him a cup, he took a seat at the island. “I apologize for dropping in unannounced.”

“It must be important. Or you wouldn’t be here.” She slid into the seat beside him. “Is this an official visit?”

“Yes and no. It concerns your friend, Marisol Dubois. More specifically, her boyfriend. Michael Farrar.”

“Oh. Well, they’re not together anymore.” A frown crinkled her brow. “She’s not in any trouble, is she?”

“No. But I’m glad to hear she’s not involved with him any longer.” He glanced at her. “It goes without saying that this stays between us.”

“Of course.”

“I’m sharing this information with you *only* because of your previous concerns about Farrar. You suspected he might be involved in something shady.”

She nodded. “Art forgery, to be exact.”

“Last night he was involved in a minor accident. Officer Scott responded to the call.”

"I know. I was on my way home when I saw the Jaguar, and I stopped to check on Marisol. She and Michael spent the afternoon together."

"Farrar wasn't too happy. The damage to his car was minimal, but the other driver's rear bumper was crumpled."

"He was furious," she agreed. "He blamed Mari for the accident, said her talking distracted him. She was pretty upset."

"I'm sorry for your friend, but the accident was a stroke of luck for us."

"How so?"

Morelli met her gaze. "When Lucas ran him—"

"Ran him?"

"Ran a background check. He discovered that Michael Farrar isn't who he claims he is. He's a convicted felon. And his real name is Ben Jennings."

Thirty-Four

No wonder he didn't want the accident reported," Phaedra said slowly.

He shrugged. "Changing your name isn't illegal. People change their names every day, for a number of reasons. Perfectly legal reasons."

"So why did Michael—sorry, Ben—change his name?"

"He and his sister grew up in foster care, got bounced from one place to the next. He ran away several times, had brushes with the law as a minor. When he was nineteen," Morelli added, reaching once again for his coffee mug, "he got busted and served five years in prison for grand larceny. Specifically, accessory to art theft. When he got out, he left his old life—and his real name—behind."

Her fingers tightened around her mug. "Marisol was right. He's copying my father's painting. He must be planning to return the forgery, say it's the restored work, and sell the original. If he can prove its provenance as a previously unknown work by James Brighton, he stands to make a lot of money. At Dad's expense." She pushed her chair back. "I have to warn him."

"No."

She stared at him in disbelief. "Why? My father deserves to know the truth. We can go to the gallery right now and get the painting. And then you can arrest Michael—or Ben, or whoever he is, and throw him in jail."

"Proof, Professor. As in, there is none. It's all conjecture at this point. If you tip your hand and let Jennings know we suspect him, he'll take that painting and disappear faster than you can say 'art heist.' Not to mention," he added as she opened her mouth to argue, "he's a convicted criminal. If he feels threatened, there's no telling what he might do or how he'll react. I won't let you put yourself or your dad in danger."

"Meaning, I can't tell him Michael's real identity."

"No. You can't." He swallowed the last of his coffee. "Like I said, this stays between the two of us."

"But not knowing puts my father at a disadvantage. Right now, he thinks Michael Farrar is a legitimate businessman, an art gallery owner. Someone he can trust."

"And that's good," Morelli said. "As long as Malcolm believes Farrar is who he says he is, he won't rouse suspicion. Giving me time to gather sufficient evidence to put Ben Jennings where he belongs—behind bars."

"Did Clark Mullinax talk to you?" Phaedra asked, abruptly changing the subject. "He claims he has a potential new suspect in the 'chocolate box poisoning.'" She grimaced slightly. "His words, not mine."

"If you mean Biddy Bondurant, yes. He told me."

"I can't believe she'd do that. But Clark says Michael's assistant saw her put the box on the counter."

"I'll look into it. See if any of the local shop owners remember her buying a box of Chiles chocolates." He stood up. "Thanks for the coffee. I'll be in touch."

"Wait." She placed her hand on his arm. "Before you leave, I have something for you."

He followed her into the living room, where she knelt beside the Christmas tree and pulled out a small package wrapped in dark blue paper with a gold bow.

She straightened and handed it to him. "Merry Christmas, Detective."

He stared at it, then at her. "What's this?"

"It's called a Christmas present." She laughed. "It isn't much, just a token of my appreciation. Something to keep you company on your next stakeout."

"I didn't get you anything."

"I don't expect you to. You can open it now, or later."

"My powers of observation," he said as he lifted it and shook it beside his ear, "tell me it's a book."

"I invoke the Fifth."

A reluctant grin lifted one corner of his mouth. "Fair enough, Professor. Thanks. And Merry Christmas."

"Merry Christmas, Detective."

Late that afternoon, as the sleet changed over to snow flurries, Phaedra arrived at the Poison Pen to put in an appearance at her mother's holiday open house.

Already, cars lined both sides of the street, coated in a light dusting of snow.

In an attempt to be practical as well as festive, she wore a dark green sweater dress and low-heeled black boots, with her hair hanging over her shoulder in a French braid. Her only jewelry was her grandmother's brooch, a vintage Christmas tree fashioned of tiny pearls and beads.

She wiped her boots on the mat and slipped inside. Low-key holiday music greeted her, along with the buzz of conversation and the occasional trill of laughter. There was no sign of Lucy or her sister, Leah.

"Hello. Professor Brighton, isn't it?"

A young woman with short dark hair and red lips approached. "Amelie," Phaedra said. "Michael Farrar's assistant, right?"

"You remembered. Your mother was kind enough to invite Mr. Farrar and myself." She sipped from her martini glass. "He couldn't make it, unfortunately."

Thank goodness, Phaedra thought as she fixed a polite smile to her lips. "Sorry to hear that. I'm glad you're here." She frowned. "But I'm surprised. Marisol told me—"

"Phaedra, you made it." Her mother hurried over and thrust a glass into her hand. "Cranberry and vodka, your favorite. If you'll excuse us for a moment, Amelie?"

"Of course. I'm leaving, anyway. Ciao." She set her glass aside and departed.

Nan turned back to her daughter. "I want you to come and meet Mark's father."

"Mom," she protested, "I just got here—"

But Nan Brighton was on a mission, and there was nothing to do but follow her mother through the throng until they reached the reading room at the end of the hall.

A Christmas tree took up one corner, and the reading table stood against the wall opposite the windows. She glimpsed a selection of hors d'oeuvres, a punch bowl, and a tempting array of bite-size desserts.

Her mother tugged her forward. Two armchairs occupied the corner opposite the tree. One of them held her father, who greeted her with a smile and a raised glass.

The other chair held the Honorable Judge Selden.

"Judge Selden," Nan said, "I'd like to introduce my daughter, Professor Phaedra Brighton. Phaedra, this is—"

"Geoffrey will do." He rose and extended his hand. "A pleasure to meet you, Professor."

His grip was firm and his gaze direct. He spoke with a slight British accent. Years of working in the US judicial system had eliminated most of it.

"Phaedra, please." She smiled. "It's lovely to meet you as well. I've heard a lot about you."

His hair was white but still thick. "None of it complimentary, I'll wager. I understand you and my son are seeing each other."

"I . . . yes." Evidently, more than his gaze was direct. "We are."

"You met at Somerset University?"

"Yes. We're both on the English Literature faculty."

"I never approved of his academic career, you know. I fully expected him to follow me into the law, just as I followed my father, but Mark had his own ideas."

"He's an excellent professor," she said. "His students love him."

"He would've been an excellent QC." At her puzzled glance, he added, "Queen's Counsel. But my son had no interest in taking silk. Stubborn. Willfully so. Still is."

She opened her mouth to respond, then closed it. What a charmer Geoffrey Selden was.

"Phaedra," her father said mildly, "would you mind getting me another Scotch and soda?"

"Not at all." She took his glass, glad of a reprieve, and turned to the judge. "Geoffrey? Another drink?"

"No, I'm fine. Thank you."

She couldn't get out of there fast enough.

"Now I know what a crusty humbug is," Phaedra muttered as she arrived at the drinks cart around the corner and replenished her father's glass with Scotch.

"What did you say?" Hannah asked as she joined her.

"Nothing. You look great." She eyed her sister's black wool dress and single strand of pearls and glanced past her. "I didn't know you were here. Where's Charles?"

"Stuck in traffic on route twenty-nine. The snow's starting to stick and accidents are everywhere." She poured a glass of chardonnay. "You look very festive. But stressed."

"I just met Judge Selden." Phaedra splashed soda into the glass. "He couldn't wait to tell me what a disappointment Mark is. Because he didn't become a barrister and carry on the family tradition."

"How very feudal of him."

"He's one of those people who sees everything as black or white. No shades of gray. Innocent, or guilty."

"Well, he is a judge."

"He's certainly judgy." Phaedra steeled herself. "Time to return to the scene of the crime." She held up the glass. "Dad wants a refill."

"Sounds like he'll need it. I'll take it if you'd rather avoid Mark's father."

"No, I've got it. I'm not staying much longer."

Hannah wandered off, and Phaedra returned to the reading room. As she neared her father's chair, she realized he was deep in conversation with the former judge.

Without interrupting, she handed over his drink and he nodded his thanks.

Phaedra's phone rang, and she stepped away. "Marisol? Where are you?"

"Watching TV. Feeling sorry for myself. Wishing I'd gone home for Christmas but glad I didn't."

"I know exactly what you mean." She paused. "I hoped you might stop by. Mom and Dad are having their holiday bash at the bookstore right now."

"No, thanks. I know I said I'd come, but . . ."

"You can't spend Christmas Eve alone."

Marisol sighed. "Turns out, I can."

"Have you heard from Michael?"

"He called to apologize. I let it go to voice mail."

"Good. Promise me you won't talk to him. Don't even think of giving him another chance. He doesn't deserve it."

"I'm not, don't worry." Curiosity undercut her words as she added, "Why? Do you know something I don't?"

Phaedra hesitated. "I had a visit from Morelli earlier. He . . . told me something. About Michael."

"Does it have anything to do with the painting?"

"It does. I'm supposed to keep it to myself, but I know you share my concerns about Michael, so . . ."

"Phae, tell me. What did Detective Morelli say?"

"When Officer Scott responded to the accident, he ran a background check on Michael."

"Okay . . ."

Phaedra lowered her voice. "Turns out his real name is Ben Jennings. He has a criminal record. He's a convicted felon, and he served five years in prison for art theft. He isn't who he says he is. And he may be dangerous."

Thirty-Five

After a sharp intake of breath, Marisol lowered her voice. "Hang on. Someone's at the door." She rented the top floor of a subdivided Queen Anne house on Tyler Street, in a neighborhood comprised largely of student housing.

Phaedra waited, but heard nothing. No sound of a door opening or voices talking. She glanced up as her father edged past on his way down the hall.

"Mark?" he asked as he saw the phone pressed to her ear.

She shook her head. "Mari."

"Wish her a merry Christmas. Or should I say, a 'Mari' Christmas."

She rolled her eyes as he chuckled and turned away. A moment later, Marisol returned.

"Phaedra, he's here," she breathed. "Michael. His Jag is parked out front."

"What does he want? Did you talk to him?"

"No. He probably wants to apologize, but I'm not interested. Not after what you just told me."

"Are you afraid? I can call Officer Scott right now—"

"Please don't. After the way Michael acted at the accident

last night, yelling and throwing a temper tantrum? I'm still embarrassed. Lucas is the last person I want to see."

"Why? The bad behavior was on Michael, not you. Lucas is a good guy, Mari. And I think he likes you."

"Really?" She didn't sound convinced. "Can you see me dating a cop, though?"

"Better a cop than a convicted felon."

"Good point." Marisol paused. "Wait. I think . . ." Her breath whooshed out in relief. "He's stopped knocking. I think he's leaving."

"Peek out the window," Phaedra advised. "Don't let him see you, but make sure he leaves."

"Okay. There he is. He's walking over to the Jag," she reported. "He got in. He's pulling away. And, he's gone."

"Go take a look outside your door. See if he left a note, or a Christmas card, or something."

"I didn't think of that. Hang on, I'll be right back."

As Marisol went to check the hallway outside her door, Phaedra waved away the offer of a passing tray of hors d'oeuvres. She returned to the front of the bookstore to look for Hannah but didn't see her sister anywhere.

The phone crackled in her ear. "Phae? You were right. Michael left a card propped against the door. Probably a Christmas card. Or a note." Her voice was doubtful. "The envelope is nice. Thick, cream cardstock. Looks like an invitation."

"Don't keep me in suspense. Open it." She waited as Marisol lifted the envelope's flap and withdrew whatever was inside. "Well?" Phaedra prodded. "What is it?"

"It's an invitation. Rachel Brandon requests the pleasure of my company at a private party at Delaford on New Year's Eve."

"That's the event Hannah's catering for Rachel." She frowned. "Kind of odd that Michael left it at your door. I'm surprised Rachel didn't mail it out."

"She probably overlooked it. Or added me to the guest list at the last minute. I don't even know why she invited me. I barely know her."

Phaedra sank down into an armchair in the corner. "Michael's a successful local gallery owner," she said. "Or he pretends to be. Rachel must've invited him. And he must've asked her to invite you."

"Why, though?" Marisol wondered.

"Maybe he wants a chance to talk to you," Phaedra suggested. "To apologize in person. Will you go?"

"And risk seeing Michael?" Her question vibrated with indignation. "No way."

"I can't say I blame you," Phaedra agreed. "But . . . it does present us with a unique opportunity."

"A unique opportunity for what? And what do you mean, 'us'?"

"We know he's up to no good," she said. "And we know he has a criminal record. But Morelli needs proof. Evidence. If you go along as Michael's date to this party, you could do some intel. See what you can learn. After all, he has no idea you suspect him."

"I'm not crazy about the idea, to be honest. What if he realizes I'm snooping? Who knows how he might react? What he might do?"

"You're right." Phaedra sighed. "I can't ask you to put yourself in danger."

"Maybe there's another way." Marisol paused. "I'll decline the invitation, and you can go to the party instead. You're much better at this stuff than me."

"There's one problem, Mari. I'm not invited."

"But Hannah is. She's catering. Offer to give her a hand. You can circulate with trays of shrimp toast while you keep an eye on Michael. Or, should I say, Ben."

"It could work," Phaedra mused.

"And while you're at Delaford, I'll do a little recon at the gallery. I know the updated code for the security keypad."

"I'm surprised he told you. You haven't been dating that long."

"He didn't. I watched him enter the code after the break-in attempt."

"Why, Marisol Dubois," Phaedra said in admiration, "that's positively devious."

"Thanks. Which also means it wouldn't be breaking and entering. Technically."

"No. It's still too risky. Even if you find evidence, there's a good chance you'd contaminate it. And illegally obtained evidence isn't admissible in court. Not to mention—what if he catches you in the act?"

"He won't. And like you said, he has no idea I know his real identity," Marisol pointed out.

"What if you trip the alarm and the police show up? How would you explain it? No way. It's too dangerous."

"Okay, then," Marisol said. "How about this? You go to Rachel's party under the guise of helping Hannah, and I'll go as Michael's plus-one. We can have each other's backs in the event something goes wrong."

"That's what worries me," Phaedra said. "Something going wrong." She knew what Detective Morelli would have to say about their tag-team scheme. "Ill-advised" and "harebrained" were two immediate possibilities.

"It'll be fine," Marisol promised. "You'll be passing out hors d'oeuvres and I'll be on a date. At a party, in a house full of people dressed to the nines, ready to bring in the New Year. How dangerous could it be?"

When Phaedra returned to the carriage house a short time later, it was dark. At least Hannah had left the outside light on.

As she'd done many times since Mark left, she took out her phone and checked her text messages. Nothing.

She returned the phone to her evening bag and reached for the key fob with leaden fingers. Where was he? Why the silence? Had she done or said something to offend him?

But she knew she hadn't. They'd parted on good terms. After his first, and only, text from England—Arrived safely. Miss you already—she'd heard nothing more.

Was her brief romance with Mark Selden already over?

If he truly was ghosting her, there was nothing she could do about it. No point sitting in the dark brooding and feeling sorry for herself.

Besides, there was a logical explanation. There had to be.

She got out of the car and made her way up the walk to the carriage house, her steps careful in the light covering of snow. She unlocked the door and reached for the lamp on the hall table.

"Wicks," she called out as she snapped it on. "I'm home."

Poor Wickham. He'd be outraged to be left alone in the dark all this time.

As she took off her coat, Phaedra paused. A thick cream envelope lay on the entry hall floor. She'd nearly stepped on it. She hung her coat and knelt to pick it up.

Her name was scrawled on the envelope. Inside was an embossed invitation requesting the pleasure of her company at Delaford on New Year's Eve.

"Well, well. I've been invited to the party at Rachel Brandon's house," she told Wickham as he ambled up and threaded himself leisurely between her booted feet.

His uplifted blue eyes telegraphed his indifference at the news. *And you're telling me this, why?*

"Now I won't need to go as Hannah's assistant," she mused. "No need for subterfuge."

Wonderful. Whatever "subterfuge" is. Now, kindly let me out. Posthaste.

She opened the kitchen door and let him out, and watched as he padded distastefully through the slushy remnants of snow on the ground.

Who, she wondered, would be at Rachel's party? Michael and Marisol, certainly; Hannah and her staff; maybe Vanessa Cole, Rachel's producer, and possibly Rachel's soon-to-be ex-husband, Kyle. Although after his churlish behavior at the Farrar Gallery the night of Colette Parrish's showing, Phaedra would be surprised if he put in an appearance.

As she put the kettle on and took down a box of chamomile

tea bags, Phaedra frowned. Detective Morelli was right about one thing. They needed to focus on finding Anna Steele's killer. And right now, although the evidence was circumstantial, it pointed to Rebecca or Biddy Bondurant as the most likely suspects.

Both had attended Hannah's grand opening. Rebecca was at the Poison Pen the day the chocolates were left on the counter. According to Amelie, Biddy was there, as well. Rebecca bought a murder mystery featuring aconite, the poison injected into a single chocolate—hazelnut crunch, her father's favorite.

The sisters sold Chiles Chocolates at their shop.

She pulled a mug down and dropped in a tea bag. Who, other than herself and her immediate family, knew of Dad's partiality for hazelnut crunch? Again, Rebecca and Biddy presented the most plausible explanation.

Although her mother dismissed the apothecary as "new age fiddle-faddle" and rarely visited the shop, her father occasionally stopped in for a tin of hard candies and a chat with Rebecca. He enjoyed sparring with her on all manner of subjects, from politics to college football.

Which made it possible that he'd mentioned his candy preference to one or both of the sisters.

Still, she found it difficult to believe that either of the elderly pair had gone to such lengths. While it was true Biddy had a motive, believing the James Brighton painting rightfully belonged to her, why wait so many years to act on it? Why *kill* for it? And how did Anna Steele fit into the picture?

Was she murdered? Or was her death an unfortunate accident? Was Malcolm Brighton the intended target?

Or was Phaedra?

She poured hot water into her mug and breathed in the comforting fragrance of chamomile as she took a seat at the island. So many questions, so many still unanswered.

She needed to convince not only her father but also Detective Morelli that Michael Farrar planned to forge the painting, return the copy, and sell the original. She needed proof before it was too late and the painting disappeared forever.

Nonetheless, finding whoever had targeted her father took absolute priority. No question. The killer—or killers—had to be stopped before another innocent person died.

Thirty-Six

Happy Christmas, everyone!"

Charles Dalton, his arms piled with presents, entered the Brighton kitchen, where Nan was taking the turkey out of the oven.

He peered around the stack of brightly wrapped boxes. His face was flushed, his from cold, Nan's from a hot oven and a morning spent preparing their holiday meal. Hannah followed behind him.

"Merry Christmas, Charles," Phaedra said. "I'll take those." She relieved him of the presents and carried them out to the Christmas tree in the living room.

"Charles!" Nan set the turkey down on the counter and flung her oven-mitted arms around him. "Merry Christmas! It's wonderful to see you again. Malcolm," she called out as she drew away to give Hannah a quick peck on the cheek, "come and greet your future son-in-law."

"How long are you here for?" Mr. Brighton asked after welcoming Charles and handing him a tumbler of whiskey.

"Only through the weekend, unfortunately. Then I'm off to London to visit the parents for a few days."

"Have the two of you set a date yet?" Nan asked as she removed her oven mitts. "A June wedding would be lovely."

"Too predictable. And too hot." Hannah glanced at Charles. "We're thinking fall, or early winter."

"Winter? You run the risk of snow," Malcolm said.

"I love the idea of a fall wedding." Phaedra glanced at Hannah's fiancé. "What about you, Charles?"

"I'll do whatever it takes to keep my bride-to-be happy." He leaned forward to give her a quick kiss. "Whatever she decides is fine with me."

After serving the last slice of turkey, Nan leaned back and glanced around the table. "Who wants coffee?"

"Perhaps later," Charles said, and glanced at Hannah. "Are you up for a walk? Incinerate a few calories?"

She nodded. "See you all later," she said as they went to retrieve their coats.

Phaedra stood to help her mother clear the table, but Nan waved her away. "Stay. I've got this. I'll bring out the coffee in a few minutes."

"Glad you stopped by the open house," Malcolm told Phaedra as Nan left. "I didn't think you'd show."

"I would've skipped it, but I wanted to meet Mark's father."

"And? What did you think?"

"I'm sure he was an excellent judge. But not the best father."

"He has dizzyingly high expectations," he agreed. "He makes no secret of his disappointment in his son's failure to follow him onto the bench." He paused. "Have you heard from Mark?"

She shook her head. "I'll check my phone when I get home. I left it behind so I could focus on everyone without any distractions."

She wanted to enjoy Christmas without any talk of suspects, or poison, or murder.

With customary tact, her father dropped the subject. "We're invited to Rachel Brandon's New Year's Eve bash."

"You and Mom?" Phaedra couldn't quite keep the surprise from her voice. "How did that happen?"

Malcolm shrugged. "Hannah probably wrangled the invitation. Or Nan's relentless charm left a lasting impression on Rachel when they met at your sister's grand opening."

She gave a wry smile. "My money's on Hannah."

"I suspect you're right." His expression grew serious. "I couldn't help but overhear part of your phone conversation with Marisol last night." He made no secret of his curiosity. "Who is Ben Jennings?"

She stared at him, unable to summon a reply. She wanted to tell him the truth about Michael. But the memory of Morelli's words stopped her. *"He's a convicted criminal. If he feels threatened, there's no telling what he might do or how he'll react. I won't let you put yourself or your dad in danger."*

"I've caught you off guard." He waited as Nan reappeared with two cups of coffee and set them down.

"I'll get the cream and sugar." She gathered up two more plates and left.

"Does it have to do with the poisonings?" he asked, lowering his voice. "Or the police investigation?"

Phaedra waited as her mother returned with the cream and sugar, then departed. "It's nothing to do with that."

"Ah. Then I won't press you." Disappointment flickered over his face. "I'd hoped the police had found a viable suspect. I'd like to see this thing solved."

"We all would."

They took their coffee into the living room. A light snow had begun to fall, and flakes drifted lazily past the large bay window.

They sat in companionable silence, drinking coffee and watching the snow, listening to the hum of the dishwasher in the kitchen.

The subject of Ben Jennings did not come up again.

* * *

When Phaedra returned to the carriage house that evening, it was ten thirty and the snow had stopped. This time, in addition to the outside light, she'd left a lamp on inside.

Charles and Hannah left shortly after dessert. They didn't specify where they were going, and she didn't ask. She was happy for her sister and glad she'd found love with Charles Dalton. They deserved some alone time.

How had Mark and his mother spent the day? Did they stay in or go out? Raise a pint at the local pub?

She unlocked the front door and took off her coat. As she hung it up, she heard her phone ringing upstairs.

Wickham lifted his head from his reclining position atop the sofa, his ears pricked forward as she dashed by on her way up the stairs to the loft bedroom.

"Hello?" Her voice was breathless from the sprint.

"Phaedra? Where've you been?" Lucy demanded.

"Christmas dinner with Mom and Dad. I left my phone behind. And where," she added, "were *you* last night? I looked for you, but you and Leah never showed."

"Yeah, about that. We had an unexpected visitor."

She guessed from Lucy's lengthy pause who the visitor had been. "Your mother?"

"Yes. To make sure we show up for dim sum tomorrow."

"And?"

Another pause. "Leah wants to go, but I'm not sure. But that's not why I called. How'd the egg custard tarts go over?"

"They were a huge hit. Mom said they disappeared in twelve minutes flat."

"Good. Hang on." She covered the phone and shouted something in Chinese. "I made more tarts this afternoon, and my pig of a sister—" She raised her voice. "Has already eaten most of them."

"Sorry, but I'm Team Leah on this one." Phaedra perched on the edge of her bed. "We should get together next week. Do something fun before our break ends."

"Agreed. Massanutten or Wintergreen?"

"Skiing? You know that's not my thing." She paused. "Actually, I need to go shopping. For a new dress."

"What's the occasion?"

"I'm invited to Rachel's New Year's Eve party next Sunday. You want to come along? I can bring a guest."

"Thanks, but no. Can you imagine if I left Leah alone on New Year's Eve? The mind boggles." Lucy paused. "Will Mark be back by then? Maybe he can go with you."

"Doubtful. Guess I'll be flying solo, then."

"All the better for gathering intel."

"I have no idea what you mean."

"Marisol," Lucy replied. "She filled me in on everything. And I'll tell you exactly what I told her."

"What's that?"

"Be careful. Michael, or Ben, or whatever his name is, could be dangerous. Especially if he learns you're both onto him."

"I promise we'll be careful."

"Okay." Lucy didn't sound convinced. "I'll hold you to that. Merry Christmas, Phae."

"Merry Christmas, Lu. To both of you."

As she ended the call, Phaedra noticed an unread text notification. Mark had left a message. She thumbed it open.

> Hello! This is Trudy. Mark is in hospital but recovering nicely. He wishes you a very Happy Christmas and will see you in the New Year. All best xx

Bewilderment, relief, and panic surged through her. Who was Trudy? His mother? His nurse? Why was Mark in the hospital? What on earth happened?

Why hadn't he texted her himself?

Is Mark all right? she typed back. What's going on?

She waited, but there was no reply.

And there wouldn't be one, she realized as she looked at the time. It was eleven p.m. in Laurel Springs but four in the morning in the UK. The message had been sent several hours earlier while she was still at her parents' place.

At least now she had an explanation for Mark's lack of communication. He was in the hospital.

If she wanted more answers, she'd just have to wait until he—or the mysterious Trudy—responded to her text.

Phaedra didn't believe in bad omens.

But after hearing the weather forecast for New Year's Eve—flurries, with an eighty percent chance of snow—and after snapping a high heel on the way out the door, she wondered if she shouldn't forget about going out that night and stay home.

While she enjoyed parties in general, and New Year's Eve parties in particular, and welcomed the opportunity to wear her glittery new gold evening gown, she'd prefer to spend the evening with a book and a glass of wine.

At least she'd heard from Mark. He sent a brief text to assure her he was fine and ready to come home. He promised to explain everything when he returned after the New Year.

Her thoughts returned to Rachel Brandon's upcoming soiree. While everyone drank champagne, nibbled hors d'oeuvres, and sang tipsy renditions of "Auld Lang Syne," Phaedra planned to find answers.

Who was Michael Farrar, aka Ben Jennings? Was he copying her father's painting as she suspected? How could she prove it?

She returned upstairs, had a quick rummage in the closet, unearthed a replacement pair of strappy heels, and slipped them on. Halfway down the steps her phone rang.

"You haven't left yet, have you?" Malcolm asked.

"I'm just about to. Why?"

"Your mother's not feeling well. One of her migraines. The Wagon's out front, all warmed up and ready to go. Why don't I stop by and pick you up? No sense taking two cars."

"The Wagoneer?" she asked doubtfully. "Is that thing even roadworthy?"

"Runs like a top. And it has snow tires. Which, if you've heard the forecast, we may need later tonight."

"Okay, I'm convinced. I'll be waiting."

"Your mother's disappointed she can't come," her father said as he turned the Wagoneer onto Afton Mountain Road ten minutes later. "She bought a new dress."

"I'll have Hannah make her a plate. And I'll text her a few photos."

"Good idea. She'll like that."

They lapsed into companionable silence as he negotiated a curve, focusing his attention on the road.

In a perfect world, Phaedra thought, she wouldn't be traveling up Afton Mountain with snow looming large in the forecast. She'd be in front of the television, waiting for the ball to drop in Times Square, with a bowl of popcorn in her lap and Wickham curled up beside her.

In a *truly* perfect world, she'd be spending her first New Year's Eve with Mark.

A few desultory flakes pirouetted in the beams of the Wagoneer's headlights. Good thing Hannah and her staff had taken the catering van to Delaford earlier that afternoon to get everything transported and set up.

She thought of her sister's hors d'oeuvres and bite-size French pastries, and frowned. Rebecca had mentioned that she and Biddy were invited to the party. What if one of them really *had* poisoned that box of Chiles Chocolates? What if they tampered with Hannah's appetizers, or poisoned one of her tiny desserts?

Telling herself she was being ridiculous, she reached for the radio knob. "How about some music?"

"Too late." Her father slowed the Wagoneer and turned off the road. "We're here."

"So we are." She'd been so lost in thought she hadn't realized they'd arrived.

Delaford sparkled like a jewel on the side of the mountain as they arrived. Malcolm followed the line of cars to the front portico, where a valet opened his door.

As Phaedra and her father went up the steps to the entrance, she noticed the parking area was crowded with sleek sedans and expensive SUVs.

"The old Wagon doesn't fit in with all these fancy vehicles." Malcolm chuckled. "Decent turnout. Not as many here as I expected, though."

"The weather forecast probably kept people away."

He cast a quick look at the clouded night sky. A few flakes drifted past. "So far, so good. If it starts snowing in earnest, we may have to leave early."

Phaedra nodded and lifted the flap of her envelope clutch to check the status of her lipstick, phone, and—just in case—her Swiss Army knife.

She closed it and looked up to see Michael's Jaguar parked by the fountain. "Marisol's already here."

"Are she and Michael still an item?"

Phaedra hesitated. Although she wanted to fill him in on their planned reconnaissance mission, she knew he wouldn't approve. The less he knew, the better. "Tonight, they are."

"Ah. Now, there's a nonanswer if I ever heard one."

"Sorry, Dad. But Marisol likes to keep her private life . . . private."

"No matter, I completely understand. It's none of my business anyway." He held out his arm. "C'mon. Let's go have some fun."

They'd barely surrendered their coats and taken flutes of champagne from a passing tray when Rebecca Bondurant sailed forward to greet them.

"Professor Brighton! And your delightful father. How lovely to see you both." She wore a black silk dress and low heels, with a purple cashmere wrap draped around her shoulders. "I understand Mr. Farrar brought your restored painting with him. I can't wait to see it."

Malcolm sipped his champagne. "Yes. He's out of town next week, so he's handing it off to me tonight. Speaking of which," he added as he surveyed the glittery crowd, "I need to find him. Excuse me."

"Where's Biddy?" Phaedra's gaze followed her father as he wove his way across the great hall and disappeared into the drawing room. "I don't see her."

"She didn't sleep well. I suggested she stay home and watch the festivities on television." Rebecca took her by the arm. "Come along, and let's get ourselves a nibble. Your sister's done an outstanding job. You must try the devils on horseback. Scrumptious!"

"Phaedra! There you are." Marisol, her hair arranged in a simple Grecian knot at the nape of her neck, hurried toward her a short time later.

"Mari, you look fantastic. Dark blue suits you." She stepped back to admire the slinky, diamante-studded gown.

"Never mind that." She lowered her voice. "What's the plan?"

Her gaze went to Michael, currently conversing across the room with Rachel and her father. "I thought I'd slip out and find Dad's painting, take a look. See if it's a copy or the real deal."

"Will you know the difference? You're no art expert."

"No. But I've looked at it enough times over the years. I'll know." Her gaze slid to Michael, talking once again to Rachel. "Any idea where it might be?"

"He stashed it in the wine cellar downstairs. Said he didn't want anything to happen to it."

"Why hide it? If it's a copy, it's of no value. And even if it *is* the original, according to him, it isn't worth anything."

"Good question."

"Did you learn anything useful?" She glanced once again at Michael. As if he sensed her attention, he gave her a brief nod. She forced a smile in return.

"Nothing," Marisol admitted. "I didn't push too much. Afraid I'd raise his suspicions."

"Smart. If he won't confide in you, he certainly won't tell me anything." Phaedra took a tiny sip of champagne. "How do he and Rachel know each other?"

"I have no idea. They're in close contact, though. The last time I snuck a look at his phone, quite a few calls were from her."

"Interesting. I wonder why. What could a gallery-owner-slash-convicted-felon and a Home Channel media maven possibly have in common?"

Marisol shrugged.

Phaedra set her flute down and turned to Marisol. "Stay here and keep an eye on our mutual friend while I have a look around."

"Be careful." Anxiety edged her voice. "He's smart, Phae. If you're gone too long, he'll notice."

"I'll be back soon." She glanced at her diamond wristwatch. "I need to find more than that painting. I need to find a connection."

"What kind of connection?"

"I'm not sure. But something tells me Rachel and Michael are in this together." Phaedra frowned. "They're up to something. I just don't know what yet."

Tucking her clutch under one arm, she headed across the grand hall as quickly as possible. Snow fell steadily outside the windows and had begun to stick to the ground.

She hesitated. Maybe she should forget the plan. Find Dad and leave before the roads became impassible.

As she turned back to retrace her steps, the sound of someone tapping a fork against a crystal glass rang out.

"As you may have noticed," Rachel announced as the hum of conversation died, "the weather forecast has changed. Snow is falling and it's starting to cover the ground."

Her words caused a stir among the guests.

"If you'd like to stay," she went on, "we have plenty of rooms." Her glance flickered to Michael. "But if you prefer to leave, I urge you to go now. The roads are getting slick and there's a good chance they'll be impassible by tomorrow."

Most people began to leave, saying their goodbyes as they headed for the door to retrieve their coats.

Just a quick look, Phaedra told herself. She was so close. It would take literally moments to determine if the painting was a forgery. Then she'd come back upstairs, find her father, and go.

No one noticed as she slipped down the hall and turned the corner, no one saw her randomly opening a succession of closed doors. The sound of clattering plates and raised voices told her she was near the kitchen.

". . . more stuffed dates, please. And check the choux pastries. These people eat like *vultures*."

Hannah's voice. Phaedra hadn't seen so much as a glimpse of her sister since her arrival.

Opening another door, Phaedra faced a square of darkness. The basement, she realized. Had to be. She felt along the wall just inside the doorway until she located a light switch. Sure enough, shallow stone steps sprang into view, sweeping down into the shadows.

She groped for her phone and switched on the flashlight. The feeble overhead bulb did little to illuminate her surroundings. The temperature grew cooler as she reached the basement, and she shivered. The thin silk of her gown offered little protection against the chill.

Sweeping the flashlight beam around her in a quick, exploratory arc, she deduced that the wine cellar was to the left, under the center of the main house. At least there was no danger of her father's painting being exposed to too much heat down here.

She rounded the corner and let out a sharp yelp as something gossamer soft yet clingy brushed against her bare arm. What in holy heck . . .

"A cobweb," she whispered, brushing it aside with equal parts relief and revulsion. "It's just a cobweb."

As the passage opened up ahead, she saw floor-to-ceiling wine racks built into the arched bricked walls, the racks filled with bottles, some dusty, some brand new. Banded wooden casks took up the far end. She thought of Edgar Allan Poe's short story, "The Cask of Amontillado."

"The thousand injuries of Fortunato I had borne as best I could, but when he ventured upon insult, I vowed revenge."

The story's narrator devised a fitting and horrible revenge for his enemy, Fortunato.

Another, deeper shiver passed down Phaedra's spine. What was she doing down here alone?

"The painting," she reminded herself, gripping her phone a little tighter. "You're here for the painting."

She forced herself to move forward. The floor was hard-packed dirt, and uneven. It made walking in thin, strappy heels difficult. Phaedra reached out to steady herself, recoiling as her palm touched the cold, clammy stone of the passageway.

Where was the painting?

Her hopes sank. What if it wasn't here? The wine cellar was enormous. Perhaps Michael had lied to Marisol; it wouldn't be the first time. He could have stashed the painting anywhere.

But she didn't think so. Hiding her father's painting in this cellar, with its cobwebs and silence and dusty racks of wine, not to mention a darkness so impenetrable it felt like being inside a tomb, made a twisted kind of sense.

There was no risk of anyone stumbling across the painting, no chance of anyone getting a closer look.

So intent was she at eyeing the spaces between the casks, searching every dark corner and crevice with her phone's flashlight, Phaedra didn't hear the footfalls until they were almost upon her.

She whirled around and opened her mouth to scream.

"Dad!" she croaked, her heart thrashing against her rib cage as she saw him. "What . . . What are you doing down here?"

He handed her coat over. "Looking for you. I saw you talking to Marisol earlier, and when everyone started to leave, I saw you slip around the corner. I knew you were up to something. I decided to follow you."

"Marisol said Michael put the painting—*your* painting—down here. I need to find it and take a good, long look at it. See if it's authentic . . . or a copy." She set her phone and clutch aside and slipped gratefully into the coat.

"A copy? Phaedra, we've been through this before. If Farrar really is an art forger, you need to let the police deal with him."

"It's got to be here somewhere. Now that you're here, you can help me look."

"Never mind the painting," he urged. "It doesn't matter. The snow's really coming down." Malcolm glanced at his wristwatch. "We need to get out of here."

"I'm afraid you're not going anywhere," a voice in the darkness behind them said with regret. "Either of you."

Thirty-Eight

Phaedra turned to see a tuxedoed figure blocking their exit. His face was in shadow. “Michael,” she breathed. “How did you know we were down here?”

“I told Marisol the painting was down here. I knew she’d tell you, Professor, just as I knew you’d go looking for it.”

“We’re anxious to see your efforts on the restoration,” she said, trying to inject a note of normalcy into her words. “Marisol said you did a great job.”

“Did she? How kind of her.”

She saw the gleam of something metallic in his hand. A snub-nosed pistol. And it was pointed at the two of them.

“Where is it?” Malcolm asked him, his voice level. “Where’s my painting?”

“Right now,” Michael said, stepping closer, “I’d say that’s the least of your worries. Wouldn’t you agree?”

The gun remained firmly trained on them.

“But to answer your question,” he went on, “your painting—the one worth six figures—is safely stashed in the trunk of my car. Where it’ll remain until I leave this Podunk town. By then,” he added, “you and your oh-so-clever daughter will die in a tragic New Year’s Eve car accident.”

Phaedra stiffened. "What are you talking about?"

"I'll tell the police your father was inebriated but insisted on leaving. Against my advice, of course." Concern warmed his words. "You both wanted to get home. The roads were bad, you must've taken an icy curve too fast, and off you sailed over the side of the mountain. Just like Thelma and Louise."

"Look," Malcolm said reasonably. "There's no need for any of this. You want the painting? You've got it."

"I knew that painting was worth a bundle the moment you showed it to me." He stepped closer, and Phaedra shrank back against her father. "But there's still a matter of unfinished business between us, Counselor. A loose end to tie up before I send you and your daughter on your way."

"And what's that?" Malcolm asked grimly. "Enlighten me."

Phaedra's fingers closed over her father's arm as footsteps hurried up behind Michael, and a flashlight swept over them, momentarily blinding her.

"Don't," Rachel said, her voice breathless and strained. "Please, Ben. Don't do this. Let them go."

In a flash, Phaedra connected the pieces. What was it Detective Morelli had told her, just a few days ago?

"He and his sister grew up in foster care, got bounced from one place to the next."

And her father, only tonight, had mentioned an old case that ended in tragedy.

"He lost control of the car and struck and killed a young single mother. She had two kids, four and six. A boy and a girl."

"You're Ben Jennings," she said slowly. "And Rachel is your sister."

"Very good, Professor." Grudging admiration gleamed in his eyes. "Although that's not her real name. Any more than mine is Michael."

"I remember the case very well," Malcolm said. "I defended the man who went on to kill your mother." It was obvious saying the words pained him. "Two days later, he robbed a bank. There was a high-speed car chase."

"The judge let him go."

"He had no choice. The defendant wasn't read his Miranda rights. It ended in a mistrial."

"It was your fault she was killed." His words were like shards. "We had no one. Nowhere to go. I was six years old when we went into foster care. It wasn't long before a wealthy family adopted my sister."

"I had every advantage growing up," Rachel admitted. "But Ben . . ." She let out a tremulous breath. "He wasn't so lucky."

"I was angry." He shrugged. "Hard to handle. No one wanted me. I bounced around from place to place. Until I was old enough to run away."

"I'm sorry," Phaedra said, and meant it. "What that man did, what he took from you and your sister—it was tragic. Unforgivable. But it has nothing to do with me. Or my father."

"That *man* was your father's client," Michael snarled. "But the good counselor here failed to put him behind bars. He went free. And so my mother was killed." He glanced at Rachel. "We were just collateral damage."

"It was you, wasn't it?" Phaedra stared at Michael's handsome face. "You poisoned that cupcake. Just like you injected the chocolate and left the box at the bookstore."

"Guilty on both counts. But both times, it went sideways." He shook his head. "The cupcake was meant for you and your father. A twofer. But that stupid woman grabbed it. And the chocolates?" He glanced at Malcolm. "He mentioned a fondness for hazelnut crunch the night I stopped by to look at his painting. I made sure to inject that one." His face congealed into something hard and ugly. "But you knocked it out of his hand, Professor."

"It's too late, Ben. Let them go. Please." Rachel laid a hand on his arm, but he shook it away. "This won't bring our mother back. You can't change the past."

"No. But I can change the future." He studied his sister

with a thoughtful frown. "However, you make a good point. I should let them go."

Before either of them could react to this sudden shifting of gears, Michael lifted the gun and gestured Phaedra and her father into the passageway behind him.

"There's an exit at the end of the passage," he instructed them. "Rachel, go ahead of us and open the door. Make sure everyone's gone."

"You're . . . you're letting us go?" Malcolm said, exchanging a glance with his daughter. "What's the catch?"

"No catch. Change of plan."

They retraced their steps on the packed dirt. Phaedra stumbled, righting herself on her father's arm. "Why are we leaving this way? Why can't we go back upstairs?"

"This is more convenient. Closer to your car." As they arrived at the end of the passage, he preceded them up a flight of worn stone steps until they emerged into the frigid night air. "Looks like yours is the only one left."

The observation amused him.

Snow fell thickly, with a couple of inches already covering the ground. Michael wasn't kidding, Phaedra realized with a jolt of dismay. Everyone else was gone. Only the Wagoneer remained, parked several yards away.

He jerked the gun toward his sister. "Give her your phones."

Phaedra balked. "What if we break down on our way home? The roads are treacherous."

"You're smart. You'll manage. Phones, please."

Reluctantly, they did as he commanded and relinquished their cell phones to Rachel.

"We'll go to the police the minute we get back to Laurel Springs," Phaedra said.

He shrugged. "*If* you get back to Laurel Springs. You haven't a shred of evidence, so I doubt they'll believe you. You haven't convinced that detective yet." His glance flickered to the helipad. "And I'll be long gone before they arrive."

"With my painting, I assume," Malcolm said.

"Of course."

"Where's Marisol?" Phaedra asked suddenly. "What have you done with her?"

"Done with her?" He chuckled. "Nothing. She left forty minutes ago. Called an Uber to pick her up before the roads became impassable."

Her last hope, that Marisol would realize something was wrong and send for help, evaporated. She and her father were truly on their own.

"The valet left your keys in the ignition." Michael gave them a brief smile. "Good night. Have a safe trip."

"Rachel," Phaedra called over her shoulder as Michael herded his sister back toward the house. "Call the police. Please."

But Rachel didn't respond. She kept walking.

The harsh sound of their breathing and the crunch of their shoes in the snow filled her ears as the two of them descended the driveway to the Wagoneer. She couldn't walk fast; her heels were spindly and the tarmac was slick.

"I thought we parked closer to the house." Her breath plumed out with every word.

"We did. The valet must've moved it. Come on. It's not too much farther."

"I'm not exactly dressed for walking." Phaedra plunged her hands deep into her coat pockets. "And it's freezing."

They walked the rest of the way down the drive without speaking. Losing her footing on a patch of ice, she reached out to clutch her father's arm.

"I don't trust Michael," she said as they arrived at the Wagoneer. "He let us go too easily."

Malcolm, his hand on the driver's side door handle, paused. "Do you think the car will blow up when I turn the ignition?"

"Don't joke, Dad."

"I'm not."

She slid in next to him, her teeth beginning to chatter, and slammed her door shut. They buckled up, and after a moment's hesitation, he turned the ignition and started the car.

It rumbled reassuringly to life.

Phaedra reached out to switch on the heater, but he brushed her hand away. "Let it warm up for a few minutes. You'll only get cold air right now." He opened the glove box. "There's a spare pair of gloves in here somewhere."

"I can drive," she offered.

He shook his head. "I have years of experience driving in weather like this, sweetie. Trust me. I've got it."

He released the parking brake and gently pumped the gas pedal. Slowly, mindful of black ice lurking under the snowy surface, he eased the Wagoneer out of the driveway and turned right onto the mountain road.

As they headed downhill, the truck gradually began to pick up speed.

"Slow down, Dad," Phaedra said with a nervous laugh as they approached a curve. "You're going a little fast."

He pressed on the brake pedal. Nothing happened.

"The brakes." His hands gripped the steering wheel with white-edged knuckles. "They're not working."

She heard a roaring in her ears. "Not working?"

Michael's words came back to her. *"I'll tell the police your father was inebriated. . . . The roads were bad, you must've taken an icy curve too fast, and off you sailed over the side of the mountain."*

"Michael must've cut the lines." Perspiration beaded Malcolm's face despite the icy-cold air. "No wonder he changed his mind and let us go."

They were gathering speed at an alarming rate. "We should jump out while we still can," Phaedra said, panic threatening to overtake her.

"It's too late. We're already going too fast."

Icy tree branches and cedars tipped with snow rushed past in a dizzying blur as the Wagoneer hurtled forward.

A sign loomed up in the headlights. "DANGEROUS CURVE AHEAD."

"We have to do something!" Phaedra cried. "Before we go over the side!"

"All I can do," he gritted, pumping the brakes uselessly, "is aim for that clump of bushes over there. Try to break our trajectory."

The words had barely escaped his lips when a siren wailed out in the darkness somewhere ahead of them, the sound growing steadily louder as the flash of red and blue lights coming up the mountain illuminated the night sky.

"Look out!" Phaedra screamed.

A white police SUV loomed in their headlights, both vehicles set on a collision course. Acting on pure instinct, Malcolm wrenched the steering wheel hard to the right, sending the truck into a crazy sidelong spin.

"Hang on!" he shouted.

With a judder and a sickening crunch of metal and breaking glass, the Wagoneer slammed sideways into the SUV, hitting with a bone-jarring force that hurled Phaedra hard against the passenger door.

Where oblivion claimed her.

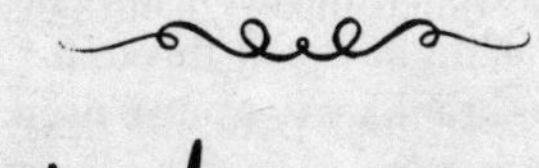

Thirty-Nine

When she opened her eyes, the first thing Phaedra noticed was silence. No sirens screamed, no engine rumbled, no branches slapped wildly at the sides of the truck.

The second thing she noticed was pain. Every muscle and bone ached and her head throbbed dully.

"Pain is good," she mumbled, disoriented. "Pain means I'm still alive."

The collision. They'd crashed, thankfully not head-on, slamming into the side of a police SUV. Reaching out in the darkness, she croaked, "Dad? Dad, can you hear me? Are you all right?"

He stirred beside her. He lay sideways, thrown by the force of impact halfway across the bench seat. He let out a low moan but didn't answer.

She tried to sit up but fell back against the seat as dizziness overtook her. "Have to . . . get help."

What about the police vehicle? Was the driver injured? Why had no one come to check on her and Dad? Where *was* everyone?

She closed her eyes, semi-aware of the warm trickle of blood on her cheek and voices rising and falling in the darkness, growing closer, of feet crunching through snow. The beam of a flashlight arced through the cabin of the Wagoneer and she shrank away as it splayed over them, momentarily blinding her.

"Phaedra!" Detective Morelli appeared at the passenger window. Relief and concern warred on his face as he took in the scene. "Phaedra, can you hear me?"

She managed a nod.

"An ambulance is on the way," he said, his voice strong. Reassuring. "Can you tell me what happened?"

"He . . . cut the . . . brakes."

"Who? Michael Farrar?"

"Yes. Didn't know . . . until . . . too late."

He said something to someone nearby. "We're going after Farrar right now. An officer will stay with you and your dad until the ambulance arrives. Okay?"

"He . . . has a gun." She paused, alarmed as the distant sound of a helicopter grew closer. "Helipad." She struggled to finish. "Hurry. Or he'll . . . get away."

Saying the words, giving him the warning, exhausted her, and she closed her eyes.

Later, as the ambulance waited to take them to the nearest hospital, Phaedra gave Detective Morelli a brief statement.

"I'm fine," she protested as a pair of paramedics secured her to the gurney. "I cut my cheek. It's nothing."

"You're going to Somerset General," Morelli said as the EMTs transported her to the back of the vehicle. "Don't even try to argue. I'll get a more detailed statement from you and Malcolm tomorrow. If you're up to it."

"Where . . . is he?" Panic bubbled up as she lifted her head. "Where's Dad?"

"He's already been loaded into an ambulance. He's pretty banged up, but he'll be okay."

"Thank God." She fought against another wave of exhaustion. "You're not . . . injured?"

"I'm fine. I left my car at the station. When the call came in, I signed out a police cruiser and followed Officer Scott in the SUV."

"Who called? To come looking for us?"

"Your friend Marisol. She said you and your father disappeared from the party, and so did Michael. She was worried. Not long after that, Rachel Brandon called."

So she *did* call the police. "Rachel . . . is Ben Jennings's sister."

He nodded. "She told me everything. How she and Ben went into foster care, and she was adopted pretty quickly, but her brother wasn't. How he was in and out of foster homes. There was abuse. Mistreatment. He ran away numerous times.

"Eventually, he fell in with the wrong crowd. Thieves, forgers. Found he had a knack for copying artwork."

"Why didn't she reach out to him? Try to help him?"

"She did. She wrote letters, sent him cards, but they were all returned unopened. She finally gave up."

"He blamed my father. And maybe . . . maybe he's right. If Dad's defendant hadn't been released, none of this would've happened."

"It wasn't your father's fault, Phaedra. If Ben blames anyone, he should blame the families that tried to foster him. They failed. Miserably."

Now she understood why Rachel had dropped her champagne flute at the art showing. "Ben must've told Rachel he was her brother that night at the gallery. She hadn't seen him since he was six years old. She dropped her champagne flute."

"Must've been quite a shock."

"I saw his car at Delaford last week and I wondered why he was there. Now I know he was visiting his sister." Her eyes searched his. "Was he blackmailing Rachel? Is that why she didn't say anything sooner?"

"Not blackmail, exactly. He guilted her into keeping his secret, said it was the least she could do for him."

Before she could ask Morelli if he'd arrested Michael, an EMT informed him the ambulance was ready to go.

Phaedra reached for the detective's hand and clung to it. "Thank you," she said, her words simple but heartfelt.

He squeezed her fingers gently and smiled. "Just doing my job, Professor."

Forty

After an overnight stay in the hospital, Phaedra was treated and released.

"You look great," Marisol enthused as she arrived in her Toyota to pick up Phaedra. "Other than a nasty bruise on your cheek. Nothing a little makeup can't cover up."

"Thanks. I think." She slid onto the passenger seat while her friend stowed her evening gown and shoes on the back seat. "And thanks for bringing a change of clothes."

She'd had plenty of time to think in her hospital bed, about a number of things.

First and foremost, she was glad her father's quick reflexes had saved their lives. Grateful he was okay. Thankful the police showed up when they did, preventing the Wagoneer from hurtling off the side of the mountain. And she was thankful Marisol had called to tip them off.

Ben Jennings was behind bars, where he'd be staying for a long time.

She was also relieved to realize that Rebecca and Biddy had nothing to do with the poisonings. The elderly pair might be a bit eccentric, and Rebecca never hesitated to speak her mind, but for all their faults and peculiarities, at least they weren't killers.

They were part of what made the Laurel Springs community unique.

"Have you heard from Mark?" Marisol asked as she waited for a car to pass and pulled away from the curb.

"No. He's due back tomorrow."

"Does he know what happened? You should tell him."

"I will. But I'd rather tell him in person. Too much to explain in a text." Phaedra leaned back against the headrest. It might take a few days to get her energy back. "What about Lucas? How's he doing?"

"Lucas?" Marisol betrayed herself with a blush. "He's fine. His bruises are healing. I only stopped in to see him because his hospital room was right next to yours."

"Uh-huh." She smirked. "With a giant bouquet of gift shop flowers and a balloon in hand." Her smile faded. "I'm sorry things didn't work out for you and Michael."

"What can I say? He was perfect, until he wasn't." She signaled a lane change. "But despite all the terrible things he did, I can't help but feel sorry for him. To be six years old and lose it all, just like that. His mother, his sister, his home . . . his whole life was upended."

They both fell silent, counting their many blessings.

"Thanks for calling Detective Morelli." Phaedra gazed, unseeing, out the window. "If the police hadn't shown up when they did . . ."

Her father would have lost control of the Wagoneer at the first curve, plunging the two of them to certain death.

Marisol reached out to clasp her hand. "But they did," she said firmly. "Now, let's get you home."

At half past eight that evening, the carriage house doorbell rang.

Phaedra, curled up on the sofa in a T-shirt and pajama bottoms, peered over the rim of her reading glasses at her sister. "Are you expecting anyone?"

"Nope. Charles left hours ago." Hannah glanced at the door. "You don't suppose it's Mom, do you? Or one of your tea party friends?"

"Tea *Society*," she corrected. "And no, we're not meeting until later this week."

"Guess I'll see who it is, then." With a huff of exasperation—she was in the middle of rereading Clark Mullinax's *Clarion* article about Michael Farrar, aka Ben Jennings—Hannah went to the front door.

"Oh!" she exclaimed, her voice drifting out from the foyer. "Come in, please. Let me take your coat."

Phaedra heard a polite murmur of thanks. A polite murmur of thanks with a distinctly British accent.

Before she could untangle herself from Wickham, who'd settled himself on her lap, or wish she'd applied at least a touch of lip gloss, Mark entered the living room.

His customary scarf hung askew around his neck, his hair was a dark and tousled mess, and he looked like someone who'd just flown for eight hours with very little sleep.

He was also the most singularly wonderful sight she'd ever seen.

"I'm going." Hannah grabbed her coat. "Be back in a few." She opened the door and slipped out.

"Mark," Phaedra breathed, gently thrusting Wickham aside as she pushed herself to her feet. "Why didn't you tell me you were coming?"

"I didn't know myself until I asked the driver to let me off here. I hope you don't mind."

"Of course I don't mind! But—" Her brow puckered as she saw the carved stick he leaned on. "What's that?"

"This," he sighed, "is my walking stick. I had a spectacular fall down the stairs in Mum's cottage the first night I arrived. The stairs are so steep and narrow, you can't imagine. I was lucky I didn't break my neck. Or so the doctor told me. Spent most of my holiday in traction."

"The text from Trudy?"

"My nurse."

"Oh, Mark."

She flung herself into his arms—well, *arm*—and he kissed her, and she was laughing and crying, and it was all very romantic and more than a little awkward, but somehow, perfect at the same time.

"You said you sent the driver away?" Phaedra asked when she finally drew back and glanced out the window at the empty, darkened street.

"I did." He hesitated. "But I realize your sister's staying here, and I know she sleeps on the sofa. Not sure what I was thinking, actually. I'll call for another car to come and pick me up—"

"No," she said firmly, "you won't. Wait here."

He waited, puzzlement on his face, as she darted over to the Christmas tree and unearthed a small package wrapped in silver foil and stuck with an extravagant blue bow.

"For you." She held it out to him. "Open it."

"But . . . I haven't got anything for you. Well," he amended, "I do, but I don't have it with me."

"Open it."

He did, his fingers slow and clumsy as he set his stick aside and tore at the wrapping paper.

"I didn't know what to get you," Phaedra admitted, "so . . ." She paused as he withdrew her gift. "I hope you like it."

He stared down at it, then glanced up at her. "It's a key." He held it up, bemused. "With a dark green tassel on the end."

"It's a key to the carriage house. *Your* key."

He stood, quite speechless, in the middle of the living room floor.

"It's so you can come over whenever you like."

"I see."

Her face fell. "You don't like it." How had she misjudged things so badly? Could it be that she was ready for the next step, but he wasn't?

"No, I don't like it." He reached for her, his eyes never

leaving hers. "I love it. It's absolutely the most perfect gift anyone's ever given me."

"I'll make up the sofa bed," she said, in between kisses, "and Hannah and I can share the loft."

He regarded her in dismay. "The sofa bed? Oh. But I thought—"

"One step at a time, Romeo." She tugged gently at his scarf. "You've had a long flight and you're exhausted."

"I am," he admitted, and pressed his forehead to hers. "But I promise to make it up to you. As long as I can sleep for about nineteen hours first."

"I think that can be arranged."

She opened up the sofa bed. By the time Phaedra returned from the linen closet with an extra blanket, Mark was sprawled face-down across the bed, sound asleep.

She eased off his shoes and arranged the blanket over him. Then she turned off the lamp.

"'Night, Romeo," she whispered.

"It's official." Malcolm Brighton beamed at his wife and daughters gathered around his hospital bed the next day. "I'm out of here tomorrow."

As everyone welcomed the news, Phaedra in particular, he added, "One more announcement. The painting that hung on my law office wall for so many years has been verified as an undiscovered work by James Brighton."

"That's fantastic, Dad." Phaedra couldn't stop smiling. "I promise I won't say 'I told you so.'"

"As you and Mrs. Bavier suspected, it's worth a staggering sum."

"Will you sell it?" Hannah asked.

"I'd prefer to keep it for sentimental reasons, but I have to be realistic. The painting should be stored in a safe and temperature-controlled place. A place where someone like Michael Farrar can't get their hands on it.

"Which is why," he went on, reaching out to clasp Nan's

hand, "I'm selling to a private collector and donating half the proceeds to the Historical Society. After all, if it wasn't for Mrs. B. and her research, we'd never have known the value of that painting. Now the restoration work on the old Morland estate can be completed."

Nan nodded. "An archeological dig starts on the site in two weeks. Who knows what they might unearth." She gave a delicate shiver. "It's rumored the house is haunted."

"Haunted?" Phaedra raised a quizzical brow.

"I have news of my own," Hannah said. "Charles and I have set a wedding date."

"Oh, my goodness," Nan cried, "that's the best news I've ever heard!"

"Better than owning a painting worth a bundle and Dad getting out of the hospital?" Phaedra teased.

"Those things are wonderful, no question," she agreed. "But now I have a wedding to plan."

"You mean, *I* have a wedding to plan." Hannah exchanged a *Here we go* glance with her sister.

"Well, yes," Nan agreed distractedly. "But you'll want your mother's input, won't you?"

Hannah wisely stayed silent.

"What are you doing with the other half of your money?" Phaedra asked her father. "A trip to Cancún? A tour of Europe?"

"I'm buying a new truck to replace the Wagoneer." He smiled at Hannah. "And I have a wedding to pay for."

Acknowledgments

Once again, my thanks to the amazing team at Berkley Prime Crime: to my editor, Sareer Khader, for taking my words and making them so much better; Farjana Yasmin and Victoria Fomina, for creating another unique and eye-catching cover; narrator Jennifer Jill Araya, for bringing my characters to life; and everyone else who contributed to the making of this book. Thanks also to my agent, Nikki Terpilowski; to the librarians, booksellers, and the cozy mystery community; to the readers (seriously, where would us authors be without you?); and to my husband, Mark, for believing in me right from the start.

Ready to find
your next great read?

Let us help.

Visit prh.com/nextread

Penguin
Random
House